LADY OF THE LOCH

Jennifer Sanders

and

Christen Stovall

Printed in the United States of America

First Printing, 2022

ISBN: 978-1-7362662-6-7

For Saria and Callie C.

Contents

Acknowledgements

Cover design by Sabrina Watts, Enchanted Ink Studio. Our thanks to everyone who took the time to read our drafts and bring this story to completion.

Chapter One

The Professor's Assistant

Charlie Whitfield squinted out over the rippling waters of Loch Ness, shading her eyes against the glare of the afternoon sun. The chores were done for the day and all that remained was to clean up, get dressed, and see that Uncle Elias was presentable for the autumn gathering and bonfire at the Lochmuir Inn.

Best get to it then, she thought, turning from the glistening water to hurry back to the house. Charlie opened the door to find things just as she'd expected: the house was quiet, with the light from her uncle's study serving as the only evidence of his presence. She hung her coat on the hook by the door and glanced at the clock on the mantel, then double-checked the invitation on the kitchen table.

Charlie resisted the urge to grind her teeth at the use of her given name, 'Charlotte,' knowing that it was to be expected, despite repeatedly asking innkeeper Fergus Shaw and his son, Oliver, to use the abbreviated form. The evening's festivities were set to start in a few hours, which meant Charlie had better begin nudging her uncle immediately, and with a certain level of urgency.

Uncle Elias often lost all track of time, and usually forgot to look after himself when he was certain he was on the verge of discovery. He'd been in something of a frenzy for the past few weeks. Livestock had recently been brutally slaughtered by some sort of predator on some of the local farms. Some were blaming the creature of Loch Ness for the carnage. Uncle Elias was determined to disprove this theory

Charlie worried that his single-minded obsession with proving the existence of the Loch Ness monster would drive him to an early grave. He was all Charlie had, and she loved him dearly, despite—and because of, all of his eccentricities.

As a man who'd devoted his life to the study of the mysteries of the natural world, Elias Whitfield had hardly known how to care for a small girl when he took Charlie in twelve years ago. She'd been a sad and frightened eight-year-old, reeling from the loss of both parents, far from everything familiar. Yet they'd managed to find a pattern and contentment in their strange life together, and if it meant that Charlie was now stepping into the role of caregiver, she was happy to do it.

Charlie tapped lightly on the door to the study. When no answer came pushed it open to reveal the usual chaotic jumble of papers and books that were scattered throughout the room. Uncle Elias was snoring softly at his desk, his head pillowed by the day's work. With a shake of her head, Charlie hurried round the desk to gently nudge her uncle's shoulder.

"Uncle, it's time to get ready," she coaxed him from his sleep. "Come now—you're sure to be terribly stiff if you don't get up and stretch a bit before the party."

"Mm, what?" Elias mumbled as he lifted his head, His hair was disheveled, and his spectacles hung haphazardly askew across his nose, none of which seemed to be of the slightest importance to the man. "Charlie? Oh, oh dear, is it afternoon already?

"It is, and you've spent the entire day in here. I really wish you wouldn't push yourself so." Charlie started straightening the papers on his desk, trying to lend some sense of organization to the chaos.

Elias straightened his glasses and patted her hand absently. "Yes, of course, my dear, but discovery waits for no one, you know."

"Yes, I know, Uncle," Charlie replied, setting a now orderly stack in front of her uncle. She offered him a helping hand as he started out of his chair with a grunt. "Come now, let's get you presentable."

"Hm? Oh yes, of course, the bonfire at the inn," he said, too busy shuffling through the papers Charlie had just put in order, re-cluttering the desk immediately.

"Uncle," Charlie scooped up the papers and made short work of tidying the stack a second time. "You need to change and wash up. Why don't you get ready and then you can tell me all about it on the way there, hm?"

It took a bit more urging, but Charlie was finally able to pry her uncle out of his study and into his room where she *hoped* he was changing, and running a comb through his hair. More than likely she'd have to knock on the door a few times to offer gentle reminders of the time.

To Charlie's relief, he proved to be more focused than usual; she only needed to knock on the door once to inform him of the time. Even more impressive, he'd managed to remember to change into his good Sunday waistcoat, and only had to spend a little while trying to figure out where he'd placed his spectacles when he washed his face. The result of which was that they were only running a few minutes behind by the time they were outside with the wagon hitched and ready to depart.

"Care to tell me what's had you so engrossed today?" Charlie asked, climbing up onto the wagon and settling into the seat beside Uncle Elias.

He clicked his tongue at their dappled gelding, Tobias, and pulled away from the cottage before answering. "It's these blasted reports of mutilated livestock. The idea that the creature could be doing it is utterly absurd." He frowned and spared Charlie a quick glance. "Everything we've found to support its existence points to an aquatic animal, hardly suited to land travel, let alone agile enough on land to be capable of running down and killing cattle and sheep."

"Why do you suppose they believe the creature is responsible?" Charlie asked. She shifted in her seat, pulling her shawl up around her shoulders to ward off the autumn chill.

"Oh, who knows? Half of them scoff at the very idea of the beast until there's a drought or some other disaster. Then it's all the fault of the creature of the loch," Elias grumbled. "Yet they have no interest in anything I have to offer on the subject. My status as an Englishman has me firmly on the outside."

"I'm sure it's just a wolf or some other animal that roams the highlands. Whatever it is will move on and life will go back to normal," Charlie tried to reassure him. If she was being honest, there was something strange to the recent attacks. The bite marks and feeding patterns seemed *different*. There was a brutality to the killings that was difficult to explain away.

Elias grunted in response, clearly unconvinced by Charlie's suggestion. He clicked at Tobias again, giving the reins a shake. For a time, he seemed to be lost in his thoughts and Charlie left him to it, keeping an eye on the road to be certain her uncle didn't drive them past their turn. She was hardly eager to arrive, but if they were too late someone was sure to comment on it.

"This evening presents us with the perfect opportunity to lay some of this foolishness to rest," Uncle Elias suddenly announced, breaking his silence with a resolute nod.

That statement made Charlie perk up a bit. If her uncle only wanted to go in order to defend the beast, it gave her an objective, and everything was easier when the goal was clear. "It sounds like an excellent idea. Perhaps we'll be able to discover the source of these rumors, or some information that could identify the true culprit."

"Yes indeed, my dear! At any rate, young Oliver expressed hope that we would attend. I could hardly tell him no after he came all the way out to the farm to deliver the invitation himself."

"Oliver Shaw," Charlie repeated the name. Oliver was one of the few young people in the area who paid Charlie any attention, though it was sometimes a bit too intense for her liking. "That's hardly extraordinary, considering his father is the proprietor of the Lochmuir Inn."

Her uncle shrugged slightly. "Truth be told, I'd nearly made up my mind to forego this evening, but this latest attack at the Carmichael farm will surely be a topic of conversation, and I'm hoping to speak to Mr. Carmichael himself."

"Of course—best to hear the details from the source," Charlie agreed, eager to steer the conversation back to the business of the creature.

The inn was a twinkling spectacle of lights and music as the Whitfield wagon drew near. There were several wagons and buggies parked near the barn, and a few more dropping off guests at the front gate. Charlie adjusted her shawl as her uncle steered their rickety wagon down the lane and pulled up close to the gate for her to climb down.

The music that drifted through the evening air was filled with the energy and enthusiasm of the highland community of Lochmuir. Charlie waited by the gate as her uncle found a place to park the wagon, and together they walked through the trellis that served as the entrance to the party. She turned to study the gathered crowd, eyes lingering on the other young ladies who were happily chatting near the bonfire. None of them seemed to notice her arrival, and even if they had it wouldn't have garnered a friendly greeting. No one was cruel to her, but Charlie was *other*, her interests vastly different from theirs. Occasionally, awkward attempts of inclusion happened, but it generally led to uncomfortable small talk that ended in equally uncomfortable silence.

"I was hoping you'd be here this evening, Miss Charlotte." Oliver sidled up next to Charlie. His smile was eager, his eyes alight. "You look lovely, but then you always do."

"Oh, well, my uncle thought it would be a good idea," Charlie replied, tucking a stray lock of hair behind her ear. The compliment threw her off guard. The addition of 'you always do' gave the words more weight than a general remark on her appearance.

"Thank you, it is kind of you to say so. All of the ladies look quite lovely this evening."

He bowed over her hand. "Are there any other ladies here? I hadn't noticed."

Charlie felt her cheeks go hot. She pulled her hand back slowly, trying to detract from the movement by pretending to adjust the collar of her dress. "I believe Maggie Graham would be disappointed to hear you say so." She pointed at a round-faced and rosy-cheeked brunette who was watching Oliver with thinly-veiled interest. "You ought to see if she would share a dance with you."

But as usual Oliver was impervious to hints, tucking her fingers into the crook of his arm and holding it there with his free hand, leading her away from Uncle Elias, whose entire focus seemed to be fixed on scanning the crowd. "Come, let me serve you some refreshments."

Charlie shifted her hand slightly, pulling her fingers out from under his. She was hardly in need of refreshments and Oliver's focused attention was uncomfortable enough without the attention it drew from others. "Mr. Shaw, you are one of the hosts and it would be wrong of me to monopolize your hospitality. Besides, I think it would be best for me to stay close to my uncle."

Oliver's eyes narrowed for just a moment, then resumed their guileless expression. "If you think it best, of course. I hope you will save me a dance?"

"Oh, I am sorry, but I don't know any of the dances." Charlie was quick to take the escape thus presented, and it had the added benefit of being the truth. She smiled at him. "But there is no need for you to miss out on anything this evening. It is very kind of you to offer your guests such a warm welcome." She looked over her shoulder, searching for her uncle and hoping he hadn't wandered off already. To her relief he was still lingering near the gate. Charlie slipped her arm away from Oliver. "If you'll excuse me, I believe my uncle is gesturing for me to join him." That *was* a lie.

"Let me escort you," was his aggravating reply, and there was nothing she could do to dissuade him. Oliver led her to her uncle's side and deposited her there with a bow and a rather ridiculous flourish. It might have passed muster in a society ballroom, but at a country dance it just seemed silly.

Uncle Elias smiled at Charlie as Oliver wove his way through the throng of people. Elias rubbed his hands together. "Mr. Carmichael is standing with our host, Fergus Shaw. Shall we make our way over and see if we can talk some sense into everyone?"

Charlie was quick to agree, for turning their efforts to the defense of the beast provided a way to avoid Oliver's attempts at charm. Though they'd been friends in the early years of her sojourn at Lochmuir, something had changed from their childhood days and in recent years his attentions had grown more persistent. The change put Charlie on edge whenever she had to be around him.

Uncle Elias started weaving through the assembly of neighbors and townsfolk, exchanging greetings with the few people who acknowledged him. Charlie followed as closely as possible, though she started to fall behind when several children dashed in front of her, squealing and laughing as they chased one another.

Standing quietly in a corner, carefully watching the crowd, was their neighbor Lorna Alvin, a widow of indeterminate age who'd been unfailingly kind to Charlie over the years. She caught Charlie's eye and smiled, lifting her glass in greeting. The friendly gesture made Charlie's shoulders ease into a more relaxed position. She smiled at Mrs. Alvin, waving to her before moving to catch up with Uncle Elias.

Lorna disappeared briefly and then resurfaced nearby. She reached out for Charlie, taking her hand and following along. "I see your uncle is on a mission again—I had hoped he brought you simply to socialize, but that was clearly optimistic of me. What sort of bee is in his bonnet this evening?"

"Oh, I don't mind, I enjoy helping him," Charlie was quick to point out, and she didn't... much. She cleared her throat and leaned closer to the other woman. "He's disturbed that the recent attacks have been attributed to the creature of the loch. He was hoping to speak to Mr. Carmichael."

The older woman frowned. "Do you mean old Ian Carmichael's sheep up along the ridge pasture? That's not even... the creature lives in the loch, for pity's sake. How would it get up to the ridge pasture?"

Charlie lifted a brow even as she inclined her head. "My uncle's thoughts exactly. The idea makes little sense, and will do nothing to prevent the predator responsible from striking again." Speaking of the creature was an easier topic than whether or not she ought to be there for social reasons alone.

At least Lorna seemed to be on their side. It was typical of the residents of Lochmuir that the existence of the creature was rarely debated—only what the beast was like, what it was capable of. Their neighbor was firmly of the opinion that the mysterious beast was of benign intent and ought to be left alone, unlike much of Lochmuir's citizenry who relished a good drama. The fact was that something had been killing some of the local livestock—killed and mutilated, like a mad thing. So it was not truly surprising that the blame was being placed on the ready-made monster of the loch.

Mrs. Alvin held steady at Charlie's side. "And Elias hopes to defuse the situation here? Now?" She huffed out a breath. "Of course he does," she answered her own question, just loud enough for Charlie to hear. "One sort of gathering is surely exactly like another, and all is wheat that comes to the scythe. Perhaps," she added more loudly, "I may be able to help."

However, Uncle Elias had already cornered Mr. Carmichael. Charlie picked up the pace, knowing full well that her uncle was rarely as diplomatic as a situation might call for. Indeed, by the time she sidled up next to him, her uncle was already in the midst of a logical, if tactless, explanation for what might have happened to the unfortunate sheep on the ridge.

"So you see, Mr. Carmichael, it's highly unlikely that that the creature is the culprit. Everything we've compiled points to an animal that rarely—if ever—makes landfall and would have extremely limited movement outside the lake," Elias explained emphatically. "In fact," her uncle continued. "I think it fair to hypothesize that the creature is entirely aquatic. If these killings are the result of some kind of predator, I would hypothesize it to be a wolf suffering from some sort of physical or behavioral malady. It is undoubtedly something far more commonplace than the lake beast to be sure."

Fergus Shaw broke in. "Nonsense, Whitfield. We're a community of farmers—most of *us* have been here for generations. D'you really think we know our business so little as to not recognize the attack of a wolf? That, you'll excuse me, is a very Sassenach point of view." He shook his head. "Those sheep weren't simply attacked and eaten, as a wolf or other predator would do. They were savaged, Whitfield—dismembered, their throats punctured by great sharp teeth, this big around," he demonstrated by touching forefinger and thumb together. "Show me a wolf with teeth like that, hm?" He turned to the rest. "A wolf, he says."

The expressions on the faces of the surrounding onlookers ran the gamut from outright amused to suspicious to hostile, a reminder that despite living among them for over a decade, the Whitfields were not part of the community, and therefore not to be trusted.

"Surely you can see that it is equally ridiculous that a creature supposed to dwell in water heaved itself to shore, lumbered across miles of uphill terrain, then ran down several healthy and well-fed sheep," Uncle Elias returned, apparently oblivious to the attention he was drawing. "Have you no respect for science—or logic, at the very least?"

Charlie put a hand on her uncle's arm, trying to draw his focus from their host and Mr. Carmichael, who looked as though he would have liked to melt into the stone wall behind him. "Uncle, perhaps this is not the place for such discourse after all."

Shaw lifted his hand and snapped his fingers in Elias' face. "There's for your science," he said. "You waste a lot of air tellin' us how you know everything about a creature you know nothin' of. This is a celebration, Whitfield, not a place to air your foolishness. We've had a good harvest—another subject about which you know nothin'. Take yourself off, if you've nothing better to offer." He glanced at Charlie. "My apologies, Miss Charlotte, but y'must allow that there are limits."

Lorna Alvin spoke up with some asperity. "Such disrespect to a guest in your home, Fergus Shaw! For shame! Professor Whitfield," her tone became gentler as she turned her attention to the older man, "surely y'see that this is a gatherin' for the young people to make merry, and the older to make fools of themselves," she cast a withering look at Shaw. "'Tisn't the place for your learned discourse."

Elias finally seemed to take note of the crowd that was now watching with avid interest. He took off his spectacles, shaking his head a bit as he cleaned them, a gesture Charlie recognized as a sign that he was merely gathering steam.

Charlie squeezed his arm and began to tug him gently away from Mr. Shaw. "Perhaps we ought to let the matter rest for the evening." She nodded toward the refreshment table. "We can help ourselves to the cider and... and..."

"But if folk erroneously blame the beast, they won't be hunting the true culprit and more havoc will be wrought," Uncle Elias continued doggedly, replacing his spectacles.

Fergus sighed and threw up his hands. "Saints preserve us all from your obsession, Elias!"

"The pursuit of knowledge should be the obsession of all men," Elias' voice was mild, but gaining in volume.

Charlie tried to pull her uncle away from Fergus Shaw again. "I think we should save this conversation for another time, uncle."

"There now, y'see? Even your young niece can see the sense in leaving the monster to its own for the evening," Fergus said. "'Twould be a pity if I had to ask y'to leave, and she missed the evening's fun. I'd loathe doin' it, but I've a responsibility to my other guests."

That seemed to finally penetrate her uncle's need to argue a point. Elias opened his mouth to reply, but shut it just as quickly. He looked from Charlie to the other guests, then once more at his niece. "Very well, Mr. Shaw. I'll let the matter rest, but I would very much like to come examine the sheep myself, Mr.

Carmichael. Perhaps I can offer some possibilities that would help you prevent any further losses."

Charlie almost felt bad for Mr. Carmichael. His cheeks were a vivid shade of pink, and his eyes darted between the two men nervously before he offered Elias a quiet invitation to come by the following day.

Fergus' jaw tightened. "Do as ye will then, but now that you've made your arrangements I expect ye to drop the matter while ye're on *my* property. I'm a patient man, Mr. Whitfield, but this is a night of celebration, and I'll not have you scarin' my guests out of their wits with your nonsense."

Charlie had to work to keep her expression passive, inwardly seething at Fergus Shaw's manner toward her uncle, but there was little enough she could do about it without making matters worse. He would undoubtedly show them off his property without another word. She took a deep breath and focused on her uncle. "Come, let's leave Mr. Shaw and Mr. Carmichael to enjoy the festivities."

Elias frowned but nodded his agreement without further ado. "Yes, of course, my dear."

"That's right." Mrs. Alvin tucked her arm through Charlie's on her other side. "Let's let this party be a party, hm? Y'need to spend time with some folk your own age—and not that Shaw boy, for all he seems to think your attention is his for the askin'. Plenty of other young folk to socialize with." The older woman shook her head and lowered her voice. "As for Fergus Shaw, don't let him upset you. He's a tedious man, needin' to be in the right all the time, but he's all bluster and no bite."

Charlie nodded. Fergus Shaw's attitude toward her uncle was hardly noteworthy. Most of the locals thought Elias Whitfield's research to be Sassenach silliness, or outright madness. Were it not for the patronage of a society in London simply called 'the Agency', he would have been forced to give it up long ago. "I'm sure everything will be forgotten and forgiven before the evening is over."

The Whitfields made a show of enjoying the festivities until enough time had passed for them to leave without causing offense or feeding the gossip mill any further. The ride home was quiet, but by the time they drew to a stop outside the barn, Uncle Elias was already preparing a list of equipment to take to the Carmichael farm.

Though her uncle's conscience seemed clear, Charlie spent most of the night tossing and turning. Even the familiar and soothing sounds of the farm outside or the gentle lapping of the loch beyond couldn't quiet her thoughts. Eventually she huffed out a frustrated breath and tossed aside her blankets. Pulling the quilt from the bed and wrapping it around her shoulders, she slipped out of her bedroom, shivering a bit in the night air. The house was quiet and dark as she made her way up the creaky staircase to the small cupola on the roof, a comical oddity in the local architecture but Charlie's personal refuge when she needed to think things through.

Nearly a week after the gathering at the inn, life around the loch returned to normal, in the absence of any further attacks. For the Whitfields, however, the mystery remained as prevalent as ever, another piece to be examined and placed within the puzzle. The visit to the Carmichael farm had only created more questions. The evidence left behind was inconclusive at best, but seemed to eliminate any of the ordinary predators known to inhabit the highlands. Uncle Elias was determined to get to the bottom of the matter. He spent hours locked in his study, muttering to himself as he went through his books, and papers. Charlie helped where she was able, but with her uncle so distracted, most of the work around the house and farmyard fell to her.

"Charlie, my dear, I think I will go to my research camp tomorrow," Uncle Elias proclaimed as they sat down to dinner.

Charlie carefully finished filling her plate before answering. "Has there been another attack?"

"No, but I've gathered the most evidence for the beast in that area. If the creature is indeed leaving the waters to hunt, I suspect that would be where it makes landfall. I want to see if I can find any evidence to support the idea that it is capable of hunting on land." He laid his paper on the table and turned his attention to the meal.

They were silent for a time, only the sounds of silverware clanking on plates filling the small space between them. Then, finally, Uncle Elias spoke again, looking at Charlie earnestly. "As much as I hate to admit it, I think we must at least consider the possibility that the creature is behind the attacks, if for no other reason than to be able to say that we've examined the situation with a fair and open mind."

Charlie's hand stopped with a forkful halfway to her mouth. Until now, her uncle had dismissed the connection as utter nonsense, and as such it had been easy to put any potential danger from her mind. But to hear Uncle Elias suggesting that the creature upon which their lives was centered could be responsible for the slaughter of animals on land made the gruesome mutilations seem closer to home, and more threatening by far. She placed her fork back on her plate. "Are you suggesting the creature may be dangerous after all?"

"What? Oh, no, no, my dear," Uncle Elias assured her. "I find the idea ludicrous, personally, but

I wish to approach the matter with an even hand. Mustn't jeopardize the scientific method, you know."

"Of course, uncle," Charlie replied, returning her attention to her meal, though the uneasiness of the idea remained. "When shall we leave?"

"No need for you to inconvenience yourself. I thought to go on my own this time." Her uncle's attention was on his meal. "I'll take the boat in the morning, see what there is to be found, and return home in time for supper."

"But Uncle Elias, surely it's best not to be alone if a predator is stalking the shores." Charlie hated the prospect of being left behind, and was even less fond of the idea of her aging uncle wandering the wilds without a companion to see that he was properly caring for himself. "I can be of help. Two sets of eyes are better than one, after all."

"Now, now. Nothing to fret over, my dear girl. I shan't be gone long." He offered her a reassuring smile. "This expedition is a formality, nothing more. I must consider all options, regardless of my own opinion. I'm leaving you here to see that our research does not suffer for it."

Charlie's lips thinned but she offered no further argument. Her uncle had made up his mind; once done, there would be no persuading him otherwise. And in fairness, if he was correct and there was nothing to be found, there truly was no reason to put their research on hold for the day. "Very well, uncle, but do be careful."

"My darling girl, you take excellent care of a silly old man—but you worry entirely too much." Uncle Elias shook his head, and returned to his dinner.

Despite her disappointment at being left behind, Charlie set about her day with determination after Uncle Elias departed in the morning. The needs of the farm came before she could turn to academic pursuits. She hurried through feeding the animals and cleaning out the stables, gathering the eggs, and then put a loaf of bread in the oven for dinner. When the tedious work of the household was finished, Charlie situated herself in her usual chair in Uncle Elias's study to collate their findings thus far, and was soon wholly absorbed in the quest for the Loch Ness monster.

The mystery of the beast was one that had filled her childhood, and yet the riddle remained unsolved— irresistible to Charlie's inquisitive mind. It didn't bother her that she lacked a circle of peers her own age, despite well-meaning Lorna's worries. Charlie had more important things to concern her than needlepoint, or finding a husband. The world was so much broader than all of that, and if her interest in understanding more of that world meant that she suffered a bit of loneliness now and then, it was just the price to be paid. That thought blunted the quiet emptiness of the house now.

So engrossed was she that the passage of time slipped Charlie's mind entirely. Eventually she realized she'd been squinting at the pages of the book in her hands and looked up from her work to a nearly dark house. The shadows outside the window were deep, and the solemn cries of the night birds were slowly replacing the more energetic tunes of their daytime counterparts.

Charlie closed the book and frowned. Uncle Elias should have been home hours ago. Even with the family habit of losing track of time, he was always home before supper. She set her work aside and headed for the front door. Perhaps he'd come home and was distracted by something outdoors, or maybe the wind was working against him and rowing back was taking longer than usual. Even as she tried to rationalize her uncle's absence, anxiety worked its way through her mind, knotting in her belly and shoulders.

The farmyard was peaceful. The chickens were out pecking and scratching at the ground; the cow, Nan, was contentedly munching on grass in her paddock. Charlie ran her hands over her hair and set to preparing the farm for the night. Nan needed milking and the chickens would have to be put back in their coop before it got much darker. Focusing on the practical work helped to keep Charlie's mind from brooding over her uncle's tardiness. Deal with one task, then move on to the next. It was controlled, methodical, and that always helped the world make sense.

Charlie was nearly finished with the evening milking when she thought she heard splashing coming from the landing. She heaved a sigh of relief and gave Nan a quick pat on the rump. It was silly that she'd let herself get so worried. Uncle Elias had simply lost track of time after all. She finished with the cow, grabbed the lantern, and went to greet her uncle and help him unload the boat.

"Hello..." Charlie's voice trailed off when she stepped out of the barn to find the landing empty. There was no sign of her uncle, and the boat was still gone. She crept further from the barn, lifting the lantern high and squinting into the quickly-dimming twilight.

Charlie's heart began to pound as she drew closer to the water. The splashing was still there, distinctly different from the usual lapping of the waves. It seemed to be moving back and forth near the shore. Whatever the cause, the sound implied something of substantial size.

Suddenly, the images of the mutilated animals and the more colorful stories told of the creature came racing back into Charlie's mind. She was keenly aware of her solitude and just how dark it was, but even as her hands began to tremble, she took another cautious step toward the water, curiosity overwhelming fear.

Tiny lights were flickering over the water just offshore. They bobbed and flitted, diving under the waves and then bolting high into the sky. A low sort of keening drifted toward her from the dark water, filling the air with a haunting, inhuman cry. A shadow began slinking closer to the shore, the call and the splashing growing louder.

Charlie took a step back, then another, and then she sprinted for the house and bolted the door behind her. She hurried to light every lamp in the sitting room, and wrapped herself in a blanket as the sound first intensified, and then slowly moved away.

Chapter Two

The Queen's Agent

On the train from Inverness, Asher Burton, member of a little-known cohort of agents to Her Majesty, Queen Victoria (known generally as the Agency), reread the telegram once again, sucking on his teeth in bemusement. He knew Elias Whitfield well; the professor occasionally helped out Her Majesty's agents with one thing and another. He liked the man, eccentricities and all—and chief among those eccentricities was a staunch belief that there was a heretofore unknown creature living in Loch Ness.

A month ago Asher himself was on the side of the benevolent naysayers, believing that old Elias must be softening in the brain pan to believe such nonsense. Judging from the tenor of the telegram he'd received, that was still the consensus at the home office.

Recent events, however, had opened up Asher's experience of the world beyond what was easily encountered or explained. After seeing—and participating in—the literal resurrection of his best friend, aided by an otherworldly creature from the sea that defied belief, he felt that perhaps he'd been too hasty in his previous dismissal of all things supernatural.

In any case, Elias was an old friend of Asher's superior, William Melville, and had been of use to Her Majesty in the past; thus his disappearance was of concern. He knew the name of the concerned nephew as well: Charlie Whitfield had contributed much to his uncle's work, and thereby assisted in several cases for the Agency. He, at least via his letters and research, seemed not at all the chap to sound a false alarm, and it was he who had reached out to the Agency about Elias. Hence Asher's assignment to the case, to try and discover if the old man had met with an accident, lost the last of his marbles and wandered away, or if something more sinister was afoot.

The train arrived at the Lochmuir station a little after luncheon, and once Asher had checked his suitcase into the luggage room and received directions from the porter, he headed for the local police station to pick up his brief and any new information before trying to find Elias' nephew to get details of the disappearance.

Lochmuir was a small and unremarkable town—the sort that one passed through and quickly forgot. Its proximity to the lake was likely the only reason the train stopped there at all. The main street contained a few small shops: a general store, a smithy, some sort of tinker's workshop, a small tea room, and what served as the headquarters for the local authorities.

Inside the station a young woman stood at the front desk, verbally wrangling with the sergeant who manned it. "Sergeant," she said, her voice beautifully modulated, without the Scottish lilt he'd expected, but with a more familiar English accent and an unmistakable chord of exasperation, "I assure you I have been thorough in my examination of the situation. If you would just take a look at what I've compiled I am certain you would find it most helpful."

She looked at Asher briefly and he felt winded by the force of that glance. Objectively speaking, the girl was an absolute stunner: satiny, creamy skin; spun-gold hair, braided in a coronet to show off the curve of an elegant neck; vivid green eyes, deeply intelligent. Asher shook himself as she dismissed him and turned back to her quarry.

The harried sergeant huffed out a breath. "And as I've told *you*, Miss, we've been out to the campsite. No sign of anything having happened to your uncle. Now then—a police investigation is no place for a lady to meddle. Leave the papers here, if you like. We're keeping an ear to the ground, and we'll call you if we find anything."

She studied the sergeant for several moments, a slight narrowing of the eyes the only sign of her annoyance. After a moment she relented and set the papers on his desk, gloved fingers drumming lightly on the pages. "Very well, Sergeant. I will do as you say, but before I go I must ask that you sign this page here." She pointed to the top of the first piece of paper.

Entertained, Asher continued to observe this spectacle play out. Beautiful, calm, self-possessed: this young woman was—at least in his opinion—the equal of the condescending sergeant, even if the man didn't know it. The sergeant looked askance at the paper she indicated. "And this is?"

"A receipt for the information you are asking me to leave here with you," she replied calmly, handing him the pencil that sat on his desk. "And date it as well, if you don't mind."

He did so, giving her a skeptical look. Asher hid a smile behind his hand.

"Thank you, sergeant." The young woman stood straighter, her features perfectly composed. "I'm certain you will reach the same conclusions I have, and when you do I'd like there to be a record of when this information was brought to your attention."

The policeman stared at her for a moment, then cast the pencil aside with an air of disgust. "Good day, miss."

"A good day to you as well, sergeant." The lady dipped her chin and then turned to make her way toward the door without another word. She walked through the office, holding her head high, despite her lack of success. Asher held the door open with a bow.

"Thank you, sir." She offered him a slight nod, a most becoming blush painting her cheeks.

Lovely girl. Asher smiled warmly and went to speak to the sergeant. "Asher Burton," he introduced himself. "I believe you have a package for me?"

The sergeant's mood was still sour. "I do, sir. Let me just get rid of this female nonsense and I'll retrieve it for you."

Asher's curiosity got the better of him. "What female nonsense?"

The sergeant pursed his lips. "Got a bee in her bonnet about her uncle's disappearance, up by the shores of the loch. Thinks it has to do with the old crackpot's research, God help us all." He gathered up the pile of papers.

"Wait—may I have a look, while you retrieve my package?" Asher's brows drew together. How many crackpot uncles had disappeared this week from the shores of Loch Ness?

"Suit yourself." The other man rolled his eyes with a dismissive wave of the hand before he went after Asher's brief. Once alone, Asher himself sorted through the young woman's report–clear and concise it was, with attention to detail. He thought he recognized something of his old friend's touch in her report.

The sergeant returned with the requested brief, and upon request, released the woman's report to Asher. In another moment he had picked up the sheaf of papers, acquired his brief, and hastened after the girl. She was at the end of the block, about to cross. "Miss?"

The woman turned around with an unmistakable look of confusion as she pushed an errant lock of golden hair off her forehead. "Yes? Is there something I can help you with, sir?"

He held up the papers, hurrying to catch up to her. "This report–this is yours? You're Charlie Whitfield?"

"Yes." she answered slowly. "I'm Charlie—Charlotte Whitfield. I'm afraid you have me at a disadvantage, Mister...?"

"Asher Burton." He bowed again. "Am I to understand that you were the Professor's assistant?"

"Yes, I *am* his assistant," Miss Whitfield replied, assessing him with those intelligent green eyes. "Are you familiar with my uncle's work?"

Asher nodded. "I am–and more to the point, I've been assigned to his case, to investigate his disappearance. Would you perhaps take tea with me, Miss Whitfield?" He offered her his arm.

There was another pause, and further consideration before she accepted his arm. "A cup of tea would be lovely." Whatever else Miss Whitfield might be, she did not seem to be a woman of haste. "You do not have the look of a police investigator.

Would I be correct in assuming you are associated with a certain Agency my uncle and I have assisted in the past?"

Asher added 'perceptive' to his mental list of Charlotte Whitfield's qualities, studying her face. "You would."

"Then your employer believes that my uncle's disappearance is not as simple a matter as the local authorities have deemed it?" Miss Whitfield asked, and Asher got the sense that the question was something of a test.

"Let us rather say that my employer believes in taking no chances with people deemed important to the Agency." He smiled at her as they began to walk, his companion gently guiding them down the main street. She indicated that they should cross to the other side of the street. "Why 'Charlie'?" Asher asked. They moved toward a building with window boxes burgeoning with fading salmon-pink chrysanthemums, setting it apart from the generally unadorned and practical appearance of the rest of the town.

"You were expecting to meet with a man, no doubt," Miss Whitfield replied, her lips curving into a smile that revealed a charming set of dimples. "My uncle found himself charged with raising an eight-year-old girl. I believe he found it a bit daunting, and 'Charlie' made the prospect easier, to his way of thinking. Or perhaps he felt a new name would make a new beginning easier."

He nodded. "And did it?"

"I suppose it did in some ways," she said with a shrug. "And it is who I am now. I see no reason to change that."

The flower-adorned building proved to be the tea room, a rather small and simple affair. Asher released Miss Whitfield's arm and opened the door for her, following closely behind.

There were only three tables inside, each adorned with a simple white cloth and a bouquet of the same flowers that grew in the window boxes outside. The tea room lacked the elegance of London, Asher thought, but it was adequate for the business at hand. They were led to a table near the window by a short, stoutly-built woman of middling years by the name of Mrs. Wilson, who greeted Miss Whitfield warmly and cast a polite but curious look over Asher. She stayed long enough to take down their order, then left them to themselves.

They stuck to the pleasantries as they waited for their tea. Asher thought it best to let the details of the case rest until they could do so without interruption from the hostess. Mrs. Wilson bustled to the table with a tray a few minutes later. She put everything in order and disappeared again, though Asher had the sense that she was discreetly observing them even as she made a show of folding napkins in the corner.

"You say that you've been sent to investigate the circumstances of my uncle's disappearance," Miss Whitfield tilted her head slightly, a brow rising thoughtfully. "Your accent implies you are not from Scotland, yet you can't have traveled far. I only sent the telegram to Agency headquarters in London a day ago."

Deductive reasoning. Interesting. "I am from London," Asher told her. "But I was already in Scotland when I received word, so I just came ahead." He poured the tea and offered Miss Whitfield one of the tea cakes.

Miss Whitfield accepted it, though she merely picked at it, leaving a plate full of crumbs. "It's fortunate you were nearby. As I understand it, time is of the essence in cases such as this." A line of frustration appeared between her brows. "Thank you for coming so quickly. I'm afraid the local authorities are not taking the matter as seriously as I would have hoped."

"I'm sorry to hear it," he replied courteously, though in some ways that would make his job easier. "I suppose your uncle's research..." Asher let the sentence drift off.

"Yes, his research has left him with something of a reputation here." She looked up from the cake and met his eyes for a moment. "Most think his fascination with the Loch Ness Monster *eccentric*, at best."

He chuckled. "You've a gift for understatement, I see."

"I was raised by Elias Whitfield. One of us had to be understated." Her lips quirked upward in a half-smile, amusement reflecting in her eyes.

"A fair point," Asher allowed.

Miss Whitfield looked at the clock and sighed, pushing away her plate. "As lovely as this has been, Mr. Burton, I'm afraid I must cut our time short. With my uncle... away, I'm left to see to the business of the farm on my own. I still have supplies to collect at the store, and need to return home to tend the animals before dark." She stood, gathering her gloves. "Where are you staying, in case I need to reach you?"

He stood up as well. "At your farm, if there is room. In the stables, if need be—but I must be on the spot to do my job properly, and you should not be alone, Miss Whitfield, not with the possibility of mischief abroad."

"I suppose you're going to insist." Miss Whitfield glanced up from the task of putting on her gloves.

He looked at her over the rims of his spectacles. "I am."

"Very well, Mr. Burton." She nodded, though it was difficult for Asher to guess what she thought of his answer. "However, I think I can do better than to stick you in the stable with Nan. I'm sure my uncle would not object to you using his room while you're here." She gathered the last of her belongings and headed for the door. "Do you have a horse of your own with you? It's a bit of a drive if you'd rather ride in the cart."

"Thank you, I'll settle the bill here and engage a horse. You drove a cart?"

Miss Whitfield chuckled, turning back to look at Asher over her shoulder. "Well, it didn't drive itself." She stepped outside where she waited at the door for Asher to pay the bill and join her.

When all was done, she beckoned for Asher to follow. She led him back down the street, and then down a small alley to the back of the general store. She continued to a small wagon, with a dappled gelding hitched and waiting. "Do we need to stop off to get your belongings?"

"I'll gather them and meet you, say in half an hour? Where?"

"Here will suffice. I'll go inside the store and do my shopping for the week," she replied, climbing into the cart. "When that is finished we can drive back to the farm and start the search for my uncle." Asher nodded and strode off.

Half an hour later Asher met her at the store, having engaged a large and hardy Dales pony named Whiskey. He tossed his suitcase into her cart, and pronounced himself ready to go.

The drive through the countryside proved to be a pleasant one, with all the color of the Scottish autumn on full display. Mysterious creatures and missing persons aside, the scenery surrounding Loch Ness was breathtaking. An hour or so later Miss Whitfield and

Asher pulled to a stop in front of a weathered barn that stood several yards from a small cottage, with very little remarkable in its appearance save for the cupola on the roof.

"You can put your things in the house while I put the cart away and see that Nan, our milk cow, gets her evening milking." She hopped down from her seat, gesturing to the house.

Asher stripped off his gloves and slipped easily from Whiskey's back. "If you like, I can see to Nan after I've put Whiskey away."

A slow, mischievous, and utterly charming grin crept across Miss Whitfield's face. "Are you used to handling an udder, Mr. Burton?"

"I believe I understand the general principle, yes." He smiled back at her.

"In that case, I shall leave Nan in your tender care." She started to unhitch the gelding, which she called Tobias, then paused and shot Asher a quick look. "Do be aware, she tends to kick the bucket halfway through."

He nodded. "I shall use my gentlemanly wiles and charm her into submission. Failing that, I'll just hold the bucket with my feet." Asher gave her a brief salute and headed for the barn, Whiskey in tow.

"The bucket is in a cabinet by the door!" Miss Whitfield called after him.

Asher acknowledged her final instruction with a wave, and led Whiskey into the barn. He found the milk bucket with relative ease, along with the rest of the stable equipment, and gave Whiskey his rubdown and mash. Miss Whitfield brought Tobias in just as Asher was turning his attention to the recalcitrant Nan.

His hostess saw to Tobias' care without comment, filling his feed trough with grain and giving the horse a quick brushdown. Asher had Nan tied to the milking stand and was settled on the stool at the cow's side when Miss Whitfield finished with Tobias.

She filled another bucket with grain and hung it on a hook at the head of the milking stand. "Seems you have everything in hand," she commented dryly, taking up a position on the other side of the cow. "She seems content enough for the time being."

"I'm told I have a very gentle touch," Asher replied, his eyes on his job.

"Oh? Converse with many cows, do you?" Miss Whitfield bent down to look at Asher from underneath Nan's belly.

He flashed her a quick grin. "Not at all. But I imagine females of any species are much the same in their appreciation of being kindly treated."

Her quiet reply came after a thoughtful pause. "Kindness seems to be something you excel at, Mr. Burton." She straightened with a sigh and a contemplative expression that was marred by subtle lines of sadness. "I'll leave you to this and see what's to be done for dinner."

Asher straightened up and watched her go, wiping his glasses on his handkerchief, his gaze speculative. Lovely, intelligent, clever, devoted... what was Elias thinking, keeping a girl like that in this isolated, lonely place? Or did she prefer the isolation, like her uncle?

By the time Asher finished the milking and joined Miss Whitfield in the house she was standing at the stove in a small and organized kitchen, well into the task of chopping potatoes and carrots. The home was surprisingly cozy—no doubt a result of her presence—and the smile with which she greeted him was a warm one. "I'll have supper ready soon. I can show you my uncle's study after we've eaten, if you like."

"At your convenience, of course. May I help you chop?"

The offer scored Asher another smile from Miss Whitfield. "If you wish." She stepped aside and handed him a second knife. "As brilliant as my uncle is, food preparation was never a skill in which he excelled. It only took a few months of eating his cooking to convince me that I should take over the task. Thankfully, our neighbor, Mrs. Alvin, was willing to teach me the basics." She finished with the potatoes and leaned against the table as Asher chopped his way through a carrot.

He smiled at her and picked up another carrot. "I'll do my best to exceed expectations, then."

"Exceed? Meeting expectations isn't enough?" Miss Whitfield asked, and Asher got the distinct impression that the question was another test.

He shrugged. "If your uncle's kitchen skills were so execrable that you felt a need to take over at the age of eight, it seems to me that the desired level of competency is set rather low. Luckily, my own mother required some expertise in the culinary arts from all her children."

"If I believed in something as capricious as luck, I would say that was lucky indeed, at least in regards to our dinner." There was a pause, her eyes lit up, and she started to laugh. It was not the demure and simpering laugh of the ladies in London, but a warm and genuine one. "I just realized how silly that must sound when you consider that I'm helping my uncle research the existence of the Loch Ness monster."

"Capricious indeed." Asher chuckled. "Tell me— what are your own beliefs?"

Miss Whitfield nibbled her lower lip thoughtfully before answering. "I believe that there are things about this loch that are as of yet unexplained.

My uncle has made some very compelling discoveries, but if you're asking if I believe that the waters and surrounding area are stalked by a bloodthirsty monster, then no. Whatever is out there has a logical explanation. Even if we have not found it yet."

He nodded thoughtfully, recalling his own recent experience with an entirely illogical, relatively bloodthirsty monster, though in lieu of provoking either derision or disbelief he merely presented her with a pile of chopped carrots. "Anything else to chop?"

"An onion, if you're brave enough to have a go at it." She plunked the onion down in front of him. "They make my uncle tear up terri..." Miss Whitfield stopped, and swallowed, eyes and nose going red. She took a deep breath and shook her head as if to physically banish the break in composure, then scooped up the carrots and potatoes, turned away from Asher to deposit them in a pan of water on the stove.

Poor woman. Asher took up the vegetable without a word and diced it efficiently, not a tear to be seen. "The secret is to leave the root on until the end," was all he said, adding the onion to the pot.

"So it seems." Miss Whitfield replied, turning back to him with a smile that lacked any true joy. She gave the pot a quick glance and then studied Asher for a moment. "Milking cows, chopping onions, and investigative sciences to boot. You seem to be a man of many talents, Mr. Burton."

"My interests are varied," he allowed. "What are you making, if I might ask?"

"Just a simple vegetable stew, I'm afraid." Miss Whitfield turned back, features composed. "I was not expecting company for dinner and with the trip into town I didn't have time to prepare anything more extravagant. But there is a supply of herbs that we can add to the soup, if you'd like to make it more interesting."

Asher was thoughtful. "Have you eggs?"

"Of course, over there in the basket." She nodded toward the table. "Our small flock of chickens keep us well stocked."

"Would you mind if I...?" He took off his coat, rolling up his sleeves. Maybe he could lighten the atmosphere a little for her.

"By all means." She stepped aside and held a hand out toward the dinner preparations. "Uncle Elias was always far too engrossed in his work to take much note of what he ate. What do you have in mind?"

He seemed to have caught her interest. *Good.* "Have you ever had tagliatelle?" Asher began scooping flour onto the cutting board, making a well in the center, breaking eggs into it.

"No." Miss Whitfield shook her head, watching him with curiosity. "Though our neighbor did show me the fundamentals of the culinary arts, I have had little experience beyond the scope of local cuisine. I've come up with a few recipes of my own through a bit of trial and error, though I'm afraid my personal collection is still somewhat limited."

"Then allow me," he replied. "Have you any cheese?"

She went to the cupboard and pulled out a small round of cheese. "Will this do?"

"*Perfetto.*" Asher kissed his fingers, clowning a bit. "Here—cut off a piece of the rind and pop it in the soup, and then grate up a handful or two, will you?" The dough under his hands was becoming smooth and stiff.

Asher heard that warm laugh again as Miss Whitfield set to the instructions he'd given, following them to the letter. When she was finished she moved closer, leaning over to examine his work. "A skilled touch indeed," she commented as she watched him knead the dough.

"Years of practice," he assured her. "Rolling pin?"

"One moment." Miss Whitfield pulled the rolling pin from a drawer and held it out to him.

Asher rolled out the pasta exceedingly thin, then deftly cut it into strips, coiling those loosely. "Now we let them dry for a bit, until the soup is just about finished."

His companion reached out, lightly brushing delicate fingertips across a piece of pasta. "I'm the host and yet I've already set you to work twice this evening." She glanced sideways at him. "You will spoil me, Mr. Burton." He merely smiled. Miss Whitfield met his eyes for a moment, her green gaze assessing him, but revealing nothing of her thoughts. "I'm just going to go tidy myself up a bit and I'll be back in time to set the table." She hurried out of the room without another word. The sound of footsteps on the stairs was followed by that of a door closing.

Asher cleaned up the kitchen while she was gone, gathering up the debris from the pasta-making in a cloth and shaking it out the kitchen door with a snap. Miss Whitfield's reaction to the tagliatelle seemed to confirm his earlier musings on her life here, and he resolved to have a firm chat with Elias once he found him. Not finding him was simply not on the table any longer, not after witnessing the lovely young woman's loneliness and grief. There was only one acceptable outcome, to Asher's mind. Miss Whitfield needed her uncle back.

Dammit, Elias, where are you?

Perhaps ten minutes later the sound of footsteps heralded his hostess' imminent return. A sudden whiff of something floral—lilacs and the scent of summer rain, Asher thought—and then Miss Whitfield stepped through the kitchen door. She'd obviously tidied her hair, for it was smooth and glistening in the lamplight. Her fingers drifted to a delicate chain around her neck, upon which dangled a single pearl.

"This is as close as I've come to hosting a dinner party," she explained, cheeks going a little pink. "I thought it fitting that I mark the occasion."

Asher hurried to finish rolling his shirtsleeves back down and shrugged on his coat, giving her as elegant a bow as he could manage. "I am honored."

Her blush deepened as a sweet and somewhat shy smile revealed those dimples again. She glanced down, hands smoothing her skirt. "Though, I did put you to the task of cooking, so I suppose hosting is something of a joint effort this time." Miss Whitfield cocked her head to the side for a moment. "Perhaps we should invite the chickens in to serve as guests." She shrugged and her expression grew playful. "Though they are not known to be particularly interesting conversationalists."

Asher dropped the fresh pasta into the boiling soup. "I would think that depends on whether you speak fluent chicken or not. I believe it's a very idiomatic language."

"With a surprising number of different dialects," she shot back without missing a beat.

"Oh, yes," he agreed, giving the soup a stir. "Locally, I'm given to understand, there are a few primary dialects. Do you speak Dumpy or Grey? Perhaps Orpington?" He was trying not to smile, but was pretty sure he was failing.

"I'm most fluent with Grey," she replied, green eyes sparkling. "But one does pick up a few of the nuances when visiting the parlors of the henhouse." Her lips twitched.

Asher dug a noodle out of the pot and blew on it. "Perhaps," he replied as he cut the noodle in half, "you would be so good as to accompany me as translator the next time I have tea with a chicken." Chuckling, he offered her half a noodle to test, popping the other half in his mouth.

"If I'm available. The farmyard does fill one's social calendar," Miss Whitfield accepted the noodle, eyes fluttering closed for a moment as she chewed. "Delicious, Mr. Burton. I believe I have just the thing to finish off the menu." She hurried to the cupboard and pulled out a loaf of bread, perfectly golden, with seeds and flecks of seasoning crusted on top. "I like to add herbs to it. Took a bit of perfecting but I finally got the combination just right, I think."

He broke off a morsel and tasted it. "Mm! Divine, Miss Whitfield. I bow to your superior skill," and he did, again, because she'd seemed to like it the first time.

The food was excellent, if plain; the company congenial, and Asher, for his part, was sorry when it was over. After the meal and general tidying-up he retired to Elias' room, surprisingly neat given what he knew of the man, although perhaps the hand of his niece was in evidence. In any case, he unpacked his few belongings, including his pistol and ammunition, and settled on the bed to read his brief and the packet Miss Whitfield had left at the police station.

A concise document, giving a breakdown of local events in the days before her uncle's disappearance, a sketch of the latest alleged attack site, and a summary of Elias' research into the other 'attacks'. When Asher was finished he removed his glasses, rubbing his eyes. There was nothing specific to grab hold of, but he agreed with Miss Whitfield's overall conclusion: something very suspicious was in the air.

Chapter Three

Company and Comfort

Charlie woke before dawn, her thoughts an unsettled jumble. Though she had rested better knowing that someone was there, she still found it difficult to sleep through the night when her uncle's safety and whereabouts remained in question. Yesterday evening had brought the loneliness of the past few days into harsh focus. She missed Uncle Elias desperately, but just having another person around the place soothed that terrible, empty ache more than she imagined it would. Mr. Burton seemed a comfortable companion, and despite the newness of their acquaintance, he'd created a sense of safety and hope where none had existed before.

Though the bed was warm and the idea of climbing out of it to pad across the cold wooden floor an unpleasant one, Charlie knew she'd slept as much as she was going to. Besides, the chores had to be attended to, and there was a guest to feed. Getting up and being productive seemed a better option than staying in her bed and finding more reasons to fret. Uncle Elias was depending on her, and now she had the help she needed to succeed.

By the time the sun was up she'd already milked Nan, gathered the eggs, and started breakfast. With the extra time that her early rise provided, Charlie put far more effort into the morning meal than she normally would have. She whipped up a batch of sweet rolls, one of the few vices her uncle could not resist, and then grated the remainder of the cheese from dinner the night before, fried up a pan of bacon, and laid out a variety of options for omelets.

Mr. Burton came into the kitchen, not from the direction of her uncle's room as she'd expected, but from outside, his arms full of newly-split kindling. The shirt he wore was only partially buttoned, leaving plenty of surprisingly muscled chest on view. His hair was damp and curling wildly, his spectacles were nowhere to be seen, and his cheeks and chin were freshly shaved. "Good morning, Miss Whitfield." He dumped the kindling in the wood box and surveyed the table. "I hope you won't go to such trouble for me every morning," he said with a chuckle.

"I..." Charlie's gaze settled on her companion, noting the way his muscles tensed and shifted as he moved, how striking the blue of his eyes were when framed by those dark and wild curls. She'd never been alone with a man who was not family, let alone a man who was so.... objectively attractive.

That thought startled Charlie back to the present and caused her cheeks to heat. She cleared her throat and focused on fussing over the table setting, hoping he hadn't noticed how openly she was staring. "It was no trouble at all, Mr. Burton. I was up early and had the extra time. There's coffee." She composed herself and turned back to him. "It seems I was not the only one up early though. When did you wake? I didn't even hear you go outside."

"Oh, I was up to see the sun rise, learning the layout of the place. I'd noted that you were low on kindling last night and thought I should make myself useful." He finished buttoning up his shirt and ran his fingers through his unruly locks. "Forgive my state of dress—I'll go change before we sit down to break our fast."

"That's quite all right, Mr. Burton." Charlie replied quickly, pausing in the trek to the china cabinet to retrieve cups for their coffee. She wasn't certain whether it was the desire to have company, or that she... enjoyed the way he looked, but the response had left her lips before she'd even considered the words. "There's really very little need to stand on formality here. The nearest neighbor is two miles away, and I don't expect you to dress up for me. Thank you for seeing to the firewood, though."

He bowed, with a smile. "Your servant, miss." Asher scanned the table again. "So what are we making this morning? Our collaboration turned out exceedingly well last night, I believe. I find myself eager to repeat it."

"Everything is nearly done." Charlie smiled at him. "I didn't know what you liked in your omelets so I set out what I had for you to choose from." She gestured to the cutting board for him to inspect the gathered ingredients. "I also made sweet rolls, a specialty of mine, and they are ready. I admit to having a bit of a sweet tooth. Your arrival seemed a good justification for indulging."

Her companion chuckled and helped himself to a roll. "As I am used to eating whatever is put in front of me, I shall defer to your judgment with regard to omelet ingredients. This roll looks almost too good to eat—though, you observe, that will not stop me." He took a bite and groaned, nostrils flaring in delight. "Ambrosia. Cinnamon, I detect, and... what is that? It's delicious!"

"There's a secret trick to them." Charlie smiled, deeply satisfied by the compliment. "My uncle still hasn't figured it out." She put a finger to her lips and began contemplating the omelet ingredients before carefully making her selections.

Breakfast proved to be a very pleasant start to the day. Charlie and Asher conversed comfortably; he asked her questions about the currents of the loch, the research she'd been conducting. Charlie asked her share of questions as well, particularly concerning what sort of travel he'd experienced, and whether or not he'd ever visited any of the other bodies of water reported to contain mysterious creatures.

When they had both finished, Mr. Burton insisted on doing the cleaning up and Charlie took the opportunity to continue the research her uncle held so dear. He would return—anything else was unthinkable—and when he did, Charlie would report that she hadn't been lax in their work.

The morning had warmed some during breakfast. The sun was shining at any rate, and there was little in the way of a breeze, allowing the sunlight to ease the autumn chill. Though Charlie set out with more optimism than she'd felt in days, it didn't take long before the work began to darken her mood. The process of checking their live traps and collecting samples of the water had always been a task that she'd carried out with her uncle. It had been nearly a week since they'd shared this task, nearly a week since her uncle had bidden her farewell and rowed away. Charlie knew all too well that with each day that passed, the chances of finding him alive and well diminished.

It all came cascading down on her like a relentless avalanche. Uncle Elias was gone, and unless they were able to find him, life would never be the same. She would be alone. It was all too much to confront, and her legs refused to support her under the weight of such loss. Charlie's eyes filled with tears and with a quiet sob she sank down to sit on the ground. She covered her face with her hands and gave in to the grief that was making her throat ache.

A warm hand gently touched her shoulder.

She jumped a little, scrubbing at her cheeks as she tried to regain control. Yet, for all her efforts the tears would not abate, the aching wouldn't ease. "F—forgive me, Mr. Burton." She hiccupped. "I am not usually..." The weeping intensified, stealing her breath, and doing little to ease the burden. She turned her face away from Mr. Burton, but was vaguely aware of movement at her side.

"Come," he murmured, and astonishingly, warm arms wrapped around her shoulders as he pulled her into a hug His grip was gentle but firm, warm and reassuring.

Charlie leaned into that embrace, clinging to the man, letting him hold her, accepting the comfort he offered. Under normal circumstances she would have been horrified to lose control of her emotions in front of someone she had so recently met, but the strain of her uncle's disappearance was too much to bear alone. Charlie needed this release, and she suspected that Asher Burton knew it as well as she did.

He let her cry, merely stroking her hair or rubbing her back while she did. He didn't offer any hollow reassurances or empty platitudes, which was all to the good, for they would have broken the simple yet profound sense of comfort that his quiet compassion provided.

It took several minutes for Charlie to settle herself, but she finally managed to draw a full breath. She pulled away, wiping her eyes and sniffling a little. "Thank you."

Mr. Burton offered her a large and snowy handkerchief. "Perfectly understandable."

"I'm not generally prone to falling to the ground in a puddle of tears." Charlie accepted it with a grateful smile. "It's just—well, it's been five days, Mr. Burton. I know that each passing day reduces the probability of finding my uncle."

"My dear Miss Whitfield," he replied, his blue eyes serious, "I would be surprised if you were not distressed. But you have my solemn promise—I will find him. And I will bring him home."

His words eased that ache a little. "I believe you will," she managed quietly. After a moment more Charlie nodded wearily and gathered herself.

Mr. Burton stood, rolling to his feet with graceful ease, and held out a hand to help her up. "Come inside, Miss Whitfield. Let's see what we have to go on with."

She took the hand that was offered to her, holding tightly as he pulled her to her feet. The steadying strength in his grip was like a tether, helping Charlie regain her emotional equilibrium. "How would you like to begin?"

"With you, if I may." He tucked her hand into the crook of his elbow and began leading her back to the house. "Tell me where he was going, the last time you saw him."

"The last morning that I saw him, he took our boat to a remote area on the loch. He has a research camp there, and hoped to find a way to disprove the creature's involvement in the recent slaughter of some local livestock. He was certain that if the creature existed that would be where he'd find it." Mr. Burton opened the door, but Charlie paused on the threshold. "It's rather a long ride from here, but I will take you as soon as we can make arrangements for someone to tend the farm in our absence."

"I would appreciate that, if you feel you're up to it."

Charlie's gaze drifted out over the water before responding. Wherever her uncle was now, he needed her and she would not fail him. "I am up to it, Mr. Burton. I must be." She gave a slight but resolute nod and stepped inside.

He offered her a small smile. "What must we do to see that the farm is taken care of in our absence?"

Focusing on the practical would help put her mind in order, or at the very least provide a distraction. "We can leave extra feed for the chickens and close them up in the henhouse. The eggs will keep if they go ungathered for a day." Worry began to creep past the details. She nibbled her lower lip, trying to regain her focus. "And Nan... well, I'm not certain what to do about the milking," she admitted, coming up blank on that account. "I suppose she'll keep for a day as well. Though it won't be comfortable for the old girl."

Asher was thoughtful. "Is there a neighbor, perhaps, who would be glad for the milk?"

Charlie nodded, feeling silly for not having thought of it herself. "There is a farm a few miles up the road, belonging to my nearest neighbor, Mrs. Alvin. 'Twas she who taught me the basics of cooking, and how to mend clothing. She is a skilled maker of cheese—I should think the extra milk would be appreciated."

He rubbed his hands together. "Excellent. If you and Tobias will take Nan to the Alvin farm, I'll see to the rest here. Will you?"

"Of course," Charlie was already heading back toward the door by the time she finished speaking. She stopped and turned to look at Mr. Burton. "There should be plenty of food in the cabinets to get us there and back, but I'll return shortly if there's anything you can't manage on your own."

He jogged after her. "Let me help you—I'll saddle Tobias if you want to halter Nan, or vice versa."

It was a kind offer, and one that Charlie was happy to accept. Between the two of them the job was done in record time, and soon Charlie was atop Tobias as he plodded down the dirt road, with Nan lagging behind, the latter stopping often to attempt a go at the grass that grew alongside the road.

Lorna Alvin greeted Charlie warmly, promising to look after the cow, and expressing her condolences over Elias' disappearance.

Charlie thanked her, both for her kind words and for caring for the cow. She was about to take her leave when it occurred to Charlie that she ought to give Mrs. Alvin a detailed account of where she would be going, and what she'd be doing while away. It was entirely by surprise that she found herself explaining the details of Mr. Burton's presence at the farm. Mrs. Alvin listened patiently and without any show of disapproval. The older woman merely nodded and wished Charlie success in her investigation.

On her return to the farm she found Asher waiting in front of the door with a rucksack and a large lidded basket at his feet. He'd produced thick hobnailed boots from somewhere, and a long woolen greatcoat, as well as a wide-brimmed felt hat which was perched upon his curly head, leaving his face in shadow.

"You look ready to brave the wilds," Charlie commented, swinging her leg over the saddle to climb down. "Give me a few minutes to change and I'll be ready to set out as well. Did you think to pack what was left of the sweet rolls?" He grinned and lifted the basket lid to show it fully packed. "Industrious. I shall add that to the list," Charlie said, not bothering to disguise her pleasure. As much as she adored her uncle, it was refreshing to have a companion who was a bit more organized.

"List?"

"Yes." Charlie paused at the open door. "No doubt my uncle will want to send his thanks to the Agency for sending someone, and I intend for him to include a list of the qualities that aided in his safe return." With that she stepped inside the house, leaving Mr. Burton to make of it what he would.

He had both horses at the post when she came out of the house dressed in one of Uncle Elias' heavy wool coats that had grown a bit tight for him in recent years. Mr. Burton laced his hands together and offered her a leg up into the saddle, which she accepted gratefully. It was still a few hours before noon when they guided their horses away from the cottage, ready to begin the search for Elias Whitfield.

Even with the sun shining brightly, the weather was chilly. Despite the earlier calm, the breeze was picking up now, the wind whipping up from across the loch. Charlie turned Tobias off the beaten path and into a break in the trees. The trail was little more than a narrow gap in the underbrush, but it was the most direct route, and it provided some moderate shelter from the wind.

Her companion followed her closely, occasionally encouraging Whiskey with a click of the tongue. Once, when she looked back, she saw him turning up the collar of his coat against the gusts of air rising off the loch.

After a few hours, Charlie pulled Tobias to a stop and looked skyward to judge the time. The sun was past its apex and from the way her stomach was beginning to grumble, she suspected it was at least an hour past noon. She glanced back at Asher. "I think we should stop for a little while. We should let the horses rest, and I am more than ready to have a bite to eat."

"As you like." He slipped easily from the horse's back and went to help her dismount, holding up his hands.

Charlie paused. No one had helped her off of a horse since she was a girl, and though she was capable of dismounting on her own, the idea of Mr. Burton helping was a pleasant one. Her mind immediately summoned the image of his well-muscled chest, showing through the unbuttoned top of his shirt, sending warmth rushing to her cheeks again. "Thank you, Mr. Burton," she replied as she leaned forward and allowed him to wrap his hands around her waist.

"Your servant, Miss Whitfield," he replied cordially as he lifted her down with ease and set her upon the ground. "Shall I light a fire?"

"I was going to offer to do just that," Charlie indicated. "You looked a little cold while we were riding." And as she said this she made a mental note to see to it that he had a scarf before they rode out again. She had some blue yarn at home—a Christmas gift from her uncle—and she thought the shade would go nicely with Asher's eyes.

"Merely a brisk breeze," he demurred, and then belied the statement by pulling off his gloves and cupping his hands over his mouth to breathe on them. After another moment he flipped Whiskey's reins around a branch low enough to let the pony crop what grass there was, and began to gather stones to make a fire pit.

Charlie set to the task of gathering kindling and a small bundle of branches, narrow enough for her to break with a sturdy stomp. It wasn't the most efficient method, but they only needed enough wood to provide an hour's warmth while they enjoyed their luncheon.

It took a few minutes, but when Charlie was satisfied with her offering she returned to the stone circle Mr. Burton had carefully laid out, and began to arrange the wood in the way her uncle had shown her. "You never said why you were in Scotland," she began conversationally. "Were you on another assignment?"

He glanced up at her as he opened the match safe. "A friend's wedding," he replied. "Well—not initially. But that's what it turned out to be."

"I've only been to one wedding," she answered conversationally, finishing with the firewood and brushing off her hands. "I was six, but I remember thinking that everything seemed to glitter, and being quite pleased that I was allowed to wear a new pair of lace gloves." She hadn't thought of that day in years, but the gloves had been the epitome of finery to her young mind. She'd felt so proud and grown-up at her mother's side. "My congratulations to your friend."

Asher chuckled. "I'll relay them. It's as well I left when I did—I think there might have been something in the water, for we had not been there above a fortnight before another friend married rather suddenly as well." He was grinning as he lit the kindling.

"It sounds as though Cupid was hard at work," Charlie replied with a laugh. "It must have been quite the series of parties."

"It was, rather. My stay seemed to be bracketed by celebrations of one kind and another." A small frown came and went between his brows. "All's well that ends well, as the Bard would say."

Charlie wondered what the source of that frown was: it seemed an odd, albeit fleeting, response to the happy occasions. "Let us hope there is yet another happy ending to be had," Charlie held her hands out toward the flames now sputtering to life, and hoped that moment of concern hadn't been an indication of doubt concerning her uncle's well-being.

The frown returned and he leveled that unsettling blue gaze on her. "I will find him, Miss Whitfield."

Charlie met his gaze and offered him a smile. It seemed to her that there was something more to the talk of his friends' weddings. There was a shadow in his gaze, as though his memory was haunted by something. Not that she knew the man well enough to hypothesize about such things. Perhaps it was nothing more than melancholy. "We should eat. There's still a fair stretch to cover and we'll want to be back in the saddle soon if there's to be any hope of getting there while the lighting is good."

He nodded and opened up the basket, passing her a fried egg sandwich–a little cold, but not unpalatable. He'd added dill or something to the butter. "Your order, madam."

The dill proved to be an excellent touch that added interest to what would have been an otherwise simple meal. It was not something she'd have thought to do, but decided to add the trick to her repertoire. *'Always look for the opportunity to expand your* knowledge, Charlie.' Her uncle's voice was so clear that Charlie could almost imagine he was sitting with them now.

Mr. Burton's voice broke into her musings. "All right?"

"Forgive me, I let my mind wander," Charlie said, taking a deep breath, and then another bite, which she washed down with a long swig from her canteen. "He'd have liked the sandwiches. My uncle, I mean. He wouldn't have been able to pinpoint the use of—dill, is it?"

"Got it in one." His lips curved, but the smile didn't quite reach his eyes, which were still studying her. "I found some cold meat in the larder and brought that along for supper, with the last of your excellent bread."

"And the sweet rolls," Charlie added, trying for a bit of levity to lighten the underlying current of disturbance that had snuck into their luncheon. When the hint of trouble remained in her companion's countenance she gave up and decided it was better to have out with it. "Is everything all right, Mr. Asher?" A silly question, considering the circumstances, but she'd asked it and there was little point in attempting a retraction.

He sighed. "Apart from your uncle's disappearance, you mean? Yes," but she had the impression he was reminding himself rather than her. "It's—I just want you to know that I won't fail you, Miss Whitfield. I'll find him and bring him home."

Charlie reached out to place a hand on his, feeling the need to offer him comfort even if his words had been meant to comfort her. "I believe in you, Asher Burton. No matter what happens," and here she raised her other hand to forestall any further promises. "I must at least acknowledge the unhappy possibilities, though I choose to have hope. Whatever the outcome, I will not believe you failed me."

He was staring into the fire, and maybe it was the heat of the flames that tinted his cheeks, but they seemed to grow rosy. Still, he nodded and cleared his throat. "I've a few apples in the basket, if you'd like one."

"I think I've had my fill for now," Charlie declined the offer after finishing off her sandwich. She felt the urge to be on the move again but forced herself to sit still. There was no need to force the man to choke on his sandwich to accommodate her restlessness. "I'll save mine for breakfast."

She needn't have worried; Asher finished the sandwich in two bites. "I'll bury the fire, if you're ready to go."

"The sooner we leave, the sooner we can be out of the saddle again." She rubbed at her lower back as she stood up. Though it wasn't the first time Charlie had made the ride to the research camp, the pace with her uncle was generally slower with more breaks.

Asher kicked dirt over the fire and stomped on it to be sure it was fully extinguished, then tossed her into the saddle before swinging up onto Whiskey. "Lead the way."

Chapter Four

Partners

Asher contemplated the straight back of the woman riding before him. Tougher than she seemed, she was; worried for her uncle, but brave and determined enough to make this trek with a near-stranger.

He'd been distracted by thoughts of Ross, about what it had been like to lose his best friend, to be unable to find him for nearly two weeks. Then when he'd finally returned, Asher'd had to watch him die.

He said nothing of this to Miss Whitfield, of course. They hardly knew one another. She was already under enough strain, worrying about Elias; and Ross was alive again, and that thought deserved more examination than Asher had been willing to give it so far. Now was not the time, so he shoved it back down out of sight again and forced his attention to the current situation.

From what she'd said, Charlie herself had not been to this campsite since her uncle's disappearance. Asher wasn't sure what to expect; he hoped that there would be something that might hold some kind of clue—and that he'd be clever enough to recognize it should such a thing be found.

Miss Whitfield reined her horse in and pointed to a clearing a few yards away. "That is where Uncle Elias does his research in this area. He would not have gone somewhere else without letting me know."

Asher nodded and swung down from Whiskey's back, helping Miss Whitfield from the saddle before walking over to the campsite. A roughly constructed lean-to and bedroll, he noted, the latter used; the thick layer of dirt on the campfire indicated that it had been put out deliberately. An iron kettle with coffee dregs, a pot with the moldy remnants of beans in it, an unwashed tin plate... "Was your uncle careless about his campsite?" Asher asked, squatting to examine the ground around the lean-to.

"Never," Charlie answered without a trace of hesitation. She knelt at Asher's side. "Despite the state of his study, he was always meticulous about keeping this site tidy."

Asher stood again and held out a hand to help Miss Whitfield up. "How did he get up here? Do you have another horse?"

"We have a small rowboat, he used it to get here. The journey is much faster by water. There's a bit of an inlet just past those trees. Unless he left without cleaning the dishes, the boat is likely to be tied there." She pointed absently, her eyes carefully scanning the perimeter of the camp.

Asher excused himself and went to look. The inlet was exactly as she'd described, and the rowboat bobbed placidly in the water, secured to a low-hanging branch.

He pursed his lips. The presence of the rowboat seemed to confirm that Elias hadn't intended to leave the campsite; but the lack of any signs of struggle argued that he had done so under his own steam. Whitfield was a meticulous researcher, he knew of old, and his niece had said that this same level of care extended to this campsite, which only made sense as it would have served as a sort of field laboratory. Was it rash to assume that while Elias might have left voluntarily, he'd done so in some great disturbance of mind?

His gut sank a little, a familiar feeling that sometimes told him that he'd grasped a good thread to follow, even if he wasn't sure in the moment why or how. Fine, then—Elias had left the campsite abruptly and in some distress of mind, perhaps. What did that mean, and where did he go? Asher looked about a bit longer, but there was no sign of anything having been amiss with the boat. Frowning, he returned to the camp.

Miss Whitfield was in the process of gathering more wood and piling it beside the cold firepit. "Did you find the boat?"

He nodded. "It's there," he told her. "So Elias didn't leave that way. Why he left the campsite in this condition and where he went are still a mystery." He didn't much like the way signs were pointing.

"We'll have to figure out how to get it back to the farm," she mused, dusting off her hands as she finished with her work. Despite her careful demeanor, Asher detected the depth of her anxiety in the way her lips thinned. "It doesn't make sense," Charlie muttered, taking off toward the inlet herself. She stopped at the break in the trees and ran her fingers over the rope wrapped around a low-hanging branch, keeping the vessel tethered close to shore. Her eyes drifted out over the water, its surface reflecting the sunlight as it shifted. After a minute or two she turned to Asher. "There must be something at the camp. Some clue to indicate what happened. If he made a discovery he would have written it down in his journal, and he would have taken that journal with him."

Asher nodded, following his companion back to the camp. The one place he hadn't examined yet was inside the lean-to, but he intended that Miss Whitfield use it that night, so he might as well glean what he could while there was still light.

He dragged the bedroll out of the lean-to, and began methodically shaking out and folding each blanket. After he finished with the first, he lifted the second to find a leather-bound journal tucked within its folds. Asher held it up. "Look familiar?" he asked.

The expression on Miss Whitfield's face was enough to break his heart, and to confirm that the journal was familiar. She lifted a hand to her mouth, blinking back tears. "He—he took it everywhere with him. I half-hoped we wouldn't find it."

Asher felt awful for her, but the journal would have to be searched. "May I?"

She nodded and moved to sit on the trunk of a fallen tree, taking a few moments to compose herself before speaking again. "If he found anything here, it will have been recorded in that book."

Asher nodded and set the book down and finished searching the bedroll before diving back into the lean-to to discover what else was in there: a candlestick with a mostly-burned tallow candle in it, some pencils, a change of clothing, and a crock of soap. Satisfied that he'd seen all there was to see, he squatted on the ground and paged through the book.

It became clear very quickly where Miss Whitfield had picked up her thorough record-keeping habits; most of Elias' observations were of things he hadn't seen. In one or two places he recorded seeing strange ripples in the water, but for the most part the statistics were measurements and percentages and proportions and degrees of the scenery around the loch.

He turned the page dated a week earlier and found the next page blank. Frowning, Asher turned back, and then forward again. There ought to have been at least one more day—his fingertip caught on something and he pressed the book farther open. Two pages had been torn out.

He contemplated this development, smoothing his fingers absently over the blank page, when it dawned on him that he could feel something—ridges where an impression had been formed. Asher held the book up to the light—yes, there was something there, but... no, he couldn't make it out. He chewed on his lip for a moment, then remembered the pencils and went to grab one.

Lightly he rubbed the lead over the page. There was definitely something there: E... U...

At last he'd covered the page and sat back.

Eureka.

Asher heard a sniffle and then the sound of Miss Whitfield exhaling slowly. She stood up and came to join him beside the lean-to. "Have you found something?"

"I don't know how much further it gets us, but..." Asher nodded and showed her the page. "He found something. Do you think...?" He glanced up at her, belatedly taking in her distress. "Oh, Lord, I'm sorry. Sometimes I get a bit wrapped up in things, and I forget—here, let's get set up and comfortable, at least."

So saying he put the journal down and got up to work on starting a fire in the pit.

Miss Whitfield was quiet throughout the process, applying herself to one task and then another with a little frown creasing her brow, though her eyes remained dry. When all was put to order, and they were comfortably arranged around a fire she finally broke her silence. "You needn't be, you know. Sorry for getting caught up in your work, that is."

He shook his head. "No—it's unforgivable that I should have forgotten, even for an instant, that this isn't a case to you." He took off his hat and rubbed a hand through his curly hair, making it a little wild. "My only excuse is that I generally work with a partner, and he is much better at the personal side of things— comforting people and that sort of thing." Quinn occasionally seduced a witness in the name of comforting them, but Asher wasn't going to get into that. "I do apologize."

Her response was quick, and surprising. "Then it's fortunate that your partner is not here."

Privately Asher was of the same opinion—Miss Whitfield was not a woman to be taken lightly, he thought—but his brows rose. He was interested to hear her reasoning. "Is it?"

Miss Whitfield sighed. "I suppose some would prefer to be fussed over and coddled, or left to their fretting. But I find it easier to focus on the task at hand, to approach it as a puzzle to be solved." She offered him the ghost of a smile that seemed a little embarrassed, even apologetic. "It's been easier to handle things with a... partner who has a similar approach."

Asher smiled in response, though internally he was distracted by calculating whether her beauty would tempt Quinn, or her inexperience put him off—or tempt him more—and found the entire train of thought annoying. "I hope," he replied after an appreciable silence, "that I can continue to ease the situation for you, until Elias is safe and sound at home."

"So do I, Mr. Burton." She tilted her head thoughtfully. "May I ask you something?"

"Of course."

"Do you enjoy what you do?"

He was surprised by the question, and had to consider the answer. "I enjoy putting puzzles together, as you mentioned," he began slowly. "I like feeling that I'm working toward the good of my country. Occasionally," he shifted a bit and poked at the fire, stirring it up, "it's enjoyable to teach a short, sharp lesson to those who deserve it." He softened that with a smile. "I don't much enjoy being shot, or being *taught* a short, sharp lesson myself. But overall I'm suited."

"You've been shot?" Miss Whitfield's brows arched in surprise. "And here I get aggravated when I prick my finger on a fish hook."

Asher chuckled. "Well, fingers are very sensitive, you know."

Charlie laughed as well, and Asher was gratified that his response seemed to have brightened her mood. "Do try not to get shot while you're here, Mr. Burton," she said, eyes twinkling a bit. "I would be terribly put out if you did."

"I would never want to cause you any distress, Miss Whitfield," he replied, glad to see her spirits continued to lift, and he held up a hand. "I solemnly swear that I will do my best to dodge any bullet that might come my way."

"I appreciate that, it's very professional of you, agent," she answered, those green eyes locking with his, solemn despite the curve of her lips. She exhaled, clapping her hands on her knees in much the same way

Asher had seen Elias do. "Well, as you so kindly passed out lunch, I shall see to our supper."

"If I can help," he began.

She stopped in her trek toward the picnic basket and turned the most beguiling smile on him. "You already have, Mr. Burton."

He blinked, feeling a bit like he'd been clubbed over the head by that smile—and by her statement. After a moment Asher returned his attention to the journal, to see whether he could glean anything else useful from it.

Supper turned out to be surprisingly pleasant. Miss Whitfield was not satisfied to simply pass out slices of cold meat, and set to warming everything over the fire, including the apples, which she drizzled with a small amount of honey that she pulled from her saddlebag with a grin. All in all, it made the campsite feel cozy even when the sun sank beneath the horizon and the night chill set in, the only light their fire, the moon, and the dancing reflection of stars on the water's surface.

Her concoction went incredibly well with the herbal bread, and Asher was lavish in his praise. "Where did you come up with this? I haven't tasted anything like it since my last assignment in Morocco!"

She blushed, tucking a long, wavy lock of hair behind her ear. "Necessity is the father of invention, Mr. Burton. We do not always have sugar, and sometimes one is in need of a little treat."

"True enough." He nodded. "The flavor put me in mind of bastilla—it's a Moroccan dish with lamb, or chicken, wrapped in pastry and dusted with sugar and cinnamon. Delicious—but this is much better." He took another bite.

"High praise from one with such experiences to inform their opinion." Her cheeks were nearly as rosy as the apple peels. "I imagine it must be quite fascinating to see distant places. My uncle has books about the ancient civilizations in Egypt and Greece, and I've always wondered what it might be like to see the exotic places of the world, and try new ways of living."

"Mm." Asher swallowed his last bite. "I imagine much the same. My experiences are hardly those of the average tourist, and I think probably far less enjoyable."

"Come now, you must have had some fun traipsing the globe," Charlie polished off her dinner and set her plate aside. She studied him for a moment. "If I were to venture a guess, I'd think travel was one of the appeals of your profession."

"Seeing new places, all the world has to offer...? Yes, I suppose it is." Less appealing were the seedier underbellies to which he and Quinn were so often exposed, but Asher didn't mention that.

"And yet, you're unpracticed in the dialects of Dumpy and Grey," Miss Whitfield teased. She sighed and shook her head slightly. "I shall have to make note of that lapse in training to your superiors."

Asher held out his hands. "No—wait! I'm a quick study, I can learn! My partner—my other partner," he allowed with a quick smile, "says that all it takes for him to learn a new language is a beautiful woman to teach him." He paused. Why on earth had he said that? Too much time spent with Quinn, he was certain. "Maybe I could chat up one of your hens back at the farm," he added, to try and retrieve the situation.

"Fluff their feathers with flattery and I'm sure they'll tell you all the latest gossip," was her dry response.

"Oh, no." He shook his head. "I have a sister, and the one thing I know about women is that they know empty compliments when they hear them. Flattery is pointless. I only ever tell the truth in my compliments."

"He that loves to be flattered is worthy o' the flatterer," Charlie quoted.

"True for you—and for the Bard," he replied, impressed. "I stand by my principles—though it must be admitted, a little practice doesn't hurt. Look at Miss Austen's Mr. Collins." Asher chuckled. "Perhaps I should practice my compliments on you rather than in the mirror. I suspect you could give more constructive feedback."

Miss Whitfield laughed a little, lashes lowering. "If it would help in carrying out your missions successfully." Her eyes met Asher's across the fire. "What would you say?" She turned pink again. "To the mirror, of course."

"The face I usually see in the mirror holds no interest for me: black hair that curls all the wrong ways, blue eyes that don't see very well beyond the end of my nose." He studied her for a moment, at the way the firelight seemed to dance along the tendrils that had come loose around her face. "Maybe... your hair looks like it's been spun from sunbeams," and what in God's name was he saying? "Feathers, I meant feathers, of course. Or perhaps—your beak is looking particularly keratinous this evening, Miss Grey." *Good Lord.* Asher looked away across the lake, watching the stars' reflection on the water—or perhaps they were glow-worms.

She was quiet for a little, then in a tone that was carefully light. "'Keratinous' is it? I believe such compliments would earn you a full education in the dialects of poultry."

"I am relieved to hear it." He needed to end this conversation *now*, before he really put his foot in it. "And I should get to cleaning up before dark fully falls."

Asher rose and began to gather the dishes and cookware, including what Elias had left behind.

Chapter Five

A Visitor in the Night

Charlie nestled into her bedroll, tucking the blankets tightly around herself to stave off the cold. The lean-to was far from comfortable, but had to be more hospitable than a bedroll with nothing but the overhanging tree branches that served as shelter for Mr. Burton.

She rolled onto her side and peeked over the edge of her blanket, considering her new companion. He was unlike anyone she'd met before, with interests and experiences that broadened the world to more than the little corner that Charlie had experienced with her uncle. And yet, he had a way of talking about things that didn't make her feel naive, or foolish, and not once did he behave in a manner that implied he considered the life she lived to be improper or strange for a young woman.

Not that she could have blamed him entirely if he thought it was. She didn't remember much about the life she lived with her parents in London, but what she did recall was different. Everything had been orderly and refined... and, well... different. It was no secret to Charlie that the lifestyle she enjoyed now was not the same as other women of her age.

Charlie sighed and resituated herself onto her back once again. Blast it all, it was just like her uncle to build a lean-to over a tree root. He could sleep anywhere, and through anything, but Charlie could claim no such indifference. Her frustration quickly turned to guilt and then sorrow. She'd spend the rest of her life sleeping on roots if it meant he was home safely.

Movement from Mr. Burton's direction caught Charlie's attention and she rolled back toward the open side of the lean-to. Mr. Burton was sitting up, the blankets from his bedroll having fallen away to reveal a well-muscled, lean torso. He got to his feet, all his attention on the loch beyond the little circle of light from their campfire.

It was then Charlie heard it: heavy splashing, followed by the same sound she'd heard the night her uncle went missing. Somewhere between a song and a moan, a whistle and a cry, it skittered up her spine and set her hair standing on end. The first time she heard that call, it had filled her with terror and seemed like an ominous portent.

Mr. Burton walked to the edge of the light, eyes narrowed as he perched his glasses on his patrician nose.

Curiosity and the knowledge that she was not alone overwhelmed the fear that rose at that call. Charlie cast the blankets aside and was on her feet in an instant. The sound was haunting, and enticing, like something from a dream one could barely remember. She crept across the camp to join Mr. Burton, partially out of curiosity, but more out of a need to be near another person in the presence of that cry.

He glanced at her and she realized that he held a pistol in his other hand, but loosely. His brows drew together briefly, and before she realized what he was doing, he'd picked up one of the blankets from his bedroll and draped it about her shoulders, still warm with residual heat. He held his finger to his lips and stepped out of the light of the campfire toward the loch.

That call sounded again, and Charlie couldn't say if it was closer or further away. Glimmering orbs of light appeared over the distant waves, just as they had the last time she'd encountered that unearthly sound. Their size and color seemed more varied this time, but the movement was unmistakably that of something living. Charlie reached out without thought, and grabbed hold of Mr. Burton's hand as they edged toward the shore, her other hand clutching the blanket close at her neck.

His fingers wrapped around hers, warm and secure. With the light from the campfire so near and little light from the moon, it was almost impossible to make out anything past the shoreline beyond those dancing lights, and the waves occasionally glistened in the distance.

Mr. Burton let out a sudden breath, and after a glance at him Charlie followed his line of sight. A shadow—huge, rounded—hove into sight, then sank with a heavy splash.

Silence seemed to fall over the area like a heavy blanket, even the usual creeping of nocturnal wildlife was gone. The little lights dipped beneath the surface of the water, distorting for a moment before they vanished entirely. The call had gone quiet, and the only sound that remained was the soft lapping of the waves on the shore. Charlie tightened her grip on her companion's hand. Her mind was filling with questions, but it felt wrong to be the first to break the silence.

A nearby owl did not seem to share this sentiment, and after another minute or so gave a loud hoot before launching itself from the branches of the nearest tree. Charlie jumped, sucking in her breath and letting it out with a huff. "That was..." She turned to look at Mr. Burton, and stopped mid-sentence, eyes tracking down his bare torso, the curves and details of his muscle highlighted in the moonlight, scant though it was.

"Oh," he said, and scrubbed a hand over his face, shivering a little. "Let me just—" He strode back to his bedroll and scooped up his shirt, pulling it over his head and adding his coat. "I should—um—stoke up the fire a bit."

"The fire?" Charlie asked absently. "Oh—yes! You must be cold." She shook her head a little and returned to the fireside, glad to know that the darkness probably hid what must have been a truly brilliant blush.

The smile he offered her was perfunctory as he laid more wood on the fire. After a moment he sat back on his heels. "What—um—what do you think that was?" he asked.

Charlie went to the lean-to and retrieved one of her own blankets before answering. The movement helped her to refocus. "I don't know, exactly, but I have heard it before," she finally replied, passing his blanket back to him, though the warmth from it seemed to linger a little. "It was near the farm the night my uncle was supposed to return. There's a sense of life to the sound. Some sort of animal, perhaps?" She was at loss as to what animal might have produced such a call, but it was the most logical explanation she could come up

LADY = LOCH

with at the moment, and an unfamiliar call was hardly concrete proof of the existence of the Loch Ness monster.

Asher nodded, staring into the fire.

"May I?" Charlie asked, indicating a spot on the ground at his side. "My nerves need to settle a bit before I try to sleep again."

"Oh–of course." He seemed distracted, but made a place for her beside him. "Are you warm enough?

After situating herself at his side, with her own blanket draped over her shoulders, Charlie gave him a nod. "As warm as I'm likely to be under the circumstances." She drew her knees up and propped her chin on them. "Have you any theories about what that was?"

He gave a slight snort. "Of course I do, and I feel sure you have the same ones."

"Perhaps I added a bit too much spice to our dinner?" she offered, knowing good and well that what they heard was nothing so mundane.

"Mm. Perhaps it was the *Turbinia*, having lost its way," he retorted, naming a well-known ship. "Or... perhaps it was exactly what it seemed to be."

"Eureka?" Charlie cocked a brow at her companion.

"Eureka," he agreed, his voice soft. He glanced over at her. "I don't think your uncle is mad, or even just wrong. I think he found the creature–and I think maybe it just found us."

That made Charlie's mind still. Hearing Mr. Burton say what she'd been avoiding made it impossible to continue doing so. She frowned into the flames as a lifetime of theories and research shifted into something more solid, stepping out of the world of idea and into a real and physical possibility. "It would change... everything." If her uncle had found the creature, or proof of its existence, it was sure to reshape the pattern of their lives. Having even one person—this person, Asher Burton—express belief made life feel different. "Then I'm glad you were present to hear it too."

He huffed out a short laugh. "I'm only glad you weren't alone. There are things beyond what we know..." He shook his head. "You should try to get more sleep."

"*Any* sleep," Charlie corrected him, rubbing at her neck to emphasize her statement. "Tree roots make poor mattresses."

Asher frowned and scooped up his bedroll, crossing to the lean-to and adding his blankets to hers. "Here—this should be comfortable enough. I'll keep watch."

The gesture delighted Charlie, though she knew she ought to be concerned for the comfort of her companion. "What of your sleep?"

"Oh," he actually chuckled, though there was no humor in it, "I'll get no more sleep tonight."

Charlie considered insisting he try, but decided against it. The man was an agent for the Queen. If he felt he needed to stay awake and watch through the remainder of the night, then she would trust to his experience, and to his abilities. "Very well." Even so, she made a mental note to see that he took his leisure in the morning before they packed up. "But I insist that when morning comes, you get what rest you can, while I see to breakfast and pack up the camp for our return to the farm."

Something in the quality of his expression changed and somehow Charlie felt that he was really seeing her for the first time since hearing the creature.

His smile warmed; his blue eyes did too, and he took a moment to see her settled on his bedroll.

Sleep came more easily than expected this time. Whether it was from the added cushioning of Mr. Burton's blankets, or the knowledge that he was keeping watch, Charlie did not know, and she did not care to examine it in depth. She simply accepted the blessing for what it was and allowed herself the escape of sleep.

Even so, morning seemed to come with unusual rapidity. She was certain that she'd only just closed her eyes when the sounds of birdcalls and lapping water forced her to open them again. Charlie sat up with a small groan, rubbing at her face and pushing away the hair that had escaped her braid. "Do tell me you thought to pack the coffee beans." Another attempt at rubbing the sleep from her eyes. "And the grinder."

Asher's expression was that of exasperated amusement. "I assure you, Miss Whitfield, this is not my first time sleeping rough. For your information, I ground the beans while you were taking Nan to your neighbor's, and the water is already in the kettle." He gestured to the fire, where the coffeepot did indeed hang from an iron tripod. "I'm afraid I can't offer cream, though I believe there's some honey left."

"I do not think there is another person who could be more heroic in my mind at this moment," Charlie returned, digging in her bag for a hairbrush before unbinding her braid to sort the ridiculous mess with efficiency. In a matter of minutes her hair was brushed and braided once again, and Charlie felt ready to face the work of the day.

Asher poured out two cups of boiling coffee and set them on a flat rock. "Let the coffee cool for a moment," he told her, and beckoned. "I think," he said gently, leading Charlie toward the shore, "that we should probably leave as soon as possible. Look."

There in the mucky sand were the imprints of their feet from the night before; and not six yards away, another imprint: a huge, triangular flipper.

The fog in Charlie's mind cleared instantly. "Oh! I should take measurements, perhaps sketch it." She knelt down to examine it in greater detail. "A pity I didn't think to bring plaster!"

There was silence from Asher; after a moment Charlie looked up at him to find that he was staring at her, brows nearly to his hairline. All at once he began to laugh. "Here I've been trying to think of a way to break it to you without frightening you! Miss Whitfield," he said between gales of laughter, "you are an extraordinary woman. By all means, let us measure and sketch."

"*I'll* measure and sketch. *You* will get some sleep," she said, straightening. "And after we've finished our breakfast we'll start for home."

But he didn't lie down to sleep, instead packing up the campsite while she worked.

It hadn't even occurred to her that this discovery might be considered frightening. On the contrary, the existence of proof, real and tangible proof, was nothing short of absolutely exhilarating. The only dark spot was that Uncle Elias was not here to share in it, though from the evidence of his journal, he had experienced the thrill of discovery himself.

When Charlie was satisfied that the print was sufficiently documented, they polished off the last of the rolls and were soon in their saddles and heading in the direction of the farm. The excitement of the discovery wore off as the tedium of the ride wore on. Going home meant returning to a place that reverberated with the absence of her uncle.

They were still a few miles from the house when the wind switched and turned decidedly colder. The sky, which had started clear and blue, was blanketed with angry grey clouds. Charlie pulled her coat tighter, though it only provided a nominal improvement. She considered stopping to pull a blanket from her bedroll, but decided against it.

Beside her, Mr. Burton clicked his tongue and prodded Whiskey into moving a bit faster. "Better for them to stay warm," he called above the blustering gales. "Come on."

Charlie would have laughed if her teeth hadn't been chattering so much. Instead she managed a shaky. "Mmhm." She nudged Tobias' sides and drew up next to Asher. "I hate to remind you, but we still have Nan to re-re-retrieve," she stammered.

"No." He shook his head. "You'll write a note to Mrs. Alvin, telling her I'm to pick up Nan. Or we'll wait until tomorrow." He squinted at the sky. "Once this storm moves in, you'll stay put."

Charlie turned to him, brows raised. "I have managed through storms before, Mr. Burton."

Asher thumbed his hat back on his head. "I've no doubt of it. But Elias is by way of being a friend of mine, and he wouldn't thank me for not taking care of you when it's in my power to do it." He considered her for a moment. "I won't be here forever, Miss Whitfield. Best take advantage of me while you can."

Charlie licked her lips slightly. "Very well. If the weather doesn't clear, Nan will just have to wait until it does. In the meantime I'll enjoy the care you're willing to give."

It was the storm itself that put the final statement on their discussion. With another mighty gust, the heavens opened and a heavy drops of freezing rain began pelting down on them. They spurred Tobias and Whiskey forward, and galloped the last mile or so to the cottage. By the time they made it inside the barn, both horses and riders were soaking wet and freezing cold.

Asher jumped down from Whiskey and lifted Charlie from Tobias' saddle. "Go get dry," he told her. "We can switch when you're changed." So saying he began to unload the saddles, paying no further attention to her.

Charlie did not argue, for she was shivering so intensely that her entire body felt ached. She ran into the house and straight to her bedroom, stripping off her sodden coat and tossing it on the floor near the door. It would have to be hung up by the fire, but the sooner she changed, the sooner Asher would be able to dry off as well.

She put on the first dress she could find, toweled off her hair, and then headed back down the stairs, stopping long enough to throw her uncle's heavy winter coat on before hurrying out to help Mr. Burton tend the horses and check the other animals.

He'd managed to rack the saddles and was in the process of wiping Tobias down when she returned, though his teeth were chattering and his entire body shaking.

Charlie put her hand over his, stilling it. "Go, get dried off before you catch pneumonia." She considered offering him her uncle's coat but knew he'd refuse to take it. "I'll finish and then gather the eggs." He met her gaze and then nodded, hurrying from the barn.

Care for the horses was nearly complete, and it only took another minute before that was done and Charlie was in the henhouse gathering the eggs. She'd been in such a rush to relieve Asher of his post that it had slipped her mind entirely to bring the egg basket out with her, and she was forced to collect the eggs in the gathered folds of her skirt. It hardly mattered—the dress wasn't one of her favorites, and certainly not the first time it had been used for the job.

By the time she returned to the house she was nearly as wet as she'd been before. "Well, I doubt the rain will stop before it's dark. I suppose Nan will just have to spend another night away from home. You have no more business out in this than I do." Charlie said, hanging the now drenched coat on the hook. "The rain is turning to ice."

In her absence Asher had lit the kitchen stove and the fireplace in the sitting room, and was holding another set of drying sheets for her. His hair was still wet and unruly, curls falling into his face, but he'd stopped the full-body shivering. "Here," he said. "I can make something for dinner, if you're hungry."

She shuddered a little even as she wrapped the drying sheet around her shoulders. The chill was the sort that set in the bones and lingered. "I detest this weather," Charlie muttered, rubbing her shoulders. "But at least we're out of it. I'll put the kettle on, and you can rummage through the pantry. We can see to dinner together."

Chapter Six

Calm in the Storm

Asher took Charlie at her word and had a grand rummage through the pantry, lips pursed as he tried to figure out a hearty meal for dinner. Heaven knew they both needed something to ground them after the last couple of days.

He began to assemble ingredients: eggs, salt cod, flour, butter. It wouldn't exactly be gourmet, but it would be warm and filling. He put the cod on to boil to leach out the salt while he turned his attention to scones, flavored with a little cheese.

As he mixed his ingredients his mind turned inevitably to what they'd witnessed by the loch: the creature. He had no doubt that that was what it was; the cry, the splash, the print in the sand... Asher shook his head. He'd seen more fantastical things, but somehow confirmation of this kind of ancient lore still astonished him. Something lived in the Loch Ness—

something not easily explained by what was known to science.

Was it Fae, he wondered? Truthfully he wasn't sure it mattered—or how to find out, either—but as a point of academic curiosity, he wanted to know. It was difficult to imagine a mundane creature—or a group of creatures, it would have to be—simply existing in the loch like so many fish and escaping detection for centuries. That argued a level of intelligence, and *that*—he plopped the dough onto the kneading board— argued toward Fae, rather than against, at least in his opinion.

Which, he mentally allowed as he cut the dough into circles, was worth exactly nil, so there was that to be considered, and tabled the problem for the time being.

Fine. To the problem of Elias Whitfield's disappearance: did this get them any further along?

Asher prodded the softening cod and added more water. It seemed, from Elias' journal, that he'd had a similar revelation—perhaps an encounter even more persuasive. He'd recorded it, his jubilation communicating itself on the page through that single word: Eureka! And then... he'd vanished. His boat was still there, Asher had found no signs of a struggle. No— Elias Whitfield had left that campsite under his own steam. On foot, presumably, but to where?

Asher put some eggs on to boil beside the cod, trying to think like Elias. *I have proof of the existence of the Loch Ness monster, and now I'm going to take it to... where?*

He let out a breath. If they could figure that out, Asher had a feeling they'd know everything.

Soft footsteps heralded the return of Elias' niece. Charlie stepped into the kitchen, hair no longer dripping, and pinned up off her neck in a simple bun.

She checked on the kettle and then moved to the small window near the table, expression troubled.

Asher watched her, concerned. "How can I help?"

A small, cheerless smile lifted the corners of her mouth. "Can you convince the clouds to part and the sun to shine again?" She glanced at him, then her gaze returned to the storm outside. "My uncle left his coat here. It's so cold out there and..."

He pressed his lips together and wiped off his hands before crossing to join her at the window. "Don't do this, Miss Whitfield. It won't help him, and it'll drive you crazy." Asher rubbed her upper arms gently, looking over her shoulder. "Trust me on this, hm?"

There was a pause and Charlie's eyes met his in their hazy reflection in the window. "I do trust you, Mr. Burton." She smiled again, though it still failed to convey any signs of true happiness. "Forgive me. You came to find my uncle and you've spent just as much time keeping me from worrying myself to the point of illness."

"Nothing to forgive. When you love someone, it's nearly impossible not to worry, I know. But imagining each small trouble, letting them add up..." He shook his head. "It only makes the nightmare worse."

Charlie turned and contemplated him, her intelligent green-eyed gaze seeming to see straight through him. "It sounds as though you've experienced something similar."

Asher wasn't at all surprised she'd worked it out. "I have—and recently. One of my best friends was kidnapped. I was terrified." Funny thing—he'd never said it quite so baldly before, not even to his closest friends, but somehow it was easy to admit it to Charlie.

"Were you able to get your friend back safely?" There was hope in her voice and her expression.

He smiled. "Yes—he's fine." There had been a lot more to it, but it was unlikely that she needed to hear anything else right now. "Home, safe and sound." Asher leveled a look at her, meeting her gaze earnestly. "I made you a promise, Miss Whitfield. I intend to keep it."

He was rewarded with a genuine smile, brief though it was. "You did not fail your friend. I shall trust that you will not fail me either." She ran a hand over her hair, the action striking Asher as a physical echo of an attempt to mentally reset herself. "In that case, I will focus on helping find the solution, rather than wallowing in worry." A loud whistle joined the patter of the rain and howling wind. "But first, a spot of tea. Hopefully, that and a warm meal will get rid of the chill."

Asher grinned in approval and went back to the stove. Some little while later, abetted by a cup of strong tea, he served up some creamed cod over toasted cheese scones, joining Charlie at the table.

True to her word, she did not fret over dinner. Charlie tucked into the meal with enthusiasm, complimenting Asher's cooking and even helping herself to a second plateful. Conversation with her came easily, he found, even under such strained circumstances as these.

"I'm afraid my uncle had quite a time of things when he first brought me here," Charlie recalled, reaching to freshen her tea cup. "I was eight, and quite certain a monster took up residence in my closet." She laughed, shaking her head. "No amount of logical discourse would convince me otherwise, bless my uncle's efforts. In the end the only way he could get me to sleep in my own room was to build a monster trap in my closet. Of course, I insisted on helping with the design."

Asher chuckled. "Of course. How did it work?"

"Well," Charlie began, eyes dancing with merriment, "the rat that had been raiding my closet was quite displeased when it found itself trapped in a wooden crate." She took a sip of tea and glanced at Asher over the brim of the cup. "I, to the contrary, felt quite satisfied to have proof of my nightly visitor. Though I was quick to inform my uncle that it likely turned into a rat after being trapped—it had absolutely been a monster prior to that. I suspect he only conceded to the idea because he grew tired of arguing with me and wanted to return to his bed."

Asher's chuckle changed to a laugh. "If you can't beat them with logic, wear them out. A sound strategy."

"And what of you? Did you have a monster in the closet, or under the bed, perhaps?" Charlie asked.

He was still laughing. "Not I. Older brothers, and that was enough for me, I promise you." The monsters had come later, in Her Majesty's service, he thought, sobering a bit, and shook himself. He'd chosen this life, he was good at it, it was his duty, and that was the end of it.

Charlie finished cleaning her plate for a second time and sighed. "Well, I can assure you, there are no further closet monsters in this house. But should one rear its ugly head, I believe I remember how to construct that trap."

Asher pretended to clutch at his heart. "'For this relief, much thanks,'" he quoted the Bard. "''Tis bitter cold, and I am...'" he thought about it and shrugged. "Not especially sick at heart," he amended. "Concerned, more like."

Another smile—Shakespeare seemed to have that effect on Charlie. "Hamlet. Well done, Mr.

Burton." She placed her napkin on the table and stood up. "At least I no longer feel the bitter cold. I thought that chill would stay in my bones for weeks. Shall we clean up, or would you like more to eat? I've a project in mind when we're finished here."

He opted to clean up, and between the two of them it took little time. Asher snapped the dish towel as though cracking a whip and then hung it up in its accustomed place. "So," he said, rubbing his hands together. "What project?"

Charlie merely shook her head and cast a twinkling sideways glance in his direction. "That is a question you'll have to wait to find the answer to." So saying, she left the kitchen, and a short time later Asher heard her rummaging through something in the sitting room.

He liked puzzles, so he was more than willing to wait. Besides, whatever this was seemed to be keeping her sadder thoughts at bay, and that was all to the good. Asher clasped his hands behind his back. "Shall I come in there?" he called.

The rustling stopped before she answered him. "If you like."

"Eyes open or closed?"

He heard a laugh. "Is walking without sight one of the skills your training covered?" Another laugh. "Eyes open is acceptable."

It was, actually. Asher grinned to himself and followed her into the sitting room.

Charlie was situated on a rather worn settee near the fireplace, with a crochet hook in her hands and a skein of grey-blue yarn in her lap. She looked up from hooking the woolen thread through a loop and welcomed him into the room with a smile. "You may sit in my uncle's chair if you like."

He took his seat as instructed. "What are you making?"

"I am weaving a mystery," she said, eyes never leaving her work. "As I said before, you shall have to wait to find out."

Well, if she wouldn't tell him, she wouldn't. Asher considered going to Elias' study to search for any other possible clues, but the truth was that Charlie was distracted from her uncle's plight and it seemed kindest to let her remain so for a while. He looked about for something to read; his gaze lit on a small pile of blank foolscap, and so he acquired a few sheets along with a lead pencil, and began to sketch.

"I'd ask what you're drawing, but as I have denied you the details of my work, it would only be fair if you followed suit." Charlie was looking at him when Asher glanced in her direction. She shrugged and turned her attention back to her 'project' though her focus seemed somewhat false, as she almost immediately peeked in his direction again.

He hid a smile. "Don't let me disturb you."

"Nor I, you," Charlie chuckled, and turned back to her work in earnest.

After an hour, her project was beginning to take shape. A long strip, nearly six inches in width, and row by row growing in length. It was another half hour before she stopped and considered Asher thoughtfully. "I require your assistance, if you'd be so kind."

He laid down his sketch, slipping another piece of paper over it, and rose from his chair. "How can I help?"

Charlie carefully gathered her work and the rest of the skein and moved to stand in front of him. She lifted the crocheted strip and then carefully looped it around his neck, adjusting where the end fell across his chest. After another minute of fussing over it, she gave a thoughtful nod. "Yes, I believe another hour or two and the length will be just right." Asher raised his brows as he looked down at her, realizing that she was working on a scarf. She unwrapped it from his neck and returned to the settee. "It gets cold when the wind comes up off the loch. I saw you adjusting your coat to keep your neck warm."

His mouth dropped open. "That's for me?"

Color rose in her cheeks, but her eyes remained fixed on the stitches she was weaving. "It is the least I can do." A pause. "Of course you needn't wear it when you return to London, if such things are out of fashion for gentlemen."

Touched, Asher shook his head. "I shall wear it gratefully, Miss Whitfield. I'll never find any so well-made, I'm sure."

The look that she turned to him was so sweet and filled with genuine pleasure that it seemed to make the light in the room shine brighter. Dimples still on full display, the pace of her work intensified. "I'll have it finished before bed, I promise you."

He chuckled. "I don't know that I'll need it then, but I thank you for your diligence." Seeing her attention once again fully absorbed by her work, Asher bethought himself of his own small project and excused himself to the kitchen, where he examined the sketch with as objective an eye as he could muster.

Not terrible, was his conclusion, but would be the better for a little color. He glanced around the kitchen and assembled a pot of some dry onion skins and a bay leaf or two, covered them with water, and set them to boil on the stove. While waiting he lit a couple of broomstraws and let them burn to ash in a small dish, and then applied himself to the final details of his portrait. The ash served to give a grey-brown tint to Charlie's dress, and the onion-bay mixture produced a yellowish dye that served to brighten her hair a bit. He painted it on carefully with the corner of a rag so as not to smudge the lines he'd drawn, and then left it to dry on the table while he rejoined Charlie in the sitting room.

She looked up when he returned. "Are you still hungry? I heard you moving about in the kitchen." She put aside her work and moved to get up. "I could make you something if you like."

"I expect it's nearing teatime," Asher agreed, and followed her diffidently into the kitchen, hands behind his back.

The sketch was not immediately noticed, for Charlie hurried to the cupboard and began pulling various foodstuffs out. It wasn't until she moved to set a loaf of bread on the table that her gaze landed on the drying page. She stared down at it, slowly putting the bread aside. "It's me..." she looked up at Asher, but her thoughts were inscrutable.

"Just a way to pass the time," he demurred. "I hope you like it?"

"I do." She brushed her fingers along the edge of the page. "No one has ever drawn me before."

"Clearly a failing on the part of the artists' community as a whole. You make an excellent subject." Clearing his throat, Asher thought he'd better help get tea ready. "I'll—er—I'll put on the water, shall I?"

But he found that between the sound of the rain on the roof, the long ride back from the loch, and his interrupted sleep the night before, even strong tea wasn't helping him to keep his eyes open. After trying unsuccessfully to hide his third or fourth yawn, he admitted defeat. "Forgive me."

"Oh no, not at all," Charlie replied quickly. She reached out and laid a hand on Asher's wrist. It was nothing more than a tender kindness, but her fingers were warm, and the contact gentle. "You have done more than enough on less than enough sleep. Go to bed. I'll see to the clean-up, and finish your scarf. Then off to bed for me as well." She offered him a sweet half-smile. "We shall both need our rest if we are to tackle my uncle's study tomorrow."

He offered her his thanks and a tired smile as he made his way toward bed.

Chapter Seven

A Touch of the Fae

The morning's sunlight was weak and watery, as though the storm of the day before had somehow drenched it, too. Asher was up with the dawn, such as it was, and hurried to the frigid barn to see to the horses and chickens so that Charlie wouldn't have to. He mucked out Nan's pen as well so that the cow would have a clean, warm home to return to, and then went back into the house, blowing on his hands to warm them.

There was a kettle of coffee burbling away on the stove, and no sign of Charlie in the kitchen apart from the finished coffee. Asher poured out a mug of the steaming brew and went in search of her.

He found her leaning against the frame of an open door toward the back of the house. She was holding her own mug of coffee and staring contemplatively into a room that looked like it had recently been rifled. Waist-high stacks of books were lined against the wall, sheets of paper scattered haphazardly across every table and cabinet.

Asher slowed to a stop behind her. "This is Elias' study?"

Charlie slanted him a glance and nodded slowly. "It is." She took a sip from her cup. "Just as he left it."

Asher contemplated the room over her shoulder in dismay. "I ought to have called for backup."

"Shall I fetch rope to tie around your waist, lest there be an avalanche?" Charlie's lips were twitching in amusement.

He huffed out a laugh. "Seriously, though—if there is anything in there that might lead us to Elias' whereabouts, I have my doubts about whether we'd find it in time to be of any use." He looked the room over, sighing. "I suppose I'd best get started, then."

Charlie watched him enter the room then turned, disappearing down the hall only to return a moment later with the coffeepot in her hands. "My uncle claims he has a system but I have never been able to puzzle it out." She stepped inside and carefully cleared a spot on the desk for the pot. "I suspect we'll need this and more if we're to excavate anything of use."

"There's a system?" Asher ran a hand over his face. "Oh, Lord. I suppose we'd better preserve as much of it as possible, then." He began to divide the room into sections. "Have you got an empty crate we can use to sort out anything that might be worth looking at?"

For answer, Charlie left the room again. It was several minutes before she returned this time, two battered hat boxes in hand. "Will these do?"

"Perfectly." He'd created a sort of mental grid and began to carefully sort through the first square, putting aside a paper or two for a second look later. Asher explained his methodology to Charlie and she began on the opposite wall. "Anything dated more recently than, oh, three months; anything that seems out of place; anything pertaining to the creature," were the guidelines he gave her, and they worked with a will for a couple of hours.

By that time, it was late enough in the morning that he could pay a call on the neighbor to retrieve Nan. "Could you write a note to them, explaining who I am?" he asked Charlie as he shrugged on his coat and wrapped his new scarf around his neck.

Half-corralled by stacks of books and papers, Charlie brushed her hands off and carefully moved through the path of organized chaos they'd created. She searched for a sheet of blank paper, but gave up less than a minute into the pursuit and simply went to the sitting room and used one from the stack Asher had spotted the night before.

"Here," she said, handing him the note. "Mrs. Alvin lives two miles up the road, in a house behind a copse of trees. It can be easy to miss if you are not paying attention."

He grinned at her. "I'll pay attention," he began, and then paused. "Lock the door behind me, and don't open it for anyone, hm? I'll call out the word... 'hippocampus' if everything's all right. If you don't hear that word, don't even let me in." Asher leveled a look at her over his spectacles. "Promise."

That seemed to have caught her by surprise; worry clouded her expression. She glanced around them and nodded. "I promise: 'hippocampus'." There was a pause and then she moved toward the door. "Would it be better for me to come with you? I did say that I would, and it would likely reassure Mrs. Alvin if I was present."

He studied her face. "I had thought to spare you the trouble, but... it'd likely be safer, if you're willing."

The look of relief on her face held such vulnerability that it nearly broke Asher's heart to see it.

"I'll come along. The turn really is easy to miss, and it would hardly do for you to be wandering country roads in search of the cow." She glanced at the door again, and Asher saw a hint of fear. She didn't say anything else until they were at the front door and putting on their coats. She turned after he helped her into her coat, and met his gaze solemnly. "Do you think... do you think whatever happened to my uncle might happen to me?" Her voice was very careful indeed.

He felt like a gold-plated arse. "No," was his emphatic reply. "No, absolutely not. My precautions were merely force of habit. If I truly thought there was the slightest chance of anything happening to you I would never have suggested that you stay here alone, even for just an hour." That part was true, at least, though he ought to have known that the password suggestion would frighten her.

"Ah," she said, fastening her coat. She finished and went to the door, turning to look at Asher over her shoulder, green eyes twinkling once more. "Perhaps you ought to suggest the password to the chickens, as an added precaution should the local foxes grow more clever."

"An excellent suggestion," he replied gravely. "I believe I did mention a language barrier. If you would be so good as to speak to them, I would be much obliged."

Charlie shook her head with a laugh and stepped outside, Asher following close behind. "I doubt they could manage the word."

Relieved to see her smiling again, Asher made a mental note to tread more carefully, and started toward the bard to saddle the horses, while Charlie locked up the house.

They were on the road a few minutes later, and though the wind had calmed, the cloud cover maintained the chill. The scarf proved to be as warm and well-made as Asher had predicted, and the ride to retrieve Nan was comfortable enough despite the weather.

The Alvin home lay back a bit from the road, as Charlie had described, and Asher very nearly did miss the turning. It was a picturesque place, complete with thatched roof and plumes of smoke wafting from the chimney.

The lady of the house came to the door and watched them approach, the greater part of her attention clearly on Asher, though it was to Charlie she called. "Come to retrieve Nan?" she asked. "Come in for some tea, I've just put the kettle on."

"Hello, Mrs. Alvin," Charlie returned as she dismounted and led Tobias toward the barn without waiting for help dismounting. She gestured for Asher to follow, then turned back toward the other woman. "We'll just tie the horses off in the barn and then come to thank you properly for looking after Nan."

As soon as the horses were settled inside the warm barn they returned to the house, where Mrs. Alvin remained on the front step. "Well, now," the older woman said, clearly giving Asher a full once-over as they approached, "isn't this nice."

Charlie hurried up the steps and allowed Lorna to usher them into her home. After taking off their coats and warming themselves by the fire per their hostess' instruction, they settled at the table and Charlie gestured toward Asher. "Mrs. Alvin, this is the gentleman I spoke of, Mr. Burton."

"Och, of course he is, anyone can see the clever comin' off him in waves," her neighbor exclaimed. She filled their teacups and placed a plate of muffins beside the cream. "Handsome, too." She held up her hand. "And well I know that 'tisn't needful for a man to be handsome to do a job of work, but if there must be someone pesterin' you with questions and deductions and the like, might as well have a face that won't frighten the horses, as my mam used to say. Milk in your tea?"

Entirely nonplussed, Asher nodded. "Yes, thank you."

"Mm." There seemed to be some sort of judgment attached to his acquiescence, but for the life of him Asher couldn't decide whether it was in his favor or not. "And Elias? Any sign of him?"

Asher glanced at Charlie, unsure how much confidence to place in this woman.

Charlie lifted her teacup, but Asher caught the way her lips turned down just before the cup reached her mouth. She took a sip and then placed the cup back on the table before answering. "We haven't found him, but we also have not found anything that indicates he is..." Charlie cleared her throat. "There is reason to hope he's alive somewhere."

"And no reason to think otherwise," Asher added definitively.

"Good." Lorna was equally emphatic. "He'll be home soon, safe and sound, Charlie dear. You'll see." She shifted her gaze to Asher. "Mind you make sure of that, Mr. Burton." There was something unsettling about the way she was watching him, but Asher couldn't put his finger on why. She reminded him of someone... Ross' mother, that was it. Mrs. Alvin had a similar sort of directness, a way of making one feel as though she could see right into one. Of course the senior Mrs. McInerny *could* see right into... oh, now *that* was an interesting thought. Asher sat up and examined their hostess more closely.

And if he hadn't been looking for it, he would have missed it entirely: when she refilled Charlie's cup, light flared very briefly from her fingertips. Mrs. Alvin was Fae-touched.

Charlie's gaze settled on Asher, her expression no longer clouded with grief. "Mr. Burton has been a godsend during these difficult times. He's quite good at compiling and examining evidence, as well as keeping me from pacing a hole in the floor." She looked away from Asher and smiled at Mrs. Alvin.

"I'm glad to hear it," the other woman replied. "My offer to put you up here with me is still open, should you need it. But it's good that you're not alone." She contemplated the two of them. "It's a good place for unlocking secrets, Loch Ness. I've no doubt you'll find Elias—and y'might find more than that along the way."

"What do you mean?" Asher asked.

"Just what I've said: this is a good place for unraveling that which is tangled, for opening doors that have been closed. You'll find what you came for, I make no doubt." Lorna got up and took the teapot to the sink. "I'd offer you a noonday meal, but I was only planning on a boiled egg for myself. Perhaps you'd like to come for a meal another day, when I've been to the market." She chuckled a little.

"Perhaps," Charlie agreed. "It was kind of you to offer us the tea. We really only meant to collect Nan, but the day is far too cool to turn down such warmth and hospitality." She stood up, bustling her own teacup to the sink as well. "We ought not keep you any longer."

Asher pushed up from the table and helped the ladies finish the tidying up. "We have more work to do back at the farm as well. Thank you for your help with Nan, and for the tea."

Shortly thereafter they were on their way to the Alvin barn when Asher patted his pockets, an expression of chagrin on his face. "I seem to have dropped one of my gloves," he said mendaciously. "Won't be a moment," and he jogged back to the house, walking in without knocking, hoping to catch her by surprise.

In that he was disappointed. Lorna Alvin stood by the sink watching him, a brow raised. "Twigged, did you?"

"You're Fae-touched," he replied.

"Aye. You've met us before, seems like."

Asher nodded. "Is the creature Fae?"

She smiled. "Tellin' you that *would* put me in the soup. Try another."

He frowned. "What can you tell me, then?

Mrs. Alvin nodded. "Better. I don't know much, but I can tell you: there's Fae afoot. I can't put my finger on it, exactly, but I can feel it in the wind. We're near the realm, here, and something's crossed over." *Something bad.* He didn't need to hear the words to know what she meant. "Mr. Burton," she went on after a moment, and he glanced over at her. "You should tell her."

"Tell her what?" His brows drew together.

"Whatever it is you're trying not to talk about." Mrs. Alvin studied him a moment longer. "You've encountered something—seen something. Something terrible, and you've been avoiding thinking about it because you're afraid it's what's happened to Elias."

Instantly the image rose in his mind of the docks at Balmaclaren, and Hamish Maclaren's gruesome end. He could feel himself blanch. "Do you know what I saw?"

Mrs. Alvin moved closer, reached out to touch his forehead, and let out a breath. "Aye. Deep magic, that was, and dreadful. You're right to be afraid—but not of the creature in these waters. That much I can say, I think."

Asher nodded and tugged his 'missing' gloves out of his pocket. "That much and no more, is what I'm hearing."

Lorna laughed. "You've acute hearing for a man." She laid her hand on his arm. "I'll help where I can. But you need to help yourself, too. Tell Charlie what you know—for both your sakes."

"I'll... think about it. Take care of yourself, Mrs. Alvin," he said, stepping back outside to return to the barn, where Charlie was waiting.

She already had Nan's lead tied to her saddle, and was astride Tobias near the barn door. "I see you found your gloves," she said, nodding to his gloved hands. "Good thing too, it's likely to stay cold until the sun comes out again, and who knows when that will be this time of year."

Asher nodded absently as he swung up into his saddle, mulling over what Mrs. Alvin had said. *'Fae afoot.' Not Fae-touched—she means something truly otherworldly.* The idea was deeply unsettling.

The ride home was uneventful, which was just as well since Asher was entirely distracted by his encounter with Mrs. Alvin. After a worried query from Charlie, however, he determined to table his internal struggle until he had time to figure out what he ought to do.

Nan the cow seemed grateful to be returned to her pen, even if she was rather lax in expressing her gratitude for the mucked out stall. The two humans were glad to be back as well, given all they had to do, and after a quick meal of bread and cheese, Asher was back in the study with Charlie.

But returning to the den of disaster that served as Elias' Whitfield's study made the entire undertaking all the more daunting. They'd spent the better part of the morning trying to respect Elias' 'system' as they sifted through the stacks of books and notes, finding precious little to aid in their search for the missing professor. Asher shook his head and reassessed their approach. They simply were not going to make any headway without putting the room in proper order. Elias would just have to put things back the way he liked them afterward, and perhaps the safe return home would be enough to soften the blow.

They were just settling into a rhythm, and finding that the study did possess a floor, when a knock at the door startled them both.

Asher glanced at Charlie. "I'll get that," he told her. Perhaps it was an excess of caution, but Asher was a cautious man by nature, especially in situations where he simply didn't know enough to decide differently. He went to the door and opened it, making sure to block the interior with his body.

The young man standing on the other side of the door took a step back, surprise obvious on his face. "Who..." he cleared his throat and looked around the farm. "Is Charlotte here?"

Asher gave the man a brief but comprehensive examination. Fair of hair and skin, eyes an indeterminate greyish-bluish-green, decided chin, squarish jaw—from the description in the brief he'd been given, this must be the innkeeper's son, he guessed. "Depends on who's asking."

His regard was returned. "Mr. Oliver Shaw. I am a friend of Charlotte's." He craned his neck and tried to look past Asher. "Who are you?"

It was at this moment that Asher discovered he'd taken a wholly unreasonable dislike to Mr. Oliver Shaw. He called over his shoulder. "Charlie? Friend of yours?"

Asher heard the sound of approaching footsteps before he sensed her at his back. "What are you doing here?" The question was one of surprise, her tone polite. She did know him apparently.

Oliver Shaw smiled triumphantly, looking past Asher to focus on Charlie. "I found your boat. My father didn't think I needed to bring it back, but..." now he glanced at Asher, with thinly veiled suspicion, "but I wanted to see how you're holding up without your uncle."

The boat that they'd left securely tied at the campsite? What a curious thing to do. Interest caught, Asher spoke up again. "Why would your father think my cousin wouldn't want her boat back?" A spur-of-the-moment cover, yes, but he trusted Charlie's ability to improvise, and he didn't trust this person's ability to read a situation correctly—or worse, go blabbing about it.

"I have it in the back of the wagon," he replied, pointing a thumb over his shoulder, and blatantly ignoring Asher's question. "I can take it to the lakeshore for you."

"No need." Asher took his coat from the hook by the door and shrugged it on, slipping out of the house and closing the door behind him. "Where's this boat, then?"

Oliver Shaw studied Asher, not glaring, but with a less-than-friendly demeanor. "In the wagon, just as I said before. Charlotte never mentioned having a cousin."

"No?" Asher grinned, obscurely pleased to have caught him off-kilter. "She never mentioned you, either. Shaw, is it? No," he pretended to think about it, "I'd've remembered. Though we've traded a lot of letters over the years, so maybe not. Asher Burton." He held out his hand.

Oliver glanced down and though he took the hand offered, the shake was stiff and ended quickly. "How long are you staying?" he asked, turning to lead the way to the wagon at the edge of the barnyard.

"As long as Charlie needs me," Asher replied. "It's hardly safe for her to be on her own with Uncle Elias gone." He dropped the tailgate of the wagon and assessed the rowboat: he'd portaged worse. "Excuse me." Asher reached forward and began to tug the boat toward him.

The other man was absolutely silent, neither stopping Asher nor making a move to help. Then, voice low, "She isn't on her own."

"No," Asher agreed with a sunny smile. "She's got me." With that he hefted the rowboat onto his shoulders and headed for the shore.

"Well, since you seem to have everything in hand, Mr. Burton. I'll leave you to it and go see to Charlotte." Shaw's voice was light. He turned on his heel and made for the cottage.

Asher ground his teeth, at the same time wondering why this Shaw person annoyed him so much. Was he a suitor of Charlie's? Nonsense—the fool insisted on calling her Charlotte. Hadn't she said... no, he mentally replayed their conversation, she'd never said she didn't like the name Charlotte, only that she didn't use it. Maybe it was reserved for this Shaw person.

He levered the boat over his shoulders and onto the shore, dusting off his palms. *Get yourself in hand, Burton,* he thought. Charlie's—Miss Whitfield's—choice of friends or suitors was none of his concern, unless they could reasonably be suspected of having kidnapped Elias.

Which technically can't be ruled out yet, he added to himself, and glanced at the rowboat. While he was thinking about it, what to make of Shaw's assertion that his father had said he needn't return the boat to the Whitfield farm? Asher definitely had questions.

Asher headed back toward the house, routing through the barn to expedite the trip and reduce the time Charlie was left alone with Oliver Shaw. He found the man standing with her on the porch—she hadn't let him into the house, for which Asher mentally praised her.

"Ah, there my cousin is now," Charlie said, stepping away from Shaw and moving to greet Asher. To his surprise, she wrapped her arms around him and offered him a small hug before looking back at her 'guest.' She cleared her throat. "I was just telling Mr. Shaw about the lovely recipe for that pasta dish your housekeeper sent along." She ran a hand over her hair and casually returned to the porch. "He asked what the latest news from London was."

Asher grinned at Shaw—he couldn't help it after that hug. "Have you friends in London, Mr. Shaw?"

Shaw looked spectacularly put out for some reason. He shook his head and addressed Charlie. "I shouldn't linger. My father tasked me with clearing some branches that were torn down during yesterday's storm." He glanced at Asher and reached for Charlie's hand. "But please, Charlotte, know that you can call on me if there's any comfort I can offer in this difficult time. The loss of a loved one is not to be borne alone. You have only to ask..." He broke off. "I will be here in an instant, I swear it."

Charlie blushed a little—no, it wasn't a blush, what Mr. Shaw said had made her angry, Asher realized. All the same, her response was polite. "Thank you, and my uncle will thank you for your care as soon as he's safely returned."

"Charlotte," Shaw held her hand, patting it a little. "I hope you're right, but..."

"Well, this *has* been lovely," Asher broke in on this tender moment. "I'm sure Uncle Elias will appreciate your concern for his welfare. We'll be sure to send for you if we want you for anything. Charlie, my dear, I don't think you ought to be kept standing out in the cold like this. Do go in and put the kettle on—I'll be in to make us a cuppa as soon as I've helped Mr. Shaw turn his wagon around."

Charlie pulled her hand away from Oliver Shaw without a moment's hesitation. "Thank you, Mr. Shaw," she repeated. Then to Asher, "I will see you inside."

He offered her his best smile. "Anon," he replied, and then to Shaw, "I'll direct you, hm?" He paused. "By the bye, where did you find the boat, Shaw?"

"Adrift," was the other man's noncommittal answer, and Asher noted it with interest. Shaw was looking at the door that closed behind Charlie. "You needn't direct me. I can handle matters well enough." So saying, he turned his back to Asher and marched to the wagon. He did indeed manage to back out of the drive, but doing so was something of a production, with a great deal of whinnying protests from the horse before the wagon was ambling back down the lane and away from the farm.

Asher chuckled to himself and went into the house.

Charlie was waiting at the door, a little frown on her face. She took hold of Asher's hands, her slender fingers cold in his. "Did you see everything settled?"

"Good Lord, your hands are like ice!" He rubbed them between his own. "Come, let's make that cup of tea." He suited deed to word, putting the kettle on the stove, and indicating that Charlie should sit at the table. "I must congratulate you, Miss Whitfield," Asher began, "on your nimble acceptance of a very odd situation—for not giving away that we had seen the boat at the campsite, and for letting me be your temporary cousin."

She offered him a little shrug, eyes twinkling. "I've never had a cousin before. I thought the idea an intriguing one." He chuckled and offered her his arm to escort her to the table.

Chapter Eight

A Pointed Message

She ought to have known the sun wouldn't stay long. Charlie rubbed at the knotted muscles at the base of her neck. Outside the study windows clouds had rolled in again, obscuring the sun, and before long fat raindrops were splattering on the paned glass.

Charlie sighed and moved away from the window to stir up the fire in the little black stove; but the truth was that here, surrounded by memories and worry, she was finding it hard to find any sense of warmth.

After her third or fourth shiver, she glanced up to see Asher's blue gaze assessing her. "We ought to stop for a little while," he said. "I think my eyes are crossing."

Whether his statement was true, or simply his way of providing a reason to stop that wasn't an obvious show of sympathy, Charlie couldn't tell, nor did she care. The break would do her good. It was difficult to spend so much time in her uncle's sanctuary and not feel his absence more keenly.

Charlie stood up, dusting her hands off. "Very well. Sometimes stepping away for a little while helps one see things anew. Perhaps some tea, and there is a tin of biscuits in the cupboard."

"An excellent idea." Rubbing his hands together, Asher led the way to the kitchen, where he filled the kettle at the pump and then placed it on the hob. "There was mention of biscuits, I believe?"

Charlie was already digging in the cupboards, shoving things aside until she found the tin. Her uncle would have eaten them all in one sitting if they'd been visible at a glance. "There was indeed," she replied, turning around to hold the biscuits out to Asher. "Just enough to help us rejuvenate."

Again she was aware of that assessing gaze. "I may need a little more rejuvenation," he said. "That study is a bewildering place. Though I believe I saw a gramophone in the corner?"

"You did. Uncle Elias keeps a small collection of recordings on hand. It's our Sunday tradition to listen to music after luncheon." The Sunday before Uncle Elias disappeared they'd been too busy to uphold that tradition, which left the gramophone half-buried in his study. "Would you like to listen to something while we enjoy our treats?"

"I would," he replied. "The weather's become dreary–I think a little music would be just the thing. I'll go get it." He strode off in the direction of the study.

In the meantime, Charlie focused on the task of setting the table while the water heated on the stove. Feeling the need to further brighten the mood and chase away the autumn chill, she decided to use what served as the 'fine china' which consisted of two slightly yellowed teacups and saucers with a delicate ring of forget-me-nots painted around the rims. Mrs. Alvin had given them to her when she was twelve, and Charlie rarely had occasion to bring them out. She arranged the biscuits on another plate and removed the kettle from the stove, then stepped back to examine her handiwork. It was likely to be unimpressive compared to the parlors of London society, but it added a sense of charm to an otherwise ordinary tea.

Asher grunted slightly as he maneuvered the gramophone through the door. "Where do you usually place it?"

Charlie bit her lower lip and gave the man an apologetic look. "There's a corner cabinet in the sitting room where we store the records. That's generally where we put it on Sundays." She looked around the room, not wanting to ask him to carry the heavy thing any further than needed. "But there's enough space on the other end of the table." It was true: the tea setting only took up one end and the table was plenty large enough to accommodate both.

But Asher eschewed the table, choosing to take it into the sitting room instead. "What would you like to listen to?" he called.

"Your choice. I've heard everything there more than once," Charlie called back, adding some finishing touches to the table.

Before long the familiar strains of a waltz filled the air. Asher returned to the kitchen and bowed to Charlie, elegance in his movements despite the rough clothes he wore. "May I have this dance, Miss Whitfield?"

Charlie looked at his outstretched hand and felt a little flutter of excitement, followed almost immediately by nervous knots. Her focus shifted to her companion's face. "I'm afraid I..." Charlie looked down, her cheeks going hot. "I... don't know how."

"Oh—" He paused, then went to hold out her chair. "Then we should fortify ourselves, for no one should go through life without a good waltz. I'll teach you."

"You are one the bravest men I know," Charlie replied solemnly, taking her seat. "I salute your toes, and wish them a speedy recovery." She grinned at him as she gave a quick salute.

Asher laughed. "I'm sure I've suffered worse. Come, drink up and let's have a good spin around the sitting room."

Something about the idea of dancing with Asher made the weather outside seem brighter and the chill that had settled in her bones warmed suddenly.

The rattle of the kettle on the boil followed shortly. Asher insisted on seeing to the tea preparation, pointing out that Charlie had done the work of setting the table. He made quick work of it, and before long the two of them were chatting over their tea and biscuits.

When they'd had their fill Charlie downed the last of her second cup in one long, un-ladylike gulp and followed her would-be dance instructor to the sitting room. She took up a post at the end of the settee and gestured to the open space in the center of the room. "You're the expert: will this do for our activity, or do we need to clear more space?"

"Hm." He took the time to push the chairs and tables back against the walls. "Better." After a moment's deliberation over the music selection, Asher placed the needle down on the record and went to face Charlie, bowing before her for a second time.

Ordinarily, this treatment would have made Charlie feel self-conscious, but with Asher there was nothing uncomfortable about it. Even more than that, the gesture made her feel elegant and lady-like. Charlie curtsied a little and then stepped closer to him. "Where shall I put my hands?"

For answer, Asher took her right hand in his left and guided her left to his shoulder. "Of course if your dress had a train, you'd hold that instead. Shoulders back, chin up," he instructed, and with his right hand around her waist, tugged her close, lifting his chin. "Now. We are going to make the shape of a box with our feet, to this rhythm: one, two, three, one, two, three. You'll go back on the right foot first. All right?"

"Sounds simple enough," Charlie replied with a little nod. She matched her mental count with the music and followed as Asher took the first step. Her eyes dropped to their feet almost immediately.

"No—look at me. You can trust me, Miss Whitfield. I'll guide you through the dance."

"Oh, sorry," Charlie murmured absently, slowly bringing her head back up to meet Asher's eyes. "Some show I'm making of it," she laughed.

He twinkled at her. "And—one, two, three!" A few awkward steps and then they were whirling about the room. "Yes—you've got it!" he praised her, and dipped her before bringing her back up and into another dizzying spin.

Dancing with Asher was a new kind of delight. Suddenly Charlie was in an elegant ballroom, surrounded by men and women dressed in their finest, with no thought of the dreary clouds outside. She laughed and spun, following his lead around the cleared out space. It was as though he'd found a way to spin magic into the steps, and dance her further and further from her woes.

"You're an excellent teacher," she huffed out breathlessly, coming back into his arms after a spin.

"As you are my first and only pupil, I fully intend to retire while I'm ahead," he replied with a laugh. The music ended and so, regretfully, did their dance, with another of those elegant bows. "An unqualified pleasure, Miss Whitfield. I and my toes thank you."

Charlie would have gladly spent the rest of the days dancing away the doldrums, but Asher was hardly here to entertain her. Or at least that was what she told herself, in an attempt to dull the sudden ache that rose up at the absence of his touch. She tucked a loose curl behind her ear. "Thank you, Mr. Burton. It was the perfect diversion." After a quick glance around the room she returned her attention to her partner. "Perhaps we ought to set the room back to rights and then continue with our work in the study."

"Perhaps." He went over to the gramophone and changed records, then returned to her. "But as I've already moved all the furniture, it seems a shame to waste the effort. One more?" Without really waiting for an answer he swept her into his arms and guided them in another glorious circuit of the sitting room.

Charlie turned onto her side and wrapped her arms around her pillow. She closed her eyes and tried to clear her mind, but her imagination immediately conjured the image of Asher's face close to hers, the sensation of his hand resting on her waist. It left her feeling feverish and unsettled.

The clock in the hall outside her room began to ring out the hour. *One, two, three, four.* Charlie sighed and threw the covers aside. She'd slept a little, not enough to feel particularly rested, but enough to make falling back to sleep with a head full of new ideas and possibilities impossible. *Not much point in staying abed and fixating on the matter*, she decided. *Heaven knows I've enough to worry about.*

Deciding that she was not ready to dress, Charlie reached for her dressing gown, tying the sash securely before she stepped out of her bedroom. Asher was likely to be asleep for a little while longer. She'd have a cup of coffee, and perhaps read for a bit while the house was still and quiet.

She tip-toed down the hall and then the stairs, careful to avoid the floorboards that creaked the loudest. She was nearly to the kitchen when an odd sound at the front door caught her attention. The wind had picked up a bit during the night, and something seemed to be fluttering at the front door. It was likely nothing, she told herself, even as her footsteps grew more cautious, but best check.

The sound continued, and grew unmistakable the closer she drew to the door. It was paper rustling, or flapping. Charlie unlocked the bolt and slowly cracked the door open, peeking surreptitiously around the edge before opening it wide. It took a moment for her eyes to focus in the cloudy pre-dawn, and then she saw it. A sheet of paper pinned to the middle of the door, held in place by an ornate dagger, the blade strangely translucent and wickedly curved. Scrawled on the paper were the words:

MORTAL, A WARNING
THINK NOT TO INTERFERE LEST DEATH FIND YOU AT MY HANDS

Charlie jumped away violently, upsetting the small table in the hall. She staggered backward, the door itself still open and swinging in the wind. "Mr. Burton!" Her call wasn't quite a scream, but close to it.

There was immediate noise—thumping and cursing—and seconds later Asher came down the stairs at a full sprint, barefoot and bare-chested, his braces flopping around his mis-buttoned trousers. "What is it—are you hurt?" He grasped her upper arms, looking her over anxiously, then looked out the door. "Miss Whitfield, what is it?"

Charlie lifted a shaking hand and pointed to the note. "Th–there," her teeth chattered as she spoke.

Asher gave her a reassuring squeeze, scowling at the dagger, and urged her to move farther into the house. "It's cold outside," he muttered absently and pulled the dagger from the door, reading the note. His expression went from worried to wrathful and he strode out the door, heedless of his state of undress, to glare about the yard.

Charlie watched him, still trembling, tears streaming down her cheeks though she wasn't sure when they'd begun. She knew she ought to try to think through the situation, but the more she tried to calm herself, the more intense the shaking became. She backed against the wall and slowly slid to the floor, drawing her knees up to her chest and burying her face in the folds of her nightrail.

He came in after a moment or two. "I don't see any–oh, no." His hands were cold where he grasped her arms again, urging her to stand. "Here–you're chilled. Let me make some tea." Asher helped her into one of the kitchen chairs, and then set about filling the kettle and teapot.

Even with the door shut, and settled in the kitchen Charlie felt half-frozen. She stared at a dark spot on the wooden table, trying to focus on the contours of the blemish, but the image of the dagger embedded in the door, and the undeniable threat of that note seemed to keep the chill of the night close. "Whoever left that—they said 'lest death find you at my hands'. They're *watching* us. What if..." Her trembling intensified. What if this person had already killed her uncle?

Asher set a cup of tea in front of her, scooping in plenty of sugar. "For the shock." His expression, when she glanced up, was grim. He took the seat across from her. "I know this is frightening, Miss Whitfield, but it's important to understand what it means. No one would bother warning us off if there was nothing to be found. They wouldn't be this concerned about us finding a body—far too easily disposed of in the loch. And that means that more than likely, Elias is still alive. As to watching us..." Asher shrugged. "They'd be fools not to. I expected as much. This simply confirms that someone has taken your uncle—and most importantly, that he still lives. There's hope, Charlie."

Charlie forced herself to take a slow, deep breath and worked to still her hands enough to lift the teacup to her lips. The process was still rather wobbly, but after a few sips the warmth of the liquid, and the comfort of the familiar taste helped her feel a measure of calmness, small though it was. "Then, in this case, a death threat is a good thing?" She attempted to make the question sound less serious, but the way her voice cracked a bit at the end undermined that effort.

"Exactly so. They're trying to frighten us off— but what that really means is that there's something for us to find." His blue gaze was steady. "We'll find him. I promise."

Another sip of tea, more deep breaths, and Charlie was able to push the fright far enough away to consider the situation with greater objectivity— something she did not think would have been possible, were it not for her companion's composure. "Perhaps they were watching my uncle's camp, and our visit there tipped them off to our investigation."

"Possibly," he agreed. "It hardly matters now— this is a misstep on their part. We had little to go on, before. Now we have something." His lips curved in a somewhat wolfish smile. "I don't need much, and they've just given it to me."

"I believe I like the idea that they've inadvertently given us the key to finding my uncle. To see this incident as a mistake on their part helps ease the threat... a little," Charlie replied, though she did shudder again. She shifted her attention to Asher, smiling weakly but genuinely. "I am glad you were here. You seem to have a gift for making dark situations seem brighter somehow."

Color rose in his cheeks. "I've done very little," he demurred. "I've only told you the truth." All at once his expression shifted and he dropped his gaze.

"Which is why it brings me comfort." Without thinking, Charlie reached out and touched his hand. "You are not the sort to offer hollow reassurances."

Asher turned his hand over and squeezed her fingers briefly. "Do you think you can get back to sleep? I'll stay up and keep watch, in case our friend decides to give us another clue." He offered her a small smile as he said it.

Charlie huffed out a humorless laugh, the idea that she might find sleep again seemed as impossible as the notion that Nan might suddenly sprout wings and fly south for winter. "I should probably try. I don't feel confident in success, but it would hardly serve my uncle for me to stay awake all hours of the night."

He was quiet for a moment. "I have something you could take—a mild sedative, if you think it would help."

Charlie considered the offer. On the one hand, the idea of sleeping was somewhat unnerving when the homestead was clearly being stalked, and yet, Asher had said he would remain awake and keep watch. He would not allow anything to harm her, of that Charlie was absolutely certain. "Perhaps that would be wise. Thank you, Mr. Burton, for everything."

"It's why I'm here. Won't be a moment," and he hurried toward out of the room and up the stairs, returning a short while later buttoning a hastily-donned shirt, a pair of socks hanging out of one trouser pocket. He dug around in the other pocket and came up with a small vial of something greenish. "A friend of mine makes this. Very effective, and it won't leave you feeling drugged or logy—might even give you pleasant dreams." He offered it to her and then sat to pull on his socks.

"I'm afraid it would have to be potent indeed for pleasant dreams to happen tonight," Charlie said, accepting the vial. She pushed away from the table and stood up slowly, a little unsure as to whether her legs would hold her, and relieved when they did. "I shall bid you a good night—or rather, a better night than has been had thus far." She thanked him a final time and started back toward her bedroom.

The familiar shadows cast by her belongings seemed ominous now, but Charlie refused to allow her imagination to get the better of her. Asher would think she was little more than a frightened child if she went running back into the kitchen over something as harmless as the shadow cast by a hat.

Determined to be the rationally-minded person her uncle had raised, Charlie climbed back into bed. Once she was settled under the blankets she uncorked the vial and took a sip of the oddly colored liquid within. The stuff had a strange taste to it, like the way lavender smelled, but there were other notes, earthy and soothing, and perhaps a little sweet.

The muscles in Charlie's back and shoulders relaxed almost immediately. She sighed and put the cork back in the bottle, carefully placing it on the bedside table. Warmth spread through her limbs, the bed seemed to cradle her. Charlie's eyelids began to grow heavy, and bit by bit the fear that had clenched around her like a clawed fist was replaced by a general sense of calm and well-being.

Charlie skipped along the lakeshore, closely following the little boy ahead of her. He always moved faster than she did, but she was still better at catching frogs. Even so, Charlie hated being left behind. "Wait! My legs aren't as long as yours! You'll scare all the frogs away if you get there first!"

Her companion gave her an exasperated backward glance. "We're nearly there, Charlie." The little boy did slow down though, grinning at her when she finally caught up. "I bet that cave will be full of frogs."

The clouds overhead shifted, the sunlight dimmed and suddenly Charlie was standing at the mouth of the cave, the water flowing lazily into the darkness. She craned her neck and squinted to peer into the darkness, but nothing could be seen save for the dancing lights that seemed to beckon her further.

"Charlie..." her friend called to her, but his voice was different now. "Come inside, I found something."

Charlie lingered at the entrance. There was something here, something that both enticed and terrified her. She took a careful step forward, sliding along the narrow, rocky lip along the cave wall.

Boyish laughter echoed through the tunnel. "Come along, Charlie, don't be afraid. Come see what I've found."

She moved as fast as she could, determined to share in the wonder of discovery. Perhaps it was the creature, and wouldn't Uncle Elias be proud if she could bring him proof of the beast? The dancing lights were all around her now but their movement was different; it was no longer graceful and relaxed. Now the little lights seemed agitated, they zipped from one side of the cave to the other, the colors shifting from white, to blue, to red. The lights swirled and swarmed around Charlie's face. She batted at them and nearly tumbled into the water.

Ahead the cave opened up to reveal a verdant forest that glittered in the sunlight. It was breathtakingly beautiful and inviting, with petals drifting down from the blossoming boughs to float on the surface of the river below. Charlie tried to push forward, but with each step the little dancing lights became more aggressive. They were swarming her like angry bees, flitting through her hair and tugging at her clothes. It felt like tiny hands were touching her, grabbing, pinching, attempting to pull her back.

Charlie tried to bat them away even as she pressed against the cool rock at her back.

"Help me!" she cried, genuinely fearful that the little light creatures would pull her off the ledge and into the murky channel that ran from the lake to the forest just beyond the cave.

"Don't be afraid, Charlotte," came the response from beyond. There was another peal of laughter, this one different from the laughter of her friend. "Hurry, they want to meet you. They have cakes and cordial!"

She managed another step forward and then another after that. The way out was so close, only a few more steps now and she would be in that beautiful forest. The air suddenly filled with a strange, low keening, or moaning. The sound was deep and reverberated against the rocky walls, but Charlie was at the mouth of the cave now. "I'm coming! Leave some cakes for me!"

The keening grew louder and something swirled beneath the dark water of the river. Charlie backed away from the water and started into the trees. She could just make out figures standing in a shadowy clearing not far from her. They beckoned to her, waving indistinct and glimmering hands.

"Come, child, come, your friend is waiting," called a voice more beautiful and melodious than anything Charlie had ever heard before. She started to move deeper into the trees. "That's right, join us."

A sudden scream rent the air. The figures in the trees suddenly looked darker, with eyes that glowed. Charlie tried to back away, but the ground was boggy and her feet wouldn't budge. One of the figures started drifting through the trees toward Charlie. "It is far too late for that, child."

Terrified and frantic, Charlie bent down and tried to pull her feet loose. She scrambled to untie her boots. If she could just get free, just get home to her uncle... The figure was drawing closer—in a few more steps it would be near enough to take hold of her. "Please, please let me go," Charlie whimpered, half praying.

"You have trespassed where mortals should not tread. You belong to us now," the figure hissed.

A sudden flurry of activity erupted behind her. Water exploded into the air, spraying Charlie from head to toe. She ducked instinctively as the mournful cry turned to an outraged roar. An enormous head, attached to a long and sinewy neck whipped past her, rows of razor-sharp teeth snapping at the dark figure that was bearing down on Charlie.

Charlie's feet came loose without warning and she toppled over backward. The monstrous neck hovered over her, raining lake water down on her face and clothes. Charlie stumbled to her feet again and ran for the cave. The roaring continued, but her friend's cries had stopped entirely. Heart pounding, *whole body shaking, Charlie didn't look back, she simply ran as fast as her legs could carry her.*

Chapter Nine

Lessons

Asher waited until he was sure that Ross' potion had done its work before puttering around the kitchen to make himself some extra-strong tea. Coffee would be even better, but they'd used up the last of the beans on their camping trip and there'd been no opportunity to go into town for more.

He let the tea steep until it made him wince when he drank it, and then sat at the table to try and order his thoughts. Clues in abundance he now had— he nudged the strange dagger with the tip of a finger— but what the thread was that tied them together was still something of a mystery.

Unfortunately, his wayward mind kept returning to Charlie: her fortitude, her patience, her courage, especially after this last event. With a few notable exceptions of his acquaintance, something like that would give any woman the vapors, and yet Charlie had belied her delicate appearance to show a spirit made of steel.

He shook his head. This was getting them nowhere; he had to think, and not about the shape of her lips when she spoke, or the way her eyes lit up when she caught his attempts at humor—no, still not helping.

Come on, Asher, you're supposed to be the clever one, not the impulsive woman-obsessed seducer. That's Quinn, not you.

He went into the study for a moment to retrieve some paper and a pencil. What did they know, and what could be inferred?

One: no sign of a struggle at the campsite, from which one might infer that he knew his attacker and was unafraid, or fell prey to a seemingly benign ruse. Two: the creature was real, and it seemed that Elias had found it. Given that this was his sole reason for being in Lochmuir, it seemed fair to assume that his disappearance was somehow related. Caveat: the relation to the creature might well be indirect, and that was what Lorna Alvin seemed to imply. That she knew more was obvious, but he did believe that she was saying all she could. The ways of the Fae were murky at best, and having seen all he had, Asher had no mind to accidentally put Lorna in danger.

Which brought him to the current crux of the matter: the presence of a Fae, somewhere in Lochmuir. Lorna had said it, and the note on the door, stuck through with a weirdly ornate dagger, seemed to confirm it. Charlie had mentioned the threat of death, but had evidently missed what had jumped out to Asher: the word 'mortal'.

Mortal, a warning.

Equally, the wording of the note was vague. *Think not to interfere,* and the natural impulse was to connect it to Elias' disappearance—and if that was the correct reading, then Elias was being held by this mysterious Fae for some no doubt esoteric infraction. And if *that* was the case... Asher rubbed a hand over his face. If that was the case he had no idea what to do, for the Fae were a law unto themselves and he was as likely to get them all turned into frogs as get Elias released.

It was barely possible that the note referred to something else, some other way in which Asher and Charlie were interfering, but what that could be escaped him at the moment.

He sat at the table making copious notes, trying to fit the pieces together this way and that. Every so often he'd get up and stretch his legs, or think while pacing. At one point he retrieved his boots and coat and stepped outside to check the yard, making sure that nobody was creeping about again.

He turned his attention to the dagger. The handle was some kind of black wood—dyed, perhaps, or charred—deeply incised with exotic, evocative designs, potentially symbolic. He picked it up, held it as though to attack, and immediately felt queasy. Definitely symbolic and potentially magical, he mentally revised, and put the dagger down.

The blade was another point of interest. It was curved, translucent, iridescent, with an edge and point as sharp as a freshly-stropped razor. Asher scratched at it with a fingernail: not metal. Some kind of crystal was his best guess, though he'd never seen anything like this. Most obsidian or flint points were crude: flaked or chipped into shape. This had been... shaped, polished... honed, for lack of a better word, and Asher felt he'd give a good deal to know how it had been created.

The rosy light of dawn spread across the surface of the loch at last, glinting and gleaming on the rippling water. The sun edged its way over the horizon, the light chilly but bright, and Asher got up to tidy the kitchen from the night's depredations and make a start toward breakfast.

A short time later Asher heard the door to Charlie's bedroom burst open and then slam shut. In another moment Charlie herself charged into the kitchen muttering and clutching her hair in a tight fist. "That is quite enough! Won't come untangled? We shall see about that!" She grumbled, digging through a basket in the corner. "Where in heaven's name did I put those scissors!"

"What?" Asher exclaimed, appalled. "Miss Whitfield—what are you doing?"

"I cannot get the brush through it," she said matter of fact, continuing her search for the missing scissors. "I'm just going to cut it off and be rid of it, snarls and all!" Her eyes were slightly red-rimmed, lines of stress at the corners of her mouth.

"No, indeed you shall not!" Asher grasped her hand. "It would be a sin to destroy such a beautiful thing. Here, let me help."

Charlie stopped digging and looked up at him, her green eyes even more emerald with those golden tresses loose and framing her face. "You know how to dress a lady's hair?"

"Sit." He indicated the kitchen chair. "Let us say I am a man of many talents." He began to tease out the snarl, one small piece at a time.

Charlie sat quietly, her hands folded in her lap as he worked through her long, thick hair. After a moment she spoke, her voice so soft that Asher barely caught what she said. "You... you have a gentle touch, Asher."

So engrossed—so entranced was he in his task, that he nearly jumped when she spoke. Lord have mercy, her hair felt like satin in his hands, and smelled of lilacs and summer rain, an intoxicating combination. Asher cleared his throat. "Nearly done," he murmured softly.

"Already?" Her voice was low, and Asher almost thought he detected a note of disappointment in it.

"Almost." He was as reluctant as she to end this particular chore. Once he'd rid her of the snarl, he took the brush to the rest of her hair, smoothing the silky strands in long, slow strokes.

She sighed and her head tilted back ever so slightly as he ran the brush through her hair. "Perhaps you could braid it for me as well? Lest it tangle at my own clumsy efforts, of course."

He let out a breath and began to separate the sections, his fingers gently brushing her neck, her scalp.

Charlie's breath hitched a bit when his fingers moved across her skin, but she said nothing. She simply sat in her chair and allowed him to dote on her. Asher's fingers slid down the column of her neck, and he heard another sigh, even as her head tilted slightly.

He took his time over it, pretending that he owed her the attention when he knew, deep down, that it was pure self-indulgence. But no matter how long he wished the moment would go on, at last the braid was done. Asher tied it off and moved away from her. "There we are."

"Thank you, Mr. Burton," Charlie replied in a voice barely more than a whisper. She stood up slowly, fingers smoothing down the length of her braid, cheeks flushed. "You are," she paused and cleared her throat, "You are kind to have helped."

Asher shrugged and began slicing bread, hoping the sensation of the locks of her hair sliding along his fingertips would both leave and stay. "I have a younger sister," he told her by way of explanation. "Her hair is as curly as mine, so I used to help her with it."

"Ah," was the only response she gave, and after a pause he heard her opening and closing the cupboards. "I used to wish I'd had a sister, or even a brother, I suppose." She appeared at his side, setting a jar of preserves down. "Have you many siblings?"

That made him chuckle. "I'm the fourth of five brothers, and we have a younger sister. Mother was determined to have a daughter, so they just kept going until Clover came along."

Charlie shook her head, laughing a little. "Five siblings! It must have been great fun at times. I don't imagine you ever felt lonely."

"No." He was still smiling. "Truthfully I would have appreciated a little more loneliness—or no, stillness is the word I want. School was boisterous, home even more so. And in London we had few bucolic pleasures. Growing up here must have been magical," and perhaps his choice of words wasn't an accident.

Charlie was quiet and when Asher looked at her again, he caught the ghost of a frown. But just as quickly her expression changed, though there was still a shadow lurking in her expression. "It is a pity the weather isn't warmer. There's a meadow not far from here that would be a lovely place for a picnic. I often went there as a child—all the flowers reminded me of my mother."

His interest—and his compassion—was caught. "Will you tell me of her, if it doesn't give you pain?"

"It doesn't. I think of her often. My uncle did not know her well, but he said that my father was captivated by her from the first time he laid eyes on her." Charlie pulled a couple of plates from the china cabinet and laid them on the table, and Asher realized she was using the time it took to order her thoughts. "Her name was Lillian, though to my recollection everyone called her Lily. I remember that she kept

119

flowers in every room." She leaned against the counter, smiling a little. "She used to make up stories about all the different varieties, giving them each their own personalities and voices."

"That's a lovely memory." Asher offered her a smile. "She must have been like you, I think: full of imagination. And your father was Elias' brother?"

Charlie's cheeks pinked a little. "Thank you. I don't know that I consider myself that imaginative, but I appreciate the compliment." She seemed to grow thoughtful for a brief time before speaking again. "I remember even less about my father, sadly. Uncle Elias is his older brother. Father was an officer in Her Majesty's Royal Navy, and so gone more often than not. He did have the most wonderful laugh though, I remember that—and how much my parents loved one another." She sighed. "I suppose, if my memories must be limited, the love and the laughter are the important ones to hold onto."

"Very true." Asher regarded her for a moment before cutting some slices of bread. "What happened this morning? You seemed all right when you returned to bed. Did anything else happen last night?"

Charlie wrapped her arms around herself and turned to lean against the table, the look in her eyes growing distant and troubled. "You'll think me silly for being so distraught."

"I won't, you know."

She traced her fingers along the edge of the table. "I had... a nightmare. It was so real, so vivid— almost like remembering something." Charlie shuddered. "It must have had to do with the note. I wandered into a cave and there were... creatures there. They called me 'mortal', just as the note was addressed."

He was silent for a moment. That was a bit close for comfort. Some kind of spell? A forgotten memory? Maybe they should ask Mrs. Alvin, although she was constrained in some way and might not be able to tell them anything. He set a plate of bread and a crock of butter on the table, pouring out some tea. "Tell me everything you remember about the dream."

"I remember the sense that I was being hunted, and that something terrible happened," Charlie replied slowly, her tone was distant and a little sad. She looked at Asher, and from the shadows in those green eyes, it seemed to him that the feeling remained. "It was only a dream. I'm a grown woman. I shouldn't be so disturbed by a dream in the light of day, but I cannot banish the sense that there is something *more* out there."

Lorna Alvin's words echoed in Asher's mind. *You need to tell her.* He let out a breath. "We should talk."

"That is a rather ominous response to a dream," Charlie answered, though she settled at the table and looked at him expectantly. "Tell me what it is we should talk about."

And now that they were at the crux of it, he had no idea how to begin. Asher rubbed the back of his neck, debating. Despite Mrs. Alvin's assertion, there was the small matter of his duty to consider, and the nature of the tasks that were entrusted to him, of which the whole kerfuffle with Geordie and then with Ross was a part. By Agency rules, he ought not say more, he knew it, but... it would be such a relief to tell someone. He could hardly discuss Ross' death and subsequent resurrection with Ross himself—Lord knew the man had enough pain to cope with, having been at the center of it all. But he hadn't had to watch his best friend die before his eyes, and that was a different sort of agony than what Ross had endured. Asher was more than thankful that his friend had a new wife who adored him, to help blunt those memories; but he himself had no such buffer to help stave off the nightmares when they came creeping in.

He supposed he could talk to Geordie or Quinn, but somehow... well, Geordie had his own new wife, and was still grieving the loss of his father. Losing Ross had to have been a special kind of hell for him from that standpoint, and Asher hadn't the heart to bring it up. Quinn, meanwhile, was wrestling with the guilt of having been the catalyst to everything that happened to Ross, up to and including his murder. There was no way Asher would add to that pain by asking his friend to share his personal burden.

Which left him raw and alone. He'd been here before—no doubt would be again—but that didn't make it any easier. And somehow Miss Whitfield—Charlie—seemed as though she might understand. Surely it wouldn't hurt to follow Lorna's advice, enough to ease this weight he carried, and perhaps ease some of what she was carrying too?

She was waiting for him to speak. At last he began slowly, "There is more out there. It's... I'm not supposed to..." He let out a breath. "Damn," he muttered quietly.

Charlie reached out a hand and lightly brushed his wrist. "The Agency will not hear of this from me, if that is your concern."

He vouchsafed her a glance. "No. I know you can be trusted. It's... difficult for me to break rules, that's all." Asher took a breath and settled his shoulders. "But you need to know, and I... think I need to tell you, if it won't be a burden to you."

"You are anything but a burden, Asher Burton." Charlie offered him a slight, but warm and encouraging smile. "It's been quite the contrary, you've eased the burden I've felt since my uncle disappeared. If I can do the same for you, I'm happy to do it."

He nodded, taking a deep breath. "I recently had an experience—a series of experiences—which taught me... which helped me to understand exactly what you said: that there is more out there." Asher cleared his throat. How to do this without revealing Lorna Alvin's secret? At last he began slowly, "I saw something recently that might fit into the same general category as the creature of the loch."

"Ah, during another mission?" Charlie asked. "Some sort of yet undiscovered animal." She nodded slowly. "That must have been fascinating."

Hardly, unless you mean in the same way prey is fascinated by a cobra. "It was terrifying," he replied. "Huge, with rows of teeth in a vaguely human face." He shuddered. "It saved us some trouble—and caused a miracle. But—fuel for nightmares."

Charlie frowned and cocked her head a little. "I believe I've missed something. It caused a miracle?"

When it came to the point, losing Ross was still nearly impossible to verbalize. Asher quirked a small smile, drawing invisible pictures on the tabletop with his fingertips. "You'll think me mad."

She laid her hand on top of his, stilling it. "You listened to my dream without judgment. I will not return your understanding by jumping to conclusions about your sanity."

After all, it would be a relief to tell someone. "Our quarry—the man we were after—was a murderer," he told her. "The creature dispatched him and then—" He took a breath, eyes prickling with unshed tears. "It brought his latest victim back to life. I was there—I saw everything. The victim was undeniably dead, and yet... he lives still."

"You're certain you were not mistaken about his condition?" Charlie's question was in much the same tone that Asher used when interviewing witnesses.

Asher nodded, clearing his throat again. "He was unquestionably dead. No breath, no heartbeat; his skin was grey and his body had begun to cool."

Her fingers wrapped around his. "Are you all right, Mr. Burton?" She gave his hand a little squeeze. "You've gone pale."

He shook himself and tried to smile. "Perfectly well, Miss Whitfield. It's a... difficult memory, that's all." *Understatement, Asher, old boy*, he thought, and hid behind sipping his tea.

"You know the victim, don't you?" It was her face that paled a little now.

He had to take a moment before he could get the answer out. "I do—a very dear friend, as it happens. One of my closest."

She stared down at the table in silence. "And this creature... it brought him back? He's safe and sound now?"

Not just the creature alone—it had gifted the power to Ross' wife Elsie, and she—her will, her gift, her *love*—had brought Ross back, had done what Asher himself could not. *God bless Elsie McInerny.* This time his smile was more than perfunctory. "He is, thank God." Asher turned his hand to close his fingers around hers.

He could see her weighing his words carefully. Of course she was. Even in so short an acquaintance, Asher knew Charlie rarely reacted to a situation without thought. When she finally spoke, her words were very careful. "May I ask what happened to the man who hurt your friend? You said the creature dispatched him."

Something else that haunted him: the frenzy of unearthly bodies as the creatures swarmed, the truncated scream of a man in unimaginable agony, the bloom of blood in the water. Asher rubbed a hand over the lower half of his face and nodded. "It... forgive me—it ate him."

"Oh..." Charlie leaned back in her chair, but her hand remained warm and comforting in his. She swallowed, and her lower lip trembled slightly. "That is... as you said before, terrifying." Her eyes met his, large and clouded with concern. "Mr. Burton, I believe you."

"Thank you, Miss Whitfield. And thank you for allowing me to speak of it. I hadn't been able to, before now."

Her lip trembled again. "Thank you for trusting me with such a thing. I'm honored that you did, and... I'm glad that your friend is all right now."

He gave her fingers a last squeeze before releasing her. "So am I. Thank you." Asher shook his head a little. "I did have a point in telling you all this. The Fae do exist, and I think..." He thought about Mrs. Alvin's words. "I'm certain we're dealing with one now. The warning on the note, addressed to 'Mortal', the dagger... possibly even the beast in the Loch itself, though of that last I'm not positive."

Charlie was very quiet indeed, fingers wrapping around the teacup in front of her, cheeks having gone pale again. Asher was beginning to worry that despite her assurances, she did think him touched in the head. She took a slow and very deep breath. "Everything I've been taught tells me that I should dismiss such things as nonsense, that the stories of the Fae and magic are nothing more than a way to explain what we do not understand." She looked up, eyes locking with Asher's.

"But I trust you, and as mad as it all sounds, I *know* it's true."

His lips quirked in a half-smile even as he sighed and nodded. "In the interests of full disclosure I will say there's yet more, but none of it is for me to share. I do trust you, Charlie, but when the secrets aren't mine..." He shrugged. "I hope you understand."

"I do, and I respect your discretion." She got up and began to pace the kitchen, nibbling on her lower lip thoughtfully. "Very well then, where does that leave us? We are clearly dealing with something out of the ordinary scope of things, and judging by the message we received last night our adversary is not concerned about keeping a distant watch." Charlie stopped, finger resting at the corner of her mouth as she turned back to Asher. "It seems to me that our first order of business would be to fortify the farm against any further unwanted visitors of folklore."

"A very good idea," Asher agreed. "Unfortunately, I'm afraid it's not the sort of thing covered by Agency training."

Charlie made for the door. "Then I suppose a bit of research is in order." She paused on the threshold and beckoned for Asher to follow, waiting until he was on his feet before she continued. "While I cannot claim that my uncle has much in his personal library about the Fae, he does have a limited collection of books pertaining to folklore, mostly in relation to the creature, but there may be something of use there."

Asher nodded. "Quite possible. We can divide up the books and see what we may see."

The books containing any relevant information on the Fae were indeed limited. In fact, there were only two that had anything of potential value to offer. One was a rather worn and beaten volume that seemed to have been written by a former resident of the area. It cataloged accounts of the beast, and a few colorful remedies for common ailments that the author felt were the result of Faerie mischief.

Asher pushed his spectacles up his nose. "Ash trees," he read, "red verbena, yarrow, daisies... something called St. John's wort?" He shook his head. "I know what daisies are and I understand that ash trees are a type of tree, but I can tell deciduous from evergreen and that's about the extent of my knowledge. Does any of this mean anything to you?"

Charlie looked up from the book in her lap and leaned over to examine the pages Asher was studying. "Fortunately, it does, and as it would happen I have a few of those on hand. St. John's wort I use in a tea for my uncle, to help him when his joints ache. I have a bit of dried yarrow as well." She returned her focus to her own book, holding it out for Asher and pointing to a particular passage. "I realize this is only a story, but the hero sat inside a circle of salt so that he could watch a faerie feast without being taken into their realm. I did restock our supply of salt the last time I was in town."

"A ring of salt, hm? I suppose we could just..." Asher thought about it. "Line the doors and windows, or even surround the house, although that seems like something of a waste. I've never heard that a Fae could walk through a solid wall. But if it would help...?"

"Have you heard that they cannot?" Charlie asked, but from the slight smile on her face, Asher decided the question was not a serious one. She closed her book and put it aside. "This is all theoretical, and we can hardly be assured of the validity of our sources. However, this is our course and we may as well commit to it. Therefore I suggest we use the yarrow and St. John's wort to make four..." she paused and shook her head slightly. "I can hardly believe I'm saying this, but I believe we should fashion charms of a sort, bundle them and hang them at the edges of the property, one in each of the four directions. Then we apply the salt at the windows and doors just as you've suggested."

Asher got up and rubbed his hands together briskly. "No time like the present. What's the yarrow for?" he asked as an aside. Ross would no doubt know— or he might have a different application for it entirely. Either way, Asher was curious.

Charlie was busy putting the books back in their proper places. "Oh, it helps with a number of things, according to Mrs. Alvin, but I most often use it when Uncle Elias or I catch a chill."

According to Lorna Alvin, hm? That seemed to answer that, at least to a point, and Asher grinned to himself.

He took the small wooden barrel of salt and walked around the perimeter of the house, leaving a trail in front of each doorway and window, and then did the same inside, climbing the stairs to the cupola to make sure it was lined along the inside as well. He didn't, after all, know what this Fae was capable of, and it was imperative that Charlie be protected.

When he came back down the stairs it was to the accompaniment of a growling stomach and he was reminded that he'd had nothing more than a slice of bread for breakfast. "What do you say to an early luncheon?" he asked Charlie, who had finished up her talismans. "We can hang these along the property line first."

Her stomach answered for her, gurgling as if in response to the question. "That would be a yes," Charlie laughed as she placed the roughly-made charms in a basket and headed for the door.

They made quick work of posting the charms around the farm, and were back inside with luncheon laid out in record time. The tension of the morning seemed to have evaporated with the work of their research and the proactive—albeit eccentric—steps being taken toward the security of their home base.

Asher was thoughtful during the meal. Something more needed to be done to keep Charlie safe, in case this bastard targeting her managed to get past him—the very idea of which infuriated Asher, but he had to be practical about the situation and put his pride and worry aside. Most women of his acquaintance, with only three possible exceptions, would be unsuited for what he was about to propose, but he rather thought Charlie Whitfield was exactly the right sort of woman required.

He let out a breath and took his dishes over to the sink. "Miss Whitfield," he remarked calmly, "I believe you should know something of self-defense, just in case. Would you be willing to learn?"

Charlie paused in the process of gathering her dishes, and seemed to think the proposal over before giving him a small nod. "Under the circumstances I believe it would be utterly foolish of me to refuse."

He offered her a smile. "Then let us adjourn to the yard as soon as we've finished cleaning up."

In a quarter of an hour they were outside facing one another. "Have you done anything of the sort before?" Asher asked, wanting to gauge any potential knowledge. He thought likely it was zero, but on the other hand, Elias was a practical man and might have taught her something.

To Asher's surprise, Charlie's cheeks colored a little. She glanced at him and then quickly shifted her gaze to the lake. "Uncle Elias did tell me where to strike a man, should he try to force... unwanted attention."

Asher couldn't help the grin that curved his lips. "Well done, Uncle Elias. I wish all men cared enough to convey that sort of vital information to the women they love." He chuckled aloud. "As my intentions are benign, I trust you won't feel a need to practice that particular maneuver on me."

"Oh, certainly not! I'd never hurt you, Mr. Burton." Her response was so quick and genuine that it seemed to have overpowered her earlier bashfulness. She cleared her throat and squared her shoulders, offering him one of those dimpled smiles. "At least, not intentionally. I suspect lessons in defending oneself might prove a little hazardous to both teacher and student."

"I'm prepared for that," he allowed. "The point, after all, is to teach you to cause harm if necessary." Asher organized his thoughts. "Of paramount importance," he began, "is that there are four places on any person that are most vulnerable. Hitting someone in the chest, for example, is pointless—Nature has devised excellent protection in the form of the ribcage. Those vulnerable areas are the eyes, the nose, the throat, and—er—the area your uncle mentioned." He watched her to be sure she was following him and not being overcome by finer feelings.

She was nodding thoughtfully, and Asher could all but see the notes being written in her mind. "Eyes, nose, throat, and groin," she repeated back, apparently moving past sensitivities to focus on the technical aspects of the lesson. "I assume there are right and wrong ways to attack, methods that are more effective than others?"

He ought to have known she would engage that scientific mind of hers, Asher thought, and ceased to worry about the niceties. He moved next to her to demonstrate how to properly make a fist, and various ways to strike an opponent without harming herself too much. Charlie repeated his movements a few times, first slow and precise and then at the proper speed.

Asher nodded with approval. "Those strikes and the use of your legs—to kick or to run—are the main components in defending yourself. Of course the primary objective is to prevent any assailant from approaching too close in the first place, and the best way to do that is to do exactly what your uncle advised. First you must stabilize yourself, prepare to lift one leg with good balance." He demonstrated how and where to kick a man to disable him quickly, giving Elias' instruction some added clarity. "Once he's down, as always, run."

Charlie practiced as instructed, only wobbling a little when she kicked forward, her foot catching slightly in the fold of her skirt. She huffed in irritation. "There are times I think men's fashion far more practical than all of this nonsense," she muttered, gesturing to her attire.

"A fair point. Here—forgive me," he said, and moved around behind her, his hands settling on her hips. "Shift this way a bit, to put your weight behind the kick, and try grasping your skirts as you move forward to pull them out of the way. You want to make contact with your shin or the ball of your foot, not the top."

Charlie repositioned herself, her hips moving easily under his hands. She shifted her weight as he recommended and repeated the action. This attempt was met with more success, and she turned a bright, triumphant smile toward Asher. "Excellent suggestion! This is quite enjoyable."

The weight of her hips in his hands coupled with her sudden shift back toward him caught Asher by surprise, and his mind went to some very untoward places before he reined his thoughts back in. "I'm glad you're enjoying it," he returned, though his voice was a bit rough and he had to clear his throat. "What was I going to say—oh, yes. If somehow the person gets too close for you to do a full kick, abruptly raising your knee will have the same effect."

"Raise my knee, yes," she nodded, and followed the statement by demonstrating her understanding, gathering her skirt to make the move a smooth one.

"Well done." Asher stepped back so her hips would stop grazing against his. "Unfortunately not every assailant will have the good manners to approach from the front, so I think it would be wise to learn how to escape from an attack from behind. But before we do that, let's discuss how to land an effective blow at close quarters. In these cases it's often more effective to use your elbow. The advantage to this, as you see, is that you can strike both forward and back."

"Repeat those motions, if you would," Charlie replied, and as Asher demonstrated again she moved around him, watching thoughtfully. When she finished her inspection she came to stand in front of him again, a finger resting lightly on her plump lower lip. Charlie studied him briefly before she turned her back. She angled her head, chin just over her shoulder. "Ready, Mr. Burton."

He closed his arms about her, setting his jaw, pointedly ignoring the scent of lilacs as it rose from her golden hair.

She gave a very quiet gasp, and then the slightest of tremors. "I doubt anyone bent on harm will be so gentle. You'll need to apply yourself, Mr. Burton."

Focus, Asher. "Very well," he went on after a moment. "To escape from such an attack, the steps are thus: bend forward—suddenly is better, to throw off your assailant's balance—and from that slight crouch, hit backward with your elbows, one after the other." They went through the moves slowly. "Very good. When your attacker's grip loosens for you to step away, turn to apply a closed-fist downward blow to the neck, grasp his shoulder for leverage to lift your knee into his groin, and then run."

Charlie stepped out of his arms and turned to him with a look of confusion. "A downward blow to the neck?"

"Yes. You see, when you bend suddenly you will pull him forward, off balance." He showed her again. "Here—perhaps we are doing this too slowly. I shall apply myself, as you said." Asher moved behind her again and this time pulled her snugly to him. Charlie bent forward, her hips pushing back against Asher's. Her whole body tensed against his as she prepared to strike.

He was genuinely caught by surprise when desire roared to life, so much so that she landed the first hit to his head with rather more success than either had intended, knocking his spectacles askew. She completed the rest of the maneuver with ease, fortunately sparing him the knee to the groin. Asher lay in the dirt for a moment, contemplating the sky.

She dusted her hands with a look of satisfaction that quickly turned to concern when her eyes came to rest on Asher. "Are you hurt, Mr. Burton? Oh dear, I should have asked if you were ready for me to begin."

"You did exactly as you should," he demurred. "Manners have no place in this sort of activity, and I suffered no hurt that I won't recover from. Do you want to run through it again?"

Charlie offered him a hand up. "Manners may not have a place in a true fight, but you'll hardly be able to complete the lesson if I knock you senseless."

That made him huff out a laugh. "Miss Whitfield, if you knock me senseless, you may consider the lesson completed." This time he gave her no warning, grabbing her around the waist roughly from behind. He was prepared now, and thus the maneuver was completed with him once again on the ground but far less discombobulated. "Very well done! I have one other variation to show you."

"I'm ready for it!" She lifted her chin and folded her arms across her chest. "Do your very best, Mr. Burton."

"As my... er... personal wellbeing will be even more in jeopardy, let us walk through it first." Asher positioned himself behind her again, wrapping his arms around her upper torso to trap her arms in his grasp. "All right. You cannot attack with elbows in this case, so what you will want to do first is to shift your weight not forward, but to the side, thus exposing your attacker's... um... liabilities." She moved as instructed. "Now: closed-fist strike downward, aiming for the groin." Charlie brought her fist down, stopping short of connecting. "Thank you. I promise you that if you hit hard enough your assailant will be temporarily incapacitated," he let go of her, directing her to spin out of his grasp, "but if needed, keep attacking with your knee—to the groin, yes," when she hesitated, then carefully followed his instructions, again without making contact, "and with a kick to the face, if the opportunity presents itself. And then, as always, run."

Charlie ran through the process a few more times, moving slowly and with careful precision. After a fifth attempt she stepped back. "I would suggest we try it in earnest, but I believe this step ought to remain theoretical. I'm not certain we could run through it without you suffering for your efforts."

"I heartily agree," he replied good-naturedly. "Do you feel you have the theory in hand?"

She gave him a confident nod, and then an assessing look. "I will wash your clothes for you. After all, you were only laid flat in the dirt to help me. Fair is fair."

"Not at all," he replied, waving a hand. "All part of the service."

"In that case, back to work," Charlie replied. She turned on her heels and headed for the house. Halfway there, she looked back at Asher. "Thank you. Knowing I'm equipped to defend myself, at least to some extent, helps."

"Good." He gave her a nod. That confidence was what this lesson had been intended to confer: a formidable woman made yet more so. The fact that he had his own lessons to take from the experience did not escape him, but those thoughts were better left to a more contemplative time.

Chapter Ten

Beneath the Surface

Shortly after luncheon the following day, Charlie found Asher contemplating the loch. "I keep trying to think what I'd do if I were Elias," he replied when she asked what he was doing. "He had the boat up at the campground. Maybe all he did was take it to the site, but maybe he went out in it. I should go out in it, see if I can work out what he was looking at." He sighed. "And see where the currents might lead from there, if the worst happened and we need to trace his—er, where he might have ended up. I don't think it did," he was quick to add, "but it's best to be thorough."

Charlie swallowed a little, focusing on a pebble near her feet until she could think past the very real possibility that despite all hope, her uncle might indeed be gone. She exhaled slowly and looked to Asher with a small nod. "As much as I hate to admit it, I do have to consider all the possibilities. I'll pack a little food—rowing is hungry work—and we can head out straight away." The suggestion of packing food was as much a practical concern as well as giving her time to steel herself if the worst became reality.

Once the boat was loaded with adequate supplies for their afternoon expedition, Asher and Charlie set off on the murky waters of the loch. "You said getting to the research camp was quicker this way— I'd like to begin there, see how much quicker it is so I can have a clearer idea of the timeline," Asher explained, exerting himself. Soon enough he'd removed his coat, declaring that with all the exercise of rowing, he was warm enough in spite of the cold.

It was much quicker by boat—Charlie thought it was even quicker than usual, since Asher was young and strong by comparison to her uncle. After a while the campsite came into view and they headed for the bank to drop off the supplies and salt the perimeter to ensure nothing would be tampered with while they were investigating the lake. When all was sorted they climbed back into the boat again and drifted back out onto the loch.

A little chilled herself, and after noting that Asher's pace was beginning to slow, Charlie offered to take a turn at the oars. "It will be a nice distraction, and I'm more familiar with the loch than you are."

His face was a study, warring between gallantry and practicality. "Very well," he said at last. "For a little while."

Shaking her head slightly and chuckling at his response, Charlie took hold of the oars. His concern for her was touching, but paddling about the lake was hardly a new activity for her. She dipped the oars into the water and pulled them back, propelling the boat expertly. "I've spent many an hour out on the—" She strained a little as she pulled again. "—On the water, Mr. Burton. Rowing is quite good for one's vitality."

He pulled his coat back on. "As you seem to have more than the customary amount, I cannot help but agree, Miss Whitfield." He paused, attention caught by something ahead. Asher took his spectacles off, polished them on his waistcoat, and put them back on. "What...?"

Charlie propped the oars on the side of the boat and twisted round to see what had her companion so visibly confused. A short distance from where they drifted Charlie spied the mouth of a cave, large enough for the boat to pass through with ease, with a spattering of toadstools surrounding the mouth. Odd, Charlie thought, it was late in the year for mushrooms of any kind to be up.

A ripple of disquiet fluttered through Charlie's mind. She'd seen this place before, but she couldn't quite recall when. Even as the cave unsettled her, it seemed to call to her, to invite her in. She couldn't pull her gaze from the shadowy opening.

As Charlie continued to stare, she realized there were small lights flashing and moving about within the dark opening. Glow-worms? No, they'd never be out so late in the year, but the lights twinkled and moved as though alive. No, they were not glow-worms, these were floating in midair—floating over the water just as they'd done the night her uncle disappeared.

"Mr. Burton?" Charlie turned back to her companion, wondering if he had any explanation.

"I don't know," he replied. "Some sort of electrical phenomenon, perhaps? Here—let me take over rowing again. If we are thinking like Elias, those lights warrant further investigation."

"It is exactly the sort of thing that would have caught his attention," Charlie agreed, and so saying passed the task of rowing back to Asher. Free of the work, she took the opportunity to examine the cave of swirling lights with greater care.

Apart from the out-of-season mushrooms, and the little lights, the cave itself was unremarkable, yet Charlie couldn't shake the sense that it was familiar, that it was something *more*. She shook herself mentally and tried to think logically; ridiculous flights of fancy were of little use scientifically. The cave seemed familiar, yes, but that was hardly a surprise considering how many boating trips she'd taken with her uncle. The late mushrooms and lights were fascinating but... but... the sense of strangeness was a nagging one, and no amount of rationalizing thought could dismiss it.

Asher paused and turned around. "I've heard of such things at sea, in the rigging and such, but never..." He backpaddled, bringing the boat to a stop. "I ought to take you back to the camp, perhaps."

Not bloody likely, Charlie thought, but decided not to give voice to it. Instead she fixed what she hoped was a stern look on the man across from her. "Mr. Burton, I am a student of the natural world and I would be a poor one if I did not investigate this phenomenon thoroughly." She softened a little. "Besides, I have no intention of sitting on the lakeshore while you investigate such an intriguing puzzle." The way the place called to her as if whispering her name over and over was a fact she chose not to share.

Asher studied her face for a long moment, then chuckled softly. "All right. If you're electrocuted, on your own head be it." He dipped the oars back into the water and began to urge the boat toward the mouth of the cave.

Charlie refrained from pointing out that if she were to be electrocuted, he was just as likely to suffer the same fate. She'd won the battle in any case, and there was little reason to give him cause to change his mind. She folded her hands in her lap and waited for the boat to approach the entrance to the cave.

Each stroke of the oars revealed a new and intriguing detail about their destination. The tiny flecks of light seemed to move independently of one another, without the usual arcs and jagged edges of an electrical current. In fact, she could swear there was an intelligent purpose to their relentless shifting. Moreover, each twinkling orb was slightly different from the next, in shape, or size, even in color. Charlie reached out and put a hand on Asher's wrist to still him. "Look! They seem... alive."

The prow of the rowboat passed the cave's threshold, and now Charlie could see the lights under the water as well, sweeping in one direction, swirling in another, much like flocks of birds in the sky. As the rest of the boat drifted into the cave, the quality of the light changed, and the darkness before them lifted. It became brighter, more golden, with a shimmering quality, like dust motes drifting through rays of light between the boughs of the trees. The scientist in Charlie grew silent, giving way to wonder as the small craft drifted out of another opening, suggesting that they'd been in a sort of rocky tunnel, rather than a cave.

Tall, twisting trees lined either side of the stream they were floating down, their roots curling into the water. The banks were blanketed in pale green moss that twinkled a bit in the sunlight. Strange sounds echoed from the shadowy world beyond, at one moment like the cry of a dove, and then more akin to the sound of high tinkling voices murmuring or—or... singing.

Asher stopped rowing. "What is this place?" he murmured, as though unwilling to disturb the atmosphere.

Another world, thought Charlie, though she felt the same hesitance to disrupt the sense of wonder and power. The dancing lights that drew them to the cave in the first place were more numerous here. A few of them flitted closer to the boat before darting back into the surrounding forest.

Quite without thought, Charlie leaned over the boat and dipped her fingers into the water. There was a moment of absolute stillness, and then... the nearest of the swimming lights moved toward her. It paused for only an instant and then wove around her outstretched fingertips, feathery-soft and warm, leaving a tingling sensation wherever it made contact with her skin.

Asher pulled his spectacles from his face, his eyes seeming very blue in the golden light. "This... is no place for folk like us."

"It's beautiful," Charlie replied in a dreamy voice. She longed to go further down the stream, to walk under the glistening branches that surrounded her. But, Asher's words managed to break through whatever enchantment called to Charlie. Breathtaking though their surroundings were, there was also something... unsettling about this place. She pulled her fingers from the water and looked from one bank to the other. A small shiver skittered down her spine. They were being watched, of that much she was absolutely certain. "Perhaps... perhaps you're right."

The stream was wide enough to turn the boat, which Asher did, though carefully, and then began to row back toward the cave from which they'd emerged.

There was a moment of sadness for Charlie when the vessel moved back into the shadows of the tunnel, a tug at her heart that urged her to wander back toward the woods, but then the singing ebbed and the sunlight vanished entirely. She wrapped her arms around herself as the air grew chilly again.

Asher continued to row, and Charlie was certain they'd break into the daylight soon, but as the boat emerged from the cave, it was not to a sunny Scotland afternoon, but to the deepening purples and blues of dusk.

"What?" Charlie blinked, shifting around in her seat, mind grabbling to apply some kind of rational explanation.

Asher too was looking around in astonishment. "We've lost time somehow," he said, and applied himself to the oars. "We should get back to the campsite at least."

"This is not possible," Charlie shook her head, as if refusing to admit to the evidence before her would change the night to day. She stopped and glanced to the nearest shore. "Hours, or... do you think it might have been days?"

"No way to know." Asher grunted as he pulled on the oars. Up ahead the contour of the lakeshore became familiar. "There's the camp—we might need to—"

Without warning the rowboat tilted sharply and then overturned, spilling both occupants into the shockingly cold loch.

The air was knocked from Charlie's lungs as the water enveloped her. She was too stunned by it to react immediately. There was nothing but cold and darkness, and the relentless pull of the weight of her soaked skirts. Charlie pumped her arms and her head broke the surface briefly. "Ash—" she tried to call out, propriety forgotten in the struggle for survival. The water closed in over her head again, cutting off her desperate plea.

A soft glow permeated the water rising up from the depths; a short distance away she could barely make out two figures struggling in the water. Through a haze of fear Charlie realized that one was Asher. He was locked in combat with a form both human and vaguely animal. The limbs were slightly longer and thicker than a man's, the back and shoulders broad, and it moved with frenzied intent.

Bubbles spiraled upward, obscuring Charlie's view; the fabric of her skirts twisted round her feet and pulled her deeper into the water. More wisps of light floated up from the depths; something huge streaked by below her. The need for air was nearly excruciating, and the edges of Charlie's vision was starting to blur.

Things were beginning to go black and then Asher's face materialized in the murky water, close to Charlie. He grasped the sides of her head and pressed his mouth to hers, forcing her to open to him, and then he filled her lungs with air before attempting to drag her to the surface.

Charlie tried to help him, but her skirts were so heavy and kept twisting around her legs. Even with both of them stroking toward the surface they were making little progress. The physical exertion burned through the precious air Asher had provided and soon Charlie's lungs were searing again.

All at once she felt something under her legs, lifting her upward, rushing them toward the surface of the loch. Her head broke the waves seconds after Asher's and they were both speeding toward the shore and then... the pressure under them fell away and Asher was dragging Charlie toward the rocky beach by Elias' camp.

Asher helped her stumble onto land and toward the firepit. He was shivering visibly but he immediately set to building a fire. "Get those wet things off, quickly," he told her tersely, stacking the wood.

Charlie herself was shivering so badly that she could barely force her limbs to obey commands. She staggered toward the lean-to and began fumbling with the buttons of her bodice. After a bit of struggling she managed to unfasten the last of them and peeled her wet shirtwaist off, tossing it aside to turn her focus to her skirt and underthings.

She disposed of her soaked and heavy skirts with relief and took hold of her corset, frantically twisting to loosen the busk. Unfortunately, her fingers seemed to have decided gripping was no longer a function they cared to practice, and try as she might, she simply could not keep a steady hold. Charlie let out a little whimper, though it was a rather wobbly sound.

The fire had just taken hold of the kindling, thanks to Elias' tin of waterproof matches, and Asher was in the process of shucking his coat. He took in her predicament and strode to her. "Forgive me," he murmured, placed his hands on either side of her breasts, and with a quick motion of his wrists the busk came entirely undone. He let out a breath, looking down at her: his glasses were gone, his curly hair wet, and his breath was coming quickly. She could almost feel the weight of his gaze as it fell on her mouth, and then he stepped back, catching the corset before it fell to the ground entirely.

He shook his head as though trying to dislodge something, and moved further back, his stride hitching as he went. "You'll need to take... that off too," he gestured to her chemise, and turned away.

Charlie's eyes dropped down to her chest and she suddenly realized that completely soaked, her chemise was all but transparent. Her first instinct was to wrap her arms across her breasts and try to cover up, though his words, and the sensation of freezing cold fabric across her skin, broke through her embarrassment.

She looked around the lean-to and spotted her uncle's chest of supplies, dragging it close. Sure enough there were woolen blankets inside, and Charlie pulled the dripping chemise over her head and tossed it to the ground, wrapping one of the blankets round herself. She glanced back toward the fire and looked away just as quickly as Asher's sodden trousers and drawers hit the ground, revealing a lean and muscular backside.

"Mr. Burton," Charlie cleared her throat, and tried for all the world to sound more dignified than she felt. "There is a second blanket here—better to fight the cold, I think." She pushed Uncle Elias' chest out of the lean-to and turned her attention to the loch.

"Forgive me," he said again, and there were rummaging sounds behind her as she stared out toward the waters. "I'm covered," he said, but when she turned back it wasn't entirely true: his torso was still exposed and he was inspecting several long and bleeding lacerations along his ribs.

Charlie almost dropped the blanket that was wrapped around her body. "Mr. Burton, what has happened to you?" She resituated the top of her covering and moved to inspect the wound.

"I believe I met the creature that's been disemboweling sheep." He touched one side of the worst gash, hissing a bit. "That was no accident—there was someone—some*thing*—in the water. It overturned us, I fought it a bit and then it swam off suddenly." He inspected the wounds again. "Claws, I would guess."

"Here, sit down, let me have a look at that," Charlie tucked the top of the blanket firmly under itself, just below her arms and hurried to see to the man's injuries. The information that the capsizing was part of an assassination attempt seemed less important when Asher was bleeding freely. "We must see the wounds are clean at the very least."

"Oh, I expect they got a thorough washing," he replied, trying to look at the bloody lines that ran parallel down his side. "Deepish, though." He relaxed his arms and pulled up the edges of the blanket. "That middle one should probably be stitched, I'm afraid. Do you feel up to that, or shall I cope?"

Charlie carefully nudged his blanket back down and leaned in to get a closer look at the gash on his side. 'Deepish' was being optimistic—the middle wound was wide open, and leaving it unstitched simply would not do. "I can't say that I've ever stitched flesh before, but I'm afraid this cannot be left for later."

He nodded. "That's my own conclusion, but as I said, I can cope with stitching it myself if the idea upsets you. I have a first-aid kit in the box with the supplies, if you wouldn't mind retrieving it."

Charlie shot Asher a look that she hoped conveyed exactly how ridiculous she thought the suggestion that he could stitch the injury himself was. "Mr. Burton, while I have no doubt that you are capable of stitching a wound, I would be shocked if you were capable of the contortions required to do so with this one." So saying, she got up and went to retrieve the first aid kit.

It was either fortunate or a sad commentary on his life choices that the kit Asher mentioned was well-stocked with bandages, heavy suturing thread, curved needles and the like. There were also a fair number of vials and jars, though the handwritten labels indicated that these were not commercially prepared medicines. Charlie brought the kit over to where Asher was seated.

When she had her workspace settled, Charlie picked up the thread and one of the needles, holding them up in the dim light of the fire. "Do you know if I should begin sewing from the bottom or the top, or does it matter?"

"I rather think from the center out," he replied. "I believe there's a jar in there labeled 'Sine Sensu'? I'd appreciate if you'd apply that first—it's surprisingly effective at numbing pain entirely. Very handy in these sorts of situations."

"Entirely?" Charlie asked. She placed the threaded needle back in the kit and found the jar he named, examining it closely. It was impossible to get a sense of the true color, but there was a slightly shimmering quality that could just barely be made out in the firelight. "This is... not conventional medicine." Charlie's gaze shifted from the salve to Asher's face. "Is this magical in nature?"

There was a pause. "It is," he admitted. "I could bite on a stick instead if the idea makes you uncomfortable."

Charlie removed the lid and used the corner of one of the bandages to scoop out a portion of the salve. "We were just saved by the Loch Ness monster and you believe a little salve to ease pain will make me uncomfortable?" She dabbed the concoction along the jagged edges of the claw marks. "You know one of the Fae, don't you?"

It seemed the salve lost little time in taking effect, for Asher sighed in relief as she applied it. "I do, yes. That was one of the—" He hissed when she got to a deeper part of the middle slash.

"One of the what?" she asked, looking up from her work to gauge whether he was ready for her to continue or not.

He gave her a nod. "One of the things I couldn't say, before. The potion I gave you earlier was from the same source."

"Ah," she returned thoughtfully, resuming her efforts and coating the entire area around the gashes. There was something more to it. He'd told her the Fae existed; it seemed odd that mentioning his own acquaintance with them was beyond what he could share, but if he was bound to secrecy she would not push the issue. "How does it feel now? Shall I begin the stitching?"

"I can feel some light pressure. Are you touching the wound?"

That answered that, Charlie thought, returning the jar to its place in the kit and lifting the needle. "Very well, I believe the salve has done what it was meant to." Her hand hovered over the wound, needle poised to begin. It was with some measure of satisfaction she noted her hand was steady, even if her stomach was turning a bit. "I'm beginning now."

With those words, Charlie placed her free hand on the edge of the cut, carefully pressing the edges together as she started the first stitch. It's only a bit of sewing, she told herself. Simply focus on the task and not the materials. It was difficult to think beyond the details with the first stitch, but as she grew accustomed to the feel of the work it became easier to continue.

"The salve still doing its work?" Charlie asked, after completing a few more stitches, fingers sliding gently down his torso to reposition for the next section.

Asher's breath seemed to catch, but he replied in the affirmative, though his voice was rough.

Charlie stopped her work to check him more thoroughly. "Are you certain?" His physical response seemed contrary to his words. "I'm not yet half done, but I can stop if you need a moment."

"No, I'm..." He took a breath, seeming to shake himself. "There's no pain. Mind's wandering a bit, that's all. Carry on."

Perhaps it was part of his training, taking his mind away from the present to avoid the pain, or perhaps the salve was working as well as he claimed.

Either way, there was a job to be done, and Charlie would not fail him.

At last the final stitch was in place and tied off. Asher twisted himself a bit trying to see her handiwork. "Well done, thank you. I'll gather more wood in a moment—let me just catch my breath."

Charlie held her hands out awkwardly, looking around the space for something to wipe the blood from them. After a minute or two she gave up and simply went to the water's edge to scrub them thoroughly. After that she rifled through the basket of food they'd thankfully left at the camp and produced a bottle of whiskey she'd thought might help ease the chill after their foray onto the lake. She uncorked it and took a swig, to soothe the frazzled nerves she'd managed to keep steady until she finished working.

Asher held out a hand, raising his brows at the bottle. "Share?"

Charlie passed it to him with a little grin. "It does take the edge off the cold, and I suppose a patient as well-behaved as you deserves a nip."

He chuckled, taking a draught at the bottle. "That does hit the spot. If you can pass me a roll of bandages, I'll trouble you no further for any surgical procedures. And then I'll go gather more wood before the Sine Sensu wears off."

"You gave me the very breath from your lungs; I believe it was the least I could do," Charlie replied over her shoulder as she returned to their limited store of supplies and sifted through for something to prepare for dinner.

Fortunately, Asher seemed to have anticipated an appetite after their exertions—though he could not have known what form those exertions would take—and so she found some bread, the last of the cold lamb, and a few potatoes—as well as an assortment of her dried herbs, which meant that he'd been listening carefully when she'd explained them to him, something Charlie found pleasing.

Asher finished wrapping the bandage around himself and secured the blanket as best he could, much as she would imagine a denizen of ancient Rome to do. "I'll get that wood—won't be long."

He returned with an armload of deadfall, fortunately dry, and stacked it not far from the fire pit, adding a couple of larger pieces to build up the flames. Charlie could see that he was shivering again, and no wonder, really.

"You should come warm yourself and allow your body a little time to recover," she insisted. "You've suffered blood loss as well as a frigid dunking."

Asher nodded in agreement, teeth chattering, and joined her by the fire. "Only doing what needed to be done, I swear. I'm finished." He let out a shuddering breath. "It's a good thing we spread the salt when we dropped off the supplies—I haven't the energy to do it now."

Charlie shifted around, pulling the blanket tighter around her torso, and trying to find some measure of comfort. She glanced at her companion, knowing that for all her discomfort he was likely to be in worse shape. "How does it feel? Is the salve still easing the pain?"

"It is. I expect it'll work for a while yet—my friend isn't one to do things by halves," he replied. He added a few nearby sticks to the fire, watching the flames leap. "Are you warm enough?"

Charlie laughed at that, she wasn't shaking from head to toe any longer, but 'warm' was a bit of a stretch. She raised a brow at him. "Are you?" she asked dryly.

"I've been warmer," he acknowledged, and added more wood to the fire, poking at it with a stick.

Sitting still was doing nothing to help her feel any warmer, and so Charlie fixed all her focus on producing a hearty, and blessedly warm meal to aid in the endeavor. Cooking over a fire proved to be somewhat awkward when also doing her best to keep the heavy woolen blanket in place. Yet, with a bit of patience and ingenuity she managed to pull it off with a reasonable measure of success. The blanket only slipped a little, once, and thankfully Charlie managed to catch it before Asher got an eyeful.

"Thank you for doing all of this," he said quietly, after the first hungry bites.

"Cold and hunger always seem worse when paired. Besides, you have done enough," Charlie replied. She took a swig of the whiskey and coughed a little as she passed the bottle back to Asher. She turned away to stare into the flames thoughtfully. With a hot meal helping to warm her, Charlie was able to turn her mind to the events of the day. "I don't think we lost more than hours in that cave. The fact that our food has not spoiled indicates it was not more than that," Charlie said, looking up at Asher for a second, suddenly realizing why the cave had seemed familiar. "I also think... I think I've been there before."

Asher frowned. "What do you mean? When?"

Charlie reached for the stick that Asher had been using to stir the campfire. Having a physical activity to focus on helped her to order her thoughts, and to find a little distance from the fear that was creeping closer and closer. "The nightmare I had before... it took place there. I went into that cave with someone." She felt tears burning in her eyes and sniffled a little, determined not to let them fall. "I think

I was the only one who came back out." She shuddered, remembering the sound of a child's scream.

Asher reached out and touched her back through the blanket, offering support. "Do you think it was a memory, rather than a dream?"

She wanted to say no; she wanted so very badly to be able to claim it was nothing more than a nightmare. It would be so easy to deny it, and yet when she opened her mouth to do just that, Charlie knew it would be a lie. A tear slipped free from her lashes and she dashed it away quickly. "I wish I could say otherwise, but I believe it was real, yes."

There was a long pause. "But you don't actually recall any of it?"

Charlie rubbed at her temple. She didn't remember actually entering the place before, but at the same time, she did. Or rather, she knew the dream was more than her mind creating the images while she slept. And then another thought occurred to her, a truly terrible one. "What if... what if everything that's been happening—the animal deaths, my uncle's disappearance—what if it's the result of my wandering where I was not meant to be?"

"No," he replied immediately. "I don't believe that. The very fact that you returned to this world from that place indicates that no one took umbrage from your first visit. As for today..." Asher was looking into the fire, his expression very vulnerable, somehow, without his glasses. "I think," he went on gently, "that you and I went somewhere we ought not have gone, and that we're lucky we only lost a few hours." He shrugged. "And I think our enemy was watching the camp, saw us go by, and took a chance on killing—well, me, anyway."

"I'm sorry you were hurt, Mr. Burton." She poked at the fire again, stirring it up and watching the little embers that floated into the air. What she had to say next was just as difficult to utter out loud, but she had to face the possibility, especially considering who or what they seemed to be dealing with. "Perhaps my uncle is lost somewhere in that... wherever we were." She took a deep breath and steeled herself for the next statement. "Or perhaps the person who attacked us... did the same to my uncle, more or less, with... different results."

"Miss Whitfield—Charlie." Asher's gaze was steady. "There has been no report of a body matching your uncle's description. If simply removing your uncle was the goal, then why all this continued interference?" He rubbed his forehead. "It makes little sense—Elias' disappearance, the spying, the note, and then this. I can think of motives for each thing separately, but all of them together—it's almost as though the perpetrator is somehow at odds with himself, unable to choose an objective. Yet they *must* be related, but... I confess I cannot yet see how." His shoulders slumped and he dropped his head forward. "A good night's sleep would no doubt help, but that's not currently on the table."

Nestling deeper into her blanket, Charlie tried to focus her mind on their current predicament. She felt heartsick over her uncle and would rather have spent the night trying to solve the mystery, but exhausting herself and catching pneumonia was not going to bring Uncle Elias home any sooner. She edged a little closer to the fire, scooting her half-frozen toes closer to the flames. "I can't imagine I'll be able to sleep any time soon." She picked at the remainder of the meal and took the bottle of whiskey for another swig. The liquid hit her belly and helped to ease some of her unrest. "Still, I suppose we ought to try."

"If it helps at all, our assailant is likely just as uncomfortable. I landed a fair few blows of my own—

I'm fairly certain I broke a few of those fangs. And the salt seems to help. I doubt he'll bother us again tonight." He offered her a small smile. "And I feel sure you must count the denouement of our adventure as yet more proof that you and your uncle are right about the creature."

"That does make me feel a little warmer," Charlie admitted with a chuckle, feeling quite justified in her belief that their attacker deserved every discomfort coming to him. "As to the rest," she shook her head. It was one thing to believe in the idea of something, but to see real evidence of it—to be saved by it—that was an entirely different experience. "I always imagined it to be nothing more than an animal, undiscovered and extraordinary to be sure, but... it, whatever it was, helped us. More than that, it saved us." It was also surrounded by the same lights they'd seen at the cave entrance, and that created more questions that Charlie was too tired to contemplate.

Asher was watching her as she spoke. "I have begun to think it a mistake to believe that simply because something isn't human, it isn't sentient." His expression reflected discomfort and she realized he must be thinking of his experience with the sea hag.

Charlie let loose with a long, tired sigh. All things considered, that conclusion was one of the most sensible she'd heard recently. "And I have begun to think it a mistake to believe anything is as simple as it seems, sentient or not."

Chapter Eleven

The Bewitching Hour

It seemed likely, Asher mused as he settled next to the fire, that it was the Fae-touched salve that had caused his current predicament; but whatever the cause, the fact remained that he could not get the feel of Charlie's hands upon his skin out of his head. The salve had made the pain of his wound recede—had it also magnified the gentle caress of her fingertips, the slim breadth of her palm?

It would be a convenient lie to hide behind, he knew, but a lie nonetheless, because the salve had been nowhere in evidence when he'd experienced sharp arousal the day before. Yes, she was a lovely creature, and he had enjoyed dancing with her a few days ago, but he'd danced with lovely women before, both in the ballroom and in the bedroom on occasion, and never experienced quite that level of visceral response. He'd thought Charlie beautiful when he met her, but now... now that he knew her mind, her heart, a little; now that he'd begun to understand the quality of the woman inside the inarguably alluring package... there was no denying his attraction to her. And when during his self-defense lessons they'd assumed a position that in other circumstances would have been carnal, his body had reacted, to his surprise and chagrin.

He rubbed a hand over his face. He knew perfectly well that this evening's circumstances were far from romantic, as he bled everywhere and she was forced to stitch up his flesh. Disgusting, he was sure, and had he been required to feel the operation he'd no doubt have been far from enamored of the process. As it was, though, for him there had been no pain, just a slight tugging, and the feel of her hands on his bare skin, and his imagination had gone rampant.

She hadn't seemed to notice, however, and that was all to the good, for he was in no position to take advantage of the situation. He had sworn his duty to Queen and country, and that put paid to any private life. He'd understood that going in, and had taken those vows nonetheless, and so courting any woman had long been out of the question. As to simple seduction... no. That was not, never had been, who Asher was. He'd never been a man to take his pleasure and walk away, unless there was experience and understanding on both sides.

The thick blanket, the whiskey, and the fire were doing their job, cocooning him in drowsy warmth; he glanced over to see Charlie slumbering peacefully, one bare shoulder peeking from her makeshift bedroll, and the sight of the expanse of creamy skin made his body harden, reminding him that he'd helped remove her corset earlier, that he'd seen through the thin and translucent fabric of her wet chemise, that she was absolutely...

Oh, Lord. He shifted to face away from her, turning his attention toward the perimeter of the campsite. Nothing but peace permeated the air, and he thought it was likely that their adversary had retired from the fray for now, or that the salt he'd laid down earlier was doing exactly what they'd hoped. Either way the silence laid heavy in the air, and he yawned widely, scrubbing at his eyes in an attempt to stay awake.

"Asher."

Her voice was so low, so sultry he'd nearly missed it, and Asher turned back toward the fire. Charlie was awake, and she... she... He swallowed, tongue stuck to the roof of his mouth. She'd dispensed with the blanket, and she was... glorious, approaching him with a hand outstretched. His body reacted immediately, filling him with hunger, and he rolled to his feet, dropping his own covering as he met her in two long strides.

"Charlie," he breathed, and then his mouth was on hers and she tasted like heaven itself, pressing her lush flesh closer to his straining body. "I want..."

"Love me," she whispered, and God, yes, it was all he wanted, everything he needed. His hands traveled over the planes and curves of her form, caressing, weighing, molding, and he lifted her, helped her slide those shapely legs around his waist. He was near to bursting for want of her. "Love me, Asher."

He wrapped his arms around her and she greedily mapped his back, his arse, his ribs with warm palms. "God, Charlie, I..." he murmured against her mouth. "I d..."

Asher sat up suddenly, the pain of his wound sharp now, and glanced back toward the fire, where Charlie slept on, oblivious to his lascivious inner life.

He rubbed a hand over his face again and moved farther from the fire in an attempt to actually stay awake this time. He briefly debated walking into the freezing lake up to his waist, then shook his head. It would solve the immediate problem, but would also leave them peculiarly vulnerable should something go wrong. No—he needed to wrangle his wayward desires into submission on his own, and more importantly, stay awake to keep watch over Charlie, as he'd sworn to do.

As the sun finally peeked over the horizon Asher allowed himself to doze, knowing he'd be good for nothing if he got no rest at all. He was able to squeeze in an hour or two before waking again. Miss Whitfield slept on, and so he carefully went to check their clothing—fortunately reasonably dry, with the exception of her corset and the heavier layers of her skirts. Though still damp, they were dry enough to get them back to the farm safely, and Charlie could wrap a blanket over her clothes if the damp proved too uncomfortable with the morning chill.

Asher went to the lakeside to splash water on his face and found the boat—still half-swamped, but pushed well up on the rocky shore. Impossible, unless... unless the beast that had saved them also understood what the boat was, or meant, at least, and had saved it for them. How did one thank a benign lake creature for its good offices? he wondered, and huffed in amusement.

By the time Charlie woke he had tipped the water out of the rowboat, put his clothes back on, and stirred up the fire.

She sat up slowly, and then scrambled to catch the blanket before it slipped down to her waist. "Our clothes are dry?" she asked, not looking at Asher, but the blush visible nonetheless.

"Mostly—I'm afraid some of yours are still damp, but they'll do to get you home." Asher helped her gather her things and take them to the lean-to, then was careful to keep his back to her while he packed up the site.

After a fair amount of rustling, Charlie announced that she was covered and thanked Asher for his discreet consideration. When he turned she was finger combing her hair, her ribbon having been lost the night before. After managing to apply some measure of order to her hair, Charlie discreetly excused herself and disappeared into the trees.

A few minutes of calm passed and then Asher heard her call his name. "Mr. Burton, I believe there's something you should see."

His brows climbed nearly to his hairline. Surely not... *no, Burton, of course not. Get your imagination under control.* Asher finished folding the blanket in his hands and went to find her.

Charlie was standing next to a large tree, her entire focus fixed on the bark just below eye level. She glanced up when he approached and took a step to the side, nodding toward the object of her fascination. "I believe our attacker was here last night."

The trunk of the tree had three deep gouges running parallel to each other, identical in size and shape to the gashes on Asher's side. The exposed wood was still unweathered; the marks were no more than hours old from the looks of them. Charlie pointed the next tree over. It bore similar damage, though in greater numbers, and with an almost frenzied quality to the pattern.

Asher scowled, then looked to the ground: sure enough, the marks ceased at the edge of the salt line he'd put down. He rubbed at his eyes with one hand. "At least we know that this works," he said, gesturing to the salt. "But I heard nothing, nothing at all. What the he—nhouse is this thing?"

"Angry, would be my guess," Charlie replied solemnly. She wrapped her arms around herself, casting a last glance at the damaged trees before starting back toward their camp. "It's going to be a long trek home without the boat. We'll want to get a start as soon as everything is gathered up—I have no wish to be wandering the woods in the dark."

"No need," Asher replied, following her. "Our new friend returned the boat, and one of the oars was still in the lock. It won't be quite as fast as with two, but it'll be quicker than trying to walk."

There was a pause and then Asher heard the unmistakable sound of a relieved sigh. "God bless lake monsters and their forethought." Charlie came to join him by the fire, long, golden tresses loose and blowing around her face in the morning breeze. "And God bless the warm bath I intend to take when we get back to the farm."

Asher winced a bit at the tug on his side when he picked up their box of supplies and took it to the boat. "The sooner we go, the quicker you'll have that bath," he told her. "It's likely our enemy is aware that we're here. I would just as soon we were gone."

Asher thought he saw Charlie shudder, but she made no other sign of distress. Instead, she focused her efforts on helping him pack up the remainder of their camp. The task wasn't an overwhelming one, and in a quarter of an hour everything was stowed away in the boat, and they were paddling away from the shore.

Getting themselves home was more of a chore with only the one oar and a side full of stitches. Asher found himself in a brown study, only half-concentrating on the back-breaking work of paddling first one side, then switching the heavy oar to the other.

He'd known the creature was real, but as with the sea hag, the experience far outweighed anything his imagination could have come up with. It had saved them—had pushed them to the surface, taken them to the shore, and then brought back the boat, by all that was holy. But it hadn't seemed to try to communicate in any way. Which gave him some ease, at least, for the memory of the sea hag, hissing out its deadly judgment, was still haunting.

He looked over at his companion. Charlie was just as quiet, but her expression was more contemplative than troubled. She stared out over the water, eyes searching the ever-shifting waves. Asher almost wished she'd share her thoughts, but no commentary was forthcoming.

And then, "Mr. Burton?" She was pointing to the right, where something was bobbing lazily on the water's surface. "Is that the other oar?"

He squinted in that general direction, but it was of little use without his spectacles. He was more than pleased to know that he'd brought his spare pair with him, and that his vision would be restored to usual on their return to the cottage. "Let's go see," he said, and turned the boat in that direction.

The floating object did prove to be the other oar, and after pulling it from the water Asher was able to make short work of the rest of the trip. He'd opened up the unstitched gashes on his side again with all the bending and stretching, but that counted little against knowing they were safely back at the farm.

They unloaded the boat together, at which point Charlie commented on the blood that had soaked through the bandage and his shirt. When Asher went to help her tend the animals she refused to allow it, and insisted he go see to his injuries, informing him that she'd handled the chores on her own many times in the past, and would likely do so in the future as well.

Seeing that Charlie would not be convinced, Asher conceded and went inside to carry out her instructions. He washed himself and disposed of his shirt, rummaging for the healing potion he'd forgotten earlier. Having found and administered it, he watched with interest as the wounds faded, and then spent some time cutting and picking out Miss Whitfield's neat stitchwork before putting on a clean shirt. Not wishing to remain idle, and recalling what Charlie had said about a hot bath at the camp, Asher grabbed a bucket and went to the water pump. He filled and refilled the bucket, heating the water over the kitchen fire before dumping it into the copper tub in her washroom. By the time Charlie finished with the chores and joined him in the house, there was nearly enough hot water for her bath.

The look of gratitude and relief that spread across Charlie's face when she saw his efforts on her behalf made his efforts worth it. "Mr. Burton, you are... you are an absolute treasure!"

"I am entirely recovered, thank you." Her delight about the bath made him smile, despite his mood, and he bowed. "Miss Whitfield, I am happy to be of service."

Two more buckets of hot water, and a few more of cold, and the tub was ready for Charlie, and Asher left her to soak away the memories of the last twenty-four hours.

It was some time before Charlie finished with her bath and joined Asher in the kitchen, dressed and clean, with her hair in a single long braid down her back and a contented smile on her face.

They collaborated on dinner, and by the time the meal was done, Asher found his spirits lifted enough to set aside the disturbing details of the past twenty-four hours.

He sat across the table and contemplated her. "I know you are made of sterner stuff than most of my acquaintance, Miss Whitfield," he began, "but anyone would blanch at our last twenty-four hours. How are you faring?"

She let out a slow breath, eyes going distant and thoughtful before she responded. "To be perfectly honest, I hardly know how to answer that. Did we even truly experience twenty-four hours?" Charlie shook her head and then took a sip of water. "I can't decide if it feels like less or more, even with those hours we lost."

He knew what she meant, but she hadn't answered his question. "I suppose not, technically speaking, and yet those we did experience were..." He thought about the wounds that had decorated his side, the area tingling a bit still. "Exhausting. Are you all right?"

"I'm sound in body, but I won't be all right until my uncle is safely home." Charlie stood up to carry her plate to the sink, and Asher got the impression the action was as much a matter of distancing herself from the emotional impact of their experience as it was to tidy up. She remained there, her back to him for a few seconds, before turning back with an answer. "I'm certain my nightmare was a memory now, and that I was in that... place. I think whatever attacked our boat came from there, or perhaps it even followed us out. Either way, its intent was clear enough, and that puts a new lens on... everything."

He stretched his legs out under the table. "How do you mean?"

"You got a better look at it than I, but even underwater and in the dark I could see that it was neither human nor animal." She huffed out a rather mirthless laugh. "I suppose that leaves Fae. The note, your injuries, the trees... I believe it's likely the culprit behind the attacks on local livestock. I always thought I was safe here, but now that my eyes have been opened I cannot ignore the danger."

"Do you feel unsafe here?" he asked. "Perhaps you should take Mrs. Alvin up on her very kind offer to stay with her for now."

"Mr. Burton, after what we encountered do you really believe a few miles will eliminate the threat?" She gave Asher an incredulous look and returned to the table. "Home feels safer, even with an angry Fae stalking the area."

What he privately thought was that staying with a Fae-touched would eliminate the threat, but of course he couldn't say so. "If there is anything I can do to help you feel safer still," he began, "I will gladly do it. I ought to reinforce the salt lines in any case. That does seem to work well."

"I'll go with you. Being busy keeps me from overthinking the situation. Besides, I will not be any safer for being idle." Charlie was up again and halfway to the kitchen door before she finished speaking. Asher had given up on the idea of trying to convince her to allow him to carry out such tasks alone. Charlie Whitfield was not one to sit meekly in the parlor when there was a course of action to follow.

She accompanied him out to the yard, where they reinforced the lines he'd placed around the house, and then returned inside to check the salt at the doors and windows. Once satisfied that everything was as it should be, the pair settled in the sitting room with a cozy fire.

After watching her attempt to do some mending, only to lose her attention to the dancing flames, Asher offered to read to her from Collins' 'The Woman in White', giving it his dramatic all when she acquiesced.

It took very few chapters to wear them out, however, though the well-crafted prose had at least calmed Asher's jangling nerves, and he hoped had done as much for Miss Whitfield. A stifled yawn and some surreptitious eye rubbing from his companion confirmed that the activity had served its purpose, and after finding a good stopping point they wished one another pleasant dreams and went upstairs to find their rest.

Chapter Twelve

Under the Pale Moonlight

The following day saw the investigation once again focused on Elias Whitfield's study. Charlie was situated on the floor, sifting through her uncle's notes. Asher was at the desk, feverishly scribbling notes of his own, presumably a log of their investigation thus far.

The events of their expedition on the lake were too much to be examined deeply outside the safety and comfort of home, and on some level that had been a relief for Charlie. Now, however, she couldn't avoid the questions that the experience had created. They'd left this world entirely, entered into the Fae realm itself, and doing so had made Charlie's recent nightmare a reality.

She'd been in that place before, and whatever dangers she'd narrowly escaped the first time clearly were not confined to that realm. It could be no coincidence that their boat was attacked mere minutes after returning to the familiar waters of Loch Ness. If it had not been for the creature itself, neither of them would have made it back to shore, of that much Charlie was certain, and her mind shied away from that distressing conclusion.

To distract herself she glanced over at her companion, admiring the set of his broad shoulders, envying the sun that so comfortably landed on his neck and jaw. She found Asher Burton a singularly fascinating man. He was kind, intelligent, selflessly brave, and undeniably handsome both in appearance and in spirit. It was that latter part that tended to drive Charlie to the point of absolute distraction.

None of the men around Lochmuir made the very sun shine brighter simply by walking into the room. She'd never wondered what it would be like to touch or be touched by any of them. But her stomach flipped at the mere idea of Asher's touch, a veritable colony of butterflies taking wing. And on the occasions he had touched her—to help her stand, or dismount, or when he'd wrapped his arms around to demonstrate how to defend herself—the contact sent little shivers across her skin.

Even at night, when she'd lay awake in her bed trying to quiet her mind and find sleep, it wasn't only the concern for Uncle Elias that made her restless, but also thoughts of Asher's blue eyes, his smile, and thick black curls. More than once as they'd gone about their day she'd found herself wondering what it would be like to run her fingers through his hair, and then remembered the way she had felt when he had brushed and braided her hair, how his fingers had danced ever so lightly across the back of her neck. That was a memory that enjoyed making its way to the front of her mind several times throughout the day. Her preoccupation was frustrating and exhilarating all at once, and Charlie wasn't sure she wanted it to end.

And now Asher had asked her something and she'd missed it. "Miss Whitfield? Should I collect the eggs when I milk Nan?" he repeated, getting up from the desk. "Or will it upset the chickens?"

Charlie jumped like a child caught sneaking sweets before supper. She dropped the page in her hand and cleared her throat. "Forgive me, I was distracted. Is it already time for the milking?" she glanced out the window, noting that it was indeed time to tend to Nan. "I'll go with you.

He opened his mouth, and Charlie felt sure he was about to protest, but in the end he simply offered her a small smile. "As you like."

Charlie smiled in return, unable to keep her lips from curving as she set her work aside to follow him outdoors. She liked being with him, whether in the study or the barn. What she would have liked more was hearing her name on his lips, or to know what it might be like to feel those lips on hers without the threat of drowning hanging over them.

It was exactly that thought that preoccupied her as they crossed the yard to the barn for Nan's evening milking. Rather than looking where she was going, Charlie was studying the way the evening light made his mouth seem softer and somehow more enticing. So distracted was she that she did not notice the bit of old root sticking out of the ground until the toe of her shoe hooked into it and she began to stumble forward.

Moving swiftly Asher turned and caught her, his arm around her waist, his face so close to hers she could feel his warm breath. He looked at her for a long moment, searching her face; he took a soft breath and dipped his head, and for a second she thought—

Charlie slipped her arms around his shoulders, allowing her fingers to graze the hair at the base of his scalp. Heat seemed to flare up between the two of them, and she felt warmer despite the coolness of the evening. Her skin felt more sensitive, every tiny twitch of his fingers on her body creating a sort of static buzz that made it difficult to draw a full breath.

He had gone very still, his own breath quick as he studied her face. She watched a myriad of expressions chase themselves through his blue eyes, though what they meant she couldn't guess. At last he set her upright, though he was slow to release her. "Careful."

Her glance drifted to his lips as he spoke and every instinct urged her to close what little space remained between them. Without intending to follow that urge, she pressed against him, only just stopping herself from closing the distance between their lips. "You... you caught me."

"Of course I did," he replied, his voice unaccountably rough. "I told you I'd protect you."

"Yes." Charlie swallowed and her fingers twitched where they rested on the back of his neck, lightly brushing his skin. Again that excited flutter danced through her; she wanted so badly to reach up with those same fingers and lace them through Asher's hair and pull him to her. She felt a hot blush blaze across her cheeks and was suddenly struck by the notion that if she didn't move away from him now, she'd never have the willpower to do so. "Thank you, Mr. Burton."

He made sure she had her balance, then withdrew his grasp and bowed. "Your servant, Miss Whitfield."

"Yes... thank you. I believe I'm ready," Charlie replied, her own voice so husky she barely recognized it. "To see to Nan, that is." She stepped back, straightening her skirt and running her hands over her hair. "We should get the milking done."

"Yes, of course," he agreed, his unsettling gaze still on her.

She stared at him, trying to ignore the fact that her body seemed to ache with the need to wrap her arms around him again. Heaven's sake, but those eyes of his were beautiful! Nan lowed loudly, breaking the spell. Charlie laughed a little. "Poor dear, she's probably ready to kick the door down." She understood how the cow felt.

He bowed again. "After you."

They carried out the evening chores with efficiency, completing each task from the milking to putting the chickens away for the night, while keeping a careful distance from one another. Dinner was prepared with equal care. As much as Charlie felt a pull to be near Asher, she also felt the need to catch her breath and regain her mental footing. What had happened—or rather, what had almost happened — seemed to have left a kind of tension in the air, and they needed to keep their attention focused on the business at hand.

After the meal, Asher excused himself to continue writing his report, opting this time to do so in his borrowed room, and though he did not close the door entirely, only the slightest crack was left open.

Charlie found working alone in her uncle's study a bit too difficult as the shadows closed in around the house. Eventually, she gathered up a stack of papers from the desk and moved her work to the sitting room instead. She began the task of sifting through each page, organizing them by date and subject, and it quickly became evident that most of what she'd grabbed was of little use. Charlie was about to put the entire batch aside and go back to the study for a new stack when something in the pile caught her attention.

The invitation to the bonfire at the inn was mixed in with her uncle's notes. She picked it up, hefted the paper for a moment, holding it up to the light and then turning it over again. Nothing specific in the wording itself drew the eye, but there was something about the invitation that nagged at Charlie, and created an inexplicable sense of uneasiness.

"Mr. Burton?" Charlie called, rising from the settee to hunt Asher down.

Footsteps from the stairs heralded Asher's approach and a few seconds later, he came into the sitting room, pen in hand. "Did you call me?"

She held the invitation out to him. "Is there anything about this that catches your attention? I found it among my uncle's things. I was about to dismiss it entirely, but there's something about it that I can't quite puzzle out. Perhaps a fresh pair of eyes is what's needed." Perfect blue eyes, she thought, but did not voice the observation.

He perched his spectacles on his nose and read the note. "No, at first glance I must say I see nothing remarkable about it. Does it seem unusual to y—" He frowned and looked again.

"It's not that it strikes me as odd, but there's something about it..." Charlie leaned forward, looking down at the sheet of paper, trying and failing to connect the dots. "What do you see, Mr. Burton?"

"I think—excuse me for a moment." He dashed back up to his room and returned seconds later with the note that had been attached to the door a few nights earlier. "Look," he said after a moment. "The paper is the same, right to the watermark. And the writing is very similar as well."

"You're right!" Charlie took hold of both pages, holding one in each hand. "This could indicate that whoever has Uncle Elias is either staying at the

Lochmuir Inn, or is in some other way affiliated with it. This is not the same stock sold at the general store."

Asher contemplated the writing. "I would venture further," he said slowly. "I think the same hand wrote both of these notes."

"Then we have somewhere to begin looking." She glanced at Asher, and smiled with satisfaction. "We make a good team, Mr. Burton."

He returned her smile. "We do indeed, Miss Whitfield."

"So, what is our next course of action?" Charlie handed both the invitation and the note to Asher and put her hands on her hips. "The inn is not far, though it would be best to ride, and certainly better to wait until the light of day to do so."

"I should like to speak to the innkeeper," Asher replied decidedly. "But you're right about the need for patience."

Charlie glanced down. "And what should I do while you meet with him?"

"I want you nearby," he began, and then flushed with color. "So I may protect you if need be," he clarified.

"Then you wish me to go with you?" She kept her tone carefully neutral, but chanced a glance at him.

"I do."

"Very well." Charlie nodded before a slow smile spread across her face. "I would have refused to stay here in any case." If these were written by the same hand, then there was every chance that the evening's discovery was exactly what they needed to bring Uncle Elias home.

Charlie lay in her bed staring up at the ceiling, her mind racing over everything that had happened that day. Making the connection between the invitation and the note left on the door had given her renewed hope for her uncle's safe return. But with that hope, a sense of sadness had begun to coalesce in her mind.

Asher was there to solve the mystery of Uncle Elias' disappearance, and when that mystery was solved, he would leave. Her mind wandered back to the moment he'd caught her, the way it had felt to have his arms around her, his breath hot on her skin. The very idea of going back to her usual routine around the farm without him by her side caused a dull ache in her chest that would not be soothed.

She rolled over on her side and closed her eyes, fighting against the urge to cry. She wanted her uncle back, worried about him every hour of the day and night. But the idea of saying goodbye to Asher Burton left her feeling bereft and unbearably lonely. She felt guilty and selfish for it, but she couldn't deny it either. It was ridiculous. She didn't even know if he shared her feelings.

After what felt like hours of trying and failing to find sleep, Charlie tossed the blankets to the side and reached for her dressing robe. She went to the kitchen and poured herself a glass from the pitcher of water on the counter, taking a deep gulp of the cool liquid and trying to settle her thoughts. She walked aimlessly through the house for a few moments before deciding what she really needed was a quiet place to think and gain perspective.

Charlie wandered the house for a few more restless minutes before she went back to her room and pulled a blanket out of the trunk at the end of her bed. Tossing the blanket over her shoulder, she carefully tip-toed down the hall to the narrow door that opened onto the staircase for the cupola. It would be cold up there, but the view was sure to bring the clarity she so desperately sought.

She climbed up the staircase, trying not to make too much noise on the creaking steps. Just because she couldn't sleep was no reason to disturb Asher. She reached the top of the staircase and moved to her favorite window, one that had the perfect view of both the lake and the sky. She sat down, wrapping the blanket around her shoulders as she did and looked up at the night sky, pondering the stars and letting the vastness of the heavens settle her mind.

Asher could hear her creeping about. He lay in bed, debating with himself over the propriety of going to her to see whether there was anything he could do to ease her mind further. In fairness, there was nothing truthful he could offer: he'd sworn to keep her safe and to do his best to find Elias Whitfield, and that was all he could really do. But the urge to comfort her remained, and it was unsettling.

He rolled over, too warm in the stifling room. Yes, all right, fine, the girl was lovely. He'd seen lovely girls before, there was no need to get all worked up about it. And yes, fine, she was intelligent, with a droll sense of humor. *What of it?* he asked himself truculently. One would think he'd never seen an intelligent, lovely girl with a sense of humor before.

But then the vision of her sorrow rose in front of him, when he'd found her weeping and she'd clung to him for comfort, for all the world as though he was a lifeline. Asher sat up and swung his legs out of the bed, running a frustrated hand through his hair. That was when she'd gotten to him, when things had changed. Almost any other girl of his acquaintance, with very few exceptions, would have turned that moment into something awkward or inappropriate or pseudo-romantic, possibly in an attempt to secure his affections. Charlie, though... Charlie had merely accepted the comfort he'd offered for what it was intended to be, and that, more than any other response she might have offered, crept into his heart and stayed there.

Not that he was besotted with the girl. Not that he ever thought about the scent of her hair, or the way it felt in his fingers; not that he cared when her lower lip trembled in an excess of emotion, or that he ever exerted himself to amuse her, just to watch her smile at him. Ridiculous to think his heart leapt when she looked at him with pleasure. Nonsense to believe he'd ever wondered what her lips would taste like.

Well, he'd done that last, in spades, when she'd tripped in the yard and he'd caught her, bloody hypocrite that he was. Excellent practice, Burton: find a woman fraught with grief and proceed to make violent love to her. Even better if she has no protector.

He was an idiot, and he knew it.

Asher jerked his nightshirt over his head— stupid bloody thing was far too warm—and dragged on his trousers and shirt, though he only buttoned it perfunctorily. The sounds from the kitchen had stopped, so perhaps she'd retired after all. It couldn't hurt to find out.

The kitchen, as predicted, was empty. Feeling twelve kinds of a fool, Asher climbed back up the stairs and glanced down the hall toward her room. There was a faint light from within, and the door stood ajar. Berating himself mentally, he nonetheless trod towards the open door, to just peek inside, make sure all was well.

The room was empty, and Asher's heart stopped. Had someone taken her, right from under his nose? He hurried from room to room, but the house seemed deserted. "Miss Whitfield? Charlie?" he called, worry nearly overwhelming him.

"Mr. Burton?" There was a shuffling sound coming from above, of all places.

Of course—the cupola. He dashed to the stairs and looked up, panic in his wide blue eyes. "Char—Miss Whitfield? Are you all right?"

Charlie's head peeked over the stairs. A long lock of wavy hair, highlighted by the silvery moonlight, dropped forward as she did. "Yes, I'm all right. I thought you were asleep. I'm terribly sorry—I didn't mean to cause you alarm."

Asher blinked. "What on earth are you doing up there?" He climbed up the stairs, emerging through the floor of the cupola to find her waiting there, swathed in blankets. He took her by the shoulders and examined her face. "Truly? You're all right?"

"Yes, I'm—I couldn't sleep. My mind just wouldn't stop running in circles." Even in the moonlight he could see her cheeks color. "I come up here when I need to find clarity. I like the stars." She glanced toward the windowed wall, then back to his face. "I should have considered the current situation, though. Forgive me for causing you distress."

His fingers convulsed on her shoulders, and then he let her go. "No, not at all. I should be wary of jumping to conclusions."

"Under the circumstances it's hardly unjustified." Charlie offered him a half smile, one dimple appearing. "If it would make you happier we can go back downstairs."

"No need. I rather like it up here." He looked around, then back at her. "Unless I intrude, in which case I shall leave you to it."

"No, no, not at all." Her smile broadened. "Here, come sit." She took hold of his hand and led him to a further pile of blankets.

"What *are* you doing up here?" he asked again, picking his way carefully across the wooden floor in bare feet.

She glanced at him over her shoulder as she came to a stop. "Stargazing." She made a wide gesture to the night sky.

Asher glanced up, a smile creeping across his face. He looked back down at Charlie's upturned face. "Beautiful," he murmured.

"Indeed it is, Mr. Burton." She settled on a blanket that was spread out under the window. "Aside from the meadow I told you about, this is my favorite place to be. I look up at the night sky and suddenly all the problems that plague my mind seem insignificant."

He sat next to her, leaning on one arm, the other propped on his knee, and squinted up at the sky. "And which stars do you gaze at in particular, Miss Whitfield?"

To his surprise she lay back and her partially unbound hair fanned out beneath her. She let one hand rest on her chest, and lifted the other to point up at the sky. "Do you see that grouping of stars, just there? It is the constellation Andromeda, my favorite of the classic formations."

After a beat Asher joined her, laying back on the blanket as well, only slightly concerned with the propriety of it all. But if Miss Whitfield was unbothered, who was he to cavil? "She who was more beautiful than the Nereids and was rescued from Cetus by Perseus? You are a romantic, Miss Whitfield."

She laughed softly and turned her head to look at him. "You'll note there's a monster in that story." She fixed a sweet smile on him. "But yes, I can be romantic from time to time."

He chuckled softly. "Nothing wrong with that, after all."

"Nothing at all," Charlie whispered before returning her attention to the night sky. "The stars I truly favor are not among the classics, though."

"No?" He shifted to look at her, propping his head up on his fist.

"No," She paused for a moment, glancing up at him with those wide, green eyes, then lifted her hand and pointed skyward. "If you look just below Andromeda and to the left you will see a group of stars, all swirled together." She turned back to Asher, her gaze soft. "Those are my favorites. I call them 'The Rose.'"

"As good a name as any," he agreed, casting them a perfunctory look. "And why are they your favorites?"

"I like the way they seem to be dancing with one another. When I was younger my uncle read Romeo and Juliet to me. I often imagined all the characters in their glittering finery at the Capulet banquet, and thought they must have looked like that group of stars." Her voice was soft, the moonlight lighting her skin and reflecting in her eyes as she spoke. "That's where I got the name. I knew no matter what I called them they would ever be beautiful: 'that which we call a rose by any other name would smell as sweet'."

Asher chuckled. "I always thought Romeo a bit of a mug, myself. Leaving Juliet in that fix to face everything alone."

Charlie looked at him thoughtfully, her eyes twinkling in the starlight. "True. I suppose not all men can be as valiant as yo—others." She quickly focused on the stars again.

He blushed. "I don't know about valiant, but it certainly seems impolite to marry a girl underhand and then scarper without her."

"And what of Juliet? If she'd had any sense at all she would have gone with him."

He shrugged. "I'll confess, Juliet is a favorite of mine. Her speeches, her wisdom; it isn't her fault that she's so subject to the whims of the men who rule her life, all of whom seem to me to be singularly lacking in sense or compassion." Asher sighed, laying back on the floor. "I think she would have gone with Romeo, had she the choice."

"Ultimately, she did," Charlie pointed out. "I find myself understanding her more and more as I experience more than a life of research. It is a daunting thing to be faced with a future without the one you care about."

"No, I refer to earlier in the play: the Nurse's speech." Asher thought for a moment. "'Stand up, stand up; stand, and you be a man: For Juliet's sake, for her sake, rise and stand.' But he doesn't, he just blubs about being banished, and leaves her behind to face the consequences."

"We speak of Romeo and Juliet and yet it is the practical Nurse you quote." Charlie chuckled. "A far more interesting choice than most would make." She sighed, nestling more deeply into the blanket. "You are correct, though, Romeo is a bit of a sop. He's not my idea of a romantic hero."

Asher chuckled again. "I am gratified to hear it. Who is your ideal, then?"

"My ideal hero?" Charlie glanced up at him for a moment.

"Yes! Are you intrigued by d'Artagnan, for example, with his headstrong temper and passionate nature? Or perhaps Mr. Darcy, shy and aristocratic, or Heathcliff, brooding and dominating, or Mr. Rochester, equally brooding and somewhat morally questionable?" He chuckled. "Cinderella's prince—

certainly charming but not, perhaps, the cleverest chap, unable to recognize his true love except from the ankle down?"

"I think you've given this more thought than I have." Charlie laughed. "Perhaps someone like Mr. Darcy, with just a touch of mystery and dashing deeds. But truly what turns my head more than anything is genuine kindness, intelligence, someone who is just as happy to listen as he is to speak, and who thinks before he does speak."

"And have you found such a man?" Asher asked after a thoughtful pause, his voice low, wondering why her answer was so important to him.

"I... well, I'm not sure. At any rate, it would not matter if I had, if he did not share those feelings." Charlie sat up, her fingers twisting into her hair nervously. She was silent for a moment. "What of you, Mr. Burton? I have revealed my ideals, it seems unfair that you should not do the same."

Asher laughed aloud. "You want to know what my masculine ideal is?"

"No, of course not!" Charlie turned back to him, laughing as well. "Your feminine ideal, you goose!" She gave his shoulder a teasing nudge, laughing again.

"Oh, that." He shrugged. "I've never thought about it, really. I don't plan to wed, so it hardly seems to matter, doesn't it?"

"I suppose not." She sobered. "And yet, you're terribly concerned with what a lady might think the ideal man?"

"Not concerned, merely curious. I've had similar discussions with my sister—I wanted to know your views, by contrast."

"Of course, Mr. Burton." Charlie lay down again and looked up at the stars. "I'm hardly the woman to ask. I haven't spent a great deal of my time dreaming of a hero, or what sort of man I might marry. I've always been more focused on other things."

"Such as the Loch Ness Monster." He gave her a friendly smile.

"Among other things. There are a great many mysteries in the world, begging to be puzzled out and solved." She glanced at him. "Surely, you can see the appeal of an unsolved riddle?"

He nodded. "I can, indeed."

"I suppose you have seen your fair share of the world's mysteries." A soft smile curved her lips. "Including the Fae themselves. No doubt this quiet little farm is dull compared to that."

It was on the tip of his tongue to contradict her, tell her his experience with true Fae was actually very limited. But that would be revealing the secret of the Fae-touched, and that wasn't his to share, so he merely nodded. "Sometimes I realize that I've seen real magic at work—have seen it save life, take life, and restore life—and I can't help but feel a sense of..." He was at a loss for the word.

"Wonder?" Charlie turned her head and looked up at him, the silvery moonlight giving her something of a magical aura herself. "Or perhaps honor that they trust you, befriend you?"

"More the latter, I suppose, though wonder is certainly part of it. And a healthy sense of humor is essential to keeping one's perspective, especially in such a friendship." He smiled, rather sweetly, put on his best Shakespearean manner and quoted, "'Thou speak'st aright; I am that merry wanderer of the night. I jest to Oberon and make him smile.'" He slanted her a glance. "And maybe sometimes Titania."

A wide grin spread across Charlie's face. "And you quote the Bard again, good sir." Her gaze lowered and she began fiddling with a loose thread on the blanket.

"Well, you know, he's got a quote for most everything." Asher rolled onto his side. "He's a favorite of yours, I take it?"

"Yes, very much so, and I am rather fond of A Midsummer Night's Dream." She released the thread and turned her full attention to Asher.

He smiled. "Things base and vile, holding no quantity, Love can transpose to form and dignity. Love looks not with the eyes, but with the mind, and therefore is winged Cupid painted blind. Nor hath Love's mind of any judgment taste; Wings and no eyes figure unheedy haste," he declaimed beautifully.

Charlie was silent, the gentle hint of a smile playing on her lips. When she spoke her voice was soft. "You do justice to those words, Mr. Burton."

Asher chuckled. "I hope so. My father would be appalled if I did any less. And Midsummer Night's Dream is a favorite of mine as well, though I think of all the Bard's works I prefer the Tempest."

"That is a good one, indeed," Charlie replied, laying her head down and pillowing it on her arm. She sighed contentedly and her eyes slid shut for just a moment.

"Sleepy?" It was a quiet question.

"To sleep, perchance to dream." Charlie replied softly, her eyes opening and closing again. "Perhaps a little. You?"

"Weary with toil," he began softly, "I haste me to my bed. The dear repose for limbs with travel tired; But then begins a journey in my head to work my mind, when body's work's expir'd." He left off the rest of the quotation, lest he reflect on the truth of it.

Chapter Thirteen

Bearding the Dragon

Charlie slept late that morning, her head filled with dreams of Asher in the moonlight: dreams of him taking her in his arms and covering her body with soft kisses, of his hands on her skin, of tasting his lips, and feeling his body pressed against hers. When she finally did wake she was breathless and filled with longing.

She took her time getting dressed, trying to settle her mind and banish the yearning of the dream before she was in the same room with Mr. Burton. To that end she fussed over her hair, agonized over what to wear, and added little drops of perfume to her neck and collarbone, telling herself it was only because they'd be going to visit the Lochmuir Inn, and wasn't at all to do with pleasing Asher.

At last she finished her morning ablutions, her hair was braided and coiled in a bun with a few wispy waves hanging down around her face and neck. She wore her favorite dress: a wool frock, dyed a vivid peacock color, which had been a Christmas gift from her uncle.

When she stepped out of the bedroom, the smell of food drifted up the stairs to her. She hurried to the kitchen, feeling a little guilty that she'd left all the chores to Mr. Burton.

"Good morning, Miss—" Asher turned to greet her and nearly dropped the pan he held. "Good morning," he repeated in an entirely different tone.

"Good morning, Mr. Burton." Charlie began to blush as images and sensations from her dreams flooded back into her mind. She nervously tucked a lock of hair behind her ear. "I must apologize for oversleeping and leaving all the work for you. I suppose too many sleepless nights finally caught up with me."

"If it gave you rest, I have no objection." He smiled at her. "For myself I felt strangely energized. The farm is entirely attended to for the morning; we may go beard the dragon in his lair as soon as we have eaten."

"Never a wise decision to face a dragon on an empty stomach." Charlie replied, chuckling. She settled at the table, taking the seat Asher pulled out for her.

The meal Asher had prepared was delicious— one of the best Charlie had eaten. Perhaps it was the company, or the fact that they had a lead to follow. Whatever it was, Charlie enjoyed breakfast immensely. "That was lovely. Thank you," she said, sighing a little as she stacked her dishes to be taken to the sink. "I cannot think of a better way to start the day."

"Thank *you*. I will confess I used some of your store of herbs to improve matters." His demeanor was sunny. "I've no clear idea what 'hyssop' is, even after your explanation, but it does seem to have improved the *pain perdu* rather a lot."

Charlie laughed a little. "Perhaps I should write it all down for you before you leave. Although if you have a cook in your employ, I would imagine any knowledge I could impart would already be known."

"A cook? Not I. I have a housekeeper who is willing enough to boil me an egg now and again, but I mostly eat at my club."

"Then I will be sure to write down any recipes or any herbal suggestions you desire." She pushed away from the table and scooped up Asher's dishes as well as her own. "But for now I believe we should finish cleaning the kitchen and see to that dragon, hm?"

"Let me just collect my armor and lance," he returned with a laugh, and hurried to help clear the last of the breakfast dishes before he went to the barn to set things in order for their departure. Charlie had the kitchen spick and span a short time later, and when she exited the house she found Asher was waiting for her in the yard, his horse saddled and ready.

"My, but you are the industrious one today." Charlie smiled at him. "Give me just a few moments to saddle Tobias and I'll be ready to go."

"No need," he replied. "Whiskey is well able to carry us both."

"Tobias will be most appreciative, I'm sure." Charlie couldn't help the wide grin that spread across her face at the idea of riding tandem with Mr. Burton.

He led her to the beast and placed his hands lightly around her waist. "May I?"

"Of course." Charlie replied softly, allowing herself to meet his gaze, wondering if he would notice the way the color of her dress brought out the touches of blue in her eyes. She put her hands on his shoulders, fighting hard to resist the urge to slide them to his neck and touch his skin.

He lifted her without visible effort and placed her gently in the saddle, then swung himself up behind, his arms around her. "Comfortable?" Asher asked, his breath ruffling her hair.

"Quite," Charlie replied. "Are you?"

He shifted slightly, a small smile crooking his lips. "Well enough." He touched his heels to Whiskey's flank and they set off.

As they rode Charlie allowed herself to cherish the sensation of Asher's arms around her, her left hand settling atop his wrist, the tips of her fingers lightly touching his wrist just past the sleeve of his jacket. She sighed contentedly and leaned her head back, letting it rest against his strong broad shoulder. She allowed herself a moment of pure indulgence, turning her head slightly and inhaling deeply. The man smelled divine— like sweet spices with undertones of leather. Under other circumstances Charlie could have enjoyed that ride for hours. She could *almost* imagine they were merely enjoying the sunshine together, but even beneath the contentment their purpose remained.

All too soon the inn hove into view, set on a bluff overlooking the loch. Asher slowed the horse to a walk as they approached. "You'll stay in the tea room while I interview Mr. Shaw, yes?"

"Of course," Charlie replied a little absently. She inhaled again, taking that scent in one last time before the closeness of the ride came to an end. "How long do you expect it will take?"

"Not long, I shouldn't think. Perhaps an hour, no more."

"Be careful, Asher." She didn't realize until she'd already spoken that she had used his first name. "Mr. Burton," she corrected herself quietly.

He smiled. "I will—Charlie." Asher slipped from Whiskey's back and reached up for her.

She smiled at him as he helped her down. He'd said her name, and it had never sounded sweeter. "Well, I suppose it's time for tea then."

As they walked through the front doors of the inn, Charlie immediately felt the tension in the room. Fergus Shaw, tall and broad of shoulder with graying brown hair, looked at them, his expression guarded.

"Good day, Mr. Shaw," Charlie began, keeping her tone congenial even though the expression on his face made her skin crawl. "This is Mr. Asher Burton. He's been looking into my uncle's disappearance."

Fergus Shaw's gaze shifted from her to Asher. "Mr. Burton." He dipped his head, but didn't offer his hand.

Asher's brows climbed. "Mr. Shaw. Might we have a word?"

The other man let out a quiet but obviously exasperated sigh. "If you insist, Mr. Burton, but I have an inn to run. I hope you understand the demands on my time." Fergus Shaw folded his arms for, looking Asher up and down. "If the two of you will follow me to my office, I will afford you what time I may."

Charlie smiled sweetly at him. "Actually, Mr. Shaw, I thought I might sample the hospitality of your tea room while the two of you speak."

Fergus looked at her for a moment then signaled to a young man working nearby. "Wallace, man the desk while I speak to Mr. Burton, and see to it that Miss Whitfield is properly attended to in the tea room."

Asher sent Charlie a reassuring look and followed Shaw into his office. She waited until the door closed behind them before making her way to the small tea room off the lobby. One of the tables provided a perfect view of the office, and Charlie settled in for the wait, hopeful that this visit would provide answers—or better yet, lead them to Uncle Elias himself.

"Is this seat taken?" A familiar hand pulled out the chair next to her, and Oliver sat down. "This is an unexpected pleasure, Charlotte." It didn't escape Charlie that he'd left off the use of her honorific.

She had to work to keep her exasperation in check. This was Oliver's family business, after all, and he had every right to sit wherever he liked. "No, but I shan't be here long. Mr. Burton and I are still looking into my uncle's whereabouts."

Oliver appropriated her hand, clasping it between his own. "You are too kind to see when you are being taken advantage of, my dear. This Burton fellow—what do you really know of him, after all? I am sorry for your loss, but you mustn't keep clinging to false hope. No doubt this blackguard has designs upon your person, and wishes to extend your acquaintance by any means necessary."

"There is nothing false about my belief that my uncle will be returned." Charlie glared at Oliver, giving up any pretense of politeness. "And that 'blackguard', as you call him, is a good and honorable man... my cousin, if you'll recall." She started to pull her hands back. "I would trust Asher Burton with my life."

"Oh, yes, your cousin. Do forgive me," and it was clear that Oliver believed none of it. He tightened his grip on her fingers. "My dear Charlotte, I have hesitated to speak out before, but now—knowing you are adrift, so to speak, with no family left to look after you—I feel emboldened to ask. You must know of my very great regard for you. Give me the right to care for you, now that there is no one else to do so. Marry me— now, today, if you like. What do you say?"

It took a moment for Charlie to navigate past the shock of what he'd said. "What? Have you—my uncle will return, and even if he—No, I am not going to marry you, Oliver."

Oliver's brows drew together. "Be very certain, Charlotte, for I will not *ask* again." He took her wrist, squeezing hard enough to bruise. "I do not take kindly to being refused that which was promised to me."

"Let me go." Charlie tried to pull her hand away again, but Oliver's grip was like a vice. "Oliver, you're hurting me."

"Perhaps it will help you to understand who is master here." Oliver stood, dragging her to her feet. "Do you recall when you were a child—the cave, the lights—the call of the Fae? You were promised to me then, and I have been more than patient. But no longer."

Ice filled Charlie's veins. She pulled against Oliver, but to no avail. He tugged her closer to him and twisted her around, clamping his hand over her mouth just as she took a breath to call out to Asher.

"Not a word, not a squeak, or I will flay the very skin from your lover's flesh," he hissed in her ear. "Reconsider my offer, Charlotte."

A very small sound did escape Charlie's lips, despite her captor's command, even as she began trembling from head to toe. Across the hall, the office door remained closed. Asher was so close, and yet he might as well have been on the other side of the world.

Mr. Shaw gestured to the extra chair in his office as he walked around the desk and settled into his. "So, Mr. Burton, how can I be of service? I can't imagine what would bring you to my doorstep."

Asher spent a few minutes getting some background information on the man, though it was more to take his measure than anything else—his brief had been thorough. Shaw seemed... uneasy, abrupt, and Asher wondered if that was simply the man's demeanor or if there was something more to it, and proceeded to scratch the surface. "I've a question about this letter, actually," he said, laying the invitation on the man's desk. "I wondered if you could tell me the story behind this."

Fergus picked up the letter and gave it a quick look. "Just a letter inviting Professor Whitfield to a gathering we had a month or so back. Several were sent out." He pushed the letter back toward Asher. "I'm not entirely sure why that's of any interest to you."

"I'm following up any leads I can, to try and locate the professor. Did he respond to the letter?"

"No, he did not, though he attended the event regardless," the innkeeper replied. "Didn't expect him to, either; the man isn't well known for socializing in the community." He leaned back in his chair, assessing Asher. "Despite his reputation, it doesn't serve my business to insult someone who may well send lodgers my way."

Asher raised a brow. "Forgive me if I've said anything that might imply that an invitation from you, or a response from him, might be construed as an insult." Shaw was touchy as hell, he mused, and wondered why.

The door opened before Shaw could reply, and Wallace walked in, a square of cloth folded in his hand. Without a word he crossed to Fergus and passed him the cloth, whispered something in his ear and then left.

"Not at all, Mr. Burton." The other man sat up, his demeanor changing completely. "In fact, I should be thanking you."

Both brows went up. "Oh?"

"Yes. You see, my boy couldn't get near Miss Whitfield with you there to protect her." He pushed the folded fabric across his desk, offering it to Asher. "And here you've brought her to me yourself." A slow, sinister smile spread across his lips. "You really could not have made it any easier."

Asher could feel his heart speed up, but he reached for the cloth with every appearance of outward calm, unfolding it. There, gleaming at him in reproach, lay a long, sunlit-gold curl. Asher's jaw set, his upper lip lifting in a snarl. "What have you done?"

"Nothing permanent, for the moment." Shaw sat back in his chair, clearly pleased with the situation. "That," he nodded to the lock of hair, "is to ensure you know which of us is in control here."

Asher shook his head, slowly, and removed his spectacles, placing them in his vest pocket. "You're an utter fool, Shaw. There you sit, congratulating yourself on your cleverness, when your own incompetence—or, more likely, that of your idiot son—is what raised my suspicions in the first place." Shaw's hackles raised visibly, and Asher knew he'd scored a hit. "And now you've simply admitted it. Incompetent. Insufferable. And in the end, insufficient, I assure you." He leaned back in his chair. "Where has he taken Miss Whitfield?"

"Enough." Shaw's voice was like the crack of a whip. He pulled a pistol from his desk drawer. "It was your own actions that made it possible for him t'take hold of that girl. It's a fair enough trade, to my mind: he gets the girl and I get my son back. You want t'know where she's being taken, I'll show you." His lip curled as he rose and gestured with the pistol. "One step out of line and he'll start cutting again, and I can promise you, the next thing he cuts off won't grow back."

A wave of fury nearly overwhelmed him, but Asher forced himself to relax. "What do you mean, you get your son back?"

Shaw sneered. "You mean the great detective from London hasn't figured it out? And y'have the gall t'call *me* incompetent." He put his fingers to his mouth and gave a sharp whistle, the muzzle of his pistol never wavering. A narrow side door in the office swung to at the sound, and a pungent fragrance—sickly sweet, like rotting flesh—filled the air. Asher recoiled as three men lumbered into the room—or no, *shambled* was more like it, their eyes glassy, their bodies emaciated and filthy. Shaw held a handkerchief to his nose. "Take him," he said, and one of the men reared back a fist, punching Asher in the jaw, dazing him. The other two took hold of him, one on either side, and dragged him out the back way.

Asher tried to shake it off, struggling as they hauled him over the bluff, but that only earned him a fist to the temple, which made everything look even blurrier than usual.

Shaw led them to a path through the woods. After several minutes the lakeshore came into view. He held the pistol to Asher's temple. "Oliver! Bring the girl out."

Two more filthy, starved men stepped out of a cave that opened onto the waters, Charlie held firmly between the them, followed closely by two others. Aside from her hair being pulled loose and her clothes slightly disheveled, she seemed well enough. Oliver strolled out behind them, his hands in his pockets.

"Asher!" Charlie began to move forward, but her captors jerked her back harshly, eliciting a slight yelp of pain. Her eyes locked with his. "It's not Oliver, he's a changeling!"

"Do not call me by that disgusting word," Oliver snapped. He looked at his father. "I said I wanted him dead."

"And I'm not your puppet!" his father retorted.

Asher gave Charlie an assessing glance, then looked at the others, though he spoke to her. "Are you hurt?"

"No, I'm not." Charlie jerked against the hands that held her.

"That's enough. You've seen the girl." Fergus yanked Asher's arm. "This isn't a picnic." He turned to the men that held him. "Get the ropes and tie him."

Asher counted the moments as the two behind Charlie and her captors began to lurch toward him, one of them with a rope in his hands. *Dilly, dilly, dilly, come and be... Now.*

He shifted his weight suddenly, throwing a hip in front of one to push him off balance, half bent over, then fisted his free hand in the back of the other one's ragged coat and jerked him clean off his feet. That one, lighter than he ought to have been, went flying toward one of the approaching thugs, who went down with a crunch and a yelp. Asher spun and shoved his knee into the small of Shaw's back, jerking the collar of his coat downward to entangle his arms, then sent him reeling backward. He grabbed for the rope in the third man's hands and jerked it toward him, then pivoted neatly, wrapping the middle of the rope around the thug's neck, choking him while he used the free end like a whip to lash one of the men holding Charlie across the face, flaying his nose wide open.

Blood spattered across Charlie's face, but despite the obvious shock she was alert enough to take advantage of the situation. She elbowed the other man holding her and scrambled back before he could recover. But rather than reaching for Charlie again, the man staggered toward Asher and threw a punch, falling forward when Asher nimbly sidestepped him and kicked out to blow his knee.

To the side, Shaw was back on his feet, fumbling for his pistol, as a couple of his men regrouped and moved back toward the fray. One of the men grabbed Asher around his shoulders; the Englishman jerked his head back suddenly and broke his assailant's nose with a satisfying crack. That one staggered backward while another tucked his shoulder down and ran at Asher to tackle him; Asher shifted his weight again and rolled easily across the man's back. He took two large steps toward Charlie and leapt into the air, striking out with his foot to kick her last captor in the face. "Run," he said briefly, and squared himself to face their attackers.

"What about you?" Charlie asked, though she was already tensing to move.

"Charlie—love—run!" he repeated, and dodged a set of fists, jamming his elbow into his attacker's windpipe, sending him reeling back, clawing at his throat for air.

A shot rang out; Asher staggered backward, fully expecting pain to bloom somewhere, but—a groan from behind him made him turn to see Fergus Shaw falling to his knees, clutching at his midsection, a crimson stain spreading across his shirt.

"Asher!" Charlie screamed, taking a step toward him, but Oliver lunged for her, a still-smoking pistol in his hand.

"ENOUGH!" he shouted, and pressed the muzzle to the side of Charlie's forehead, dragging her backward. His body changed, growing taller, thicker; his legs bent and twisted, thighs becoming haunches; claws split his shoes, sprouted from his hands. Long, pointed fangs filled his mouth as he grimaced. He was wild-eyed, panting. Asher froze, his gaze tangling with Charlie's.

"Now," said Oliver, though his voice had taken on a ragged timbre, "here is what is going to happen. My thralls are going to kill you, and then devour the old man in the cave, and then each other, for all I care. There is a boat coming—I will take what is *mine*," he snarled out the word and shoved the gun hard into

Charlie's head, eliciting a small whimper from her, and making Asher's fists clench, "return to the portal, and never set foot in this forsaken realm again."

"Like hell you will," Asher growled.

Oliver tilted his head. "You won't stop me," he returned. "I will have what I was promised, and when I have finished," he dipped his head toward Charlie and *licked* along her cheek, "I will *dine*."

"You—promised," Shaw coughed. "I brought you the girl. Give me back my boy."

The changeling gave a feral grin. "Bit of a difficulty there, old man. Your boy is—um—" He smacked his lips. "Gone."

"You monster!" Charlie reached back and raked her fingernails across Oliver's face. "I am *not* yours!"

He snarled and struck her across the face, and Asher prepared to charge the changeling—anything to get him away from Charlie, if he took a bullet for it—when all at once a huge shadow, long-necked and furious, rose from the water with a roar, tiny lights darting about around it. Oliver staggered back with a yelp.

Charlie burst into action, stomping on Oliver's instep, then jerking her elbow back into his ribcage. He released her for an instant, but quickly caught her wrists. Oliver held tight, twisting them around, but Charlie continued to fight back.

The beast thundered its displeasure again, making the very ground tremble; a sharp report echoed through the air and Oliver and Charlie toppled to the ground in a heap.

"My son," Shaw groaned, the gun falling from his hand. "He killed my... son..." Fergus Shaw slumped to the side with a rattling sigh and then went completely still.

Chapter Fourteen

Case Closed

Asher could barely feel his legs, running forward to pull Oliver from Charlie, falling to his knees on the rocky beach. So much blood—it was everywhere. He rolled the changeling over: a round black hole was centered in his forehead, his eyes open and glazed.

The beast from the loch lowered its head to mere inches from Charlie's face. The world seemed to go eerily still, but for the sound of the animal's breath. It nudged against Charlie's cheek and then drew back.

Asher couldn't breathe, couldn't think, could only repeat a supplication in his head: *Please, please, please...*

And then he saw Charlie blink. Her eyes were locked on the creature, and the look on her face was not one of fear, but of... wonder. Her hand slowly lifted off the ground and began inching toward the animal's snout. It made a sound—not a growl, or snarl, but a gentle sort of purring. Charlie's fingers brushed its nose. The beast made the sound again, its eyes closing, and then it tilted its head to press a large, scaly cheek into the palm of Charlie's outstretched hand before backing away and slipping under the waves.

Asher's whole body was trembling; he lifted a shaky hand and wiped at the blood spattered on Charlie's cheeks, tracing his thumb along her mouth. He let out a breath; the knowledge that this was a bad idea only half-formed before he pulled her close, lips blindly seeking hers. Propriety and common sense protested and Asher told both to go hang, just for this moment. Charlie was alive and in his arms and he cared about nothing else.

His mind repeated it like a litany. She was alive—she was whole—she was in his arms and he couldn't—he didn't— Asher lifted his head, searching her face, trying to think, to realize... But it was no good, he needed to take her mouth more than he needed to take a breath. "Charlie," he muttered against her lips. "I thought—I was afraid—"

"Asher," she whispered, his name little more than a throaty gasp, and then her lips pressed against his again. Warm fingers slid up his chest, his shoulders, and then wove through his hair. She made a sound, hungry and desperate, and it cut straight to Asher's core. She was leaning against him, and the world narrowed to the sensation of her body pressed close to his.

A sound from behind them broke through the haze of desperation and longing: a moan from one of the thralls lying on the ground. "What—what have I—oh God, the old man in the cave—"

Asher jerked his head back as he suddenly realized what he was doing. "I'm sorry—I—" he stammered, reality crashing down around him, and leaving him horrified at his lack of self-control. He pulled away from Charlie, rapidly scanning the scene. Oliver lay dead nearby, and his father in a similar condition across the clearing. The men who had been under Oliver's thrall lay unconscious or at least incapacitated. The first man moaned again, and Asher scrambled to his feet.

Another of the thralls was coming to, keening as though in pain. "Where am I—what—what did he make us do?"

"What man in the cave?" Asher asked the first one urgently. "Where?"

The emaciated man pointed toward the cave where Oliver had held Charlie for a brief time.

Charlie was on her feet in an instant. She hiked up her skirt and ran toward the opening. "Uncle Elias?"

Asher sprinted after her. "Charlie—wait! You don't know what you'll find—"

But if she'd heard his call she'd decided to ignore it. Charlie reached the mouth of the cavern and vanished into the dark. Asher could hear her voice echoing off the rocks, growing further from the entrance.

A string of oaths came from his mouth as he too plunged into the cave. "Charlie! Damn it, Charlie, where are you?"

As he neared the back wall Asher saw a small tunnel to the left. It curved slightly, obscuring his view, but a soft orange glow was barely visible at the bend. The sound of Charlie's footsteps was bouncing off the rocky walls and then came to an abrupt stop.

His longer stride meant that he was only a heartbeat behind her, and he nearly bowled her over when he burst into the passage. "Of all the bloody stupid," he began, "foolhardy, reckless—"

"What on earth is that?" They were standing at the opening of a small, round chamber. Charlie's eyes were fixed on the far wall, she pointed at something in the flickering light of a single torch.

There was a large object attached to the far wall, roughly the height and width of a grown man. It seemed to be made of millions of whitish strands that glimmered strangely. The object moved slightly, swelling and receding in a slow, steady rhythm. It was lumpy, and occasionally one of the lumps would bulge outward.

A muscle in Asher's jaw ticked and he grasped Charlie by the upper arms. "Stand over here," he instructed, "and do not come any closer unless I tell you it's all right. And be ready to run." He was furious with her for her earlier heedlessness, but knew better than to let it show. "I'm serious, Miss Whitfield. Will you do as I say?"

The use of 'Miss Whitfield' seemed to catch her attention. Charlie blinked and tore her eyes from the... whatever it was, looking at Asher with a little frown before she nodded. "Of course."

He studied her a moment longer before giving a nod. "Stay there," he repeated, and approached the chrysalis-like construction. One of the lumps under the surface moved again, and Asher peered at it: roughly the size and shape of a—of a man's fist—

Without further consideration he plunged his fingers into the morass of fibers, tearing at them to reveal a gnarled and elderly hand. Asher let out a succinct curse and ran his hands over the mass to where he thought the head might be, steeled himself, and began to shred the material.

A familiar face emerged. "Elias," he breathed, and set to work freeing his old friend.

"Is he—is he alive?" Charlie called, she started to take a step and then stopped herself, apparently remembering his instructions. "Uncle Elias?"

Asher felt the side of the old man's neck and found a pulse: thready, but definitely there. "He's alive." Asher glanced back over his shoulder. "Can you go back to the inn, send for the police?"

Charlie shook her head. "I want to see him first. I *need* to see him, Asher."

Asher gave a nod and made short work of the rest of the cocoon, and at last Elias fell forward limply into the younger man's arms. "I've got him—let's get him out of this place."

He heard Charlie sniffle and then she was at his side, her hands stroking her uncle's face. "He's so pale," she whispered as Asher started to carry Elias to the exit.

The missing man shifted and murmured when they got him into the sunlight. "Charlie?" he rasped weakly, squinting up at her. "Charlie, my dear child."

"I'm here," she whispered gently, taking a few quick steps so that he could see her more clearly even as she reached for his hand. "You're safe now, uncle. You're going to be all right."

Elias gave his niece a watery smile. "I knew you wouldn't give up on me." His eyes fluttered closed, and then blinked open again. "I saw it, Charlie—the creature. It's real."

Charlie sniffled a second time, dashing at the tears that were streaming down her cheeks. "I know, uncle. I know." She swallowed and Asher could see her pushing past the emotions, focusing on what needed to be done. "Is it safe to take him back to the inn? What should I tell the police?"

"The Shaws are dead," he told her, "so I think any threat from that quarter is ended. If you could meet the police, bring them back here—and tell them to bring a doctor."

Charlie cast another look at her uncle, gently touched his cheek and then took off at a run.

The dash back to the inn was a blur. Charlie burst into the lobby and hurried directly to the front desk, barely noticing the people who stopped to stare at her. She managed to relay enough information to convince the concierge to send for the police and the town doctor, and he did so immediately.

A maid asked if there was anything else that could be done, but there was a strange sort of buzzing in Charlie's head, and the only thing she could focus on was the task of waiting for the police to arrive. When they finally did, she led them to the bluff, ready to return to her uncle's side, but was stopped and pulled back to the inn before she could set foot on the path.

A woman of middling years in a crisp nurse's uniform held her by the arm, helping her back through the lobby. "Come, dear—let the men see to that and I'll see to you." She peered at Charlie's face. "Did someone strike you?"

The buzzing continued. Charlie blinked at the other woman for a second or two in confusion. "Strike me?" She lifted her hand to touch where the changeling had hit her temple. "Um, yes, it—he," she corrected herself, "he hit me, here. I need to go to my uncle."

"They're bringing him here, I believe—you'll see him as soon as the doctor has finished his work." The nurse led her into a private parlor and urged her to sit down. "Come, Miss, let's get you comfortable and out of those dirty things."

"No—where's Ash—Mr. Burton?" Charlie started to stand up, but her legs were shaking and she immediately lowered herself back into the chair. She looked down at herself. "This was my best dress." It was a ridiculous sort of observation, Charlie thought rather distantly.

"I'm sorry, dear, but I don't think it's salvageable," the nurse murmured. "Now—I apologize but I must ask, my dear, what exactly happened to you? Who hit you? Did he... harm you in any other way?"

Charlie looked at the nurse's kind expression and the fog cleared a little. "No, he didn't... He said something about—but he didn't..." She cleared her throat and closed her eyes, summoning what little calm she could muster. "Oliver Shaw hit me, here." Charlie repeated her earlier statement, pointing to her temple. She stopped and lowered her hand to stare at her wrist. Dark red marks shaped like fingers marred the pale skin, the color already deepening to an angry purple. "He grabbed me, pulled me to the loch." The changeling's words reverberated in her mind, his savagery and complete lack of compassion sapping all the heat from the room. Charlie's entire body started to shake.

"Poor child. All right, lassie." The nurse's voice was gentle. "Let's get you cleaned up."

The process of changing and cleaning the blood from her face and hair took longer than Charlie expected, though it might have been mere minutes— time felt like it was passing in bursts, and then it would suddenly seem to stop until she focused on her surroundings again. Eventually, she was reasonably clean and dressed in a loose-fitting plain woolen gown from the church's poor-box, modest enough for her to be seen by the police. Her wrist was well-daubed with arnica and had a bandage around it; her hair had been combed gently and was braided simply down her back, though one stubborn piece that had been cut too short for the style kept coming loose.

The injured men were being seen to, she was told, and after a moment of confusion Charlie realized the nurse was referring to the ones under Oliver's spell. Elias was to spend the night in the local infirmary, so he could be observed before releasing him to go home. The police took a comprehensive statement from her, surprisingly gently, and finally the nightmare seemed to be over—with one glaring exception: Asher was nowhere to be seen.

The very sergeant who'd been so dismissive of her at the start of things was headed for the door. He was just about to close it behind him when Charlie called out. "Wait, please. No one has told me what's become of Mr. Burton. Is he all right? Where is he?"

The sergeant actually chuckled. "Oh, he's all right, I reckon. Them kind of men always seem to land on their feet."

A deep frown creased Charlie's brow. She'd expected to see Asher by now. At the very least she thought that he would check to see that she was all right. "Thank you for telling me, sergeant," she managed when she realized the man was waiting for her to say something else. "But where is Mr. Burton now?"

"Here in the inn, fillin' out reports and such. No one would credit the paperwork we have to do, servin' the Law," the sergeant supplied, his tone aggrieved. "His partner's coming to retrieve him on the train. He took a room so he could rest a while before leaving."

Charlie opened her mouth to ask which room Asher was in, but realized that the question might engender gossip. "I know it is not your duty to convey messages, but I wonder—or rather, would you be so kind as to let Mr. Burton know that I would like to speak with him?" Charlie bit her lower lip, hoping the request did not sound as desperate as it felt. "I owe him my thanks for everything he's done to bring my uncle home safely," she clarified.

"Of course, Miss." The sergeant ducked his head. "I'll pass it along. He's just down the hall here—room 14."

She nodded her thanks and waited for the man to leave. When the door closed behind him she hurried to press her ear to it, listening for his footsteps. They echoed down the hall, then paused for a few minutes before coming back toward the room, and then past. Charlie popped her head into the corridor, and when she saw that it was clear she quietly made her way toward the guest rooms.

Room 14 was not far, but Charlie found herself hesitating at the threshold. No doubt the entire town knew of the confrontation at the lakeshore by now, and more attention than she liked would be turned in her direction. If she were seen doing this, that attention would increase exponentially. And yet—there were words left unspoken between them, and she could not bear the silence any longer. Slowly, Charlie reached up and tapped on the door.

She could hear footsteps within; after a moment the door opened. Asher shook his head. "You shouldn't be here."

"You saved my life. My uncle's life as well." Charlie blinked at the cool abruptness of this greeting, feeling tears pricking at her eyes despite her best effort to hold them at bay. There was a distance here, and it made her chest ache. "Where else should I be?"

His lips twitched. "Oh, Charlie." Asher glanced up and down the hall, much as she had done. "Come in, then." He stepped back to let her slip past.

Alone in the cottage, nothing had ever felt strained or improper with Asher, though they'd been more alone there with the nearest neighbor over a mile away. This, however, felt strangely inappropriate and uncomfortable. She looked around the room as he shut the door behind her, hardly knowing where to begin. What she wanted was for him to wrap his arms around her, to tell her everything would be well again. She wanted to feel his lips against hers, to taste him as she'd done at the lakeside.

Instead, she settled for the obvious. "You are not returning to the farm, then?"

The smile he offered her was tight. "No need. My job is done, and I'm called back to London. I do apologize for not being able to help you put the farm to rights."

"You needn't apologize, Asher," Charlie replied quickly, finally looking him in the eye. He'd apologized after their kiss too, and it was that, she realized, that she was referring to. However, *that* felt like uncertain ground. "What about your belongings?"

"I've a friend coming to get me," he replied easily. "He'll go pick up my things while I finish up here, get them out of your way."

Charlie felt her heart starting to crack, and despite herself she could feel the sting of tears in her eyes. "Will you be coming with him?"

Summer-blue eyes met hers over the top of his spectacles. "I don't think that's a very good idea." He let out a breath. "I'm sorry, Charlie. Miss Whitfield. I never meant—" He broke off and tried again. "This is who I am. I don't... know how to be anyone else."

"I know who you are, Asher," Charlie replied, unable to address him so formally. His use of 'Miss Whitfield' stung deeply, but perhaps it was only the setting. "Then is this..." she bit her lip, shaking her head a little. "Is this where we part ways?"

He closed his eyes for a moment, then opened them with a sigh. "I think that's best, don't you?" He held out his hand. "Thank you for everything—you were a superlative partner in helping to crack this case, and I believe you saved my life as well, down on the lakeshore." His gaze was shadowed. "I won't forget our time together. I hope the future brings you everything you want and more—you deserve it."

Charlie looked away from him and exhaled slowly but couldn't bring herself to take his hand, and after a moment he let it drop to his side. She nodded, and moved for the door. "Thank you, Mr. Burton. That was all I came to say." She stopped at the door, her hand on the knob, but couldn't quite bring herself to turn it. After another slow breath she mustered the will to open the door. "I must go see to the farm now. Nan will be waiting for her evening milking. I'll see that your things are ready when your friend arrives."

"Goodbye, Charlie," he said, so softly she nearly missed it. "Be well."

"Goodbye," she managed quickly, before rushing through the door. Charlie took a few slow steps down the hall, and then started to run. It wasn't until she was in the drive that she remembered that they'd ridden there together on Whiskey's back. Tears started to roll down Charlie's cheeks. She knew someone would offer her a horse if she asked, but speaking to anyone else was not an option. And so Charlie began the walk home.

The journey was a long and cold one, but Charlie did not care about the chill. Even so, by the time she returned to the farm she was shaking from head to toe again, and it seemed of little consequence. The house was as still and quiet as it had been after her uncle's disappearance, and that pierced so deeply that Charlie could barely breathe. She closed the door behind her and set to the task of putting things in order, hoping that focusing on the practical would keep the ache from overwhelming her.

Asher's things were arranged neatly in Elias' room, taking very little space. It was no more than the work of a few minutes to collect it all and put it in the entry. When she was done and she realized that he'd left so little imprint in her life after all, Charlie's heart shattered. She managed to make it to her room and settle on the bed before the tears began. Charlie surrendered completely to the hard, body-wracking sobs, knowing that they were caused by anger as much as pain, though she couldn't say whether she was angrier with Asher or herself. After a few minutes she curled up on her side and pulled the quilt around herself, still weeping, but the rapids had eased to a steady and quiet stream.

Eventually the tears stopped entirely, but left emptiness in their wake. Charlie sat up again, exhaling slowly. The animals needed care, and Asher's friend would be there for his things at some point, and Charlie would not have him report back to Asher that she'd been red-faced and tear-stained.

As expected, there was a knock on the door that evening, after she'd had a chance to look after the livestock and changed into her own clothes. She opened it to find a handsome, dark-haired man—but not the one she longed for.

"Quinn Rutherford," he said with a smile, holding out his hand. "I'm a friend of Asher's—I hope you were expecting me?"

Expecting, yes. Happy he was alone? No, though Asher had said goodbye, and made it clear he meant it to be a final parting. Hope could be a cruel mistress indeed, Charlie thought rather bitterly. "I was. Mr. Burton informed me you would be coming." She stepped aside to allow him entrance. "I have his things gathered in the hall."

"Excellent." Mr. Rutherford moved past her and picked up Asher's bag. "Miss Whitfield," he began after a moment, "my partner has told me some of what you went through, and I wanted to ask—do you feel safe staying here on your own? I can have some men sent up to look after the farm until your uncle is back on his feet. Perhaps there is a neighbor you could stay with for a little while?"

Charlie lifted her chin a little and offered Mr. Rutherford a small smile. "I'm well enough on my own. After so many days of acting as hostess, a bit of solitude and quiet would be restful." It was a lie, but the idea of being anywhere but home was uncomfortable. "Oh, I nearly forgot," she said, hurrying into the kitchen and grabbing the sketch Asher had drawn during the storm. She returned to the hall and held it out for Mr. Rutherford. "Mr. Burton forgot to put this with his things. It would only get lost in the shuffle around here."

He took it, looking at the sketch with interest and then shifting his regard back to her. "I see. Thank you." He studied her for a moment longer, then smiled. "Well—I expect you'll be glad to put a period at the end of all this. We'll be taking the evening train, ourselves. I thought, myself, it might be nice to have a look at the loch in the daylight," he added genially, "to see if I could catch a glimpse of the mythical creature. But Asher is insisting, and no doubt you've had a taste of his stubbornness, though hopefully not his temper. He's like a bear with a sore paw."

"Never his temper," Charlie replied softly, thinking back on all of the kindnesses he'd shown her. She smiled a little despite herself, and then felt the pang of his absence just a quickly. "I hope his mood improves quickly. Do tell him I send my—I wish you both save travels."

"I've no doubt it will." Quinn chuckled, though Charlie had the oddest feeling he was still observing her. "Honestly, one would almost think he didn't want to go." He tucked the sketch in his coat pocket and bowed. "Your servant, Miss." With that he mounted his horse—Whiskey, Charlie noted with another pang—and wheeled around, cantering back toward town.

Chapter Fifteen

Temper, Temper

Asher lay propped under the trees in the orangerie at Castle Maclaren, his hat over his face, a book in his hands.

Nearby Geordie and Quinn were seated at a small table; his friends were discussing him. Again. "What's eating him?" Geordie Maclaren, Viscount Kirkleith and owner of said castle, wanted to know.

Quinn was quick to respond—of course it was Quinn, Asher thought sourly. "He's got a leave from the home office, so he's at loose ends for a while."

"Aye, but he's like a cat dipped in paint," was Geordie's colorful reply. "I asked him if he wanted to go riding not ten minutes ago and he practically ate me."

"I can hear you," Asher replied loudly.

"So then answer the question," Geordie returned promptly. "What's roostin' up your backside?"

"Nothing. Just because I didn't want to go riding?" Asher knew full well his tone was defensive, but he couldn't seem to do anything about it. "I suppose it's not enough that I'm here when I could be anywhere else—you want me to dance like a good little puppet. And Ross is leaving in a few weeks, probably for good." He removed the hat long enough to glare at the two of them, then plopped it back over his face. "Just let me be, will you?"

"Happy to, after the end of the week—you've your own place when we go to London to see Ross off, you needn't stay at mine." Asher could hear Geordie's even temper beginning to fray, an unusual event in itself. "Why'd y'come all this way if you wanted to be left alone? What's bitin' you?"

"You know," Quinn mused, "Elias' niece was an awfully pretty girl. Smart, too, I'm told. She made quite an impression on the desk sergeant there."

Asher growled, his knuckles going white around the book.

The conversation paused at the sound of approaching footsteps. Ross came striding up, hair a bit disheveled, an irritatingly satisfied look on his face. "So, are we going riding, or not?"

Asher huffed and got up. "Fine."

"We needn't, you know," Geordie pointed out.

"No, you've been making such a..." Asher waved a hand, annoyed, "...*thing* about it that I can only conclude we must."

"Are you feeling unwell?" Ross asked mildly, though Asher suspected he'd caught some of the conversation and was trying to avoid the remark about his departure. His friend's earlier satisfaction was now carefully concealed behind a mask of concern.

"I'm fine," Asher replied shortly. "I've just got the jim-jams. Maybe the exercise will do me good."

"I see your mood is as charming as it was this morning," Ross replied, and then Asher thought he heard his friend mutter something about the horses being likely to buck at the idea of carrying a spitting cobra.

He snorted. "Maybe Apollo'll break my neck and put you all out of my misery." He stalked past the other three and went to change into his riding gear.

In his room Asher had a dram from the whisky decanter so thoughtfully placed there by Geordie's order, and stared out his window over the ocean. His friends must be thoroughly sick of him by now, and frankly Asher couldn't blame them—he was sick of himself. More than anything he longed for another assignment to give his days some structure, some meaning—but Ross was leaving in another fortnight or so, and Asher wanted to be present for that, because it would be a long time before he'd see his friend again. An assignment would only get in the way, which was why he'd asked for this leave.

But this being at loose ends was trying his patience, the more so because he was surrounded by conjugal bliss and every instance of it made him miss— no. No. That was a closed door and he would *not* look behind it again. He'd allowed himself one slip. Anything more would only end in more pain, and so he'd done his best to make a clean break. Which did not explain why he was such a mess inside.

There were two light taps on the door, and then it opened a crack. "Is it safe to enter?" Ross' voice came through the barely opened door.

Asher poured himself another whiskey. "Go without me, hm? I'm no fit company for man nor beast."

"That is not what I asked, and it isn't why I'm here," Ross replied, opening the door just a bit more.

"You don't have to go riding if you don't want to." A frustrated sigh followed. "May I come in, Ash?"

"Yes, of course." Asher tossed back the whiskey and gestured to a pair of chairs in the bow of the bay window. "Why are you here, then?"

Ross closed the door behind him and studied Asher for a few seconds before speaking. "Let me preface this by saying it is not an... easy topic for me to bring up right now." Asher caught a glimpse of the shadows in his friend's gaze before he moved to one of the chairs. Ross waited for Asher to sit, a frown on his face when he began. "You've not been yourself. Is there any chance that the changeling you encountered was a..." He stopped entirely and took a slow, steadying breath. "... A redcap?"

Caught off guard, Asher studied his friend. "No, I don't think so." He winced. "That bad?"

"Considering recent events, I thought it was worth asking," Ross replied quietly. It was the closest they'd come to talking about what happened at the docks since the morning after the encounter, and it was clear the experience was still raw. "But, to answer your question, it hasn't been good, Burton. You all but bit my head off this morning when I asked you if there was any toast left."

Ashamed, Asher hung his head. "Lord. I'm sorry, Ross." That use of 'Burton', more than anything, conveyed his friend's feelings on the matter, and Asher felt absolutely awful about it. "This is not how I want you to remember me."

"It's not how I'll remember you, you gob. A few days of bad behavior can't undo twenty years of good memories," Ross was quick to reply. He leaned back in his chair, arms folded. "I'm worried about you."

Asher was silent for a long moment. "It's—have you ever made a choice that you really believed was for the best, and for a long time it is, until it... isn't, anymore?"

His friend nodded slowly. "You've known me long enough to know the answer to that question. I can think of a few very recent examples." He regarded Asher for just a moment, then relaxed. "There have been a good many changes to our group of late. Change can be uncomfortable, or it can be wonderful." Ross smiled a little and Asher knew where his friend's thoughts had drifted to. He turned his regard back to Asher. "I don't know what happened to make you feel this way, but I am here for you. Even when I'm an ocean away and it has to be through a telegram, that won't change."

Asher smiled. "I'm going to miss you, Ross."

"I'll miss you too, but at least you'll save on your brandy expenses," Ross pointed out. He clapped his hands to his knees and got out of his chair, walking to the door. "Now, I am going to change into my riding clothes, and I will convey to the lads that you will be staying behind, but... perhaps we could enjoy a bit of billiards and brandy after dinner. Fair enough?"

"Fair enough. I might even let you win." Asher grinned at his friend.

Ross rolled his eyes at that, standing in the open doorway. "When I do finally beat you, it will be on my own merit, and if I learn otherwise, I'll have to come all the way back from America to restore my honor by trouncing you for real." With those words he bid Asher a quick goodbye and excused himself to prepare for the afternoon's ride.

Asher closed the door behind his friend, his expression sobering almost immediately. He was being selfish—and self-indulgent into the bargain—and if he didn't take hold of himself he would ruin things even more than he already had. The vision of a pair of green eyes, swimming with hurt, rose before him, and he bit out a curse and stalked back to the whiskey decanter.

Another knock, this one a familiar, coded rhythm. "Oh, come in, Quinn," Asher muttered as the door opened. "As though my telling you not to would keep you out."

"Just observing the niceties," his partner replied. "Something you could do a bit more of, frankly."

"I know." Asher let out a breath. "This last job..." He shook his head. "It got to me. Give me a little time—I'll put it behind me."

He could feel Quinn looking at him, and wondered what his friend saw. "I ought to have gone with you," Quinn replied. "Then I'd have slept with the girl and we'd all feel better."

Asher's head came up and he actually took a step toward the other man, itching to push his face in. "You bastard..."

Quinn offered him a small smile instead. "I've got something for you. Miss Whitfield asked me to return it to you, but you weren't speaking to me, so..."

"I wasn't speaking to anybody."

"Just so. D'you want this or not?" Quinn held out a piece of foolscap.

Asher took it, already knowing what it was: the sketch he'd made of Charlie, her hair gleaming in the firelight. He'd hoped she might keep it, but— He looked up at Quinn. "Thanks. Now go away."

His partner nodded, but hesitated at the threshold. "I wouldn't have slept with her, you know."

"Not up to your standards?" Asher growled.

Quinn shrugged. "No, she's lovely. But I don't poach." He closed the door behind him, and Asher let his shoulders slump.

He looked down at the sketch he'd made, then crossed to his desk. She hadn't wanted the slightest remembrance of him. Well, that was what he'd wanted, wasn't it? He'd made it clear that there was nothing between them; this was just her way of making sure. He couldn't fault her for it, though in some ways he wished she'd burned the damn thing. But maybe she'd wanted to hurt him, the same way he knew he'd hurt her—and he couldn't fault her for that either.

He pulled a folio from the desk drawer and opened it up, looking through the few drawings that lay there: Charlie by the lakeside; Charlie at the table, laughing; a careful, detailed drawing of her face, that intelligent, curious expression he knew so well. Asher sighed, caressing the cheek of the woman in the drawing with a fingertip. He added the sketch Quinn had given him and closed the portfolio.

The cottage was lonely and work no longer eased those feelings, so Charlie shoved them down and went about the chores with a sort of mechanical efficiency. The doctor insisted that Uncle Elias remain in the infirmary for a few days, and having seen the creature of the loch—touched it—Charlie found it difficult to return to the examination of evidence that only vaguely hinted at its existence. She felt like a lost child, standing at a crossroads with no way to know which direction would lead her home again.

After a day of this strange betwixt-and-between aimlessness, a brisk knock on the door caught her attention. Charlie set aside the book she'd been staring at in an attempt to distract herself. She hurried to the door, hoping to open it and find Asher smiling on the other side, ready to collaborate over the stove, or discuss Shakespeare as they sipped tea.

"Och, child, 'tis only me," Lorna Alvin said when the door swung open. "I know y'wish I was someone else. But I've somethin' for you that might cheer you a bit, I'm hopin'."

The moment of surprise and disappointment passed quickly and was replaced by a measure of relief. Charlie stepped outside the door and wrapped her arms around the other woman, clinging tightly to her. The sight of another person—a person she liked and trusted—made the fog of loneliness clear. "Mrs. Alvin," Charlie managed, sniffling just a bit.

"Y'poor lassie," the older woman cooed maternally, holding her close. "Come, let's have a cuppa before I show you what I've brought." She coaxed Charlie back into the house and put together some tea with her usual efficiency, and in a matter of minutes had two steaming mugs on the table waiting. "Now then, that's more like. Come and sit, child. I've two good ears and broad enough shoulders, if y'care t'use them."

Charlie wrapped her hands around the mug and tried to sort through her thoughts to find the words to begin. "My uncle is safe," she began, reminding herself of that much and hoping that this time it would ease the hollow ache in her chest. It didn't. "But... but nothing is the way I thought it would be." Tears welled up and then slid down her cheeks. "The creature is real. I saw it—touched it. I should be happy, but I feel... lost."

Lorna reached across the table to clasp Charlie's hand. "Sometimes when an adventure ends, it's time t'make a new beginning. But 'tisn't always easy."

"I think I..." Charlie took a shuddering breath before she continued. "I fell in love with Asher Burton, Lorna. I knew he was leaving and I let myself get carried away by it all."

Mrs. Alvin tilted her head. "And he felt nothing, you think?"

Charlie could have sworn Asher felt the same, that the kiss had been evidence of what they shared, but then everything changed and he couldn't get away from Lochmuir fast enough. She shook her head. "I believe he felt responsible for my safety. I thought it was more, but... No, he made his feelings clear when we parted ways." She dashed the tears from her cheeks and faced her friend. "I misread things, and I will recover. I just don't quite know what to do with myself now. The world is not what I thought it was."

"No, indeed. It's far more." Lorna patted her hand and rose from the table, carrying her mug. "Some doors have closed for you, 'tis true. But there are others—you only need a key to open them." She held out her free hand. "Come with me, hm? I've a message to deliver, from a mutual friend."

Intrigued, and grateful for the relief that feeling brought, Charlie took the other woman's hand and followed where she led. "What sort of message is it?" There had been some demonstrations of kindness in the last few days: cards and baked goods from members of the community, as word of the ordeal at the lakeshore had spread.

They stepped out into the yard and thence toward the loch. "One that I think will be delivered in person, as it were." They arrived at the bank of the loch, just next to her uncle's small dock. "Stand back a little, dear—she does tend to splash."

Nothing happened for a moment, and then small lights emerged from the water, dancing and darting about. The surface of the loch in front of them swelled and then broke, and a large, greenish-grey head, gleaming in the sunlight, rose from the depths.

"It's you," Charlie gasped, taking a step forward and holding her hand out. There was no fear; the creature had imparted nothing but care and gentleness when it came to her after the confrontation with the Shaws. Charlie tore her gaze from the creature and looked to her neighbor. "You knew—she?—was here. How?"

The older woman seemed to be blushing a bit; she held out a hand and the beast gently bunted its head against her outstretched palm. "She's why I'm here. Well—she, and you," Lorna clarified, which made nothing clear at all.

Charlie glanced from Lorna to the beast, torn between her desire to look at the creature and her need for answers. "What do you mean you're here for her... for me?'

"You know, I think, that there are realms beyond this—and folk beyond what we know?" When Charlie nodded, Mrs. Alvin went on. "I'm as human as you, but somewhere in my ancestry is the blood of the Fae. There are a fair few of us—Fae-touched, we call ourselves. My family has watched over Iuchair for generations, now." She rubbed the creature's nose and was rewarded with a whuffling sound.

The truth of the Fae was nothing new, and the idea that there were dalliances between the Fae and humans seemed but a step further into a world Charlie was slowly coming to terms with. "And you say your family has been watching over... Iuchair." Charlie glanced at the creature. "Is that her name?"

Lorna nodded. "No one can know what a Fae is truly named, but 'tis what she's called, aye. It means 'key'. She it is who opens that which is locked away—opens the portal between realms, among other things." She paused, and then went on. "Do you recall when you first arrived in Lochmuir?"

"I do," Charlie replied quietly. She would never forget that time in her life. Like now, there'd been so much sadness and fear that it was difficult to see the way forward. "At the time it was difficult to believe this place would ever be home."

"You made one good friend here—young Oliver Shaw. Do you remember what he was like, back then?" Lorna shook her head. "A sunny youth, he was. Friendly, kind—happy to befriend a sad little girl."

The tears broke again at the mention of her young friend. "I think something terrible happened to him, Lorna. That... person who died on the shore was not Oliver."

"No." The other woman's voice was sober. "I wish I'd known sooner. Our Oliver died years ago in the realm of the Fae, at the hands of the Unseelie. The creature we thought was him for so long was a changeling." She sighed. "I saw you go into the portal, you know. I didn't realize he'd gone in too—I was only relieved to get you out quickly."

Charlie sniffled. "I heard him scream, and then something came for me." The memory of her dream aligned with the truth of the experience. "I tried to get away, but I couldn't, not until..." She stopped and looked at the magnificent animal in the water. "She saved me. I couldn't move and then there she was and I was able to run away..." The last piece fell into place and she turned to her friend fully. "To you. You *were* there."

Iuchair whuffled again and then let out a low purr, pushing her head against Charlie's side. "You remember now," Lorna said approvingly.

Charlie reached out to stroke Iuchair's smooth neck. "She's saved me more than once. Why?"

"Och, that's easily explained." The creature laid her head down on the ground next to Charlie's feet and gazed up at her. Lorna laughed. "She likes you."

That made Charlie laugh a little as well, a relief after everything that had happened. "I like her too."

Her friend was studying her. "She's living up to her name, unlocking that memory for you. D'you feel like she might be unlocking anything else?"

"I don't know," Charlie answered honestly. So much had changed so quickly that it was difficult to sort through it all.

"Aye, well." Lorna patted her shoulder. "Perhaps the way'll become clearer when you've got your uncle home safe, hm?"

Charlie nodded, hoping that Uncle Elias' absence was all that was keeping a sense of restlessness embedded in her soul. But a small voice deep within whispered that there would be no going back to the life she'd lived before.

With a final lowing sound Iuchair dipped back beneath the waves. Mrs. Alvin looped her arm through Charlie's, and the two women went back to the house.

Days later, bundled warmly, Charlie stared out over the loch, a basket of eggs on her arm. Somewhere under those rippling waves Iuchair was watching over the loch—over her. The magnificent beast had come to her aid, it had allowed her to touch it, and had opened her mind to the possibility of a life beyond the shores of Loch Ness.

After so many years of investigation with Uncle Elias, the confirmation of Iuchair's existence was life-altering, and in more ways than Charlie had ever imagined. But that was not the only experience that had made the world shift. Meeting Asher Burton had brought Charlie face to face with the depths of her loneliness. She'd enjoyed having the company of someone closer to her own age, of sharing thoughts and ideas—feelings—that had nothing to do with the pursuit of scientific endeavors.

And then Asher had left. There were no promises of future visits, nor even letters to be exchanged. It was goodbye, and he'd made it clear that their parting was a final one. He was returning to his life, and all would go on for him as it had before. The problem was that Charlie could not do the same.

She had tried, and when Uncle Elias returned home she'd had a day or two of relief. But her uncle was recovering from his ordeal, and as life returned to a familiar routine Charlie could no longer deny that it simply wasn't enough. A broken heart was only one part of it, and her heart was indeed broken. Like a foolish and naive girl, she'd fallen in love with a man who'd never intended to stay. As sheltered as she'd been, it was not a wonder he didn't return her feelings.

For all her curiosity and education, the scope of her existence was limited to one small corner of the world. Charlie had spent the past week wrestling with that, and came to the conclusion that she was at a crossroads. Whether Asher wanted her or not was beside the point; *she* wanted more than what Lochmuir had to offer, and that had prompted her to send a telegram to one Lady Therston, an old and very dear friend of her mother's. The response received had been nearly immediate and filled with unbridled elation.

Charlie sighed and turned away from the water. She must speak to her uncle, and the matter could not be put off any longer. She trudged back to the house and hung her coat on the peg before putting the eggs away and setting a kettle on the stove.

"Uncle?" Charlie called, knowing if she did not speak now she'd never find the courage. "Could you come here for a moment, please?"

"Mm?" Elias bustled in, his hair all askew, his spectacles propped on top of his forehead. "Charlie, m'dear, have you seen my specs? I've mislaid 'em again, dratted things."

She smiled a little weakly, shaking her head and reaching to pluck the eyeglasses from his head and hand them to him. "At times one must see things from a different perspective to find the answers." Her response was equally appropriate to the topic of which she wished to speak.

"Ah." He chuckled, blinking at her happily. "What can I do for you?"

Charlie gestured to the table. "Have a seat and chat with me. There are... matters I must discuss."

He did as she asked, folding his hands in front of him. "Well, my dear?"

Charlie followed suit, trying not to think of the cozy evening spent with Asher, knowing full well that her face went red at the memories that came flooding in, despite her best efforts. She cleared her throat and fixed her attention to her uncle. "I cannot express to you how very dear you are to me, nor will I ever be able to thank you for the life that you have given me."

"Ah." He removed his spectacles and polished them with his shirttail.

"But recent events have provided me with new information, new perspectives of my own." Charlie bit her lower lip, tears beginning to brim. "And as any good scientist, which I hope is what I am, I feel that I must investigate these new ideas." It was slightly easier to frame things this way. "I have seen the creature with my own eyes. I have seen how terrible the world can be... and how wonderful." The last part was barely more than a whisper. "And I have seen that there is more that I want to learn and explore than Lochmuir has to offer."

Uncle Elias was silent for a moment, then reached across the scarred tabletop and took her hands in his. "My dear child," he said softly, "You have brought me so much unlooked-for joy over the years; but I have long known that our time was limited. Perhaps I have been selfish, keeping you to myself here." He cleared his throat. "It's long past the time when you should forge a new path. Just know that wherever I am, there will always be a home for you, should you need it. My arms will always be open for you, my little butterfly."

Her uncle's kindly reply broke through Charlie's attempt to remain calm and composed. She started to weep in earnest, even as she nodded her gratitude. "I feel like Pandora's box has been opened and I cannot put everything back as it was."

He scooted his chair closer and stroked her hair. "Recall, my dear, what was at the bottom of the box, and take heart. You'll find your path, I know it."

"I know I will, uncle, for you gave me hope in my darkest day, and the tools to clear a path," she replied, and managed to regain a small measure of control. "I have wired an old friend of my mother's, the very Lady Therston who sent me combs for my hair last Christmas." She took another cleansing breath. "She has invited me to stay with her in London for a time, to tell me more about my mother, and help me explore the life I might have lived if things had been different."

Elias nodded. "Lady Therston is a good woman—she loved your mother dearly. She will see you have all you need—I'll wire her funds first thing tomorrow." He cleared his throat again. "When do you leave?"

"She said that I was welcome as soon as a train could get me to London," Charlie answered with a little hesitation. She'd packed her trunk, but had not purchased a ticket yet. "I wanted to speak with you before I set the date for my departure, but I feel it should be sooner rather than later. I fear if it is not I might lose the courage to do this."

He nodded. "We'll go into town tomorrow and make all the arrangements. I can speak with my bank and we'll have luncheon at the Cobbler's Last, and see that everything is ready for a departure in a week. What do you think?"

"I think it's an excellent plan," Charlie answered with a mixture of relief, a bit of sadness, and a small thrill of anticipation. The kettle began to boil, and Charlie jumped to her feet. The task of preparing tea was something of a buffer, transitioning one stage of her life to the next. She turned back to her uncle. "Thank you."

Elias got up too and came over to embrace her. "Wherever you go," he whispered, "you'll have my heart with you. Bless you, my dear." He kissed each cheek and then her forehead, just as he had when she was small. "Now: let's make sure you have all you'll need."

Chapter Sixteen

What Might Have Been

The whistle of a train pierced the air, punctuating the incredible volume of so many voices. Charlie gripped the handle of her carpet bag with one hand, and held her hat in place with the other. The platform was filled with more people than she'd ever seen in one place, and it made her feel like a very small fish in the middle of a vast ocean.

She pushed through the crowd as politely as she could, certain that every person there could see how out-of-place she was. She finally managed to make her way to the ladies' waiting room where Lady Therston had instructed her to wait, heaving a small sigh of relief to find that the space seemed a good deal less chaotic.

After a rather long wait during which the denizens of the concourse ebbed and flowed, the door of the waiting room swung open to reveal a tall, dark-skinned woman in dove-grey whose attire, though neutral in color, was hardly of a retiring nature. Her walking-jacket was heavily embroidered in cream, her hat was adorned with billowing ostrich feathers in shades of grey and cream, giving the hat the look of a rather delectable, frothy dessert. Her gaze lit on Charlie and she hurried forward. "Oh, my dear child, you are the very *image* of your mama! I should have known you anywhere!" Charlie found herself embraced in the tenderest manner, the scent of orange blossoms and powder settling about her like a cloud. "Is it Charlotte, or Lottie?" Lady Therston was smiling affectionately.

"My uncle calls me Charlie," she answered, both pleased and a little flustered by such a warm greeting from someone who was all but a perfect stranger. "I apologize for my attire. My best dress was recently ruined and there wasn't time to have a new one made."

"As if I cared for such a thing, when I am so pleased to have you here at last!" Lady Therston tucked Charlie's hand into the crook of her arm and led her from the waiting room. "Have you your luggage tickets? Ah! Good. Bert!" she called, and a young man in livery made an appearance with a smart salute. "See to Miss Whitfield's luggage, if you please." She turned to Charlie. "I hope you do not mind a closed carriage, my dear. There is such a chill in the air, I could not countenance the open one."

A short time later and with little further ado Charlie found herself ensconced in a luxurious carriage, a hot brick at her feet. Lady Therston unpinned her hat and set the magnificent concoction on the seat next to her. "Now we shall have a few minutes to chat before we are home. May I call you Charlie, as your uncle does, and will you call me Aunt Callista? You needn't, if you do not like it."

Gratified to find that this woman of refinement seemed to think nothing odd about her preferred nickname, Charlie nodded emphatically. "You may, and thank you... Aunt Callista. For your welcome, and for allowing me to come stay with you while I sort matters out."

"Tsk—as if it isn't giving more pleasure than I've known in many a year. We'll say no more about gratitude, if you please, and simply be family to one another." Charlie's brevet-aunt regarded her for a moment, her expression gentle. "I know we know little of each other, but your mother was as a sister to me," she said, more quietly. "Your face is so like hers, and I've seen a similar expression on it, too. I will not pry, but—you may speak to me of anything, I promise you, and I will try to help."

"Thank—I mean to say, I appreciate the offer and shall bear that in mind," Charlie replied, blushing a bit and tucking the shorter lock of her hair behind her ear. The wretched thing refused to be tamed, and it was often a painful reminder of a difficult day. "I confess that I have little enough idea of what to expect. I'm afraid my uncle, while caring, did not worry much over the social graces."

"So few men do," Callista agreed. "Well—there is nothing so difficult about it, after all," she added. "I shall be happy to advise you, and what I cannot teach you, we will find someone who can." She thought for a moment. "I expect you're worried about dancing. When I knew Elias, he was not much of a dancer, whatever other sterling qualities he had."

"Oh yes, dancing," Charlie muttered, her one and only lesson filtering through her mind and bringing a fresh wave of heartache. Asher had been a magnificent instructor, and she'd enjoyed the activity immensely, but now it was inexorably tied to their time together and dwelling on what could not be was less than helpful. "Are there still more balls left in the Season?" The very notion that she was to take part in the London Season was quite an abstract idea, having so little reference to such things. The pursuit of new experiences was her purpose, and she was not going to start things off by balking at the opportunities presented.

"Oh, yes—this season is only just getting ready to start. It goes right into the beginning of next summer." Callista leaned forward and patted Charlie's knee. "I don't expect to launch you into balls immediately, my dear. I know the prospect can be daunting, so let us begin with what is comfortable and progress from there. Perhaps a small luncheon to start, with just a few congenial young people, so that you may broaden your acquaintance and make some friends."

Charlie felt her shoulders relax and the movement must have been visible, for her brevet-aunt smiled kindly. "I believe that sounds like a very good first step." She folded her hands in her lap and pursed her lips as she listened to the clatter of hooves on the city streets, and the bustle of so many people going about their business. "Or perhaps a second step?"

"Yes, indeed. First you must get settled, and then we must speak with my dressmaker." Callista paused. "I know you are worried, my dear—all this must seem so new. But I assure you—if I know anything of your uncle, it is that he taught you to be a good student. All you need do is apply those skills here and your first Season is sure to be a success." The coach drew to a stop and she pinned on her hat again. "Ah—here we are. Come, my love—I believe some hot tea is in order, and then you may retire to bed or explore the library or wallow in a hot bath, as you wish." Another of those brilliant smiles and then Charlie was being helped from the coach by Bert the tiger and following her brevet-aunt up broad white steps into what seemed like a fairyland.

The house was pristine, without and within; elegant steps led from the street up to the entryway. The entry floor was marble, giving way to gleaming wood in the hall, which was centered with a red-carpeted staircase that wound upward invitingly. The walls were creamy yellow, in contrast to the dark wood paneling she glimpsed through an open doorway to the right, where a fire had been lit and comfortable furniture seemed to abound. The atmosphere was warm and welcoming, much like the lady herself.

Charlie's hat and coat were taken, along with her bag. Aunt Callista made an admirably efficient job of charging the staff with the list of plans laid out in the carriage, and then turned to Charlie with the sigh of a woman ready to settle in for the evening. Charlie smiled broadly at her. "Aunt Callista, I believe I'm going to enjoy getting to know you."

Over the course of the following week, Aunt Callista proved to be an invaluable ally, and more than that, she soothed the grief left by the loss of Charlie's mother, a wound she'd thought long healed. It took Charlie a few days to summon the courage to ask about her mother, but when she did, her brevet-aunt called for a tray of biscuits and a pot of tea. She started with stories of their school days and continued all the way up to the fateful night of her parents' first meeting.

She was just beginning to describe the details of their wedding when the butler announced the arrival of the dancing master. Thus Charlie Whitfield's education in the nuances of her new adventure began in earnest.

Dresses arrived a day later, with hats, hairpins, shoes, underclothes, and much to Charlie's delight, a pair of delicate lace gloves just as her mother used to wear. Charlie stroked the lovely accessories affectionately, and for the first time in years felt like her mother was smiling down at her with pride and approval.

As per Callista's advice, Charlie applied herself to all of the changes with the same careful methodology and attention to detail that her uncle had instilled in her for their research. Table manners were refined and her dance repertoire grew with each lesson, expanding the activity well beyond the scope of the private lesson shared with Asher. With each new set of steps learned, Charlie realized that she genuinely enjoyed the activity regardless of her partner, and was eager to explore more of what London society had to offer.

It was just under a week later that Charlie found herself pacing her bedroom in a fine gown of pale lavender moiré, her hair pinned up and curled, a string of pearls around her neck, awaiting the first of her social engagements in London: the luncheon hosted by her brevet-aunt.

A tap on the door heralded Aunt Callista. "Are you dressed?" she asked from the corridor.

Charlie jumped, and then laughed at her ridiculous show of nerves. That a social gathering should have her on edge when she'd had no fear about petting what some would deem a monster was rather absurd when things were put into perspective. "Yes, auntie," she called, laughter still in her voice.

The door swung open. "I'm glad to hear you're in such good spirits, my love." Callista kissed her on both cheeks. "I have something for you—it took me forever to find it, but I think perhaps it was waiting for the right moment to be found." She held out a small book, bound in soft white leather and stamped in gold with the legend "My Year at School" and a shield with a torch emblazoned on it. "My scrapbook, from when I was at school with your mama."

Charlie took the book with a measure of awe and carefully opened it to flip through the pages. She ran her fingers along the edge, feeling a bit as if she was getting a glimpse into a time when her mother was alive, and full of youthful hopes and dreams. "Thank you. I know you said we are to be family and leave the gratitude at that, but truly... this is wonderful."

Callista held up a finger. "Here." She took the book back for a moment and then opened it to a page of small photographs. She pointed. "There. You see? Just like her." And indeed, the resemblance was striking, though not quite like looking in a mirror. Charlie tenderly touched the image of her mother's face, noting that while the others pictured bore solemn and dignified expressions, her mother's lips were curved slightly upward. It was just enough to reveal the same dimples that Charlie's own cheeks possessed.

Charlie glanced up at Aunt Callista. "Do you think she would have been proud of who I've become?"

"Oh, my love." Callista wrapped her arms around Charlie. "I know she would." She sniffled a bit, then smiled. "Now—are you ready to meet your guests?"

"As I shall ever be," Charlie replied, twisting her fingers into her pearls. She wasn't sure if she was still nervous, or if the scales were tipped toward excitement, but it was a challenge to be met, and she was determined to do so with grace.

At her aunt's instruction, Charlie waited in the parlor while Callista greeted the newcomers in the vestibule, with the result that she was able to sort out the young ladies by meeting them one at a time. It was an exercise in diligent attention for Charlie to remember faces and names, but one she found she enjoyed well enough. Spending one's life in a limited circle of acquaintance made meeting new people all the more exciting, and it seemed that Aunt Callista had exerted herself to find the most pleasant company for Charlie to sharpen her skills with. Too, there had been no one in Scotland with whom Charlie could claim any sort of girlish intimacy, and this introduction to what feminine friendship could be was a series of delightful discoveries.

One of the more exuberant maidens went by the name of Rosamond Reddisford, but "Call me Rose Red, everyone does," she insisted. "And I shall call you Rapunzel, for your hair looks of spun gold." She gave Charlie an irrepressible smile. "Though of course I hope you will find a more congenial mate in life than someone who is forever pulling upon one's scalp, prince or not." Her black eyes were twinkling at this bit of whimsy.

Charlie laughed at that. "In my experience, limited though it is, men often leave one with a headache."

Rose Red was clearly delighted with this sally. "Oh, my dear, I can tell you and I are going to be good friends indeed."

Another of the young ladies seemed to be dreadfully shy, her cheeks shading a vivid cerise if one so much as spoke to her. "A-anna Tilland," she introduced herself, though Charlie could hardly hear her. Anna licked her lips nervously. "R-rose is my cousin. Thank you for h-having us."

Rose, having stood to the side while Anna managed this speech, slipped an arm around her cousin's waist. "There, darling, I told you you could do it. Well done," she praised the other girl, and led her to the side of the room.

The next to arrive was a vivaciously lovely redhead, all smiles. "Hello—you must be Miss Whitfield!" she exclaimed. "I'm Elsie McInerny—Mrs., though I'm still getting used to that part. What a pretty frock!"

Charlie's shoulders relaxed immediately and she found herself smiling broadly, surprised by how effectively this simple and friendly greeting put her at ease. Mrs. McInerny had a warmth and genuineness that broke through the shining veneer of formality and made the newness of the experience feel comfortable. "Thank you! Your gown is quite lovely as well. Would I be correct in assuming that the 'Mrs.' is a new development?" Perhaps it was an impertinent question, Charlie thought after saying it.

"Very." Mrs. McInerny laughed. "But a very happy one, too."

"I'm delighted to hear it," Charlie replied. "And let me congratulate you on such good fortune."

"Thank you very much," Mrs. McInerny replied, and then they were called in to luncheon before the conversion could wander further.

Once settled at the table Charlie was pleased to find that she had been seated next to Mrs. McInerny for the meal. "Am I right in thinking," the redhead asked when the soup had been served, "that you have only just come from Scotland?"

Charlie glanced over at her companion, raising a brow. "Och, I've been caught." She grinned, having spent so many years on the shores of Loch Ness, the accent was easy for her to manage. In fact, as a child she'd often tried to hide her native accent around the other children. "Indeed I have, I was raised near Loch Ness."

The other young woman laughed. "Clever you! I've only recently come from there myself, though not Loch Ness. Isn't that the one that's supposed to have a creature in it?"

The image of Iuchair's eyes, gentle and intelligent, came to Charlie's mind and her smile softened. "It does have an air of... wonder to it." She looked around all the elegance and finery that surrounded them. "Though I suppose one generally thinks that of their home. Are you from London?"

"Oh, yes—well, my parents do have a country home," Mrs. McInerny lowered her voice, "which I infinitely prefer, but my father prefers the city, so we spent most of our time here. My sister's husband is Scottish, though, and I have found that I love that country. How lucky of you to be raised there."

"Home is where the heart is, as the saying goes," Charlie answered without thought, and immediately felt her throat tighten. She wasn't entirely sure where her home was, only that her heart still felt rather bruised and tender.

Her companion smiled. "I'm so glad that you decided to come to London now—had you waited another fortnight, we would have missed one another entirely. My husband and I are sailing for America— he's been offered a position as head of a clinic in Colorado." She gave a small sigh.

It was an escape from the ache and Charlie seized upon it. "America! How very exciting!" She turned to her companion, genuinely interested. "You know, there is a lake in... Pennsylvania, I believe, rumored to have a similar creature as the one in residence at Loch Ness. "

"Is there? I shall have to look into it," Mrs. McInerny returned merrily, "and if I find the creature I shall send word straightaway."

"It will likely be one of the most interesting telegrams the operator has ever sent," Charlie chuckled. Chatting with Mrs. McInerny felt... relaxed. All of the young ladies were lovely, and the luncheon a delightful affair, but the friendly redhead seemed to radiate happiness, and Charlie basked in it. She enjoyed being able to banter and chat without tip-toeing around all the little niceties. Charlie glanced around the table and then leaned a little closer to her companion "I do hope you will address the telegram or letter to Charlie Whitfield, and not Charlotte, for Charlie is what my friends call me, and I would very much like to count you among that number."

"I should be delighted to do so, if you will say Elsie," the other young woman replied. "And I have a further request: as my time here is so short, I must fill it with all the pleasures I can, and so I would be most obliged if you would come to tea some day this week. I would very much like you to know my sister as well—she was to have come today but was feeling not at all the thing, I'm afraid. Do say you will—I know I seem a madcap but my sister is all that is respectable, I promise you."

"Elsie it is," Charlie returned, so gratified by the impromptu invitation that she very nearly hugged the woman then and there, despite the table full of guests. She helped herself to another biscuit, a small treat to celebrate the success of her informal debut. "As to being a madcap, if you'd ever met my Uncle Elias, you'd know I'm quite accustomed to a little madness. In fact, I quite enjoy it in a companion."

Elsie laughed, a delightful sound. "I shall send 'round an invitation this very day, then, so we may fix a time."

As the small party came to a close, Rose Red offered a similar invitation, and Anna gave her a genuine smile, and Charlie discovered that she had acquired a small coterie of actual friends. "There, my love," said Callista, descending gracefully onto a settee in the parlor after the last guest had departed. "How was your first foray into society?"

Charlie lowered herself into a nearby chair, carefully smoothing her skirts once she was settled. "It was surprisingly pleasant way to spend an afternoon. You did an impressive job of selecting guests. Everyone was so kind and welcoming. I received not one, but two offers to come for tea." She eased back in the chair with a sigh. "Mrs. McInerny said she would send the invitation today. She is an absolute delight! It's a pity she won't be here in London for long."

Callista nodded. "I thought you two would enjoy one another. Elsie McInerny is a gem, entirely unappreciated by her parents, I'm sorry to say. Her sister, Viscountess Kirkleith, is equally lovely, and can open even more doors for you than I." She rose to her feet and came over to kiss Charlie's cheek. "I'm off to have a little lie-down before tea, I think."

A little quiet held appeal, though Charlie didn't feel the need to rest. She wanted to write to Uncle Elias and tell him all about her adventures so far. She missed his absent-minded habits, missed their discussion over dinner, and she worried he was lonely. But London had more to explore, and Charlie still hadn't found what she was looking for.

Chapter Seventeen

A Chance Encounter?

The invitation from Elsie McInerny duly arrived in the evening post and was immediately accepted; so it was that on the Thursday following their meeting, Charlie set out for the home of the Viscountess Kirkleith to take tea with the sisters.

The house she was shown into was magnificent, with a vaulted ceiling in the main entrance and marble floors. Charlie felt a bit like a goose in a swan's nest as she slowly walked through the vestibule, head swiveling from one side to the other. And yet she felt certain that all would be well. Elsie didn't seem to have a pretentious bone in her body, and Viscountess or not, Charlie hoped the same applied to her sister.

At the announcement of her arrival, Elsie herself came from the depths of the house, hands outstretched. "Welcome, welcome indeed!" Charlie found herself the gratified recipient of a hug and two kisses, one on each cheek. "Come into the little parlor—Ione and I have set up tea there so we could be cozy.

Sometimes all this," she gestured to the grandeur of the entry as they walked, "can be a bit overwhelming."

Elsie led her to a room of much more comfortable proportions, where the dark paneling was offset by gay chintzes and toiles in rosy pinks and leafy greens. The tea service was set up on a low table before a settee and a pair of armchairs; seated nearby was a young woman, not much older than Elsie herself, with glossy raven hair and vivid blue eyes. "Miss Whitfield," Elsie introduced her, "this is my sister, the Viscountess Kirkleith."

The viscountess beckoned them into the room and indicated that they should sit down and make themselves comfortable, her manners warm and welcoming, though not quite as informal as those of her sister. "Miss Whitfield, I'm so happy to meet you. Elsie has spoken of you with great fondness. I'm sorry I could not make your luncheon, but I've been rather tired since arriving from Scotland."

"Oh, not at all, my lady," Charlie quickly spoke up, sitting in the armchair opposite while Elsie took the settee. "I do understand—I was rather exhausted after coming from Loch Ness."

"And now I must shock you by breaking Society's dictates and asking you to call me Ione, as you and Elsie are already friends," the dark-haired beauty replied. She offered Charlie a warm smile, one that was as friendly as her sister's. "I am still adjusting to all the titles myself. Why—just the other day, someone announced the Viscountess Kirkleith, and I'm afraid it took a moment for me to realize it was I they meant!"

That put Charlie at ease and she laughed. "I can only imagine what that must be like."

Their tea service was especially delicious, with cakes and tiny sandwiches and crumbly, sweet biscuits, and Charlie thoroughly enjoyed the company of both women. Though the setting was one of the grandest she had experienced, the companionship and conversation could not have been more congenial.

It was halfway through their second round of tea when Ione seemed to turn a little green. She nudged her plate away, hand drifting over her mouth just a bit. "Oh dear, this is getting rather tiresome," she murmured, and it was obvious that the comment was in regards to her sudden shifting pallor and not anything Charlie might have said or done.

"Are you quite all right?" Charlie asked, brow furrowing in concern.

The other woman shook her head and managed a weak smile. "I am, but I..." she paused, closing her eyes a bit and taking a breath before she continued. "I'm afraid that the second cake is not agreeing with me. I'm sorry, but I think I must excuse myself." She pushed away from the table. "Do carry on without me," she added, even as she hurried from the room in a flurry of lace and silk.

Charlie watched her go before turning to Elsie. "Is your sister ill?"

"I don't believe so," the other woman replied, "but I will ask my husband to look in on her when he returns. He's a doctor, you know," she clarified. "I think I mentioned that we are bound for America—in some ways I cannot wait to go. The society to be found here is not always as enjoyable as my present company," she smiled at Charlie, "although I must say that this trip has been something of a revelation—for both Ione and me, I believe, though I mustn't speak for her. But you know she was only Miss Brentwood when she left at the end of last Season, and now she returns as a viscountess."

Charlie cast another glance at the empty doorway. "I imagine it does take some adjusting. I can sympathize with that." She offered Elsie a little smile, gesturing to her gown and the room. "All of this has been new to me as well. Sometimes I catch a glimpse of myself in a mirror and hardly recognize the face reflected within the glass."

"That's exactly what I mean—I had a similar experience recently," Elsie remarked, "and I entirely understand." She poured out another cup for each of them. "In my case I had become used to thinking of myself one way, and—" She blushed. "Well—when I met Ross, I found that I was quite different. And I liked the newer Elsie much better."

"It is... astonishing how the presence of one person can send such ripples through the world you've grown accustomed to," Charlie remarked quietly. "And then when they're gone everything seems to have shifted."

Elsie nodded. "I have thought about it at some length, for I did not like to believe that a single man's opinion would change me so profoundly," she replied. "And I have concluded that our truest friends and lovers are those who hold up a mirror to who we are and show us our best selves, for that is how they see us."

Charlie thought about that for a moment. "It can mean uncomfortable changes, but I suppose change is part of growth, and growth is part of being alive." She sighed thoughtfully. "I believe in thinking of change as progress, at least for myself. And as it has led me to tea in a lovely home, and the company of new friends, then I think in this case that is correct."

"Then I believe we should drink to progress, though this is only tea," Elsie replied with a grin, and held up her cup. "To progress—and to new friends!"

Charlie leaned forward, and raised her cup to join Elsie in the toast. Perhaps the friendship and company of people her own age was what she'd come to London to find. She set her teacup down again and grinned at her companion. "And now, I must hear more about these plans for America. You said your husband was offered a position as head of a clinic. Do you plan on helping him in his work?"

"Oh, yes—I try to help him all I can. He has said we make a good team." Elsie put her cup down too, and her expression grew more serious. "Charlie, I must confess something to you."

"Oh?" Charlie kept her tone level and light, though she suddenly felt a bit nervous. "What might that be?" She began fidgeting with her teaspoon, mentally bracing herself for whatever her new friend felt the need to confess.

"We have an acquaintance in common," the other woman began, "but though that knowledge might have informed my desire to meet you, it was you yourself that made me realize we should be friends, and that will not change." She sighed. "My husband's closest friend is Asher Burton—I believe you know him."

Charlie dropped the spoon, filling the room with the clatter of silver against porcelain. She righted the silverware, and folded her hands in her lap. "I do." The words were quiet, and forced through a tight throat. She swallowed and looked up at her companion. "Mr. Burton helped me through a difficult time. He did mention that two of his friends were recently married. I... hope he's doing well."

"I'm so sorry," Elsie said gently. "I ought not have said it so boldly. He is well physically, I believe; but he seems to be suffering from some disturbance of spirit."

A pang of concern for Asher filtered through the painful constriction in her chest. Had things not ended as they did, she would have rushed to him, offering what solace she could. But... "I'm sorry to hear that. He was a great comfort when I was in need." He'd been more than a comfort, he'd made the sun shine through the clouds of her despair, and he'd brought her uncle back to her. And then the sun was snuffed out and the night darker than it had been before—darker and more lonely.

Even with all the new people and experiences, that loneliness prevailed. Aunt Callista had seen something of it, and had offered to listen, but the wound was still so raw, and Charlie needed her brevet-aunt to be separate from that. Yet holding all of the pain and confusion inside felt unbearably heavy. Perhaps Elsie, so newly married and obviously in love, might understand.

"May I confide in you?" Charlie began slowly. "For there is a matter that weighs on me, and will not be eased."

"You may, with perfect confidence," Elsie replied. "Asher is a good man, but according to my husband, he can be stubborn as a badger in its den, and I suspect that what weighs on you weighs on him as well."

Charlie shook her head. "No, he made it perfectly clear that he did not wish to continue our... friendship." She fiddled with the handle of her teacup. "I thought it might have been more than that. For he... we shared a great deal together. I hope that what I say will not sully your opinion of me, but I've had no one to speak to and I feel such a fool." She finally looked up. If she was to reveal herself, it would be with head held high. "Mr. Burton and I kissed."

"You need not fear judgment from me." Elsie reached across the table to touch Charlie's hand. "It can be very easy for such things to happen when you feel close to someone."

Charlie nodded, blinking back tears. "I have never felt so close to anyone. I thought that he returned my affections. In fact, I could have sworn I heard him call me 'love'." She dashed at her cheeks. "But I must have been mistaken. We were in the midst of a terribly tense situation, and perhaps I only heard what I wanted to."

"I doubt that very much—you do not at all strike me as someone given to those sorts of fancies." Elsie was quiet for a moment, her brow furrowed. "I can't claim to know Asher well yet—I expect you know him better than I, after your recent experiences, but if I might offer some advice?"

"You may. I would welcome it," Charlie replied, hoping that Elsie's outside perspective might offer some path to relief. "To be honest, I've been at my wits' end over all of it."

"It seems to me that to lure a particularly stubborn badger from its lair, one might tempt it with something particularly tasty that it cannot find inside." Elsie tilted her head, considering. "Further, I would add that if the badger is fool enough not to appreciate what it might have if only it would set foot outside, let the fool thing starve." She offered Charlie a small smile. "By which foolishness I mean that you should show Asher what he is missing, and keep it out of reach until he comes after it. And if he does not, then he isn't worthy of your affections."

Charlie considered Elsie for a moment, then slowly smiled. "I am glad I met you, Elsie McInerny, even if you'll be off on an adventure soon."

There was a commotion from the entryway at the front of the house. "ASHER!" a man was shouting.

"I don't think we're expected—they're probably not at home—ASHER!"

Elsie looked at Charlie with the liveliest expression. "Chin up," she whispered.

Charlie's eyes went wide, her shoulders tensed. For a moment she had the most ridiculous inclination to jump out of her chair and duck behind the nearby settee. But then she remembered her recent encounter with a murderous Fae and decided that if she could face a creature like that without hiding behind the furniture, the likes of Asher Burton could be dealt with easily enough. She forced her shoulders to relax and lifted her chin, smiling serenely at her companion.

"They're here somewhere, Ross," Asher replied to his friend's assertions, marching through the house. "Even if they're 'not at home', they'd be home to us. You are living here for the next couple of weeks, after all. They're probably in Ione's parlor," and so saying he strode to that room and opened the door. "Ah! You see, here's Elsie, an—d—" A familiar golden head sat across from his best friend's wife—but—no, it couldn't be—

Elsie glanced up at him. "There you are, Asher. Do come in and join us—I'll ring for a fresh pot. I believe you are already acquainted with Miss Whitfield?" She suited actions to words, rising to ring the bell while Asher stood gaping like a fool.

Charlie's green gaze locked on him calmly. "Mr. Burton. You seem rested after your efforts on my uncle's behalf."

"I—" His face felt hot, his collar too tight. Asher swallowed. "Yes, thank you, I'm quite recovered. You look very..." Beautiful, his mind supplied. Desirable. Lovely. "Er—very well. What brings you to London?"

"A little thing called the Season," Elsie supplied, clearly disdainful, and when he looked over at her she was rolling her eyes. "Really, Asher."

"Ah. Yes. Of course." Feeling like a complete idiot, he edged into the room and took a seat. Ross stepped in behind him and joined his wife on the settee, exchanging delighted smiles with her. Not a minute later the tea trolley rolled in and the maid deposited fresh supplies on the table.

Elsie poured out again. "Ross, my love, this is Miss Charlotte Whitfield, who has very kindly come to tea. Charlie, my husband, Dr. McInerny. I may have mentioned him. I thought you were going to that lecture at the museum," she said to her husband.

Charlie chuckled, the same warm sound Asher had heard in so many dreams since leaving Loch Ness. She smiled at his best friend. "You might have mentioned him once or twice. I'm delighted to put a face to the name."

"The pleasure is all mine, Miss Whitfield. My wife has mentioned you as well—quite often since your luncheon the other day." Ross leaned forward to put a cake on a plate, then addressed Elsie. "And yes, we were to attend the lecture, but Asher decided he wasn't in the mood for the activity, and insisted we come here instead."

Charlie demurely picked up her cup and sipped at it. "I do hope you are not too put out by the sudden change, Dr. McInerny. I read about that lecture. I'm certain it would have been a fascinating oration."

Asher opened his mouth, closed it, then opened it again. "I'm sorry to make you miss it, Ross," he offered, and cast about for something else to say. "And how have you found the Season thus far, Miss Whitfield?"

246

Charlie turned her attention back to Asher, tilting her head thoughtfully. "Well, it has only just begun, but it's been marvelous thus far, full of intriguing prospects." She lowered her gaze for an instant. "I've enjoyed making new acquaintances, and seeing all of the wonders London has to offer."

"I'm glad to hear it," Asher replied diplomatically, and was dismayed to hear his voice asking (without any conscious input from him), "and have you met many new people?"

Charlie considered him for a moment. "Several, as a point of fact. Some meetings have been more engaging than others, but each new introduction brings new possibilities." She sipped her tea. "A good scholar never dismisses such things."

Asher could feel his teeth grinding and reached for a biscuit. *New possibilities?* Did she mean—what did she mean? "Excellent," he managed after a moment or two. "And what have you enjoyed most thus far?"

"I've most enjoyed meeting new and interesting people," Charlie reiterated calmly, as though he were a schoolboy unable to take in the day's lesson. "And what about you, Mr. Burton? As I recall, you were quite anxious to get back to your business here."

"Ah. Yes." Asher cleared his throat. "I'm on leave just now, so I'm at liberty for a while longer." He could feel his face heat as he realized the implication of his response.

Her eyes met his briefly, and the same hurt he'd seen at their parting at the inn was clear, even in that second of connection. "I see." She looked away, blinking a little. "I hope you enjoy your time of leisure." After another moment she started to gather her things. "I should go." She offered Elsie a warm, though somewhat strained, smile. "Thank you for having me, Elsie—it's been a delightful afternoon. Dr. McInerny, it was lovely to meet you." She rose from her seat and inclined her head toward Asher. "Mr. Burton," she said coolly, and then she headed rather quickly for the door.

Elsie's glare pinned Asher to his seat; the redhead hurried after her friend. "We'll meet again for tea," he heard Elsie say, "at a nice tea room somewhere, perhaps." Asher made it into the entry in time to see the door closing behind Charlie. He itched to go after her—even took a step or two toward the door—then faltered. A clean break was still best.

Wasn't it?

"Excuse me." Elsie returned, slipping past him in a welter of silk, the scent of heather, and an air of indignation.

Ross was standing in the doorway with a half-eaten biscuit. "That went well. I don't believe I've ever seen a tea end more abruptly."

"Shut up." Asher tried to glare at him but it was a half-hearted effort at best. "I'm trying to do the right thing."

Ross popped the rest of the biscuit in his mouth. "Because you don't love her?" He chewed for a bit, then swallowed. "Or because you do?"

A sense of complete stillness came over Asher, followed by a jumble of emotions he didn't know how to name. He let out a breath. "I'm going home," he told his friend shortly, and stalked out of the house, hat, coat, and gloves be damned.

His teeth clenched so he wouldn't shiver, Asher hailed a hansom cab and gave the driver his address, huddling in the back until the carriage stopped at his door.

He ignored the questions from his housekeeper about his lack of outerwear, hurrying up the stairs and slamming the door behind him. Of all the fool questions for Ross to ask, that one really rang the bell.

He was trying to do the right thing because it was the right thing to do. Asher's life wasn't fit for entanglements, and Charlie wasn't the sort of girl one got entangled with anyway. She was better than that, and he... was trying to be, and it was aggravating that his friends refused to see that. Weren't they the ones who knew him best? And Quinn, in particular—he was in the same line of work, and had had to break off countless liaisons, discourage numbers of young ladies with stars in their eyes. Why was this any different?

He poked up the fire and flung himself into an armchair, willfully ignoring any answer that tried to make itself known. After a long while, he got up, paced a bit, and then found his sketching materials, and began to draw a golden-haired sylph in a leaf-green dress, losing himself in the effort of recalling every detail.

Chapter Eighteen

Arias and Apologies

It was a good hour before Asher was disturbed by the sound of a ring at the front door. Another moment later, Asher's housekeeper knocked at the door. "Dr. McInerny here to see you, sir."

Asher carefully put away his sketching materials and then gave the woman a nod. "Ask him to come in, please."

The door opened a few minutes later, to Ross holding Asher's forgotten hat, gloves, and coat. "You left these at Geordie's." The expression on his face was carefully neutral, though Asher thought he detected a hint of irritation.

Asher lifted a brow. "You could have just sent them 'round, you know."

Ross put his armload on a nearby table. "And you could be grateful that I brought them back myself since, as you point out, I could have had them sent."

"Thank you." Asher studied his friend. "Would you like a brandy, or do you need to get back?"

Ross offered him a small smile. "When have I ever turned down your brandy?"

Asher actually chuckled. "When have you ever left me any?" He poured out a pair of snifters and indicated the chairs by the fireplace. "Is Elsie still mad at me?"

"Angry that you caused her new friend to rush out of the house?" Ross lifted an eyebrow at Asher, and took a sip of his brandy. "A bit, but she's a forgiving woman. She'd have to be, to put up with me."

Asher nodded. "Extend my apologies, will you? I... didn't mean what I said to come out quite like that. The whole situation caught me off guard."

Ross took another drink. "It wasn't exactly Shakespeare."

Caught by this turn of phrase, Asher frowned. "Why did you say that?"

"You were less than eloquent this afternoon," Ross returned the frown with one of his own. He sighed and did nothing to hide his exasperation. "Still a bit touchy, I see."

"No—I just thought—" Asher began, then broke off. "The Shakespeare comment. I thought you were referencing something else. Never mind." He pinched the bridge of his nose. This situation had him all turned inside out—he needed to do something about it. Maybe he should contact the home office, let them know he was ready for his next assignment. He would be sorry to miss the time with Ross, but going slowly mad wouldn't help anyone.

Ross was quiet for some time, staring into his brandy before he set it aside. He wiped his hands over his face and regarded Asher speculatively. "We were not playing at being matchmakers. I knew Elsie was having Miss Whitfield over for tea—it's why I asked you to the lecture."

"You might have said something."

His friend's counter was quick. "And you might have chosen to spend time with me instead of going to Geordie's for another pout." He sighed again. "Sorry, but you have to admit, you've been a bit... difficult to talk to. Something happened at Loch Ness, that much is obvious, and judging by the way Miss Whitfield bolted, I assume it had to do with her."

Asher stared at the fire moodily. "I'm an agent of the Queen, Ross. I can't just throw that away—what kind of man would I be if I did that?"

Ross seemed to consider that for a little while. This was not the usual easy conversation they shared over brandies. "You'd be whatever you chose to be." He reached for his snifter again and took another drink. "It's not as if that's all you've ever been."

Asher snorted. "Are you sure about that?" He shook his head. "Never mind. I just need some distance from the situation, and I'm sure, after my performance today, I'll get all I need." He looked up at his friend. "So: name the lecture, and I'm your man."

"How about a different sort of lecture?" Ross began with a smile. "A musical one, with costumes, and a very comfortable box on reserve for Viscount Kirkleith."

Asher thought about it, nodding. "It sounds like an excellent diversion. What's the opera?"

Ross shrugged and started to laugh. "I have no idea. All I know is that Elsie asked me to take her to the opera and then she kissed me and I suddenly had an irresistible urge to... go to the opera."

Asher laughed along. "Well, then I suppose we're going to the opera! I'll dust off my tails. Tomorrow evening?"

"Tomorrow evening." Ross polished off the last of his brandy in quick order. "And though my wife is a forgiving woman, a peace offering might not be a bad idea. She is very fond of Miss Whitfield." He lifted a hand in a placating gesture. "Not to steer the conversation back into troubled waters, but... it is what it is. It is also quite awkward to have my wife angry with my best friend when there is but a fortnight remaining before we sail."

Asher winced. "Any suggestions, or is this something I need to figure out on my own?"

"I'm afraid I'll have to leave you to sort it out yourself," Ross replied. "She can read me better than you can."

"All right. It's my bed; I'd best lie in it." Asher sighed. "Do pass on those apologies for me, as a start. I'll think of something." He got up. "Now go home—I can still read you well enough to know where you'd rather be, and it's not here."

Ross didn't argue that point. He looked as though he might have something more to say, but simply offered Asher a goodnight, and gave him the hour they were to meet for the opera. And in minutes, Asher was again alone with his thoughts.

In the morning Asher was up early, heading for the shops. It took him some searching, but he finally found what he wanted, and after consulting with an engraver sent a small token to Elsie with an apologetic note. He pocketed a second small token. Satisfied that he'd done all he could, he headed back to his flat, whistling.

He met Quinn for lunch at a chop house, and by tacit agreement neither mentioned Asher's recent mood. They shared a couple of whiskeys after the meal and went for a flutter at White's, and by the time he was to get ready for the opera, Asher was feeling both mellow and expansive. He'd done the best he could, and for the first time in a while he thought it might be good enough.

He dined at home and then took a hansom over to Geordie's, where he was greeted by a very pleased Elsie. She met him in the vestibule and reached up to give him a kiss on the cheek. She held up one slender arm, from which dangled the charm he'd gotten her: a tiny silver pie with the word 'humble' engraved on the back. "Well done," she said. "I hope you did as well by Miss Whitfield."

"Not yet," he admitted. "But I plan to, if you will deliver these for me. I would do it myself, but I doubt she'd take them." He gave her a letter and a small box from the same jeweler.

Elsie took them with every appearance of interest. "What did you get her?"

"A very small donkey, with my name on it," he admitted with a grin. "I hope she'll accept it. I really did not mean to be so rude."

Ross came down the stairs, pulling a bit at his collar. "The other collar fits better. This one pinches." He pulled his hand away and smiled at his wife, giving her a quick kiss on the temple. "But I'm happy to endure if your smile remains that bright through the evening." He offered a hand to Asher. "Well done— honesty often is the best charm."

Asher chuckled, feeling more like himself than he had since his return from Loch Ness. Somehow, having found a way to apologize eased some of the burden he'd been carrying, and he felt lighter as a result.

"Shall we, then?" a Scottish-tinted baritone asked, and Asher looked up toward the stairs where

Geordie and Ione were just coming down. "What's this about you giving another man's wife jewelry, Ash?"

"Merely paying a debt," he replied good-naturedly, and offered to help Ione with her cloak.

Ione smiled radiantly at Asher before she turned to allow him to drape the cloak over her shoulders. "You seem in fine spirits this evening. It's a refreshing change."

He merely smiled at her and bowed as the two couples swept through the door before him. Bringing up the rear, Quinn gave him a whimsical look and offered his arm; Asher laughed and took it and the two men strolled out to join the others in the waiting coach.

The Savoy Theatre was packed to the brim; this would be one of the final performances of 'The Yeoman of the Guard' and Asher was pleased he'd be able to see it before the new show was mounted. He enjoyed Gilbert and Sullivan's nonsense as much as anyone, especially their clever lyrics.

The box reserved for Geordie's party was in a prime position: neither too high nor low, and positioned only just off center so that they could view the show from its best angle, as well as most of the audience. Here was London society at its most elegant: the men in white tie and tails; the ladies in a veritable rainbow of colors, silks and satins and velvets, elaborately cut and ruffled, embroidered, beaded and feathered. At the front of the box Ione and Elsie had their heads together, pointing out acquaintances and occasionally waving to friends as the time for curtain drew near.

Ross was fidgeting with his collar again, and muttering under his breath about how stiff the 'damned thing' was. Asher knew that it would not have mattered how well-fitted the collar was, his friend would have fussed with it. "How late do you suppose we'll be staying?" he asked, pulling his fingers away from his neck and leaning toward Asher. No doubt a smile from Elsie would make him forget his discomfort, but with her attention diverted, his restlessness was in full force.

On Asher's other side, Quinn chuckled, shaking his head. "Some things never change."

Asher reached for his friend's tie. "Just loosen it until intermission, you knob," he said, and suited action to words.

"Oh—there's Charlie," Elsie said excitedly, and Asher nearly throttled Ross by accident.

"Sorry," he murmured, rectifying the situation, and turned to see where Elsie was pointing.

Charlie was in a box across the way, a vision in pale pink silk, embroidered with delicate and equally pale green vines. Roses in a darker shade of pink were embellished with shimmering beads. Her gown didn't bear the flurry of ruffles that so many of the other women wore, but she looked no less elegant. Her hair shone like polished gold, curls perfectly ordered atop her head with pearled combs tucked on either side.

She was smiling and laughing, fanning herself with a gloved hand as she chatted merrily with the older woman at her side. Her cheeks were rosy and her eyes sparkling.

She looked... ethereal. A stray quotation from the Bard floated through Asher's head: "...*luscious woodbine, with sweet musk-roses and with eglantine: there sleeps Titania sometime of the night, lull'd in these flowers with dances and delight.*" "Damn," he muttered, and turned to Quinn. "D'you think I could get to Geordie's and back before the end of the first act? I've forgotten something."

"I doubt it," was his friend's reply. "There was a bit of a crush at the entrance—I can't imagine they've got it sorted yet."

A gloved hand touched his arm. "Is this what you forgot?" Elsie held up the jeweler's box and the letter he'd given her for Charlie. "I didn't want to misplace it, so I put it in my reticule."

Asher let out a breath in relief. "Elsie, I could— Ross, kiss your wife."

Ross grinned at Asher for half a second, then turned and gave his wife a kiss, not wholly without propriety, but with obvious relish. He pulled away from her and looked at Asher. "That good enough, or shall I have another go at it?"

Asher chuckled as he tucked the box and letter away. "That's for Elsie to judge, but I advise waiting until the lights go down." As if by his command, the theater lights began to dim, the stage lights came up, and the first bars of the overture began. Not remotely surprisingly, Asher sensed Ross shifting back toward his wife.

Charlie was utterly transported by the spectacle on stage. She'd heard the music before—Uncle Elias had a copy of the opera—but to hear the voices in person, to see the spectacle of the costumes and sets was a different thing entirely. She was almost sad when the lights came up for intermission, but found there was more to enjoy, and looking at the finery of the audience was almost as entertaining.

She turned to Aunt Callista with a smile so wide that her cheeks ached. "It's so wonderful! I had no idea it would be like this!" Charlie wrapped her arms around the older woman and kissed her cheek.

Lady Therston laughed. "It is delightful, but all the more so for having you here with me, my love. Shall I send for refreshments?"

"Please do," Charlie nodded. After yesterday's tea she'd been rather out of sorts, but Aunt Callista had put great care into raising her spirits, and after a lovely afternoon out, attending the opera was the perfect ending to one of the most pleasant days she'd experienced since arriving in London.

"All right." Callista rose, sorting out her skirt. "I won't be long." She stepped through the box door, closing it behind her.

Hardly a minute had passed before there was a tap on the door. Charlie jumped out of her seat and hurried to open it. Perhaps Aunt Callista had forgotten something, or... She opened the door and found herself face to face with the last person she'd expected to meet.

Asher Burton cleared his throat and adjusted his spectacles. "May I speak with you?" he asked, his tone very quiet. "Just for a moment."

She blinked mutely, then shook herself and opened the door fully. "Of course, Mr. Burton. Did I leave something behind yesterday?"

His lips curved slightly. "Yes, I'm afraid so. An apology, from me." He held out a small box and a letter, sealed. On the front of the envelope, in a fine Italianate hand, it read: *'The rose looks fair, but fairer we it deem for that sweet odour which doth in it live.'* "Careful," he said when she reached for it. "I only just wrote that last bit—the ink's still wet."

"Thank you, Mr. Burton," Charlie replied, carefully avoiding the elegant letters as she opened the envelope. The action gave her an excuse to look away from Asher without seeming rude, and in doing so, cover the fact that she was slightly breathless. She felt a bit like the man she'd spent so many evenings at the cottage with had suddenly returned.

She carefully unfolded the letter inside and began to read.

My dear Charlie, it read,

I owe you an apology. I hope you will accept it, but you need not, of course. I have behaved abominably, and with no real excuse except my own discomfort and confusion, and I have passed those feelings to you, which only doubled the suffering and solved nothing.

I meant some of the things I said that day at the inn: you were an excellent partner in cracking our case, and I won't forget the time we spent together. I ought also to have said that you are an exceptional woman, who deserves the very best life has to offer, and that I valued the friendship and kindness you extended to me. I should have said that I hoped we could remain friends, though my importunate actions after confronting the changeling may have put paid to that idea. I ought to apologize for that again, but I won't, because while I am sorry for any pain or misunderstanding I may have caused, I cannot find it in myself to regret that particular action.

I have no real excuse for my boorish behavior, except to assure you that I truly did not mean my words to come out in quite that order, but my mouth does not always listen before running away with itself.

My path in life used to be so clear; it isn't anymore, but that is my own quandary to wrestle with, and I regret that I allowed those difficulties to spill over onto you.

Enclosed is a small remembrance—a token of our time together, and a portrait of my true self. I hope you will accept it in the spirit it is offered.

Yr. servant,
Asher Burton

When she finished reading the letter, she realized that Asher was holding out the small box still.

Charlie took the box from him, even as she continued to puzzle out exactly how she ought to feel about his letter. She glanced up at him, meeting his eyes briefly before opening the box. A small silver donkey shone up at her, with the name 'Asher' engraved across its side. She picked it up and held it to the light, then started to laugh.

His shoulders seemed to relax. "I hope that's a good sign," he said.

She lifted a gloved hand to her lips, and got herself under control. "It is... Mr. Bottom."

"Oh, but we're friends, are we not? Call me Nick," he invited, sharing the joke. "I have but one thing to add before I return to my seat: you rival Titania herself tonight, Miss Whitfield. I believe the London Season agrees with you." Asher offered her a last smile and a bow before slipping from the box.

Charlie pressed the letter, along with the charm to her chest, her cheeks on fire from his parting words. She sighed and returned to her seat, and though Asher had gone, her smile remained. She couldn't say for sure what this encounter had meant, but at the least they were still friends, and for that she was truly grateful.

It was several minutes before Charlie was rejoined by her brevet-aunt. "Oh, my dear, I am *so* sorry," Aunt Callista exclaimed as she maneuvered into her seat, fanning herself. "There was quite a crush at the bar, and then of course I ran into Lady Kirkleith and Mrs. McInerny in the lobby, and of course that delayed me as well. Our refreshments should arrive shortly. I hope you weren't too bored while I was gone?"

"Elsie and her sister are here?" Charlie's ears perked up at the mention of her new friends. "I cannot fault you for visiting with them. Their company is worth the delay." She slipped the letter and the jeweler's box into her bag but held the little donkey in the palm of her hand, debating whether or not she should attach it to the bracelet she wore. But no, she glanced over at her brevet-aunt and knew the little charm would have to wait to find its place. "And I had a visit from someone I knew in Scotland—a friend who wanted to set things to rights."

"Set what things to rights?" her Aunt Callista asked, but there was no time to answer as the refreshments she'd ordered arrived just then, and seconds later the house lights dimmed.

The rest of the evening held an air of enchantment for Charlie. Though everything was still new, she felt more herself than she had since they'd gone to the inn to confront the Shaws—herself and yet, as Elsie had described, not at all the same.

Chapter Nineteen

Faerie Wings and Pirate Kings

The morning's post brought excitement to the Therston household. "Oh, my dear!" Aunt Callista pushed her breakfast plate aside at the sight of the oversized envelope. She glanced up at Charlie, eyes dancing. "Oh, how thrilling! Forster!" The last syllable was nearly operatic.

The butler, thus summoned, made a hasty appearance from the depths of the house, whisking a large napkin out of sight. "My lady?"

"Lady Walsham's invitation has arrived! Send a footman 'round to Madame Lavigne at once, for she will be fully engaged by noon and we simply *must* outdo ourselves this year!"

Thus galvanized, the butler bowed and strode from the room, hollering for "Francis! Albert! Come here at once, you rascals!"

Charlie watched the entire production with a spoonful of porridge halfway to her mouth. She'd grown accustomed to her Aunt Callista's exuberance, but found it no less amusing now. "The modiste, auntie? I have only worn a few of my new dresses." A chain shifted beneath the dress she was currently wearing, the charm from Asher hidden safely away near her heart.

There was no other word for it: her brevet-aunt *wriggled*. "Yes, but this is for Lady Walsham's ball," she explained, which enlightened Charlie not at all. Callista held up the invitation. "It's simply *the* event that begins the Season—and it's *fancy dress*!" She began to nibble on her lip. "What shall we go as? Oh— it hardly matters what I wear, but you, my love, must *shine*." She consulted the invitation again. "This year's theme is Things Fantastical. What fun!"

"That is quite a broad theme," Charlie replied, laughing at the older woman's excitement. "I certainly have my choice of options." She finally took her bite of porridge and began ticking off characters in her head. The charm under her dress shifted again, reminding Charlie of Asher's parting compliment. "Do you suppose Titania will be overdone?"

Callista grew thoughtful. "I think very few young ladies would undertake the Queen of the Fairies so early in the Season, though I expect we'll have dozens of Peaseblossoms and Mustardseeds." She smiled. "An inspired choice, my love. I shall instruct Madame Lavigne to let her muse run free." She tapped her lower lip, nodding slowly. "Yes, I think Titania will work quite well."

Upon finishing breakfast Charlie found herself at the center of a frenzy of preparation. Aunt Callista applied herself to the task with the dedication of a general on the eve of a decisive battle. The woman was a marvel, and no detail was left to chance. It was not unlike Uncle Elias' ability to focus on a task, though he certainly did not carry things out with the same grace and efficiency.

Madame Lavigne arrived midmorning, sweeping into the parlor with her usual grandiose flair. "Ah, my lady Therstonne," she cried in a very French accent, "and the small golden one!" Kisses were deposited on every cheek in the room. "'Ave you decided upon the costume?"

Callista smiled and looked to Charlie to answer. Charlie smiled too, sure she was blushing wildly at the greeting. "Ah, yes, Madame. I thought perhaps... Titania would be a fitting choice."

"Ah!" and somehow even that syllable dripped with Gallic approval. Madame circled Charlie, her finger to her lips. "Oui—oui, I see it. There must be magic—the glow, the sparkle—and the secrets of the forest, flowers..." She turned to Callista, brows raised.

"Let your fancy take flight," Callista replied, her affectionate gaze on Charlie's face. "I care little for the expense—I have no one else to spend it on. Can you have it in time?"

Madame pursed her lips. "Has Lavigne ever failed my lady?" Callista laughed, and the little modiste went on. "I will consult with friends at Drury Lane and the Savoy—we shall produce a wonder for mademoiselle, *n'est-ce pas*?"

Charlie thanked Madame Lavigne and her Aunt Callista, though the latter reminded her that they were family and the joy was hers entirely. Having no clear idea what might be produced, Charlie decided to put her faith in those with more experience, and instead turned her attention to practicing her dance steps before being asked to perform them in front of all and sundry.

In this, too, Aunt Callista had been beforehand, asking Charlie's dancing-master to arrange extra time with her before the ball. "Not because I think you need it," she was careful to explain, "but because I want you to feel confident. I'm sure Titania never feels anything less," she teased.

The week was filled with fittings and dance lessons, as well as a plethora of stories shared from the 'days of old', as Aunt Callista referred to her and Charlie's mother's Season. Charlie did manage to see Elsie once during that time, and they happily chattered over their plans for the upcoming affair. The visit was a much-needed break from the cyclone of activity, and was a quiet, treasured time with her new and increasingly dear friend.

At last the day was upon them, and though remarkably cold, the glittering layer of frost that covered everything might as well have been the final touch to add a sense of wonder to the event. Charlie found herself in an elegant carriage, a fine cloak around her shoulders, and a set of airy, sparkling wings on the seat at her side, being too large and cumbersome to be worn inside a coach. She fiddled a little nervously with the bracelet round her wrist, the donkey charm discreetly positioned so as not to draw Aunt Callista's attention. Wearing it might not have been the wisest choice, but it did go with her costume, and as long as no one looked too closely, the tiny name engraved would go unnoticed.

Fortunately, apart from the frost, the weather had been dry, so there was no fear of mud, and when the carriage deposited Charlie and Callista and the wings (which really deserved their own introduction, Charlie thought), they took a moment in the ladies' retiring room to complete Charlie's costume before entering Lady Walsham's ballroom.

The Walsham home was nearly as grand as the Kirkleith manor, though situated differently, as one had to climb up a set of stairs to achieve the door to the ballroom, and then descend again to enter the ballroom. Lady Walsham herself stood upon the landing to greet her guests, and affected the fanciful custom that each guest should be introduced as their character rather than their name.

Callista and their hostess exchanged affectionate greetings. "My dear," Lady Walsham gushed, "such a costume!" Callista had chosen to impersonate a peacock, and her gown, in rich shades of blue and deep green and purple, was replete with iridescent feathers and beetle wings.

Charlie, behind her brevet-aunt, unfurled her wings, a triumph of nearly-transparent chiffon, glittering beads, and beautifully scrolled wirework. Lady Walsham gasped, clutching at her chest. "Oh—oh, my *dear!*" Charlie gave a modest spin at her Aunt Callista's behest, showing off the details of the rest of her costume. Embroidered and beaded flowers and vines twisted and curled across the sheer overdress; the underdress was of gleaming, glowing silk, white in one light, pale gold in another. Charlie's hair was piled high and adorned with sparkling, fanciful flowers, echoing the ones upon her dress, and her maid had dusted her cheekbones with a powder that caught the light like a crystalline prism. A simple yet fanciful crown sat atop her head, leaving no doubt who it was she was meant to represent.

Charlie glided forward—for the fullness of the skirt allowed for nothing less—and greeted their hostess, prettily dipping her head. "Lady Walsham, thank you for inviting me to your home, and such an evening of unparalleled wonder."

Their hostess entered into the spirit of the thing, curtseying deeply. "Oh, no, your Majesty—it is I who must thank you for gracing my home." Her eyes were twinkling when she straightened back up. "Piffle," she said to her butler, "kindly announce the Peacock and Queen Titania."

"The Peacock," Piffle cried, "and Her Majesty, Queen of the Fairies, Titania!"

Callista offered Charlie her arm. "Shall we?"

Still beaming from Lady Walsham's greeting, Charlie accepted her aunt's arm and made slow, graceful progress down the grand staircase with its glittering garlands of flowers. It was impossible not to feel like the elegant creature of magic she'd chosen to represent. She scanned the faces of those below, looking for any that were familiar, and hoping to see one in particular.

A smattering of applause rose to greet them; Callista squeezed her arm. "Next year," she murmured without moving her lips, "there will be a dozen Titanias, and none will measure up to yours."

They reached the bottom of the stairs without Charlie recognizing anyone, but the crowd was large and she had hope that there were friendly faces somewhere within the mob.

Charlie was quickly pulled into a sea of fanciful characters. Aunt Callista moved through with ease, introducing her to some, and discreetly steering Charlie away from others. It was easy to imagine the plume of feathers attached to her costume ruffling when men of 'undesirable reputation' tried to draw near. A peacock she might have been, but Aunt Callista proved fierce as a hawk when chaperoning. By the time they'd made their way toward the middle of the room, Charlie already had several names on her dance card.

A small kerfuffle caught their attention; Robin Hood and Maid Marian were making their way through the crowd toward Charlie and her aunt, mostly through Robin's judicious use of his bow to shove people aside.

"At last," Elsie said upon reaching them, slightly out of breath. "What a crush! Charlie, you look absolutely magnificent. Lady Therston, a triumph as always."

Charlie took both of Elsie's hands and gave them a friendly squeeze. "Thank you! But you are a vision as well, Maid Marian!" She leaned closer to the other woman. "I see you managed to convince the good doctor to go along with it."

Elsie dimpled. "I have my ways of persuading him."

Ross greeted Charlie and her aunt after slinging the bow over his shoulder. "It wasn't that difficult, when you consider that Quinn was trying to convince me to go as the white rabbit."

Charlie laughed, and though the response from the Irishman had been playful, the look he fixed on his wife was one of pure adoration. She cleared her throat a little. "Well, I think the two of you make a stunning pair, and I'm glad your friend was not able to convince you."

Ross tore his gaze from his wife and bowed graciously. "My thanks, Your Majesty. And if I may be so bold, might I put my name on your card?"

"Oh! Of course!" Charlie reached for her card. "Assuming your lovely wife is willing to part with you for a dance."

"Anything for the Queen of the Fairies," Elsie replied merrily. "Only I beg you, don't enchant him. I'm rather fond of him as he is."

"You have my word, as Queen, that your husband shall be returned just as he is." Charlie laughed again. She doubted even the real Titania would be able to part the two of them.

Ross finished signing up for a waltz. "Thank you for allowing a humble forest thief to share a dance."

A blue-gloved hand reached through the crowd, followed by an entirely blue-suited Quinn Rutherford. His face was painted blue and he wore a blue peruke, topped with a bright red fez; under one arm he had tucked an elaborate hookah, and on his nose was perched a familiar-looking pair of tortoiseshell spectacles. Attached to the back of his coat was a fat, segmented tail that reached all the way to the ground. He took the pencil from Ross and signed for the other waltz and a galop with a flourish. "Whoooo," he asked Charlie whimsically, "are youuuu?"

Charlie had to cover her mouth with her hand to stifle the giggles at both his appearance and the theatrical greeting. He looked nothing like the man she'd met back at her uncle's farm. She got herself under control. "Queen Titania, of the Fairy Court, is whoooo I am, and highly amused is *what* I am."

He grinned in response and bent over her hand. "Forgive the lack of a proper salute, but this blue stuff gets everywhere. You look lovely, Miss Whitfield. I hope you're enjoying the evening?"

"The trials of being a caterpillar." Charlie dimpled. "The evening has only just begun, Mr. Rutherford, but if the start is any indication of the rest, then it will be a jolly time indeed." She glanced around, wondering if Asher had come, or if he'd been pulled away and his spectacles were the only thing in attendance.

The orchestra began to tune, and she could see Prince Charming making his way over to her for the first dance. Before he quite got there, Quinn leaned in. "You may notice a rather nearsighted Pirate King milling about somewhere, if that's of interest."

It was indeed of interest, but she could hardly say so with Aunt Callista standing at attention. Even if that were not the case, her partner arrived and bowed before her with a smile that Charlie had to admit was befitting the costume. Prince Charming led her out onto the dance floor, and pulled her into the circle of twirling couples.

It was her first dance at her first ball, and her partner's skill made the experience lively and enjoyable. He smiled and complimented her, claiming that her feet must never have touched the ground. When the music stopped and he returned her to her aunt, Charlie was blushing wildly.

The next couple of dances passed in a blur of fairytale Princes (including a Frog) and Arthurian knights, and then it was time for her dance with Ross. Charlie spotted the doctor making his way toward her, again using his bow to clear a path, and she had to wonder if that hadn't been part of his decision to dress as Robin.

"Miss Whitfield," he bowed slightly. "Forgive me, but I must cry off. However, I have procured a suitable replacement so that you need not miss the waltz." He turned slightly, and nodded back in the direction he'd come from.

A rakish Pirate King followed him, his tricorne in one hand against his chest. Asher's coat was long and old-fashioned, heavily embroidered, with many buttons and deep cuffs. His billowy white shirt was open to the waist, showing his well-muscled chest; his breeches were tight, with a bright sash and several wide leather belts, a brace of pistols and daggers tucked into them. High cuffed boots and a scarf around his forehead completed the costume, his curly dark hair in dashing disarray. He stopped, staring at her for a moment, a smile slowly blooming.

"One moment, Dr. McInerny," Aunt Callista broke in. "An introduction, if you please?"

Charlie put a hand on her aunt's arm before Ross could respond. "Auntie, this is Mr. Asher Burton, the gentleman who helped in securing Uncle Elias' safe return." She looked at Asher, smiling gently. "Mr. Burton, this is Lady Therston."

Asher gave Lady Therston a most elegant bow, flourishing his hat. "My lady," he said, coming up with a genial smile. "A pleasure indeed."

Callista, after a penetrating look at him, softened a bit. "And you, Mr. Burton. Hurry or you'll miss the opening bars."

Asher offered Charlie his arm. "Majesty," he murmured, and his voice seemed a bit husky.

She slipped her hand into the corner of his elbow, and when they were far enough from Aunt Callista she shifted her wrist so that Asher could see the bracelet. "I brought Nick with me. I thought he added a touch of whimsy to my costume."

His face went noticeably pinker. "I'm glad you like him." They took their places on the dance floor, in position for the Viennese waltz, and the music began.

Charlie clutched Asher's hand and moved through the first steps, feeling a bit like the lighting had suddenly become softer, more golden. Time might have reversed and brought them back to a sitting room in a cottage on the shores of Loch Ness. She smiled at Asher, not the practiced and polished expression she'd grown accustomed to wearing here in London, but one of simple joy.

"I have practiced since the last time we waltzed," she whispered as they turned.

"Have you?" he asked, and shook his head. "You'd no need to. Dancing with you always felt like this to me."

Charlie's breath caught a little, but she tried to hide it behind a small laugh. "As I recall it is possible I bruised a few of your toes."

"I don't remember that. I thought you a perfect—that is to say, a perfectly good dancer." He was red again. "I—uh—is it difficult, dancing with those wings?"

"Not when I have such an accomplished partner, Asher," Charlie replied, indulging in the use of his name, and enjoying the sense that they'd reclaimed some of the closeness they'd shared at the lake. She met his gaze for an instant. "Then it's more akin to flying."

His lips curved slowly. "Isn't that what wings are for?" And then he tightened his arm around her waist and began to swoop her around the ballroom, his footwork as precise as any dancing master.

The other guests might have vanished entirely for all Charlie knew. They twirled around the floor together, free to simply be Charlie and Asher again, free from judgment or worries as long as they remained in the charmed circle created by the music.

"I am glad you came to speak to me at the opera," Charlie whispered. "I've missed our friendship."

"I was..." He let out a breath. "I don't know what was wrong with me, I... it was almost as though someone else was speaking through me, trying to... I don't know. I felt I'd misbehaved at the lakeside, and I was trying to..." He shook his head. "I ought to have trusted you to understand, Charlie. I'm sorry I didn't."

She wanted to reach out and stroke his face, to ease away the little lines of guilt and concern that clouded his features. But that was not possible with so many others present. Charlie resigned herself to what they were allowed. "Thank you, Asher."

"Thank *you*, Charlie. Your forbearance... means more than you know."

Charlie would have liked the dance to go on forever, but the music drew to a close as they took their final turn around the room. She curtsied to Asher, then quirked a playful brow at him. "I shall be sure to send your regards to Nan and the chickens."

He bowed, very correctly, for all he looked like a dashing rogue. "Please do," he said, and led her back to her aunt.

Charlie knew the smile on her face likely gave more away than intended, but she simply could not compose herself enough to hide the feeling of enchanted bliss. She greeted Aunt Callista with a contented sigh. "My, but this is a wonderful evening, don't you think?"

Lady Therston's gaze sharpened. "I'm so glad to know you're enjoying it, my love." She paused. "Mr. Burton is a handsome man indeed. And he is some sort of police officer?" She gazed across the room, where Asher was laughing with Viscount Kirkleith and his lady, dressed as King Arthur and Guinevere. "He certainly keeps good company."

"He is handsome," Charlie agreed absently, glancing across the floor, admiring the way his coat rested on his broad shoulders. "Kind and brave as well."

Callista made a noncommittal sound, and Charlie's next partner came to collect her. "One side," said Quinn, offering her his arm, "makes you smaller, and the other," he turned and offered her the other arm, "makes you taller."

His playful approach shook Charlie from her daydreams and she embraced the utter silliness of it all, accepting the side supposed to make one smaller. "I would not wish to step on a caterpillar before he's had the chance to become a butterfly," she replied with a laugh. It was impossible not to—the man looked ridiculous in that coat and tail, grinning like a blue-faced loon.

The galop began, and with it an impressive spectacle. Quinn was an exceptionally skilled dancer—he had to be, for his caterpillar tail seemed intent on murder and he sidestepped it nimbly as he guided Charlie around the floor. Charlie herself found that she was hopping over the blue devil almost as often as her partner.

He very nearly took out another couple dancing by, and began to laugh. "Lord, Lord, Asher is right—I need a keeper. This costume seemed so clever at the time, though."

Nearly in stitches, it was all Charlie could do to keep up with the man. When he hopped and clicked his heels she thought she might faint from the effort of laughing and dancing at the same time. "Mr. Rutherford, that tail! You very nearly caught it between your heels." The latter part of her statement was little more than a squeak.

"Not I, Miss Whitfield. It's well known that while I am a menace to society, I will preserve myself at any cost." They turned on the diagonal and headed down the center of the room. "A very good thing this is my only dance, I think."

Charlie tsked at him playfully. "You have a short memory. As I recall you are on my card for a waltz as well."

The music ended and he bowed over her hand, somewhat short of breath. "My dear Miss Whitfield," he smiled down at her, white teeth in a blue face, "you really ought to read your dance card." So saying, he deposited her with Lady Therston, bowed to both, and ambled off, fanning himself.

Frowning at his cryptic response, Charlie wasted no time at all in consulting her card. She'd been certain he put his name down for a waltz... but it was not his name in the slot.

Chapter Twenty

Maze of Hearts

Asher grinned at Quinn's return to the spot their group had staked out. "You very nearly massacred the other dancers, partner."

Quinn laughed. "I know, I know, you told me so. I haven't any intention of dancing again, however, so you will all be spared the spectacle."

"Quinn Rutherford, you are a spectacle in and of yourself this evening," Ione was quick to reply, shaking her head and sending her dark curls bouncing beneath the crown that adorned her head. "It's a wonder that blue paint hasn't speckled the entire company."

"I fully expect my housekeeper to give notice after I wash the stuff off," he agreed. "But it was for the greater good." He glanced over at Asher. "I believe there's another waltz coming up. You're engaged to dance it with Miss Whitfield."

"I—" Asher blinked. "What?"

"I wrote your name on her card. Don't stand her up." Quinn navigated his way around a glass of lemon squash, obviously trying not to color the glass blue.

"You—but—why?" Not that it mattered—it was only what Asher himself would have done if he could see more than a foot or two in front of him. But he still wanted to know.

"Because you're an idiot," Quinn growled. "Go."

Asher went.

He knew roughly where he'd left Charlie and devoutly hoped she was still in the general vicinity. Quinn still had his spectacles, and a nearsighted Pirate King would have been an absurdity, so Asher had agreed to go without for the evening. He was trained to navigate blind, after all.

There she was—those wings were as good as a beacon, he thought, and stood for a moment, just admiring her. Back at the loch he'd thought her one of the prettiest girls he'd met; at the opera she was beautiful; but tonight—tonight she was breathtaking.

His brows drew together slightly. He couldn't quite put his finger on the difference between then and now. Her features were the same, her hair, her figure... Asher was worldly enough not to be taken in by the trappings of expensive clothing or stage glitter. And yet she was undeniably lovelier this evening than she'd ever been before.

She looked up just then and met his gaze, a brilliant smile unfurling at the sight of him, and... Oh, God.

Like a kaleidoscope falling into place, Asher realized why he'd behaved so badly at the loch, why he'd been so awful to his friends, why apologizing to her and repairing that relationship had buoyed his spirits. Why he'd sketched her, over and over, trying and failing to capture her exact likeness, the elusive spirit of her.

He loved her.

And he'd never be able to have her.

He stood stock-still for a moment, until he saw her expression begin to shift, and cursed himself for a fool. He'd never have her—but he could have tonight.

His heart seemed to leap in his chest and he hurried toward her, hands extended. He had to be careful, he knew—the thought of causing her more hurt was anathema—but for the span of this waltz he would let himself love her, and then never again.

"I believe this is my dance," he said, catching both her hands in his.

Her fingers curled around his, the touch light as a feather and yet tethering him to her. "So it would seem." Those emerald eyes sparkled at him, and she tilted her head slightly. "Shall we go to the floor then?"

"It would be my pleasure." He tucked her hand into the crook of his elbow, pretending... just pretending. Asher was conscious of a swell of pride as he took her into his arms and the music began.

Like flying, she'd said, and it was, and for these moments he would soar with her.

Charlie's dimples were on full display, made more charming by the shimmer gracing her cheekbones. "You seem especially happy. Did you see Mr. Rutherford's tail when we danced? Between that tail and my wings, it's a wonder any of the other dancers made it off the floor."

He laughed. "I believe he's wanted by the authorities for attempted murder." His gaze dropped to her mouth and he remembered the feel of her lips, the softness, the warmth of her. "How could I not be happy, dancing with you?"

Her lashes lowered for a bit, gaze shifting from his eyes, and down, where they seemed to linger, and Asher allowed himself the fancy that perhaps her thoughts mirrored his own. Then her cheeks flared pale rose, and she looked up to meet his eyes again. "I could not—no one has ever—I enjoy dancing with you as well, Asher."

"I'm glad," he said, and swooped her out and back in, trying to memorize the weight of her, how lithe and strong she felt in his arms.

Her hand came back to rest on his shoulder, sliding for a second to the base of his neck, and Asher was put in mind of another time she'd been in his arms. Her fingers shifted slightly, brushing through his hair and grazing the skin above his collar. He was trapped in her eyes again, lost and found there all at the same time.

For those few minutes, Asher knew almost-perfect happiness, marred only by the knowledge that this was all there would ever be for him. She would find love—she was made to be loved—and he would go on without her, and his duty would have to be enough.

"I think this has been my favorite dance," she whispered. Her lips were close to his ear, her voice soft, almost a whisper, but enough for Asher to hear. "I'm not certain our feet have even touched the floor."

His smile felt like the midday sun. "There's a floor?" Asher shook himself. "You are a wonderful dancer, Charlie."

"I would not mind if you used the name Charlotte sometimes." She was quiet for just a moment. "I quite like the name, it is only that it used to make me miss my parents. But I do not believe it would make me sad to hear you say it."

Asher's heart squeezed. "Charlotte," he murmured, and again, because he couldn't help it. "Charlotte."

The smile that spread across her face was unlike any he'd ever seen from her before, and Asher knew it was for him alone. "I have never loved the sound of it so much as I do now."

He opened his mouth to reply, but the music came to an end, so he bowed over her hand instead, stealing the moment to press a kiss to her knuckles before escorting her back to Lady Therston. "Thank you for the dance, Miss Whitfield," he said gently. He bowed to Lady Therston and to Charlie—Charlotte— and made good his escape before he did something unforgivable. There was nothing left for him here, and Asher headed for the door.

Quinn intercepted him halfway there. "Are you all right?

"Fine. Just ready to leave."

His partner frowned. "Are you ill? Let me get Ross—"

"Quinn." Asher waited until his friend looked at him. "It's time. Let me go."

"At least come say goodnight to the others," Quinn replied, and herded Asher back in the direction of their little coterie.

The rest of the group was where Asher had left them, chatting away near the wall, Ione settled in one of the cushioned chairs with Geordie standing at her side holding two glasses of punch. Ross and Elsie were just returned from the dance floor themselves, Elsie fanning herself a little as Ross was busy slinging the quiver back over his shoulder. Ross looked up at Asher's return, opened his mouth to speak and then stopped, frowning.

"What is it, lad?" Geordie asked, looking at his brother-in-law with obvious concern.

"There's something..." Ross looked around the room, the frown on his face deepening "There's a Fae here. I *feel* it."

"What?" Asher plucked his spectacles off of Quinn's blue face and perched them on his own nose. "Where?"

His friend searched the room for another moment and then closed his eyes for just a second. "I don't think it's been here long." He opened his eyes abruptly, the color shifting from brown to green. "It's Unseelie."

Quinn did a physical double-take at their friend. "That's... a neat trick."

It was, but Asher didn't have time to ponder the implications. "Yes, all right, but where?" he repeated, scanning the crowd. All at once his attention was caught by a figure he'd not noticed before—and it was impossible that he should not have noticed. The man was tall—taller even than Geordie, and that was saying something—and elegantly built, with long ringlets of a bronzy-gold cascading over his shoulders and halfway down his back. He wore a mask of black lace, effectively obscuring his features, but as he moved through the room Asher could see that his ears were longer than the norm, and definitely pointed. His outfit was black, trimmed in purple: tails and breeches and waistcoat, fitted to a fare-thee-well. High black boots and a snowy cravat completed the picture, and the awestruck crowd melted away, parting like the Red Sea before Moses.

To Asher's horror, Charlie stood alone at the end of the passage through humanity the Fae had created, her green eyes somewhat unfocused, her lips parted a little. Asher cursed aloud. "No," he growled. "Not again."

Quinn muttered something in Portuguese, probably, and silently relieved Ross of his bow and quiver, shouldering it absurdly over his blue caterpillar coat. The two agents exchanged glances and nodded to one another but were brought up short by a warning from Ross.

"Trained or not, you can't take on a full Fae alone." Ross hissed, clamping down on Asher's shoulder.

Geordie had disposed of the punch he was holding, and crossed massive arms over his chest. "They won't be." The Scotsman turned to Ione and Elsie. "Take the carriage home. We'll get this sorted and join you there."

Ione rose gracefully, clasping her sister's hand, though her eyes were locked on her husband. "Be careful, we need you."

Geordie smiled sweetly, though the look in his eyes was grim. "Have nae fear, love. You'll have me." Elsie took her sister's arm, blew her husband a kiss, and the two women swept toward the door with every appearance of casual unconcern.

Meanwhile the four men broke off into pairs and began to move around the room. Geordie and Quinn veered off to the right, while Ross fell into step behind Asher. The ballroom had become oddly divided between guests on the outskirts who carried on as if nothing was out of the ordinary, and those who stood near the dance floor, eyes following the elegant Fae as he stopped in front of Charlie and offered her his arm. Asher picked up the pace, even as he pushed his way through the crowded room.

He scanned the room again, catching sight of a blue caterpillar hovering near the terrace doors, toward which the Fae was now making his way with Titania on his arm. Asher pointed them out to Ross, then signaled for him to move faster as they skirted the room to try and flank their quarry.

The glimmer of golden wings passed through the door and into the darkness outside. Asher could see the concern on Ross' face, and the subtle glow that radiated from his palms. "Do you know who or what this Fae is?" he whispered as they approached the doors themselves.

Anxiety coiled low in Asher's belly and he shook his head. "The changeling we encountered at the loch claimed some kind of ownership over Ch—Miss Whitfield, but he's dead. Maybe this Unseelie thinks he's got some kind of claim, too." Asher shook his head again. "Whatever obscure Fae political game this is, I'm putting a stop to it. She isn't a pawn for some kind of Fae gamesmanship," he hissed.

Quinn and Geordie were already outside where snowflakes were drifting lazily to the ground in what would have been a beautifully peaceful scene were it not for the sense that a predator lurked nearby. Quinn's entire focus was on the gardens beyond the terrace, a high hedge lining the perimeter and winding paths, obscuring the view.

Geordie turned to them, grey eyes flinty. "We saw them step in there, but can't make out where he's taken her."

Quinn was still scanning the hedge, looking for weaknesses. "Just the one opening," he muttered. "We should move quickly, while he's distracted." Asher nodded in agreement and they made their way toward the entrance to the garden maze.

The top of a stone structure could be seen above the coniferous wall, snow already accumulating on the roof. The four of them divided into pairs again, Quinn and Geordie heading off to the left, with Asher and Ross following the path to the right. The way was straight and clear, with a single turn that led to another straight corridor. Asher led Ross at a run, turning round another corner to see his other friends appear at the opposite end a second later.

There was a break in the center of this inner hedge, leading to what seemed to be a smaller square.

Quinn said something very succinct in what sounded like Russian. "Who decided this was a good garden plan?" he added, and nocked an arrow, keeping the point down. "You could have worn real pistols instead of those theater props," he said to Asher, who glanced down at the old-fashioned flintlocks tucked into his sash.

"I wish I had," he returned. "Come on."

In the center of the maze a soft glow was illuminating the snowflakes. Thunder rolled overhead; lightning flashed. There was no deliberation as to how they should continue. The four men stepped through the break and divided back into pairs, running in opposite directions to yet again meet at a break.

As they rounded another corner they were confronted with a small but straight lane with another break in the foliage. Sickly light pulsed from the opening. Asher and Ross slowed and began moving stealthily toward the opening. Quinn and Geordie were inching closer as well. They stopped short of the divide, backs against the bushy barrier.

The glow of Ross' hands intensified. "Direct it, guide, and it will flow," Ross muttered under his breath, eyes closed, brow furrowed.

Asher carefully leaned to the side to look around the edge of the hedge. He could see the structure now that they had heretofore glimpsed the top of: a small folly, shaped like a round Greek temple. There was a strange glow centered within, with the tall Fae silhouetted before it. Asher scanned the enclosed area, looking for Charlie and absently noting the plentiful array of snow-covered marble statues posing coyly throughout a complicated geometric boxwood design.

The Fae moved a bit, and suddenly Asher saw Charlie, lying still upon a raised marble plinth. There was some kind of... translucent drapery, or... no...

His stomach dropped, his tongue cleaving to the roof of his mouth. It wasn't a drapery, it was a webbing—the same kind that had held Elias in that eerie cocoon. She was being covered in the same sticky gossamer.

Out of habit he held a hand up and signed to Quinn the location of their quarry and the fact that he was alone—and that Charlie was in danger. From the corner of his eye he could see Quinn lean close to Geordie and relay that information in the Scotsman's ear. His partner followed up by lifting a hand and quickly signing back that he was going to take a shot and try to ambush the Fae.

Asher withdrew his head and relayed the plan to Ross, and then Quinn stepped into the opening and loosed an arrow. It flew true enough, chipping the stone of one of the columns of the stylized Greek temple in which Charlie lay.

The Fae spun. "Come out, come out," he sang, and gave a low, chilling laugh.

Quinn obliged, another arrow nocked to the string. Geordie was a step behind him, his prop Excalibur drawn. The brawny Scotsman swung his blade in a slow circle. "Very well, we've come out. Let the lass go," he commanded, looking every bit the legendary king his costume was meant to portray. Asher followed, scanning the area to try and come up with a strategy.

The Fae grinned. "Asher Burton and friends," he said, and there was something in the timbre of his voice that was eerie, unearthly, and yet felt somehow familiar. "How futile of you to join me."

"You have me at a disadvantage, I'm afraid," Asher replied.

The Fae chuckled. "In more ways than one, you know." The sound of stone dragging on stone whispered through the air. "Do you really not know who I am?" He lifted the mask and tossed it to the side.

The face was familiar, though the once-ditchwater blond hair had turned to shades of gold, the brows had lengthened and become winged, the smile was wider and framed with pointed canines. He was taller, too, more graceful, and his fingers had gained impossible, unnerving length. Asher went numb all over. "Oliver Shaw—but—" He shook himself, the numbness settling in his bones. "I saw you die."

"Correction—you saw the mortal part of the changeling die," was the other man's retort. "That worthless mortal flesh trapped me, but I have been unleashed, and I have come to collect that which belongs to me. I am Oliver Shaw no longer," he sneered. "You may call me—Orion."

The sound of footsteps from behind told Asher that Ross had joined him. "You have no claim here," Ross said, taking his place at Asher's side, his hand raised and glowing brilliantly, little wisps of green energy twisting around his fingers. "Go back to the Fae realm where you belong."

Orion's brows rose. "Well, well. Does the Fae-touched boy think to threaten his betters? Put that magic away, child, lest I pluck out your eyes to whet my appetite."

Quinn gave an impatient huff. "I do dislike gloating," he muttered, and loosed his arrow.

Orion caught it in midair and laughed. "Idiot mortals," he returned, and flicked his wrist. His fingertips sparked and the sound of scraping stone grew louder, and suddenly Geordie let out an oath. The other three whirled to see the impossible: the statuary across the garden was moving slowly toward them, malevolence in their blind demeanor.

A stone arm swung out toward Quinn's head only to be knocked off course by the blade of Geordie's blunted broadsword. Another statue ambled toward Asher and Ross, reaching out toward them with cold, grey fingers. Asher danced back while Ross ducked and laid a hand on the ground. Light spread across the frozen earth in spidery veins and suddenly thousands of roots started twisting up around the ankles of the statue lurching toward Asher.

Quinn growled out something in no language Asher had ever heard before and pivoted out of the way, bumping into a marble satyr behind him. Asher lashed out with a kick to the side and succeeded in knocking his marble attacker over, where Ross' vines grew up quickly and held it still.

"She's nearly mine, you know," Orion called. "You should not have interfered."

"Never!" Asher gritted, trying to run forward, but the cold hands of a dryad clutched at him, catching at his clothes, his arms, and he struggled to get away.

Geordie was bashing at the marble onslaught, sword Excalibur flashing in the sickly magical light. Quinn, a short distance away, pushed back against the satyr and then dropped, arms up, and suddenly all the statue had in its grasp was the caterpillar's absurd coat. "Go!" he shouted to Asher, and whirled to lash out at an approaching Socrates.

Asher clenched his jaw and twisted, managing to leave his coat behind as well, and ran toward the temple.

Meanwhile, Geordie was cleaving a path through statues, knocking stone limbs out of the way as he attempted to keep them from swamping Quinn. His sword was now dented and bent, and after an elegantly sculpted nymph took hold of the blade, Geordie merely released the hilt, grabbed the statue by the shoulders and slammed it into the satyr. The statues crashed together in a cloud of marble dust. The stone soldiers refocused their efforts on the viscount, their emotionless faces turning toward him. They converged on the Scotsman, obscuring him from view. Asher heard the stone slamming against stone and the frustrated roar of his friend, but the statues continued to press around Geordie until the sounds of his struggle ceased.

On of the periphery, Asher caught sight of Ross. He was on his feet again, charging toward Orion. His friend stopped short, eyes flashing green and his skin lit with golden-green light. "Call them off!" Ross' voice had taken on a strange timbre, commanding and reverberating. It resonated through the air, pulsing with magic.

The Fae stilled, and then turned to look at him slowly. "I very nearly did it," he said, his tone conversational. "You are more than you seem, aren't you?" He lifted a casual hand toward Quinn, who was nocking another arrow, and sent a wave of magic across the lawn, knocking him back into a decorative wall, where the agent crumpled to the ground and lay still. "The Lady of Illusion is seeking a consort," Orion went on thoughtfully, attention still on Ross. "I think you might do rather well."

"Sorry, but I'm already married," Ross shot back, lifting his hands and sending a blast of green energy toward the Fae.

A shield sprang up from the ground, black and sickly purple, deflecting Ross' attack. Orion grinned. "Easily enough remedied. She won't mind if you're widowed." He flung out a palm toward Ross, power scudding from his hand.

Ross threw up his hands and a brilliant, translucent barrier materialized in front of him. Orion's magic hit it and burst in a spray of purple light. Ross closed his eyes, lips moving slightly as the wind in the center of the maze began to shift and swirl. The hedge that surrounded them stirred noisily; pieces of branches snapped loose, sparking with green magic as they sped toward Orion like tiny glowing darts.

The onslaught hit Orion's shield and began to erode through it. The Fae's smug expression slipped, and took on an air of surprised strain.

His entire focus shifted to Ross' attack, allowing Asher to inch closer to Charlie. He skirted the temple to try and flank the Fae again, his heart sinking as he saw that Charlie was nearly obscured by the cocoon. Asher thrust his fingers into the fibers and tugged, trying and failing to pry them off of her sleeping form.

All at once Orion's eyes flashed brighter and the shield that was slowly dissipating solidified again. A strange buzzing filled the air and the shadows that surrounded them started to lean toward the changeling, coalescing into a swirling orb that snapped and crackled with arcane energy. Orion drew his arms back and thrust them forward, sending the ball of magic toward Asher's friend.

The orb passed through Ross' barrier like a hot knife through butter. It slammed into Ross, hitting him in the chest. He went flying head over heels and hit the hedge and then slumped to the ground, the light in his palms flickered for a moment before it went dark.

Orion slowly turned to face Asher, lips curving. This close, Asher could see the pointed canines, the too-long fingers, the bright gold eyes. He had perhaps a breath of Oliver Shaw about him, but no more, and the truth of what he'd said was clear: there was nothing human left about him.

Asher licked his lips and glanced toward his friends: Quinn, a still, crumpled figure lying against a stone wall; Geordie, just a hand visible sticking out from a pile of heavy marble pieces, unmoving; Ross, collapsed half on his face, no sign of life. Asher looked back at the Fae.

"And now the gravity of what you've taken on begins to sink in," Orion murmured, moving closer deliberately, like a predator stalking its prey. "You interfered when you should not. You stood in my way when you should not." His upper lip lifted in a snarl. "You stayed alive when you should not. But that is all about to change."

Asher straightened slowly as the Fae closed the space between them with terrifying and graceful power.

"I am going to enjoy killing you, mortal." Orion slammed his fist into Asher's face.

The blow rocked Asher back and he stumbled and would have fallen except that, impossibly, Orion was already behind him. He rebounded off the Fae and started to turn, only to receive an uppercut to the point of his jaw. His teeth snapped together and he tasted blood from a torn lip, even as he staggered back again.

This time, Orion allowed Asher to regain his balance, but no sooner was he upright again than the Fae had driven a fist into Asher's gut, forcing the wind out of him, and as he doubled over, Asher caught sight of a dagger in his belt, a match to the one that had pinned a threat to the door at Loch Ness.

Orion drove his knee up into Asher's face. The force of that blow was enough to send Asher flying backward, before skidding a yard or two more on his shoulders, finally coming to rest at the base of the garden's hedge.

"What's the matter, boy?" the Fae taunted as he closed in again. "Is your training failing you when faced with an enemy who possesses true power?"

Dazed and winded, Asher had a bare moment to register that Orion was already on him, but it was a moment enough for his reactions to kick in. As Orion moved to stomp down on him, Asher rolled to the side and managed to get back to his feet, the normally fluid movement ungainly.

The Fae snarled in anger at the missed blow and turned to face Asher, beginning to throw another heavy punch. This time, Asher was ready. He ducked beneath Orion's arm and drove his shoulder into the Fae's midsection, making a feint for the dagger, but his fingers slipped from the hilt.

Taken off balance, the move actually forced Orion back a pace, into the clutches of the hedge, but even as Asher pulled away, Orion had already regained his balance and followed him. Asher tried to move faster, but the Fae's speed was faster still and he clamped his hands down on Asher's shoulders, jerking him off balance again and shoving him down.

"What did you think you could possibly offer her?" He squeezed, grinding Asher's shoulders, forcing him to his knees. "Did you think to love her, to make her yours?"

Asher swallowed, futilely scrabbling at Orion's grip. "No—" he began, then choked off.

"You're right. You can give her nothing," Orion hissed, leaning in, his mouth close to Asher's ear. The Fae shifted his grip so that one hand was on the back of

Asher's neck while the other was free. His free hand began to glow and purple vapors started to unfurl from Orion's palm, but stopped just short of making contact. "No, you are not worthy of the quick and clean death magic would bring. I want to *savor* the bite of flesh against flesh as I snuff out your pitiful existence." Orion shook Asher like a dog with a rag and then flung him across the lawn.

Asher landed on the ground near his coat, his glasses knocked from his face. He lay in the snow, stunned and staring up into the cloudy night sky. Delicate crystalline flakes drifted down and landed on his face, tiny pinpricks of cold that helped to clear the fog. He rolled to his side and pushed himself onto all fours and began scrambling to find his spectacles. His fingers brushed against the tortoiseshell frames, and as Asher shoved them onto his nose he caught sight of the dagger, still in Orion's belt.

It gleamed ever so slightly, almost beckoning him. Asher got to his feet just as the sound of crunching snow heralded the approach of his enemy.

Asher stood up straight, lifted his chin. "What do you want, Orion?"

"I want," the Fae returned, moving ever closer, "what is mine." He stopped in front of Asher, reaching with those impossible fingers to pinch Asher's chin. "I want what is *mine*." Orion repeated, spitting each word into Asher's face with unhinged loathing. He wrapped long fingers around Asher's throat just as Asher wrapped his own fingers around the hilt of the blade, warm and welcoming and hungry.

"Let me help you, then." Asher jerked the dagger free and struck out and up, quick as lightning. "I believe this is yours," he said through gritted teeth, and gave it a final savage twist.

LADY*LOCH

The smile fell from Orion's face; his eyes went impossibly wide, then rolled back in his head as he staggered away, hands fluttering at the dagger embedded in his chest. A thin ribbon of blood leaked from his mouth as he fell back another step, then another.

The Fae's legs buckled awkwardly, bending in unnatural directions. He fell to his knees even as smoky vapors began rising up from his body. Orion's cheeks grew hollow, his eyes vanished, leaving behind empty sockets. What remained of the being took on a hazy and translucent quality as it vaporized and then drifted away on the wind. The dagger fell to the ground. It flared brightly and then vanished.

Asher ran to Charlie and began tearing at the gossamer covering her, his breath hitching when he saw that it, too, was evaporating, leaving her sleeping peacefully on the marble plinth. He fell to his knees by the marble pedestal on which she rested, hardly able to breathe until he saw the roses in her cheeks, the steady rise and fall of her chest. "Thank God," he muttered, running a shaky hand over his mouth. "Thank God." He reached out to touch her cheek, her forehead, to lightly trace her lips, and then looked about for his friends. To his astonishment he found the garden fully restored to what it had been before: every statue in place. Even the snow covering the ground was unblemished.

"*Magairlean*," muttered Geordie from the ground, sitting up and rubbing the back of his head. The man was covered in cuts and bruises, his Arthurian attire torn and bloodied. He glanced up at Asher. "I take it y'killed the bastard?"

"God, I hope so," Asher replied, shivering, though whether from cold or nerves he was hard put to say. Over by the wall Quinn groaned, looking a bit like a caterpillar who'd been stepped on.

293

"Bloody hell," Ross muttered, sitting up slowly and rubbing at his temple. One cheek bore a long, bleeding gash and the palms of his hands were dark with bruising. He looked around and then staggered to his feet. "Is everyone all right?"

Asher spotted his piratical coat lying on the ground some distance away; he went and retrieved it, laying it gently over Charlie. "See to her, will you?" he said to Ross. He turned and began to limp toward the break in the hedge.

Quinn gained his feet. "Where the hell are you going?" he asked.

"To find Lady Therston, let her know where Charlie is. And then I'm going home."

"That's it?" Geordie reached out to wrap his hand around Asher's arm as he passed.

Asher nodded. "That's it."

Ross was bent over Charlie, hands resting on her forehead, slightly aglow. "She's chilled to the bone, but I think she'll be all right." He tucked Asher's coat more tightly around her. "Elsie and Ione took Geordie's carriage home," he pointed out, eyes still on his patient. "And we're all in need of healing, including you, Asher."

Asher paused by the hedge entrance, shoulders slumping. "All right. I'll have my coach brought 'round and I'll see you all safely to Geordie's. Will that do?"

"No, it bloody wo—" Quinn began, but a commotion from beyond the hedges interrupted them.

"Charlie? CHARLIE!" a frantic woman's voice was calling from one of the outer paths. "Are you out here? Charlie!"

Asher let out a breath as Lady Callista passed him at a full run, her skirts in her hands, followed by their hostess for the evening and several more guests. He opened his mouth to say something—he wasn't entirely sure what—but they hurried past with hardly a glance, and so he shrugged and said nothing.

Behind him he could hear Ross explaining that Charlie took a fall, and reassuring the audibly distraught Lady Therston that warmth and rest would see Charlie back on her feet. He offered no explanation for his own appearance, or that of the other men.

"You'll come back to the house and let Ross have a look at you as well, Ash," Geordie said, falling into stride beside Asher.

"Honestly, there's no need," Asher began, but Quinn cut him off.

"You'll come to Geordie's or I'll put in a report tomorrow that you're not fit to serve." His partner was scowling.

Asher shrugged. "Fine. I'll come to Geordie's. For a while," he added.

Ross did not rejoin them until they were out front and waiting for the carriage. He reported that Charlie had been brought inside and taken to a guest room until Lady Therston's carriage was ready to take the ladies home.

The ride to Geordie's house was a quiet and tense affair. Whether it was just Asher's perception, or that everyone was too tired and battered from the confrontation with Orion, Asher did not know, nor did he have the heart to speculate.

Ione and Elsie were both awake and waiting for the men when they walked through the door. Ione was the first to speak, running to meet Geordie, hands stroking the side of his face, eyes clouding with concern. "Are you all right, my darling? What happened?"

"Aye, love, I'm all right. Just a few bumps and bruises—nothin' Ross can't fix. It's the same with all of us," his grey gaze lit on Asher, "mostly."

Ross pulled away from hugging his own wife, glancing around at the rest of them, before kissing Elsie's temple. "Go on up to bed, I'll be there once I see the lads sorted." She caressed his uninjured cheek, whispered something in his ear, and said her goodnights to the rest, helping Ione up the stairs.

"Brandy," Quinn declared, and Geordie led the way to his study.

Ross gave each of them a magical once over, and when he was satisfied that everyone was well and whole, he filled four snifters with brandy and passed them around. "It's a cold night," he commented as he handed one to Asher. "And you look like you could use this."

Quinn rang for some rags and kitchen grease; when those were provided he began to scrub off the blue paint. "Well?" he asked as his skin started to show through. "What was all that about? You couldn't get out of there fast enough. What idiotic idea have you got in your head?"

Asher settled into one of the leather wingback chairs and took a sip of brandy. "Nothing. I'm fine. I've got everything I need."

"That's a load of shite," Geordie observed mildly from the chair behind his desk. "You look like a sinner who caught a glimpse of heaven and is on his way to hell."

Asher almost laughed at how apt the comparison was. "Dyspepsia," he replied.

The Scotsman shook his head. "Asher, lad, I know shite when I see it, so you can stop shovelin'."

Ross crossed his arms and stared down at his friend. "Claiming a physical ailment when your doctor is standing in the same room is a pretty poor cover, Asher." He waited for a response and when none came, he uncrossed his arms and took a step closer. "Do I have to use my magic to disprove your illness, or are you going to have out with it?"

Quinn, now very shiny but mostly back to his usual color, spoke up. "Shall I take a guess?"

"No," Asher replied truculently.

His partner nodded thoughtfully. "Not a guess, then. All right. Let me give you... an opinion." He took a last swipe at his face, wet his whistle with the brandy, and dragged a chair so he was facing Asher, as close as he could get. "You're a bloody fool, Asher Burton. Why are you pushing the girl away when it's so obvious you love her?"

Asher thought about protesting, but it was pointless when Quinn was like this, and God knew he had the right of it anyway. "My life—*our* lives," he gestured between the two of them, "aren't made for love. I made a commitment—I'm an agent to Her Majesty. I can't have a wife and family—they'd be a liability in our line of work."

"What about your commitment to yourself, Ash?" Geordie asked quietly.

Meanwhile, Ross was staring at him as though he'd begun speaking in tongues. "But you *love* her. She loves you!" He shook his head. "Take a different job."

Asher snorted. "It's not just a job. This is who I am, Ross. It's all I know how to be. Tonight I let myself dream a little, but I knew that was all it was. I'll be fine in the morning."

"No, you won't." That was Quinn, and Asher realized with some surprise that his partner was so angry he was shaking. "You think you will, but you won't. There's a place inside you where she ought to be, and you'll try to fill it—maybe by sleeping with anyone who's willing, just to feel something again. Maybe by taking the most dangerous assignments you can get, because that rush of adrenaline is all that's left. And one day you'll hear that she's moved on, is loving someone else, and you'll die a little inside. Maybe you'll see her sometimes, from a distance, and you'll die a little more."

Asher tried to interrupt. "Quinn—what—"

"Shut your bloody dial and listen, for once in your life, you stubborn fool. You're at a crossroads, Asher, and you need to choose—and you need to choose *her*. Talk to Melville—get out of the field. Train the next generation of agents, maybe. Teach them how *not* to lose themselves in the job." Quinn got up and paced. "But don't throw your damn life away, not when it's within your reach." He wiped at his cheeks. "Because someday it won't be, and all you'll have left is regret."

The room was very still, but for the crackling of the fire. Ross glanced at Quinn and spoke up slowly. "Asher, it's worth everything, being with that person who makes you see who you can be." He paused, took a gulp of his brandy. "I can say with absolute honesty that I would die again to be with Elsie. Living without her would be worse than not living at all."

"Listen to us, Ash. We'd not steer you wrong," came Geordie's quiet lilt. "You know what Ione means t'me."

Asher stared into the fire, his mind in tumult. Life without Charlie—he'd accepted that it would be empty. But... what about life *with* her? Waking up to her each morning, hearing her laugh, enjoying her keen mind, her thoughtful ways... could he really walk away from that? What if... he didn't have to?

He looked up at Quinn, who was nursing another brandy, staring moodily into the flames as though some answer lay there. His partner had been describing his own behavior—his *own* heartbreak, Asher realized. He was warning Asher not to become like him.

Train the next generation of agents—teach them not to lose themselves in the job. Like Quinn had done.

Like Asher nearly had.

He got up abruptly. "Excuse me, lads. I've got things to see to."

"Asher, wait," Ross called out with the same echoing tone he'd used on Orion, stopping Asher in his tracks, but when he spoke again it was the usual lilt. "Where are you going?"

Asher turned and narrowed his eyes at his friend. "Are you using magic on me, Ross?"

His friend turned a little red. "Well you keep running off whenever—I was just trying to... Yes, fine, I used my magic on you."

"Well—stop it," Asher replied. "I need to go home—I have letters to write, and financial information to pull together. As we are not currently in Scotland, there are rules I have to follow if I want to marry." He grinned suddenly. "Can I go now?"

Quinn, by the fire, visibly let out a breath. "Thank God," he muttered, then glanced sideways at his partner. "Thought I was going to have to dart you for a moment there."

Geordie was chuckling. "If the lady is agreeable, I can speak to the Archbishop of Canterbury about a special license—and that way you can wed before Ross and Elsie leave."

"You'd do that?" Asher crossed the room and shook Geordie's hand, gave up, and hugged the man instead. "That was the one shadow in this whole affair. But first I should see if she'll have me at all."

Chapter Twenty-One

All's Well That Ends Well

Charlie opened her eyes slowly and was immediately disoriented. She was in bed... in her bedroom... and sunlight was shining through the window. Her head felt a bit like it was detached and floating, and strange images flashed through her mind. There was a man, familiar but unknown, and then she was outside in a world of glittering snowflakes and stone. She sat up slowly, blinking as she tried to mentally navigate the fog.

"Easy, dearest." Aunt Callista was immediately by the bed, helping Charlie to sit up. "You had quite an evening. How are you feeling?"

"What—what happened?" Charlie asked, looking around again. She had no memory of coming home. The last thing that she recalled with any clarity was dancing with Asher, and that memory hardly accounted for the nagging sense of trepidation that the images of a dark garden summoned. "We were at the ball, and I was..."

Her brevet-aunt stroked her hair. "You took a little tumble and had a swoon, dearest, that's all. The doctor said you should feel right as rain today."

Physically she felt fine, perhaps a little light-headed, but nothing alarming—well, nothing but a gap in her memory. "I don't remember that at all. Am I to stay in bed then, or may I get up?"

"If you feel well enough, my love, of course you may get up. Shall I ring for your maid?"

Charlie nodded absently, still trying to reconcile what Aunt Callista had said with the images of a face and a walk through a snowy garden. The memories had the same feeling that her dream of the Fae realm had, and that made her shudder from head to toe—but the more she tried to recall them, the more they slipped away, until at last she forgot entirely the source of her worry and confusion. An earlier memory in the evening was crystal clear, however: when Asher had held her in his arms, twirling them around the room, the entire world seeming to move in perfect harmony.

Her maid arrived and helped Charlie to dress for the day, taking extra care with her hair. "My lady says you're likely to have callers, miss," was the explanation when asked; but at last Charlie was deemed presentable.

By the time Charlie was dressed and making her way to the stairs her earlier disquiet had faded along with the disjointed images. Soon she was feeling quite herself again and was smiling brightly when she came down the stairs to an entryway packed with bouquets and small tokens. Charlie stopped short and stared at what could only be described as a small garden's worth of flowers. "My word, what is all of this?" she asked

Aunt Callista, as Forster the butler sought out a clear space for another bouquet.

The older woman kissed her cheek. "Tributes, my dearest. A Queen must have her court, you know."

Charlie gaped, approaching the nearest arrangement of flowers. They were for her. Each and every bud, every ribbon and card, were intended for *her*. She'd been introduced to what felt like half of London last night, but even so... True, she'd had a full dance card, yet only one person had truly meant anything amid all the enchantment and glamor of the night, and no amount of bouquets or tokens from any other would ever be enough to take her heart from him.

Even so, to be confronted by the reality of so many suitors was... staggering. Whether she wished the attention of another or not, the gifts had to be considered and polite thanks offered to the givers. She took her time looking over as many of the offerings as she could while breakfast was laid out, taking note of which she liked best, and which would suit the parlor or the dining room. But there was one that stood out above all the others.

The other tokens had been addressed to Titania; beautiful and flattering, but blind to who Charlie truly was. This bouquet was something different—a profusion of roses, all in shades ranging from the most delicate shell pink to a deep blush, studded throughout with star jasmine. The fragrance was heavenly, and the outer fold of the card bore a sketch of a donkey.

A soft smile spread across Charlie's lips as she reached for the card and slowly read the note within, heart fluttering like the wild beating of a butterfly's wings.

My dearest Charlotte, it said,

÷

Thanks to you I can never see roses without thinking of the stars—and I can never see the stars without thinking of you. I regret that I won't be able to call on you today, but look to see me tomorrow.
Your most faithful and willing servant,
Asher

Charlie folded the small paper with a sigh and slipped it back into the envelope. She leaned forward to smell the roses and her smile grew even wider. She stroked the petals of the nearest rose before asking the butler to have the bouquet taken to her bedroom.

Just as Aunt Callista predicted, the callers began to arrive by mid-morning: gentlemen with whom Charlie had shared a dance, or who had merely pushed glasses of punch into her hands. Prince Charming showed up, introducing himself, this time as Lord Frederick something. Without the trappings of his costume he was a rather unimpressive figure, but kind enough in his demeanor.

Charlie greeted each of her many visitors graciously, and only once claimed indisposition to escape the room when one fellow began reciting the most ridiculous of sonnets—self-composed—and declaimed terribly at that. Thankfully, Aunt Callista was able to tactfully encourage the fellow to return to the other business of the day, allowing Charlie to come back to the parlor for a blissfully quiet and suitor-free cup of tea.

By late afternoon she was exhausted, having received many badly written poems, several bold requests for a curl of her hair, and an invitation to go riding the following day. Lady Therston informed Forster that they were no longer at home to visitors, and their public day ended. Charlie took a moment to write and accept the invitation to go riding, and then Aunt Callista declared that an early night would be a relief for everyone in the household, and so it proved to be.

Asher was not among their callers the next morning. Charlie tried not to make a show of looking for him—but he had said he would come, though her heart beating wildly each time the bell rang would not speed his arrival.

After luncheon she readied herself for her ride in the park, rather wishing she had refused; but she'd had no real reason to do so, and the gentleman who had asked had seemed kind enough. The day was fine, if still a bit cool, and so Charlie added a velvet coat in deep rose to her ensemble, and tucked some of Asher's roses into the brim of her hat.

The ride was long and the gentleman unexceptionable—but also rather unexceptional—and Charlie was relieved to return home. Forster relieved her of her coat and hat, and after rescuing her roses she went in search of her brevet-aunt.

Callista was in the drawing room, speaking with a handsome but slightly impatient ex-Pirate King. Asher stood immediately at Charlie's entrance.

Charlie stopped in the doorway, glancing from one to the other before fixing a warm smile on Asher. "Mr. Burton," she greeted him, not bothering to hide the pleasure his presence brought. "I do hope I haven't kept you waiting long."

"I'm grateful to Lady Therston for keeping me company," was his clearly diplomatic reply. "I hope you enjoyed your ride?"

Aunt Callista rose at this juncture and excused herself, murmuring something about speaking with the cook about the evening meal, and closed the door behind her.

Surprised, but delighted by the opportunity to be alone with Asher, Charlie's shoulders relaxed. "It's almost like being back at the farm." She moved further into the room, and closer to the man she'd spent so many hours thinking about. "I must admit that even in the middle of all of this wealth and comfort I have missed those evenings we spent together."

"It's my cooking, I expect," he replied, blue eyes twinkling over his spectacles. "I could run down to the kitchen and give Lady Therston's cook a pointer or two if you like."

"It wouldn't be the same. It was our collaborative efforts that proved the most rewarding," she replied, laughing a little herself.

"How fortuitous that you should say so. I came to speak with you about another collaboration, if you are willing." His smile seemed to falter a little.

"Another case to be solved?" Charlie replied, trying to puzzle out why he seemed to have grown more serious. She gestured for him to sit, and made for a chair close to the settee. "I am at your disposal if I can be of service."

But he did not sit, instead pacing a little. "I had," he said after a moment, "a speech planned out, but I find the whole thing's fled, so I suppose I'd best just get to the point." He came and sat at the end of the settee nearest her. "The other night," he began, hesitated, and shook his head. "I've fallen in love with you, Charlie, and I've come to ask whether you might find it in your heart..." He let out a breath. "I know I've been an idiot— I was like an animal, caught in my own trap. I thought we could never be together, you see, and so I tried to put some distance between us when all I wanted was the opposite. Have I a hope, or have I pushed you too far away for forgiveness?" His expression was very stark, fear warring with hope in his gaze.

It took several seconds for his words to truly sink in, as often is the case when one is faced with their dreams becoming reality. Charlie knew she ought to reply and tell him everything she'd longed to say, but her voice was quite absent.

She reached out to put her hand on his, and in doing so, found that the words came as soon as their fingers met. "You've already been forgiven, Asher... one cannot live their life holding their own heart in contempt."

He nodded and rose again, tension in the set of his shoulders. "Then I've made a start, at least." He took a moment, seeming to marshal his thoughts. "I'd hoped—" Her words seemed to penetrate, finally, and he dropped to his knees before her, taking her hands. "Are you saying—do you mean—?"

"That I love you?" Charlie suddenly felt her eyes filling with joyful tears, she blinked a few times, laughing a little at herself. "I do, Asher, my dear, sweet Mr. Burton. I love you with all of my heart."

He blinked at her, dazed, and then pressed kisses to her hands, her fingers, her palms, finally gazing back up at her. "My love," he murmured, his voice husky, "I cannot—I will not—contemplate a life without you in it. Will you embark with me on this last, lifelong collaboration, and become my wife?"

Lost for the one word that she needed to speak, Charlie simply nodded, squeezing his fingers. She cleared her throat and sniffled just a little, allowing the Bard to answer for her. "'I am your wife, if you will marry me. If not, I'll die your maid.'"

All at once he surged to his feet, pulling her with him and into his arms. "Charlotte, my darling," he whispered, and pressed his mouth to hers.

There were no words, only Asher, and the enormity of what Charlie felt for him. She returned his kiss with all the love and longing she'd held under control for so long.

Fingers slid up his back and wove through his dark curls. Charlie moaned ever-so-slightly, and pressed closer to him.

He lifted his head and gazed at her. "I swear to you now, my love, before God, the Devil, and anyone else who may be listening: I will love you all of my days and beyond." He nudged her nose with his a little, tilting her head back, and kissed her again. His lips were soft and warm, his arms were tight around her, and when he coaxed her to open to him she obliged, a little shy but without hesitation.

The sound he made was of a man long starving who'd just been given sustenance. He lifted a hand to cup her jaw, his thumb gently stroking her cheek as he plundered her mouth in true Pirate King fashion.

A shudder coursed through Charlie, heated shivers that shimmied down her spine. Her knees suddenly felt a little wobbly, but he held her close and she knew he'd never let her fall. Seconds later—or perhaps minutes, Charlie couldn't be sure—he lifted his head, raining softer kisses on her nose, her cheeks, her eyelids. She sighed and laid her head on his shoulder. Just being close to him was like stepping into a dream. "I love you, Asher Burton. I cannot wait to see what sort of adventure our life together will be."

Asher's cheeks were red, his breath quick, and his smile intimate as he fumbled in his waistcoat pocket and got down on one knee. "May I?" He took her left hand in his and held up a ring, an amethyst surrounded by pearls.

"Oh, it's—Asher, it's the most beautiful thing I've ever..." She replied as he slipped the ring onto her finger. Charlie held up her hand and admired the way the ring glittered in the light. The corner of her mouth quirked upward playfully. "A fitting jewel to be presented by a pirate king."

"No pirate nor king," he replied gently. "Nor even an agent anymore. Just a man who loves you more than life."

And because she could not resist doing it, Charlie bent and kissed him again, though she tried not to lose all sense of propriety, knowing it would not be long before Aunt Callista would return to check on them. She pulled back and admired the ring again. "Oh, I cannot wait to tell Elsie!"

Asher chuckled and tugged her toward the settee, sitting next to her. "Geordie offered to get us a special license so we could wed before she and Ross leave, if you're willing—though if it's too soon, just say so. I'll wait as long as you need me to."

When they'd met, Elsie had said they would be leaving in a few weeks, which left precious little time for planning. Charlie looked at her beloved's face and realized that the details of the event mattered little to her. The only thing she truly cared about was the man at her side, and whether they married in a week, or at the end of the season, she would be his.

"Tell him he may ask for the license. I only want you, Asher." But Charlie stopped short on the way to kissing him again. "And we must send word, and arrange for Uncle Elias to come to London for the wedding."

Asher nodded. "I did cable yesterday to ask for his permission. I expect he's waiting to hear from you."

The drawing room door opened and Aunt Callista peeked in. "May I wish you happy, my dearest?"

Charlie grinned at Asher—*her* Asher—before responding. "Do come in, Auntie. We have quite a lot to plan."

The older woman hurried to her as Asher vacated the settee with a smile. "Oh, I am so happy for you—for you both! When Mr. Burton explained to me how very dear you are to him..." Callista clasped her hands against her breast, "oh, Charlie, how very pleased your mama would be that you have found someone so steadfast. And you are suited, truly?"

"I am, dearest auntie," Charlie assured her. Then holding a hand out to Asher. "I could not be happier."

"You know, Asher," Geordie said, roughly a week later, "some might consider three best men a bit excessive." He chuckled and finished pinning on Asher's boutonniere.

Asher chuckled. "This is as much my Charlie's choice as mine," he told them. "Once she found out what you'd done, helping me to face Orion... there was simply no other choice to be made."

"And we'd have it no other way," Ross agreed. But you must admit it's unusual."

"Not everyone's as lucky as I am," Asher pointed out with a grin, adjusting his spectacles and looking around the sacristy in which they stood.

"Truer words," the viscount agreed. "We're lucky men, and no mistake. Which got me to thinking, actually."

"That's almost never a good idea," Quinn teased, and Geordie chuckled.

"I've no wish to steal your thunder, Asher, so we'll not announce anything official for a bit yet, but," Geordie paused and looked at each man in turn. "Aye, I think three godfathers should just about be enough."

To Asher's surprise, Ross let out an audible sigh of relief. "Thank God you finally told them." He put an arm on the Scotsman's shoulder. "I don't know how much longer I could have kept it in."

"A baby?" Asher grabbed Geordie and hugged him. "Congratulations! That's wonderful!" He pounded Geordie on the back.

After a moment Quinn joined in, congratulating Geordie on his impending fatherhood. "Seems like a day for celebrating," he observed. "Though we've still got this one small matter to deal with first." He looked pointedly at Asher.

"Right!" Asher took a deep breath. "Has everyone got everything?"

Ross pulled his hand from his pocket, a band of gold slipped halfway down his pinky. "I've got the ring." He paused and reached into his other pocket. "Oh, and I found that key you gave me!"

"I've got two full flasks of whiskey," Quinn volunteered. "Emergency rations."

Asher laughed while he confiscated his house key from Ross. "You won't need that in another day, and I definitely don't want you coming to my house tonight."

"And I've got the special license," Geordie held it up with a flourish, "which I will file as soon as it's signed by the bishop."

"Then we're ready." Asher nodded and straightened his waistcoat; at his nod, Quinn went to let the bishop know everything was in order, and after a few moments, the organist began to play.

The four men filed into the sanctuary, Asher at their head, and took their places at the altar.

For having had so little time to plan, Charlie's brevet-aunt had pulled out all the stops. The chapel was a masterpiece of delicate white and pink flowers, and the floor of the aisle was blanketed in snowy petals. The doors to the narthex opened and Charlie's small party of ladies began to file in, three to match Asher's company. A young woman who Charlie referred to as

'Rose Red' was the first, followed closely by Ione, with Elsie stepping through the doors last.

And then the music changed, and so too did Asher's world. Charlie entered the chapel on her uncle's arm. She wore the Titania gown, but the theatrical flourishes from the ball had been replaced by delicate silk star jasmine. Her hair was pinned up, but several soft, golden curls framed her face. The effect was no less dream-like than the night of the ball, yet it was simpler and showed more of the woman Asher met in Scotland.

His heart felt near to bursting for love of her. Asher could feel his eyes prickle and fill, but his smile was as wide as the sky, and when Elias gave Charlie's hand into his keeping, he silently vowed he would never let it go.

The bishop began the service, but Asher wasn't listening, too wrapped up in Charlie's radiant gaze. And then it was time for the vows, which he managed without bobbling. Charlie promised to love and cherish him in that sweet voice of hers. Ross gave him the ring without incident, and Asher slid it onto the third finger of Charlie's left hand.

At last the bishop pronounced them husband and wife. "You may kiss your bride," intoned the bishop, and Asher thought that was a brilliant idea, bending Charlie back over his arm as he kissed her with élan.

It was probably Quinn who began the applause.

When Asher released his wife, for that was what Charlie was to him now, he thought he heard his friends chuckling a bit. Not that it mattered much, for Charlie was beaming at him, and had been just as enthusiastic in their embrace. Asher began to lead her back down the aisle, catching a congratulatory smile from his parents as they passed.

Charlie squeezed his arm a little, and stole another kiss once they were out of the chapel and free of the eyes of their guests. "And now we can start a new adventure, my love. Agent and Mrs. Burton will make quite a team, I believe."

"Just Mr. Burton, my darling. I've given up being a field agent." He kissed her nose before handing her up into the carriage that was to take them back to Aunt Callista's for the reception. "A man in that line of work has no business with a wife. I'll be training new recruits once we get back, working from the home office."

That earned Asher a very bright, very dimpled smile, and a kiss full of the promise of what was yet to come. "Good. I'd rather keep you close to home." She sighed a little, nestling closer to him and resting her head on his shoulder. "Our home."

"You're my home, Charlie," he murmured, tilting her chin up so he could get to her mouth. He whiled away a minute or two testing his limits, and then lifted his head. "You haven't asked where we're going for our honeymoon."

"Haven't I?" Charlie's response was breathless, her eyes only half open, but focused solely on him. She reached up and stroked back the curls at his temple. "Where are we going?"

Asher picked up her left hand to toy with the gleaming gold ring there. "Did you know that Lake Como has a monster in it?" He grinned at her.

Charlie laughed a little. "I did not." She cupped his cheek and looked up at him, expression warm and sultry. "But I have my doubts as to whether or not we'll see it. I suspect there will be more pressing matters to keep us occupied."

"Definitely," he murmured, and kissed her again.

The reception was winding down, and as the orchestra played another song, Elias came to ask Charlie for one last dance. Asher watched as they swayed to and fro at the side of the floor, while Ross and Elsie and Geordie and Ione swept past in a set of elegant figures. Across the way he noted Quinn watching them too; the other man sighed visibly and left the ballroom.

Thinking of the obviously personal nature of Quinn's words after the confrontation with Orion, Asher followed his friend. He came across Quinn in the orangerie, nursing a brandy thoughtfully, and took a seat next to him. "May I ask you something?"

The corner of Quinn's mouth quirked upward. "You may ask. I don't promise an answer."

Asher hesitated, then took the plunge. "What happened to you?"

A lengthy pause ensued; at last Quinn shook his head slowly and drew out his watch fob, opening the lid. Inside was a photo of a small boy, dark-haired and dark-eyed. He held it out to Asher.

Asher studied the photograph. "I don't understand. Who's this?" He gave the watch back to Quinn, who gazed at the picture for a long moment.

"This is my son," he said at last. "I've only met him once."

"Your s—" Asher couldn't even finish the word, his throat aching in sympathy. No wonder his friend had been so adamant, so angry when it seemed that Asher would make the wrong decision.

Quinn nodded, touching the picture gently. "When I told you you'd regret choosing the job... I made that choice, you see. And everything was taken from me." He closed the watch with some finality and looked at Asher. "I'm glad you chose differently. Now go find your wife and take her home."

Asher blanched. "Quinn, I—"

His friend held up a hand. "A bed of my own making, and nothing that should dim your lights, Ash." He stood up. "Go on, start your wedded bliss—and if you're not deliriously happy, I'll come find you and draw your cork. Now get."

That sounded more like the Quinn he knew, and Asher relaxed a bit. "Thanks, Q." His friend waved him off, and after a moment's hesitation, Asher did as he was bid.

Having been charged to indulge in wedded bliss, he went to go find the agent of his happiness. She was sitting with her uncle and Lorna Alvin, chatting happily as the reception carried on around them.

Charlie looked up at his approach, a broad and radiant smile curving her lips. "Hello, husband. Shall we enjoy another dance?"

He leaned down to murmur in her ear. "I have a different dance in mind. Shall we leave these nice people to their party?"

For answer, Charlie politely excused herself and slid her hand into the crook of Asher's arm. "Home, then?"

Asher chuckled and quoted Shakespeare. "'That is my home of love: if I have ranged, like him that travels I return again.'" He bent and stole a kiss. "Let's go home," he agreed, and they slipped away, eager to begin their lifelong collaboration together.

QUINN RUTHERFORD'S STORY
CONTINUES IN *AGENT OF CHANGE*,
COMING SOON!

ABOUT THE AUTHORS

Jennifer learned a love of historical fiction and romance from her mother, but her love for fantasy grew all on its own. Combining the two is one of her favorite pastimes, and one in which she has been indulging since her youth. She has several other novels available, including *Force Majeure, Freeing Fortune,* and *Mr. Pembroke's Ward.* She lives in Pennsylvania with her husband, daughter, and cats.

Christen is an avid reader who enjoys going on adventures whenever she can. Her love of fantasy started at an early age with fairytales and The Hobbit. She lives in Kansas in the home she shared with her late husband. She first discovered a love of storytelling on the stage. In her late teens she began writing, a hobby that helped her through her husband's death. She is the author of the Song of Souls trilogy, and its prequel, *The Twisted Path.* Christen enjoys spending days in her gardens and having adventures with her friends and family.

Lady of the Loch is the third book in the Fae-touched Chronicles, and represents the first collaboration between Sanders and Stovall. What began as a birthday gift between authors has truly taken on a life of its own. We hope you enjoy our world.